SPEAK OF THE DEVIL

When Karen Peterson first meets Mi
he is so charming. Still, when he offers her a job as hostess at his new
island hotel, she accepts with a great deal of reluctance. After all,
charm can hide a multitude of flaws. And when she meets her prede-
cessor, the very young and headstrong Cecily, Miss Peterson is sure
that she seems more than a mere employee. Even the guests have their
secrets—Mrs. Fish tells her that she is looking for her husband's murderer at the hotel.

But that first night Cecily surprises them all by announcing that she
has just killed a man who had attacked her in Mr. Fernandez's room.
Later, one of the clerks tells Miss Peterson that he had seen the devil
that night, stalking the hotel halls. Then Mrs. Fish shows Karen a
photo of her dead husband—who looks like the devil himself! But
nothing prepares Miss Peterson for murder, and that, of course, is just
what comes next.

THE OBSTINATE MURDERER

Emilia Swan calls Van Cleef at his club and begs him to come to her
aid. Someone is blackmailing her. Though he'd rather have another
drink, he agrees to visit her. But before he can leave he runs into the
son of an old friend. Russell Blackman, a supercilious young man
with a gifted intellect, has the unfortunate habit of alienating everyone around him. But he has always idolized Van Cleef, and agrees to
drive him to Emilia's country home if he can tag along.

When they arrive, they walk into a house filled with tension. Since
the death of her husband—some say suicide—Emilia has let out
rooms in her house. Staying with her are Major Bramwell, an irascible
old gent who demands that they leave immediately; Annie and Harry
Downes, neither of whom seem to like their hostess one bit; and Lizzy
Carroll, a pale, sharp-featured girl who drives the Major to distraction
with her loud music. That night Harry is stricken with a serious stomach illness. Russell thinks he's been poisoned, but no one takes him
seriously. The next night, Van Cleef himself is nearly poisoned. There
is certainly more going on than mere blackmail, but will Van Cleef
live long enough to figure out what it is?

**Two unusual stories of murder and mystery from
the First Lady of psychological suspense.**

Speak of the Devil
The Obstinate Murderer

by Elisabeth Sanxay Holding

STARK
HOUSE

Stark House Press • Eureka California

SPEAK OF THE DEVIL / THE OBSTINATE MURDERER

Published by Stark House Press
1315 H Street
Eureka, CA 95501, USA
griffinskye3@sbcglobal.net
www.starkhousepress.com

SPEAK OF THE DEVIL
Originally published by Duell, Sloan and Pearce, New York, and copyright © 1941
by Elisabeth Sanxay Holding; expanded from "Fearful Night" which appeared in
The American Magazine, June 1941. Reprinted in digest format as *Hostess to Murder*
by Novel Selections, Inc., 1942.

THE OBSTINATE MURDERER
Originally published by Dodd, Mead & Co., New York, and copyright © 1938 by
Elisabeth Sanxay Holding. Also published as *No Harm Intended* by John Lane,
London, 1939. Copyright © renewed 1966 by the Author's Estate.

Reprinted by permission of the Estate of Elisabeth Sanxay Holding. All rights reserved under International and Pan-American Copyright Conventions.

"Elisabeth Sanxay Holding" copyright © 2015 by Ed Gorman

All rights reserved

ISBN: 1-933586-71-0
13-ISBN: 978-1-933586-71-7

Book design by Mark Shepard Graphic Design
Proofreading by Rick Ollerman

PUBLISHER'S NOTE
This is a work of fiction. Names, characters, places and incidents are either the
products of the author's imagination or used fictionally, and any resemblance to
actual persons, living or dead, events or locales, is entirely coincidental.
Without limiting the rights under copyright reserved above, no part of this
publication may be reproduced, stored, or introduced into a retrieval system or
transmitted in any form or by any means (electronic, mechanical, photocopying,
recording or otherwise) without the prior written permission of both the copyright
owner and the above publisher of the book.

First Stark House Press Edition: February 2015
FIRST EDITION

Elisabeth Sanxay Holding
by Ed Gorman

*"If you want to deepen your understanding of noir's roots—
and if you want to read some crackerjack storytelling along
the way—find your way to Elisabeth Sanxay Holding.
The godmother of noir awaits you." —Jake Hinkson*

Does this sound like the "godmother of noir?"

• Attended Miss Whitcombe's School For Young Ladies
• Married a British Diplomat
• Traveled widely, settling in Bermuda for a number of years
• Published numerous romance novels and short stories
• Turned to mysteries during the Depression because the money was better

Talk about your hardboiled street cred.

But there's noir and then there's noir. Not every writer can be—or wants to be—a teller of tall private eye tales.

Elizabeth Sanxay Holding knew about the mean streets found in swank hotels, mansions, cruise ships and expensive nightclubs. She knew that the upper classes had their own special kind of demons.

The setting for *Speak of the Devil*, for instance, is an almost oppressively posh hotel in a place called Riquezas. The protagonist is a sophisticated, very bright and very cautious young woman named Karen Peterson. Not all of Holding's leading women are as capable and fearless as Karen. She can speak English, Spanish and Swedish if that tells you anything. And she trusts nobody.

She is here not because she has much respect or liking for the sleek owner, Mr. Fernandez, but simply because in the opening scene he offers her much more money than the job in Havana this cruise ship was taking her to.

Karen is dismayed to find that a lovely young woman named Cecily has been demoted to make room for her. She might have been less dismayed if Cecily wasn't such a strange, fragile beauty. Had she also been Mr. Fernandez's lover? Her fragility suggests that Cecily is unstable and she resents the dismissive way Fernandez treats his former factotum.

Karen's job is to be a Presence. To charm, beguile, reassure and welcome the wealthy guests. But there is a problem. One of Holding's skills as a writer is to make the physical circumstances of her books as severe as the paranoid observations of her characters. There is something odd, troubling, about the place itself Karen finds in the first few hours of her stay here. This could simply be the familiar gothic novel trope that goes back to Mary Roberts Rinehart. While she may owe Rinehart a small debt she is much the deeper, richer, more memorable writer.

As always with Holding, and as with much of Poe, what we have is not so much a plot (though she's as good as Christie at twists and surprises) as a phantasmagoria of despair, distrust and suspicion that consumes protagonist and reader alike.

And we soon learn that her feeling of dread—it's almost amusing to note that the most universal feeling in Holding's novels is the dread all her characters, despicable or not, share.

Cecily has a breakdown (or is this just a cunning theatrical gesture?) and admits to murdering a stranger in the hotel.

Dread is no stranger to the cast of *The Obstinate Murderer*, either.

Once again we have a "closed" setting, this time a mansion. As the critic for the excellent blog "The Passing Tramp" has noted this novel might even be considered to be an Agatha Christie Country House puzzler.

Holding had a troubled affection for eccentrics. I say "troubled" because while they fascinated her she frequently disapproves of them. Once in awhile they even prove to be murderous.

The eccentric here is Arthur Van Cleef, one of Holding's many wealthy layabouts and heavy drinkers. In the opening an eighteen year old boy named Russell Blackman shows up to remind Van Cleef of how kind he was ten years ago when Russell's Aunt Tilda died.

At the same time an old friend of Van Cleef's calls to tell him that she needs his help because she's being blackmailed. Off he and Russell go to the friend's mansion where, soon enough, a guest is poisoned. Hence the shout out to Dame Agatha.

All right. So where does the "noir" in all this show itself.

Again I think we have to posit the streets of the upper and frivolous classes have their own version of the mean streets.

For me the finest pieces about Holding have been written by novelist and critic Jake Hinkson. Here he is making his case for her:

> "If you trace the roots of literary noir back far enough, eventually you'll run into the unlikely figure of Elisabeth Sanxay Holding. Though in recent years she has been overlooked in the rush to canonize folks such as James M. Cain and Cornell Woolrich, Holding was just as pivotal in the development of noir as a distinct literary genre. Like Cain and Woolrich, she didn't write about hardnosed good guys very much. Before the term *"roman noir"* had even been coined, her specialty was isolated and desperate characters with profoundly poor decision-making skills.
>
> "In her time, Holding sold well and was highly regarded by her peers. No less an authority than Raymond Chandler called her 'the top suspense writer of them all.' The critic Christopher Morley wrote of one of her books, 'This is the kind of thing I recommend to a few like myself who find the purest refreshment in hallucinations and horrors, in damnation, dipsomania, and dismay.' And looking back on her career, the great Anthony Boucher (namesake of the Bouchercon World Mystery Convention) noted, 'Before anybody had ever heard of "pyschological novels of suspense" Elisabeth Sanxay Holding was writing them, and brilliantly.'"

Here is Kelli Stanley, the author of *Nox Dormienda*:

> "Chandler actually persuaded Paramount to purchase another Sanxay novel, *The Innocent Mrs. Duff*, and worked on its film adaptation in the spring of '46 before parting ways over its handling [...] one of those great lost scripts I'd love to unearth from a vault someday.
>
> "Now, Chandler is my favorite writer, and I take his recommendations seriously. So I purchased a first edition of *The Innocent Mrs. Duff* (1946), and found myself wondering why Patricia Highsmith is justly venerated and Sanxay Holding is largely forgotten.
>
> "A psychological suspense thriller built on a taut, perfectly structured character study, the novel ticks away like a metronome, building up an unbearable tension. One of Holding's earlier titles was *Miasma* (1929), and that eponymous sense of death and decay also informs the later story.
>
> "Narrated in the first person by a middle-aged, middle-class alcoholic snob – ambitious, deluded, and utterly narcissistic – the plot and tension are driven by his growing paranoia and suspicions of the title character [...] his beautiful, newly-married, twenty-one year old second wife.

"The book simply grabs you by the throat and won't let go. Holding can write dread as well or better than any writer [...] and like Shirley Jackson, her quiet moments and what Chandler calls her 'inner calm' fuel a palpable sense of horror."

I'm particularly pleased with Stanley's reference to Shirley Jackson because Holding is certainly as horrorific in places as Jackson. The term "suburban noir" has been coined to cover writers such as Charlotte Armstrong and other women writers who were dismissed in their time for writing "women's fiction" but who wrote troubled stories about the supposedly safe and banal Eisenhower era.

But both Holding and obviously Jackson went further into malady and madness than did the suburban noir writers. They both had a fascination with what I'd call "functional madness." Here they resemble Dorothy B. Hughes in the novel *In A Lonely Place*. Their lunatics show us, at first, only hints of their dislocation but since they are sometimes viewpoint characters we begin to see how deranged their perception of reality is. This isn't the cheap trick of them being killers, either. These are just a few of the strange folks who inhabit the upper class houses Holding favors. After the mayhem is finished they just go right back to being people who'd make you damned uncomfortable being around. Hell, Holding even manages to tell an entire novel through the mind of a man who is almost always drunk. No easy task.

Fear, betrayal, deceit, despair, violence—the same emotional elements you found in the work of the "Black Mask" writers. The only difference being that Hammett and company didn't have limousines waiting for them at the curb.

The mean streets of Elizabeth Sanxay Holding. Jake Hinkson was right. She really is "The godmother of noir."

–November 2014
Cedar Rapids, Iowa

Speak of the Devil

by Elisabeth Sanxay Holding

To Toni

I

Miss Peterson opened the door of her cabin cautiously, and glanced along the alleyway to the smoke room. And saw Mr. Fernandez looking at her. He rose.

With a sigh, she came out, closing the door behind her. She was well able to cope with Mr. Fernandez, but the weather was singularly oppressive and she felt tired; she would have preferred to avoid him. But it was too late now and she went along the alleyway, tall, broad-shouldered, and long-limbed, very handsome in her black evening dress, with her blond hair in thick braids around her head.

"Dear lady!" said Mr. Fernandez. "I haven't seen you since lunch time."

"I was resting," said Miss Peterson. "I don't like this weather."

"The glass is very low," said Mr. Fernandez.

"I thought so," she said. "You can feel it."

He drew back a chair for her, and she sat down at the table.

"It's all right on a ship," he said. "But on shore.... When I think of my new hotel!"

They were both silent for a moment. They had both felt this breathless quiet before; they had seen this slow, sullen sea before; they knew the fury that was gathering somewhere.

"What's yours, Miss Peterson?"

"Gin tonic, thanks," she said.

"Make it two, Henry," said Mr. Fernandez, and brought out his gold cigarette case.

He was, after his fashion, a handsome man; a big fellow, dark, clean-shaven, with black wavy hair that bushed out a little behind the ears. He was soberly dressed in a white mess jacket and black trousers, but nothing could disguise or subdue his prodigious exuberance.

"Well, little lady?" he asked.

"I'm five feet ten..." said Miss Peterson.

He was not to be deflected.

"Been thinking over my proposition?" he asked earnestly.

"I'm sorry, Mr. Fernandez...."

"You don't know your own heart," he said, briefly.

Miss Peterson turned her sad sea-gray eyes toward the open doorway on to the afterdeck.

"You love me," Mr. Fernandez said. "Admit it."

Salesmanship, she thought. When that man in Puerto Rico wanted me to sell refrigerators, that was the line he advised. Be positive, he said. Never negative. Tell people that they want an icebox. Be crisp. That was another thing he used to say. He told me I'd be an outstanding success at selling if I'd only give it a trial.

But I wouldn't.

The ship had begun to pitch a little; as the stern dipped she saw the leaden water that seemed not to move. The sky was leaden too, no breeze. Why do I do some things, and not do other things? she asked herself. I certainly don't act according to reason. I look reasonable; and nobody can see through me. Do we ever understand one another?

She thought about that, lost in one of her Norse reveries; one of those melancholy moods that came over her occasionally, particularly in hurricane weather.

"Well?" said Mr. Fernandez, with a fond laugh. "You're a serious little lady, aren't you?"

"I seem to be," said Miss Peterson, stifling a sigh. She sipped the gin tonic.

"If you can't make up your mind, I'll make it up for you," he said. "You're going to leave the ship at Riquezas and you're going to stay at another hotel while we put up the banns, and then we're going to be married. Then you're coming to live in my new hotel. A beautiful hotel, modern, beautiful. You'll have your own car. You'll have everything. Like a little queen. When the season's over, I'll take you up to New York and I'll buy you the finest outfit of clothes—"

"Let's come to an understanding, Mr. Fernandez," she said, suddenly businesslike. "I can't marry you, ever. There's no chance of my changing my mind, ever."

"*La donna è mobile...*" he sang in a very baritone.

"I don't know about that," said Miss Peterson. "But please take this as final. I like you, and I appreciate your offer. But I'm going on to Havana. I've got a job waiting for me there."

"You like me..." said Mr. Fernandez, seizing on that. "Liking and respect—what's a better basis for a marriage?"

"I don't want to get married," said Miss Peterson.

"That's because you don't understand," he said. "You're unawakened. You—"

She had heard Mr. Fernandez on that subject, and she did not relish it.

"No," she said, in her slow voice. And nobody could possibly think that she meant yes.

Mr. Fernandez moved his glass so that the iced clinked in it.

"Maybe you haven't known me long enough; only five days," he said. "Everybody's not like me. I make up my mind like that!" He snapped his fingers. "But that's my nature. You may be different. It may take you a long time to know...." His black eyes rested upon her face. "But once you do love—or hate—God!"

Well, if that's what you like to think, Miss Peterson said to herself. At the moment, the only emotion she felt was an overwhelming boredom.

"Another drink, little lady?"

"Thanks," she said. "I'd like it."

"Henry!" he called. "*Encore!*" He turned back to Miss Peterson. "You're low-spirited," he said. "I've never seen you like this before."

"The weather," she said.

He did not care for that.

"You're not happy," he said. "Tell me—what is this job in Havana?"

"It's in a shop," she said. "They want someone who can speak English, and Spanish, and German."

"I know how good your Spanish is," he said. "But German, too?"

"Yes," she said.

"A good job?" he asked.

"Good enough," she said.

"I wonder..." he said. "I wonder what's happened to make you go wandering around the world like this?"

"I wonder, myself," she said, with candor.

"I wonder," he said leaning across the table and lowering his voice, "what's happened to make you turn against love?"

You'd be surprised, thought Miss Peterson. It's people like you. Men you meet in planes and ships and hotels and trains, talking about love. She said nothing out loud, and he leaned back in his chair and took a sip of his drink.

"Lady," he said, "I'm going to make a different proposition. We'll forget about marriage for the time."

"I'm going to Havana," said Miss Peterson.

"Come to Riquezas," he said. "Whatever they were going to pay you in Havana, I'll double it."

She looked up.

"Come to my new hotel as hostess," he said. "You can name your own salary. You'll have a nice room and bath, all to yourself. Fine meals. Plenty of time for swimming, riding, tennis. It's a position of dignity," he added.

This position seemed to Miss Peterson very much more attractive than the one in Havana. Especially at double the salary. But she saw grave drawbacks.

"I'm afraid—" she began.

"Yes," he interrupted. "You're afraid I'd bother you—try to make love. Well, look here...." He paused. "We'll get to Riquezas tomorrow, on the twentieth of September. I give you my word I won't say another word about marriage or love, until the twentieth of November."

Miss Peterson had heard a good deal of talk about Mr. Fernandez since she had come on board at Trinidad. He was a big man in Riquezas; he had a hotel, a club, he owned the sole fleet of launches, he had an interest in the biggest department store, he was in half a dozen other things. He had his enemies; some people spoke of him with fury. They called him bullying, grasping, vulgar, even ruthless. She thought it not impossible that he might have some of these defects; but she thought he would keep this bargain.

"But you'd be thinking all the time that I was going to change my mind," she said.

"Certainly," he said, seriously. "I'm pretty sure you will, too. But if you don't—all right. I can take it."

"I don't think it would be fair to you," said Miss Peterson.

"My dear lady," said Mr. Fernandez. "Even apart from my personal feelings, it would be a big advantage for me to have you in the hotel. It is hard for me to find the right person for that job."

She liked that better. She understood very well his Latin fashion of combining love and business.

"I don't want an American," he went on. "Some of the die-hard Britishers don't like them. I don't want an English girl, because they don't understand American tourists—the backbone of my business. You're neither English nor American. I don't know what you are, and I'm not asking. Simply you'd be a Godsend in that job."

She liked him even more for this. She was wont for the most part to call herself English; she sometimes advertised for a post as 'an English gentlewoman.' Her passport was Uruguayan; but her birthplace was Minnesota. A strange rebellion of her mother's had taken her away from home in her childhood. Still in her twenties, she had traveled far and seen much. But she did not forget the farm where she was born, the wide rich fields in summer, the winter snows. It suited her to wander over the world, but her roots were back there; she had been nourished by reality, and however fantastic her experiences were, she herself was realistic, sober, a little aloof. Not romantic.

"So that if you take the job," said Mr. Fernandez, "you'll be under no obligation to me. On the contrary, you'll be doing me a favor."

"Then—thank you," she said. "I'll come, Mr. Fernandez. On two months' trial."

"*Bueno!*" he said with a sudden flashing smile.

They went down to the dining-saloon then. Mr. Fernandez sat at the Captain's table because of his importance in Riquezas; Miss Peterson sat at the Purser's table, because the Purser knew her and enjoyed her company. The other people who sat at the table had not yet come down; Mr. Wavill sat there alone.

"I'll be leaving you tomorrow," said Miss Peterson. "I'm getting off at Riquezas."

"Well..." said Mr. Wavill. "You know what you're doing."

No, I don't, thought Miss Peterson. Nobody ever does. For her Norse mood still lingered; the oppression in the atmosphere lay heavy upon her.

"I won't talk business now," she said, "but tomorrow morning I'll come formally to your office, and ask about a refund for the rest of my passage."

"Suppose we have a bottle of Sauterne?" said Mr. Wavill. "As long as this is au revoir...."

"Thanks!" said Miss Peterson. "That would be—"

"Damn!" he murmured. "Here comes Mrs. Fish."

He rose politely, and Miss Peterson looked up with a smile as their table companion approached. She was a tall, slight woman, all in black, even to her stockings, with a long-nosed, chinless face like a melancholy goose, and black hair in a somewhat untidy knot at the nape of her neck. She was amiable enough in her fashion; but she was depressing, so fatigued and silent.

"You'll take a glass of wine with us, Mrs. Fish?" asked the Purser.

"Oh, no thank you," she answered, "I think it gives me neuralgia."

The wine came, and the steward filled their glasses.

"Well..." said Mr. Wavill, raising his glass and looking at Miss Peterson with a faintly sardonic smile. "I hope you'll like—Riquezas."

"If I don't, I'll go somewhere else," said Miss Peterson.

They drank the wine and were silent in a friendly fashion. The electric fans whirred softly, stirring the heavy air; as the ship pitched, the gray water seemed to slide up toward the ports, very slow, very menacing. From the Captain's table came Mr. Fernandez's voice, loud, resonant; an attractive voice.

"One doesn't feel much like eating in this weather," said Mr. Wavill.

"No," Mrs. Fish agreed.

"Let's give up," said Miss Peterson; and they all rose. Mrs. Fish went to her cabin, and Miss Peterson and Wavill sat on deck for a time in the stifling dark; then he went to his office, and she sat alone. She remembered a hurricane in Martinique when she had been in charge of two children.... She sighed and remembered an earthquake in Chile. Life is very strange, she reflected.

"Well..." said Mr. Fernandez's voice from dark. Her chair was on the forward deck; he sat down in one beside her, he offered her a cigarette and lit one for himself, and smoked for a time in silence.

"There's one thing I'll have to explain," he said. "A complication."

A woman I suppose, thought Miss Peterson. If it's too much of a complication, I'm not going to bother with it.

"I took on a girl as hostess," he said. "But she won't do." He was silent for a time. "I was a fool."

"Do you mean she's there now?" asked Miss Peterson.

"Yes," he said, "but she's not hostess any more."

"No? What is she then?"

"Different odd jobs," said he.

"An English girl?"

"American," he said.

There was a long silence this time.

"When I first met this Cecily," he said, "I thought she'd be a fine hostess. She's very musical and so on. But it didn't work at all. She doesn't get on with people. She was unpopular. It was a business arrangement pure and simple, and I couldn't afford to keep it up. I had a talk with her. I offered to pay her fare home." He began to speak in Spanish. "*Inutil*. We had nothing but arguments, protestations. She begged to be allowed to stay in the hotel, if it must be even in the kitchen. I was sorry for her."

"And she's still there?" asked Miss Peterson in English.

"*Sí!* Yes. I gave in. I let her stay. She has charge now of the ladies' powder room."

"I don't like that much," said Miss Peterson.

"Neither do I," he said. "It was a weakness on my part and now I'll insist on her going. It's nothing serious, but I thought you'd better know."

"I don't like it," she repeated.

"Dear lady," he said, "look at it this way. You'd already agreed to come. I needn't have told you a word about this. If it is obviously what you think it is, *would* I have told you? Would I have asked you to come? No! It's nothing serious. Awkward; that's all. Cecily will leave the island by the next boat; take my word for it."

This time Miss Peterson did not believe Mr. Fernandez. Not wholly. She did not believe that he had kept on his former hostess out of sheer kindness or because he did not like scenes. Also if it had been a matter of no importance, he would not have mentioned it.

"I don't like scenes, myself," she remarked.

"There won't be any scenes," he said. "Dear lady, I'm not a fool. Remember too that I have a reputation in that island. I shouldn't be likely to prejudice my business for a girl, eh?"

There's something in that, she thought. I don't think he'd risk his reputation for anyone or anything.

"A slight awkwardness, that's all," he said. "But the girl will leave by the next boat, and we'll forget it. Have you told the Purser you're landing tomorrow?"

"Yes," she said. He rose.

"We may arrive early," he said. "You'd better turn in, and get some rest."

"Presently," she said.

He took her hand and raised it to his lips; kept it there a little too long.

"Good night!" she said, very clearly.

He left her there and she sat relaxed in her chair, her long legs stretched out, her ankles crossed. She was an expert packer and she could get ready in half an hour. She did not want to go to her cabin. It was better here, in this airless night.

"I didn't know you were going to Riquezas," said Mrs. Fish's flat, subdued voice from the dark.

"Oh, yes..." said Miss Peterson. She looked about her, but she could not make out the black figure in the shadows.

"I am too, you know," said Mrs. Fish.

"That's nice," said Miss Peterson with courtesy.

"I'm going to the Hotel Fernandez," said Mrs. Fish. "Are you?"

"I've got a job there," Miss Peterson answered. "Hostess."

"Oh. What does a hostess do?" Mrs. Fish asked.

"I'll try and make things pleasant for people," said Miss Peterson. She didn't really know what her duties would be, but she thought it would be unfair to Mr. Fernandez to admit this ignorance.

"I'm so glad you're going to be there," said Mrs. Fish. "I hear you're a trained nurse."

"I'm sorry, but I'm not," said Miss Peterson. She did not want Mrs. Fish, or any other guest of the hotel to know that she was a licensed masseuse. She had learned by experience that when people found that out, they were disposed to make extraordinary demands on her; to cure headaches, to take care of babies, to prescribe for hangovers. But Mrs. Fish had somehow found out something.

"Well, it's practically the same thing," said Mrs. Fish. As others had said. "I'm glad to think you'll be there. Such a strong personality."

"Thank you," said Miss Peterson, stifling a sigh.

There was a soft rustle, and a strong gust of perfume, lily-of-the-valley. Mrs. Fish was close to her now.

"Won't you sit down?" Miss Peterson asked, feeling that this was her duty toward a prospective guest of the hotel.

"Thank you!" said Mrs. Fish, and did sit down in the chair that Mr. Fernandez had vacated.

"You see," she said, "my husband was killed last year."

"How dreadful!" said Miss Peterson in her mild, slow voice.

"It's a nerve-strain," said Mrs. Fish. "Some day, when I'm not so tired, I'd like to talk to you about it."

"Oh, certainly!" said Miss Peterson. But it seemed to her that her new job required a little more of her. "There's nothing like travel, to take your mind off a thing like that," she added. "I should think a nice long stay in a place like Riquezas would help you a lot."

"Well, this isn't a pleasure trip," said Mrs. Fish. "I'm going to Riquezas for a reason." She paused again. "We must talk about it later on. But I'm so tired just now. I think I'll close my eyes and try to get a little sleep."

"That's a good idea," Miss Peterson said. She too, had had the idea of sleeping here, but the lily-of-the-valley perfume was so strong.... "I'll have to go to my cabin," she said. "Some last minute things.... Good night, Mrs. Fish."

"Good night," said Mrs. Fish. Her fatigued voice seemed to trail after Miss Peterson as she moved away. "You see," she said, without emphasis, "my husband was murdered."

Miss Peterson stopped, stood still for a moment. Then, with more haste than was usual with her, she went on her way. I don't want to hear any more about that, she thought. Not now. Not in this weather.

II

The sun came up in the morning, but it was a menacing sun; dull, veiled by clouds that did not seem to move. The sea had risen, there was a long heavy swell, the ship pitched heavily.

Miss Peterson staggered as she finished her packing, the light wicker chair in the cabin lurched, everything creaked and strained. The dining saloon was almost empty, Mrs. Fish did not appear, the steward came running downhill with his tray, and checked himself as the floor rose up; there were fidds on the tables.

She ate a good breakfast though, because in the background of her mind was the thought that lunch might be long delayed. She saw the Purser, she got a refund on her passage and a landing permit, and the ship stopped. It was worse then; they rolled helplessly in the long swell that came driven by the invisible fury; the deck chairs were all folded up and lashed, there was a great quiet on board.

Miss Peterson stood on deck, her nice narrow feet in low-heeled blue and white shoes planted wide apart to keep her balance, a cool blue and white print dress upon her tall frame, a dark blue hat upon her blond head. Riquezas lay before her, a flat low island looking very unimportant. A launch was coming toward them; the accommodation ladder went down.

"Disagreeable weather," said Mr. Fernandez at her side. And presently Mrs. Fish came, in a sheer black dress and a white helmet with a black puggree hanging down the back. They stood in silence watching the mail sacks go into the launch, they watched the trunks and bags of Miss Peterson and Mrs. Fish and Mr. Fernandez go down. "Well! *Au revoir!*" said the Chief Officer, and shook hands with them.

Mr. Fernandez went down the ladder first, Mrs. Fish followed, and Miss Peterson went last. The gray sea came up at her, and swooped down; the world seemed to swing in a sickening arc. But down she went slowly; she waited until the launch came up, a sailor caught her arm and helped her on board, and off they went.

The engines of the ship started, the propellers churned; off she went on her own way.

"Going to blow, sah," said the negro at the wheel.

"May not hit us," said Mr. Fernandez.

"Got to do *so*, sah. When 'ee don't come for two years, come in three years—"

"Nonsense! Nonsense!" said Mr. Fernandez.

He was, in a subtle way, changing as he sat in his launch; he was growing bigger and grander. When they reached the jetty, he stepped ashore like a king and there was a chorus of greetings from the little crowd assembled there.

"Glad to see you back, sah.... Fernandez, how are you?... Did you have a good trip, Mr. Fernandez?"

He raised his helmet, he made a vague gesture of salute with his hand, he smiled. He gave the keys of their baggage to a man in a sort of porter's uniform, and he led them along to an elegant, cream-colored roadster with a tan top attended by a chauffeur in khaki. He waved his hand again as they set off through the town.

A nice little British town, colored policemen in white gloves, a wide square after the fashion of the Spanish plaza, a bank with plate-glass windows, shop windows filled with tourist wares, a post-office with an arcade before it. But the sun was gone now; a fitful breeze stirred the dust, some of the shops had their shutters up already. They crossed a bridge, and entered the open country. They went past fields, with here and there an old estate house or a modern villa standing stark and defenseless in this flat island beneath this sky of lead.

The Hotel Fernandez was on the beach, an elaborate stone building with turrets, a patio, a colonnaded terrace. On the lawn of parched grass stood little iron tables under striped umbrellas that were shaking and straining in the rising wind.

"Those'll have to come in," said Mr. Fernandez.

They entered a large and handsome lounge. "Miss Peterson," he said, "if you'll go to the sun-deck, if you please.... Straight ahead of you. I'll look after Mrs. Fish—personally."

He led Mrs. Fish by the arm toward the desk, and Miss Peterson continued straight ahead, as he had told her, to a glassed-in veranda that overlooked the sea; there were palms and ferns in pots, a pleasing harmony of green and black chintz, comfortable big chairs and little glass tables. Mr. Fernandez joined her in a moment, followed by a waiter.

"I think we might have a little drink to celebrate," said Mr. Fernandez. "What would you like?"

"I think a lemonade, thanks," said Miss Peterson.

"A lemonade," he repeated to the waiter, "and bring me a beer."

Miss Peterson was standing by the open window and he joined her. The sea was running high, pounding on the white beach, breaking into high crests on the barrier reef. A very high sea for so still a day.

"Yes..." he said, half to himself. "Well...."

He lit a cigarette for her; when the drinks came, they sat down.

"I'm afraid I'll be very busy for a while," he said. "But I'll tell the housekeeper to look after you. Lunch in your own room perhaps. You can look around and get the feel of the place—the atmosphere, eh? And we can meet here for cocktails at—let's say five o'clock. If all goes well."

"*Bueno!*" she said.

They fell silent, and the pounding of the surf came to them, loud and ominous.

"Of course—" he began, and stopped short as a girl entered.

She was a slight girl in a black dress, and black shoes and stockings. Her long dark hair was brushed back from her forehead, her face was pale, with high cheekbones and a wide rouged mouth, her eyes were a clear, light aquamarine. She was a very unusual-looking girl, and very beautiful.

"Mrs. Barley couldn't leave just now, sir," she said. "So I came to see if I could do anything."

"Ah!" said Mr. Fernandez, somewhat wryly. "Well... Miss Peterson, this is—" He paused. "Cecily," he said. "Cecily, this is Miss Peterson, the new hostess."

The girl made a curtsey. That was a very strange thing for an American girl to do; it was either ironic, or theatrical, or both.

"How do you do?" said Miss Peterson amiably.

"Thank you, madam," said the girl. "Shall I show Miss Peterson her room, sir?"

Mr. Fernandez was more ill at ease than Miss Peterson had believed he could be. "Never mind," he said.

"I think that would be a good idea, Mr. Fernandez," she said rising.

"*Bueno!*" he said, rising himself. "Then I'll see you at five...."

Miss Peterson followed Cecily through the lounge and into the elevator; they rode up only to the second floor, they went along a corridor and around a corner where the girl opened a door.

"This is the room the former hostess had, madam," she said.

"That was you, wasn't it?"

"Yes, madam."

"Won't you sit down and have a smoke?" Miss Peterson asked. "I'm sorry, but I don't know your name, Miss—?"

"I'm called Cecily now, madam."

"Won't you sit down and talk to me a little? I'd like to get a little information."

"I'm afraid I couldn't help you, madam."

"It's for you to say of course," said Miss Peterson. "But if you feel like telling me some of the chief difficulties—?"

"My experience wouldn't be helpful, madam," said Cecily. "I failed."

"Maybe I'll fail too," said Miss Peterson.

"I'm in charge now of what they call the ladies' powder room," said Cecily, with her pale clear eyes on Miss Peterson's face.

"Well, I've never done that," said Miss Peterson. "But I've worked in a restaurant."

She felt as if she were dealing with a wild gazelle, she felt that if she made one brusque gesture, this young creature would flee. For in spite of the black uniform and the 'madam,' and her gentle voice, Cecily was wild. Certainly not the type I'd expect, Miss Peterson thought. She's obviously a very well-bred girl. And, I should say, a dangerous girl.

"I hope you'll like the position, madam," she said.

"I wish you wouldn't call me 'madam,'" said Miss Peterson. "After all, here we are. Two human beings. Two women. You've lost the job; and I've got it. The wheel turns. Who knows what's going to happen tomorrow?"

The wild gazelle took a few steps into the room, lured by Miss Peterson's calm good-humor.

"I suppose I'll have to leave the hotel now?" she said. "Even the powder room."

"I should think you could find something much more interesting," said Miss Peterson.

"I want to stay here," said the girl. "I've offered to stay without any pay at all. Just my room and meals. But now I suppose I'll have to go."

"I hope not," said Miss Peterson.

The girl glanced at her quickly.

"Of course," Miss Peterson went on, "I've just got here, and I don't know yet what's expected of me. Or what I can do. Won't you sit down and tell me what you had to do when you were the hostess?"

Cecily did sit down then, on a straight-backed chair near the door.

"I played the piano," she said. "Every morning from eleven to twelve, and in the afternoon at tea-time. And on Sunday we gave a concert in the evening. The cellist and the first violin from the orchestra, and myself. But—" She paused. "My playing wasn't liked," she said.

"Well, I don't play the piano," said Miss Peterson.

"You'll have to 'greet' people," Cecily went on. "You'll have to dance with the men, and sit and talk with the women. You'll have to get on with people. With everyone."

"I'm rather good at that," said Miss Peterson.

"I'm not," said the girl.

"Have a cigarette?" asked Miss Peterson.

The girl hesitated and then took one, and she relaxed a little as she began to smoke.

"You must have studied music," Miss Peterson observed.

"Yes. I have."

"I hear you're an American," said Miss Peterson.

"I'm half Polish. My mother was from Warsaw."

"That's interesting," said Miss Peterson. "Do you speak Polish?"

"A little."

Miss Peterson spoke a few words in a foreign tongue; the girl's clear eyes were fixed intently upon her.

"I'm sorry," she said. "I'm afraid I don't understand that."

"Well, maybe it's not good Polish," said Miss Peterson.

"Well, if it's a dialect..." said the girl.

A puff of wind came through the open window, and Miss Peterson got up and went to look out. "You've been here—how long?" she asked.

"Over four months."

"Then I don't suppose you've had any bad weather?"

"I don't pay much attention to the weather," said Cecily. "It's been hot enough, and it's rained, if that's what you mean."

"That's not what I mean," said Miss Peterson.

"Miss Peterson?" said a voice, and the girl rose quickly.

A short, gray-haired woman with a long upper lip stood in the doorway. "I'm Mrs. Barley, the housekeeper," she said earnestly, and moved to let Cecily go past her out of the room. "Have you everything you want?"

"Yes, I think so, thank you," Miss Peterson answered.

"I'm afraid," said Mrs. Barley, "that we're going to have some disagreeable weather."

"Is there a warning up?" asked Miss Peterson.

"Oh, you know then?" said Mrs. Barley. "Yes. They've just put up the flag." They were both silent for a moment.

"Well," said Mrs. Barley, "we only have five guests now, and one came by this boat. The season doesn't really begin until the end of October as a rule. We have no Americans here. Fortunately."

"Don't you like Americans?" asked Miss Peterson.

"Oh, very much!" said Mrs. Barley. "But they're more excitable. If we're going to have disagreeable weather.... I'm sending up a man, Miss Peterson, to put up the shutters."

Another puff of wind came in and stirred Mrs. Barley's hair. And Miss Peterson thought of what was coming across the water, rushing past one island, sweeping across another, giving a careless glancing blow at a third. Nobody could know where the fury would strike; at this moment, hundreds of people were doing what they could to prepare for the onslaught; men were looking at their cane fields, at the banana plantations that might vanish overnight. People were going to die.

"Let me know if you want anything," said Mrs. Barley.

Like a goddess. Suppose I answered, give me peace, thought Miss Peterson.

Her trunk and her bag came, and she unpacked them; a colored boy came up with an excellent lunch on a tray. Fried flying fish and plantains, salad, an ice, and very fine coffee. She was hungry, and she enjoyed it, and she was glad to be alone to do a little thinking.

She thought about Cecily. That's a very strange child, she said to herself; and I don't wonder that Fernandez is afraid of her. There's a terrific vitality in her, and it's exactly the other sort of vitality from his. He's exuberant and expansive, and she's channeled all in one direction, whatever it is. I should say that anything she really wants, she'll get. Even if it's Carlos Fernandez. An interesting child.... Her hair is certainly dyed; and she certainly doesn't speak any Polish at all. Because when I spoke to her in Swedish, she didn't know the difference. Interesting, and dangerous....

She finished her lunch, and then a man came to put up shutters at her windows. That was depressing, and she thought she would go outdoors while she could. But a chambermaid came to the door just as she was going out.

"Mistress, Mis' Fish say, will you please step by she room? On the next floor, mistress, three-fifteen."

I don't want to see Mrs. Fish, thought Miss Peterson, half-surprised by her own reluctance. I don't want to hear about her husband. Murdered, she said. That's no reason for disliking the poor woman, of course, but there's a sort of aura about her, lily-of-the-valley perfume, and black clothes—and death.

She sighed and straightened her shoulders. Come now! she said to herself. Be a hostess. And she walked up one flight of stairs and knocked at the door of Mrs. Fish's room.

"Come in," said the flat, tired voice, and entering, she found Mrs. Fish lying on the bed in a gloomy dusk, the windows shuttered. "I have a toothache," she said. "I wonder if you can do anything?"

"Oh, yes," said Miss Peterson, and returning to her room, she got a tiny plaster, two aspirin tablets, and three tablets of sodium bicarbonate. "I'm afraid I'll have to turn on the light," she said.

"Oh, by all means," said Mrs. Fish.

She was wearing a crimson silk kimono embroidered with gold dragons; and that made her look paler and more tired than ever; her black hair was loose, spread out on the pillow. Miss Peterson moved quietly about; she went to the bathroom and mixed her tablets in a glass, adding a brown cough drop she had in her purse, to give it a strange flavor and color.

"What's that?" Mrs. Fish asked.

"Oh, that's a secret," said Miss Peterson, who understood the therapeutic value of mystery.

Mrs. Fish sipped this exotic drink, and Miss Peterson glanced about the room. A big wardrobe trunk stood in a corner, still locked, but a suitcase was open on a chair, and a few things had been set out on the chest of drawers. There was a photograph in a silver frame, Miss Peterson glanced at it, stared at it, moved a little nearer to examine it.

It was a photograph of the Devil, a big, burly, fierce devil, with a bold nose and mocking eyes and an elegant Vandyke beard; he stood with folded arms, dressed in a mantle and a cap that revealed his horns.

"Are you looking at that picture?" Mrs. Fish asked tonelessly. "That was my husband. In a masquerade costume. It suited him very well, don't you think?"

"Oh, yes!" said Miss Peterson. She went into the bathroom and held the tiny plaster under the hot water tap until it was thoroughly warmed, then she applied it to Mrs. Fish's gum.

"Such a relief..." Mrs. Fish mumbled, and closed her eyes.

"I'll come back presently," said Miss Peterson, and withdrew, closing the door behind her. For a moment, she stood in the corridor thinking about that extraordinary photograph. The Devil... she thought. And he was murdered.

That's not right. That's not natural. Well...!

She sighed and started down the stairs. The lights were on everywhere, every window was boarded up, it was stiflingly hot. A small group was sitting in the lounge, and she did not feel like talking to them; she made her way to the sundeck, and there was Mr. Fernandez in his shirtsleeves, sitting at a table with his ledgers before him, and an oil lamp, unlit, beside them. There was a damp patch between his shoulder blades, he wiped his face with a mauve silk handkerchief; at the sound of her step he glanced up and rose.

"According to the latest wireless news," he said, "the worst of the storm will pass to the East of us. *Ojalà Dios!*"

"Here comes the rain," she said.

It came like hail, like machine-gun bullets against the boards; the wind had a hollow spinning roar. Miss Peterson sat down, pushing her damp hair back from her temples.

"Nervous?" he asked.

"Oh, no, Mr. Fernandez," she answered. "Only, coming to a new place, there are always things you want to sort out in your mind."

"Cecily, for example?"

"She seems to me to be a very interesting girl," said Miss Peterson.

"Too interesting," said Mr. Fernandez. He wiped his face again. "She came down here on a cruise ship," he went on. "And when she asked to see me, I thought—naturally—she was a tourist, wanting to stop a little longer in my hotel—my other hotel that was. I was very much surprised, I can tell you, when she said she wanted a job. But she seemed—at that time—a very sensible girl, quiet, well-bred. She played the piano for me. I'm no judge of music, but it seemed good to me, very good. She said she could give these little concerts, and that she could help to entertain the guests in other ways. I'd never employed a hostess, but she didn't ask for a large salary, and it seemed a good idea—at the time."

"But it didn't work?"

"*Por ejemplo!* Complaints began almost at once. The guests complained, the servants complained. She wanted to practice; and one morning she started at seven o'clock, waking up people. I put a stop to that, and then she started practicing at nine, when people were sitting in the lounge. She has no tact. She quarreled with the orchestra leader. She wanted to go into the kitchen, and order coffee and sandwiches for herself, and that led to a quarrel with the cook. I advised her to go home. I told her there was no future here. But she was so insistent upon staying...." He shrugged his shoulders and spread out his hands. "I'm a very good-natured man."

I wonder... thought Miss Peterson.

She could hear the surf, the waves pounding on the beach; the wind had a new note, a thin piping whistle, the rain came more furiously. There was nothing to do but wait, and to hope that the mad violence could find no crevice by which to enter, no weakness in this brave, new building, standing stark and alone by the sea.

The lights went out.

Mr. Fernandez turned on a flashlight, and by its beam he lit the oil lamp. "I'll have to reassure the guests," he said. "If you'd come too...?"

The guests were admirably tranquil. By then light of two oil lamps in the lounge they could be seen, a middle-aged couple sitting at the card table, but not playing; one old lady was knitting, another was doing nothing at all; a thin, tall man with a weather-beaten, hollow-cheeked face was moving aimlessly about, smoking.

"If you had your electric fans working properly," he said sternly to Mr. Fernandez, "it wouldn't be so bad."

"Unfortunately, the electricity has failed, Major," Mr. Fernandez explained.

"Then why don't you have punkahs?" the Major demanded. "Put some of these worthless boys to work. Gad! No air at all!"

"Do keep quiet!" said the old lady who was knitting.

"What?" the Major demanded. "What did you say, Mrs. Green?"

"I said, do keep quiet," the old lady repeated. "You have just as much air as anyone else."

"What?" he cried. "What?"

"What's that girl doing here?" asked one of the old ladies, and turning her head, Miss Peterson saw Cecily standing in an open doorway near the desk. She was outside the circle of lamplight, and in the shadowy background, she looked all black and white, a little white apron now over her black dress, and a white frilled cap on her head. It was strange to see her there, unmoving.

"Panicked," the Major observed.

Miss Peterson went over to her.

"I've just killed a man," Cecily said, in an even, very low voice.

III

Miss Peterson was accustomed to responsibility, and her first thought was to keep those guests quiet. They were all looking toward Cecily, but they were, she thought, too far away to have heard the girl above all the noise of wind and rain.

"Come!" she said, and the girl followed her past the desk and out to the sundeck. Mr. Fernandez came after them.

"I've just killed a man," Cecily said again. She spoke quietly, her light clear eyes were steady, but she swayed on her feet. "Sit down!" said Mr. Fernandez; and she did sit down on the couch, straight and rigid in her dainty theatrical uniform, the little fluted cap like a crown.

"I killed a man," she said.

"Yes, we understand that," said Mr. Fernandez. "But how? Where did this happen?"

"In your room," said Cecily. "I shot him. I killed him."

The two tall people standing before her looked down at her with no sign of emotion. She herself was quiet, but she was breathing fast.

"I was going to speak to you, Mr. Fernandez," she went on after a moment. "I knocked at your door and a man opened it and dragged me in. He tried to—make love to me, and I shot him."

"Who was he?"

"I don't know. Someone I'd never met before."

"Where did you get the gun?"

"It was there on a table."

"In my room, eh?"

"Yes," she said, and snapped her teeth shut. But still her jaw trembled. She shivered in this airless place. Miss Peterson proffered a glass of water, and the girl took a sip. Mr. Fernandez looked at Miss Peterson over the girl's head; their eyes met.

"I'll be back in a moment," he said. "In the meantime, we'll say nothing about this to anybody, eh?"

He went out, closing the door behind him, and Miss Peterson sat down in a wicker chair, stretching out her long legs and crossing her ankles.

"I didn't know the wind could be so bad," said Cecily.

"It can be worse than this," said Miss Peterson.

"Will it last long?"

"It will seem long," said Miss Peterson.

There was a moment's silence.

"Just one shot?" asked Miss Peterson.

"Yes," Cecily answered.

"Then maybe you didn't kill him."

"I *did*. I *know* I did."

Miss Peterson clasped her hands behind her head, and gazed before her at nothing.

"Well, let's hope for the best," she said. "Let's hope the police believe your story."

There was a moment's silence.

"Do you mean that you *don't* believe my story?" Cecily asked with a sledgehammer directness.

"That's right," said Miss Peterson. "I don't."

"You don't?" Cecily repeated. "But—why? What is it you don't believe?"

"Well..." said Miss Peterson, "you said you were dragged into Mr. Fernandez's room by an unknown man. He attacked you, and you found a gun lying on the table, and you fired one shot, and you killed him. If I were you, I shouldn't give the police that story."

"You mean—" Cecily began, and stopped short. One of the old ladies was trying to open the glass doors, a spare and very straight old lady in a white blouse and a long black skirt, and a broad belt about her neat waist. Her gray hair was done in two hard little rolls up from the temples, giving her an alert air. She rattled the door handle furiously in a sort of convulsion of annoyance.

"Mrs. Boucher," said Cecily. "She hates me."

"You'll remember not to say anything, won't you?" said Miss Peterson, rising. She looked at Cecily then, and the girl looked back at her, her strange, pale eyes brilliant. "All right!" she said.

Miss Peterson tried to open the doors from inside, but the old lady kept on twisting at the handle. The doors burst open suddenly, and Mrs. Boucher rushed forward against Miss Peterson.

"I want to go up to my room," she said.

"Certainly, Mrs. Boucher," said Miss Peterson, a little surprised at so ordinary a request after such an energetic struggle.

"Well, it seems that the lift's not working," said Mrs. Boucher, indignantly. "I can't walk up five flights of stairs at my time of life. And I want to go to my room. It's time for me to take my pill, and I want to write a letter. I want to go up at once!"

In the absence of Mr. Fernandez, Miss Peterson felt obliged to cope with this.

"I think we can arrange that, Mrs. Boucher," she said. "If you'll come back into the lounge, I'll see...."

She closed the glass doors as they went out, and glancing over her shoulder, she saw Cecily in her theatrical uniform, standing in there as if in a glass cage. The other guests still sat in the lounge, with three oil lamps on tables; they were silent now, in a haze of tobacco smoke. There were none of the boys about, and she borrowed a flashlight from the Major, and went out to the kitchen in search of them.

The kitchen presented an extraordinary appearance. A big room lit by two oil lamps, it was crowded with people sitting and standing; an old Negress was on her knees before a chair. "Oh, Lawd! Take away this wraf!" she chanted. "You got some good an' faithful people here, oh, Lawd! Spare them, and spare my little grandchildren over on the North Road. They *too* young, Lawd!"

Miss Peterson had a few words with the cook, a thin and sorrowful man with gold earrings, standing before the big stove in a heat that was beyond belief. He was attending to his business.

"Maybe the end of all things," he said, stirring a red sauce.

"I want two good strong boys, to carry Mrs. Boucher up to her room," she said; and the cook called two for her. They were, oddly enough, enchanted by the proposal; they found it humorous. "But you mustn't laugh!" Miss Peterson said.

"She goin' to ride up in she chair like the great golden idol!" said one of them, bent double with laughter.

"If you drop she," said the cook, "going to be calamity."

"But you must stop laughing," said Miss Peterson.

The old lady accepted the arrangement in a matter-of-fact spirit. "I hope you're quite sure the boys haven't been drinking," was all she said.

Miss Peterson picked out a wicker arm-chair, a light chair, and the old lady was light; the boys lifted her without any difficulty, and Miss Peterson went ahead of them with a hurricane lantern. In his modern hotel Mr. Fernandez had a modern fireproof staircase of stone, all enclosed, with a heavy door on each landing. And somehow this staircase caught and held the noise of the wind in a great, steady rushing roar; it pressed against the ears, it confused and almost stunned the little party mounting by the light of the lantern.

When they reached the fifth floor, Miss Peterson opened the door into the corridor, the boys set down the chair and the old lady rose. "Thank you!" she said, and set off briskly. Miss Peterson followed her to light her way; she left her in her room with a lamp lighted and everything very neat, and a vase of flowers, dead as if smothered. The boys had gone; as Miss Peterson returned to the enclosed stairs she could hear their voices from below, muffled by the roar of the wind; they were in complete darkness, and looking down, she saw a little light flash as a match was struck. The flame went out, and the voices were silent, the wind obliterated the sound of their footsteps. She went on, went fast, anxious to get out of this gloomy cavern.

A frightful yell came up to her, and she stopped with a sharp intake of the breath. For of all the sounds in the world, she most feared and dreaded a human voice screaming. Another yell came. "Oh, ma sweet *Lawd!*"

"What's the matter?" she called, holding out the lantern and looking down. She could see nothing, she could hear nothing but that eternal hollow roar of the wind. "What's the matter? What's wrong?"

There was no sense in going back up the stairs again, she thought. No one there who'd be any help. There's no other way down but this. And she went on down the stairs. She went half sideways, keeping close to the wall, moving the lantern so that she could see above and below her. As she drew near the next landing she stopped for a moment. I hope that door won't open, very slowly, she thought. She went on past the door. She had to go on down, to see what had happened to the boys, and to get out of this tomb.

I'd be very glad to see Carlos Fernandez just now, she thought.

She had lost track of the floors now. She didn't know where the boys had been when that yell came; she wouldn't know when she came to *that* door. I hope I won't go too far and come out in some sort of cellar, she thought. I hope there's plenty of oil in the lantern. This is the way it is in a nightmare. You go on, and on, and on, downstairs like this, and after a while, you try to run....

Nerves, that's all. This weather, with the glass so low.... After all, what does this amount to? I'm going down the stairs, in a hotel, and there's a gale blowing, and two colored boys yelled.

But there's a dead man somewhere. A murdered man.

And what of it? A dead man is one man we don't have to worry about. If....

She stopped short, because a door was opening. Slowly. She was two steps above it, and she waited with her back to the wall, holding the lantern steady.

A round white circle of light from a flashlight played on the wall; the door opened wider. "Who's that?" she asked.

"My dear girl..." said Mr. Fernandez. "Where the devil have you been?"

He came toward her, and the heavy door began to close very slowly after him. He laid his hand on her shoulder, looking at her with a smile. In the light of the lantern, his dark face had a copper tinge, his lips looked very red, his teeth very white; there was an air of gaiety about him.

"I was worried," he said. "Those fool boys came running down to the kitchen with some crazy story about seeing the Devil—"

"The Devil?" said Miss Peterson.

"You know the sort of thing," he said. "And you didn't come along.... I was getting dam' worried. I was afraid you'd slipped, fallen in the dark."

"I didn't hurry," she said.

"Come and have a drink?" he said, and began to push open the heavy door. Over his shoulder she could see the desk, and a young man sitting at the cashier's window, with the light of a green-shaded lamp on his bent fair head. He glanced up, and she saw his face, a wide mouth, a blunt nose; a sort of Pierrot face, half rueful, and half merry.

"Mr. Fernandez..." said Miss Peterson. "About the man in your room?"

He let the door go, and it began to close by itself.

"That?" he said. "Well, I went up to my room. The door was locked, of course. All the doors lock automatically. Well, I opened the door—" He made a gesture with his wrist. "I went in. All right! There's nothing there. No man. No gun. Nothing."

"Nothing?" she repeated.

"Absolutely nothing. Are you surprised? Did you believe the girl's tale?"

"You don't think there's any truth at all in it?"

"Not a word," he said.

No, thought Miss Peterson. That won't do. Cecily wasn't putting on an act. *Something* certainly happened. "Did you tell Cecily you didn't find anything?" she asked.

"Certainly! I went to her at once. My dear girl, I said, I've looked in my room, and I can't find any dead men. She sat there looking at me with those big, cat's eyes, and never said a word."

"Do you think you convinced her, Mr. Fernandez, that she'd made a mistake?"

"I don't know about that," he said. "I don't care. I said to her, if you're not satisfied, then later on, when the telephone is working again, call the police if you like. Tell *them* this little story. By all means."

"Is she going to do that?"

"I don't know, and I don't care," he said again. "Now let's go and have a drink, eh?"

She made no demur, and they went out through the door. The guests were still sitting in the lounge, as they had been for ever and ever.

"I've ordered tea to be served to them," said Mr. Fernandez. "Also to the two ladies upstairs in their rooms."

As they passed the desk, Miss Peterson glanced sidelong at the young man, and he looked straight at her with an odd smile; a mocking smile, she thought.

"Is your clerk an American?" she asked Mr. Fernandez.

He was struggling to close the glass doors; he got them closed at last.

"I must tell you about that lad," he said. "Sit down, dear lady. What will you have to drink?"

"Nothing, thanks," she said. "Do you know, I think the wind is letting up."

He turned his head alertly; they both listened. The hollow spinning roar went on, and that savage pounding of the surf; but the high whistling note that was like the shriek of a Fury, was gone.

"I believe you're right—as always," he said, and offered her a cigarette; he bent to light it for her, his eyes smiled into hers. Very debonair, he was.

"Six months ago I was in Havana," he said. "That's my favorite place to take a holiday. You know Havana? Little Paris.... Well, I was in a bar, having a drink, when somebody reached for the package of American cigarettes I'd laid down beside me. I caught hold of this fellow's wrist, and he laughed. He apologized. Said he was tired of the native cigarettes. There was something about him.... He was down and out, all right, jacket all buttoned up, and no shirt, pair of tennis shoes all coming to pieces. But there was something.... I offered him one of the cigarettes and a drink, and we got into a little conversation. He told me a wonderful tale, which I certainly didn't believe. But I took a liking to him. I thought he'd be an asset to my new hotel; and I brought him back with me."

"How about his passport?" asked Miss Peterson.

"You always come right to the point," he said. "I never saw such a woman. He had an American passport, all right. For Albert Jeffrey, aged forty. He said he'd come down with one of those tours, and that he'd lost his money and his luggage in a poker game."

"He's young looking for forty..." she observed.

"He is, isn't he?" Mr. Fernandez agreed. "And he seems to have grown a little since he got his passport. Two inches, I'd say." He smiled. "Still, nobody bothered much about the passport, and I don't either. If there's something in his past, some little difficulty—very well. I was glad to give him a chance. It's worked out very well, too."

"I see..." said Miss Peterson, and smiled a little herself. She thought that Mr. Fernandez would know very well how to take the fullest advantage of any 'little difficulty' in an employee's past. But about taking a chance...? I don't know how far he'd go, she thought. Or how far he *has* gone.

Because, though she had not entirely believed Cecily's story, she did not believe his story, either. *Something* has happened, she thought. Something bad.

The wind was undoubtedly moderating; it came fitfully now; the rain would come rattling against the boards and then withdraw, and the heavy artillery of the sea would advance, shaking the earth.

"It may be just a lull," said Mr. Fernandez. "In that case of course, it will come back from the opposite quarter, and possibly worse than ever. But I don't think so. I think it's missed us this time. We—" He stopped. "What's that?" he asked.

It was music; somebody was playing the piano. He sprang to his feet and wrenched open the glass doors, and a Chopin mazurka came to them, loud, very brilliant.

"No—*diga!*" he said, appalled. "No! This is too much!"

He hastened along the passage to the lounge, and Miss Peterson went after him. There was Cecily at the piano, still in her cap and apron. The mazurka came to an end, and the Major clapped. But nobody else did. She began a waltz.

"Please stop her!" said Mr. Fernandez to Miss Peterson. "It's an outrage!"

"Don't you think that perhaps it might amuse the guests?" Miss Peterson asked.

"No! I don't! Did you ever see anything of the sort in a first-class hotel? And after what she told me.... That girl is a devil! Please make her stop!"

Miss Peterson moved forward, and stopped, because above the virtuoso playing of the waltz she heard another sound; a hammering at the door.

"My God!" said Mr. Fernandez.

Miss Peterson went to the girl, and laid a hand on her shoulder; the music ceased and a little stream of fresh air blew in, exquisitely cool, as Mr. Fernandez opened the door to admit three men in rubber coats, two white men and a Negro. And two of them were police constables. Mr. Fernandez closed the door.

"Ah, Superintendent!" cried Mr. Fernandez. "Overtaken by the storm, eh? Well, it's an ill wind, eh…?"

He was too genial. And the man he was speaking to would notice that, Miss Peterson thought. He looked like a man who would notice everything; a slender, almost slight man with dark hair growing a little gray, a big bony nose, and small deep-set blue eyes.

"Quite!" he said civilly enough. "I'd like a word with you, if you please, Mr. Fernandez."

"This way, Superintendent. This way, please!"

Mr. Fernandez opened a door at the far side of the desk, he bowed the superintendent in before him, and the door closed.

"What's all this?" asked the Major. "Accident? Anything wrong?"

"I could not say, sah," answered the negro constable.

In her heart, Miss Peterson echoed the Major's question. What's all this? Something of grave importance to bring out a police superintendent in this weather…. She started nervously at the sound of stirring chords on the piano; the opening of Weber's *Invitation to the Waltz*.

"Don't!" she said.

But Cecily went on until Miss Peterson took her right wrist and raised her hand from the keyboard. The superintendent had come out and stood beside them.

"Will you ladies be kind enough to step into the office?" he said.

Cecily rose, and they followed him into a small room, hot as an oven, furnished with a flat-topped desk, a swivel chair, a safe, a glass-fronted bookcase, and two fancy armchairs with green plush seats. Mr. Fernandez stood waiting to receive them.

"Miss Peterson," he said, "allow me to introduce Superintendent Losee. Superintendent, this is Miss Peterson, our new hostess, and a great acquisition to my little hotel."

He was overdoing it. He was too flowery, his smile was too brilliant.

"Thank you," said the superintendent, and glanced toward Cecily.

"This is Miss Wilmot, Superintendent," said Mr. Fernandez. "I'm afraid she's the only one who can give you any information about this—killing. She's the only one who seems to know anything about it."

Cecily made a faint sound like a gasp; Miss Peterson, too, was startled by this sudden attack, and by the venom in his tone.

"You're not obliged to answer any questions," said Losee to everyone in general. "It is my duty to warn you that anything you say may be written down and may be subsequently used in evidence against you. Will you be seated, ladies?"

They sat down in the green-seated armchairs, Losee took the swivel chair, Mr. Fernandez sat on the edge of the desk, smoking a cigarette. He looked very debonair in his white suit; he looked too debonair, even arrogant. And Losee and his constable looked very businesslike.

Well, something's happened, she thought. I wish they'd get on with it. She glanced about the little office, and on the top of the bookcase, directly behind the superintendent's head, she caught sight of a stuffed baby alligator dressed in a constable's uniform, helmet with chin-strap, belt and so on, leaning back a little to rest upon its varnished tail. She stared and stared at it, half hypnotized by this grotesquerie.

"We have received information," said Losee, in his level voice, "that a murder has been committed on these premises."

"May I ask—how you received information, Superintendent?" Mr. Fernandez asked.

"We'll go into that presently," said Losee. "It is the duty of anyone having any information to communicate the information to the police."

"Miss Wilmot is the only one with any information," said Mr. Fernandez.

Cecily looked up at him with her clear pale eyes, and he looked back at her; it was a long and deadly glance that they exchanged.

She took time to answer.

"I killed a man," said Cecily briefly.

"Cannon," said the superintendent, and the constable brought out a notebook and a pencil.

"Do you wish to make a statement, Miss Wilmot?"

"I killed a man. I shot him—in self-defense."

"Where did this take place, Miss Wilmot?"

She was slow to answer that.

"In one of the rooms upstairs," she said at last. "I don't know which."

Mr. Fernandez looked at her quickly.

"On what floor, Miss Wilmot?" the superintendent asked.

"I'm not sure," she answered.

"You will save everyone—yourself included—considerable time and trouble, if you give me some idea—"

"I don't know," she said.

"Will you relate the circumstances which led up to this occurrence?"

"I was coming down from my room on the top floor," said Cecily. "I thought I'd stop and ask Miss Peterson if there were any orders for me. I was going along the hall—"

"On what floor is Miss Peterson's room?"

"The second."

"You were on the second floor, then?"

"I don't know. The lights were all out. I only had a flashlight. It might have been another floor."

"Very well. Continue, please."

"I saw an open door and a light inside. When I went there, a man dragged me inside. He attacked me. There was a gun lying on a table, and I picked it up and shot him."

"What did you do then?"

"I came downstairs and told Mr. Fernandez and Miss Peterson."

"How many flights of stairs did you go down?"

"I don't remember."

"What happened when you fired the shot?"

"The man fell down."

"What reason did you have for believing him dead?"

"He looked dead," said Cecily. "I spoke to him. I touched him. He *was* dead."

"Mr. Fernandez," said the superintendent, "can you supply Constable Cannon with a lantern? Thank you! We'll have to make a search of the premises."

"Some of the rooms are occupied," said Mr. Fernandez. "I hope you won't feel it necessary to disturb any of the guests, Superintendent."

"I hope not," said the superintendent. "Miss Wilmot, I'll ask you to come with us. You have a passkey, Mr. Fernandez?"

"Oh, yes. Certainly. But I'd better come too. I can tell you what rooms are occupied."

"Quite!" said the superintendent. "And Miss Peterson as well, if you please."

He looked at Miss Peterson; for the first time, their eyes met. And it seemed to her that his small, deep-set, unwinking eyes were a little like the alligator's.

IV

They went in a procession past the desk, where Alfred Jeffrey still sat; Mr. Fernandez opened the door to the staircase and they began to mount, Constable Cannon going first with the lantern.

I don't like these stairs, Miss Peterson thought. The wind was still loud here; their shadows were monstrous on the stone walls. Nobody said a word. We're going with a lantern to look for a body, she thought. Why does he want *me* along? What does he think? What information has he got, and where did he get it from?

Mr. Fernandez opened the door on the first landing.

"In what part of the corridor was the room you entered, Miss Wilmot?" asked the superintendent.

"I don't remember," she said.

"Then we'll begin here," he said.

"Allow me!" said Mr. Fernandez, and approached the door facing the staircase; he opened it with a flourish, and Miss Peterson saw him smile, vividly.

The light of the lantern showed a neat and somewhat desolate little room. Losee entered, looked in the big wardrobe, he opened the door of the bathroom. They went on to the next room, and it was the same. They turned the corner into the main corridor.

"This," said Mr. Fernandez, "is Miss Peterson's room."

"Sorry, Miss Peterson," said Losee. But he looked in there, in her wardrobe, in her bathroom. He was going to look in every room; this was going on for ever and ever.

"This is Mrs. Barley's room," said Mr. Fernandez. "She may be in there. My housekeeper, you know."

He knocked, but there was no answer. He knocked again; then he unlocked the door. A candle burned in there, and by its light they could see Mrs. Barley lying on the bed, her face flushed, her gray hair disordered. She was snoring with her mouth open, and there was a bottle of gin on the floor beside her. It was a distressing spectacle, at which Miss Peterson felt ashamed and unhappy. But undaunted, the superintendent looked into her wardrobe and her closet.

They finished with that floor, and they returned to the staircase. As Mr. Fernandez opened the door, a gay faraway voice called from below. "Ahoy there, me hearties!"

"Come up, Doctor!" said the superintendent; and they stood waiting while a man with a flashlight mounted quickly into the ring of lantern light. He was a tall man, very thin, long-legged, moving springily with bent knees; he had cropped white hair, and a brick-red face and a meaningless smile.

"Dr. Tinker," the superintendent announced, and Mr. Fernandez shook hands with him. "Glad to see you, Doctor," he said.

"Where's your corpse?" the doctor asked cheerfully. "Oh, still hunting? I had a time getting here. Trees down, wires down. We may have some more corpses. But the worst of it's over. Oh, yes. Glass is rising."

Mr. Fernandez opened the door on the second landing.

"My little suite is on this floor, Superintendent," he said. "Perhaps you'd like to look at that first?"

"We'll take the rooms in order, thank you," said the superintendent; and once more Mr. Fernandez unlocked and opened a door.

But this time it was different.

"My God!" cried Mr. Fernandez.

No one else made a sound. The light of a lantern showed a bald little man lying on his back, his eyes wide open, a pinched look about his hooked nose. He wore a singlet, and dirty white duck trousers; his heels were together and the toes of his heavy-soled shoes were turned out at right angles; his bare arms were straight at his sides.

"My—God!" said Mr. Fernandez again.

They all stood in a group in the doorway, Constable Cannon holding out the lantern so that they could see what was there.

"Can anybody identify this man?" asked the superintendent.

"That's the one!" said Cecily instantly. "That's the man I shot."

The doctor turned to look at her.

"Very well," said Losee. "Now then, kindly go down to the office and wait, Miss Wilmot. Miss Peterson and Mr. Fernandez too, if you please. Constable Cannon will accompany you."

The doctor moved forward, the superintendent took the lantern and closed the door, and the four others were left in darkness. But Mr. Fernandez and the constable both brought out flashlights; Cannon went first, holding his behind him, like a movie usher. After him came Cecily alone; as he illumined the steps, her foot in a gleaming high-heeled pump would appear. Mr. Fernandez took Miss Peterson by the arm, in a grip a little too tight. When I came down here before, she thought, that poor little bald man must have been lying there in that room, close to the staircase.... What made those boys yell? The Devil, Fernandez said. Maybe....

They went past the desk where Alfred Jeffrey was still working; the people in the lounge were still there, waiting. They went into the stifling little office, and Cannon shut the door and stood before it. Now Mr. Fernandez was sitting in the swivel chair with the alligator constable behind him. The great wind still rushed at the walls.

"Couldn't we have some air?" Cecily asked.

"Presently," said Mr. Fernandez, without interest.

The door opened, and Losee and the constable entered. Mr. Fernandez rose. "Take this chair, Superintendent!" "No. No.... Don't move, Mr. Fernandez."

"I insist...."

So Losee sat again in the swivel chair, and Mr. Fernandez sat on the edge of the desk.

"Miss Wilmot," said the superintendent. "I'll ask you to repeat your account of the occurrence."

"You mean—all over again?"

"If you please."

"I was going along the hall—"

"Can you remember now which floor?"

"No," she said. "I'm sorry, but I can't. I saw a room with a light in it, and I thought it might be Miss Peterson's room—"

"You don't know which Miss Peterson's room is, Miss Wilmot?"

"Yes. Yes, I know. But the halls were dark. I was mixed up. I knocked, and a man pulled me in—"

"Will you describe the man?"

"It was that one. The one you saw."

"You're positive of that?"

"Yes," she said. "That was the one."

"Continue, please."

"He—put his arm around me. He wouldn't let me go. I struggled with him. Then I saw a little gun lying on a table, and I picked it up, and I shot him."

"Where was the man when you shot him?"

"Standing there."

"Then you had escaped from him?"

"For the moment. But he was between me and the door. He started to come at me again. I told him to stop. And when he kept on coming, I shot at him."

"What happened then, Miss Wilmot?"

"He fell."

"What was your aim when you fired this shot?"

"I didn't aim exactly. I just wanted to stop him."

"After the man fell, what did you do?"

"But I told you. I came down and told Mr. Fernandez and Miss Peterson."

"After how long an interval?"

"Oh, only a moment."

"What would you consider a moment?"

"I came down right away."

"Miss Wilmot, did you make a telephone call to the police station at two thirty-eight?"

"No," she said, staring at him. "No, I didn't."

"At two thirty-eight, a call was received by Sergeant Brown. This call asked for police protection. According to the sergeant the call was made by a woman. 'Please send a policeman here. I'm afraid there's been a murder.'"

"I didn't say that. I didn't ring up anybody."

"This call was made just before the telephone service was disrupted. Approximately two hours before you notified Mr. Fernandez of this shooting."

"I didn't make the call."

"Were you aware of the presence of the deceased in the hotel before you confronted him in the room on the third floor?"

"No."

"Miss Wilmot," he said, "I'm going to ask Constable Cannon to read aloud to you the questions I have asked you, and the answers you have given. Go ahead, Cannon."

In a gentle sing-song voice Cannon read his notes, and Miss Peterson listened with uneasiness. The girl's lying, she thought. I can't tell which part of her story is a lie, but maybe the superintendent can.

"Miss Wilmot," he said, "do you wish to reconsider any of the answers you have given?"

"No, I don't!" she said.

"You wish it to go on record that you shot this man, and that he then fell to the ground?"

"Yes."

"Very well," he said. "I shall be obliged to place you under arrest, and subsequently to charge you with homicide. You may take with you a few articles—"

"Take...?" Cecily repeated. "But you're not—? I don't have to go—to prison, do I?"

"You are under arrest, Miss Wilmot, for shooting and killing an unknown person on these premises—"

The girl rose, her eyes fixed on his face.

"But it was in self-defense!" she said. *"That's* not murder."

"Miss Wilmot," said the superintendent, "that man was shot in the back."

V

There was a complete silence.

"Kindly get your things together," said the superintendent.

"May I go upstairs with her, Superintendent?" asked Miss Peterson.

"I'm sorry, but that's not possible. Constable Cannon will accompany Miss Wilmot to her door, and wait for her."

Miss Peterson rose and held out her hand to the girl.

"Take it easy!" she said.

But Cecily did not look like one who took anything easy. Her beautiful, narrow face had a look of proud scorn; the little frilled cap gave her, Miss Peterson thought, a Marie Antoinette air. Her fingers closed tight on Miss Peterson's.

"Thank you!" she said.

Cannon opened the door, she went out with her head high; and he followed her. Mr. Fernandez was lighting a cigarette.

"Superintendent," said Miss Peterson, sweet as honey, "doesn't the fact that the man was shot in the back invalidate her story completely?"

"Miss Peterson," he answered, "that young woman has stated three times that she killed this man."

"I thought the police were a little distrustful about confessions."

"Quite!" he said. "It's not at all unusual for people to confess to crimes they've nothing to do with. But this case has certain elements.... This young woman has had ample opportunity to commit the crime, and she doesn't seem at all the hysterical type. On the contrary. She was playing the piano when I arrived here."

Miss Peterson believed in the maxim live and let live. But for her, that meant a little more than keeping herself alive—which she did very efficiently. She was often willing to go to considerable trouble in helping other people keep alive. She had a fairly good idea of what the prison in Riquezas would be like, and how it would be there for a young white girl.

And she had an extremely good idea, based upon experience, of what could be done in a place like Riquezas by influence. Not by bribery, but purely by prestige. Which Mr. Fernandez had. She looked at him, and he raised his eyebrows and shrugged his shoulders.

"Superintendent," she said, "if bail could be arranged...?"

"Out of the question, Miss Peterson, in a homicide case. Except in most unusual circumstances."

"But self-defense...?"

"Shooting a man in the back doesn't give the impression of self-defense."

"He may have whirled around. She may have lost her head a little—been panic-stricken."

"Miss Peterson," said the superintendent, "you're wasting your time. We received a telephone call asking for police protection, and informing us that a murder had been committed. As soon as the weather allowed, we came here; and we found that a murder had been committed. A young woman on the premises voluntarily confessed to the shooting."

"She's very young," said Miss Peterson.

"Her age, according to her passport, is twenty-one," said the superintendent. Miss Peterson waited for a moment.

"Perhaps you'll be kind enough to give me the name of a good lawyer?" she asked. "I'd like to employ someone at once for Miss Wilmot."

"It's not within my province to recommend lawyers," said the superintendent. And in spite of his amiable and polite manner, she could see that he was growing more and more angry. "Our jail is completely modern, and very well administered," he said, and paused; and then said with suppressed fury, "The girl isn't going to a torture chamber, y'know."

No, I don't know, thought Miss Peterson. A wild gazelle in jail.... But I'll have to keep quiet now. I'm irritating the superintendent. And Fernandez is not going to lift a finger to help the girl; *that's* plain enough.

"Shall I go into the lounge and see if everyone's all right?" she asked.

"I must ask you to remain here," said the superintendent. "When Cannon returns, I'd like a statement from you. I shall have to question everyone on the premises, naturally."

"Naturally," Mr. Fernandez repeated. "Well.... You'll have my fullest co-operation, Superintendent." He smiled wryly. "A fine opening for my new hotel, eh? This fellow.... Off some ship, don't you think?"

"What ship do you suggest?" asked the superintendent.

"I hear that a schooner put in here," said Mr. Fernandez.

"I haven't enough facts yet," said Losee. "The very brief examination I made didn't yield anything much. No papers, nothing."

"My theory is that he's off some ship. He looks like a sailor, a deckhand. He came ashore, and when the storm broke, he wandered in here. He could have got in very easily without being noticed. There's a side entrance, for example.... He gets in, he goes around to see what he can pick up."

"All your bedroom doors lock automatically?"

"Yes, that's a fact."

"How would it be possible for anyone to enter one of the rooms?"

"Locks can be picked, eh?"

"Now, about your staff, Mr. Fernandez. How many people do you employ?"

"God knows!" said Mr. Fernandez. "You know how it is here. I have on my payroll a cook and a helper, three waiters, three chambermaids, five boys, one clerk. A skeleton staff until the season begins. But they have their relations and their friends hanging around."

"Your housekeeper, now. What can you tell me about her?"

"A fine woman," said Mr. Fernandez. "I had her in the old hotel, y'know. A very fine woman, capable, trustworthy. An Englishwoman. The only thing is, she has this little weakness—You understand."

"You mean she drinks?"

"From time to time. But it doesn't interfere with her work. Only from time to time, and only at night. This storm would get on her nerves."

"Quite. This Miss Wilmot, now?"

"Yes?"

"Did she have any love affair, to your knowledge?"

"She didn't. And if she did, it would have been to my knowledge. I assure you of that. I know very well what goes on in my hotel. No love affairs, no letters. Not one single letter since she came here."

"What do you know about her antecedents?"

"Nothing. Nothing at all. She came here on a cruise ship. She came to my hotel, and she asked me for a job. Well, I thought, why not? I thought, here's a girl of education, good manners, very musical. Why not? She had a passport; everything in order. And her conduct's been above reproach, except—"

"Except?" said the superintendent.

"She's a little hot-tempered. High-spirited."

"Any instances of violence?"

"Oh, no!" said Mr. Fernandez. "A little hot-tempered, that's all. Impulsive. She's inclined to act without thinking."

He was doing his best to close the prison gates upon the wild gazelle, and doing it deliberately.

"Did she ever, to your knowledge, possess or carry any weapons, Mr. Fernandez?"

Mr. Fernandez knocked the ash off his cigarette into an ashtray in the form of a scarlet lobster.

"No..." he said. "No." At that moment there was a knock on the door, and Constable Cannon appeared carrying a small suitcase. Cecily stood behind him. She had taken off the cap and apron, but she still wore the black dress and shoes and stockings, and she had a wide black straw hat on the back of her head. She had put on more lipstick; she looked superb, pale, beautiful and fierce.

"Have you a room that's not being used, Mr. Fernandez?" asked the superintendent. "The writing-room? Very well. Tell Humber to remain in the writing-room with Miss Wilmot, Cannon. I'll need you here."

"*Au revoir*, Cecily!" said Miss Peterson. "And remember—take it easy."

"Thank you..." said Cecily, and her clear eyes rested upon Miss Peterson's face for a moment.

That kid is frightened, thought Miss Peterson. It's a damn shame to let her go to jail, even if she gets out in a few days, even if she gets out tomorrow, it's too much.

"Now, Miss Peterson, if you please..." said the superintendent; and he began asking her questions. He wanted a detailed account of her movements since she had arrived at the hotel. He got it. He wanted a full account of Cecily's dramatic announcement.

"Quite. Did she appear agitated?"

"Very. Her teeth were chattering. She was badly upset. She told me what she told you—that the man had dragged her into a room, and that she shot him in self-defense."

"Do you recall any other details?"

Miss Peterson looked down at the floor with an air of serious concentration. She was making up her mind whether or not she would tell Losee what Cecily had said at first. That this shooting had taken place in Mr. Fernandez's room. Fernandez has got it coming to him, she thought. He threw Cecily to the wolves.

But Cecily herself didn't mention that to the superintendent, she thought. Mr. Fernandez may have persuaded her to keep quiet about it, or she may have some very good reason of her own. I might make matters worse by telling him.

"Do you recall any other details, Miss Peterson?" the superintendent repeated.

"No..." she said, slowly, deliberately giving herself a chance to 'recall' something later on, if she chose.

"Miss Peterson, before the removal of the body, I'll ask you to take another look at the deceased."

"But, Superintendent," Mr. Fernandez protested. "That's a very difficult ordeal for a young lady."

"There are a good many unpleasant details connected with any murder," said the superintendent.

"Miss Peterson's never been in Riquezas before," Mr. Fernandez went on. "She had no intention of coming now. She was on her way to Havana via New York when I met her on the ship, and offered her this position."

"Quite!" said Losee. "I'll ask you to hold yourself in readiness, Miss Peterson. And now, Mr. Fernandez, I'd like to interview your clerk—alone."

Mr. Fernandez rose.

"It won't be necessary to disturb the guests, will it?"

"I'll take your staff first," said Losee. "But if none of them is able to identify the body, I'll have to ask the guests."

"Not the ladies?" he cried. "But, Superintendent, they're not the sort of ladies who'd know a man like that! This is obviously what you might call a—an extraneous accident. The man doesn't belong here. He came in to shelter from the storm. Or possibly to steal. Some fellow off a ship."

"We'll investigate every possibility," said the superintendent. "You can count on that."

"Won't you try every other avenue, before you disturb the guests of the hotel?" Mr. Fernandez asked. "If you'd make inquiries as to whether anyone is missing from a ship—?"

"We shall use all reasonable discretion," said Losee, stiffly.

It was high time to let him alone, and apparently Mr. Fernandez realized that.

"The matter couldn't be in more capable hands," he said, with a very un-English bow. "I'll send Jeffrey in, Superintendent. The rest of the staff is at your disposal."

He held open the door for Miss Peterson and followed her, closing the door.

"Now we're going to have a nice time," he said, wiping his face with his mauve silk handkerchief. "A *nice* time... When he starts asking those boys questions, he'll hear plenty. Devils, God knows what. Well...!" He shrugged his shoulders. "Can you do anything with Mrs. Barley?" he asked.

"I can try," she answered, dubiously.

"I could wring her neck," he said. "I have a nice staff, eh? I have that Cecily, I have Mrs. Barley.... Now, if there's any little trouble about Jeffrey, that's all I need. You have a torch, eh? I'll send Jeffrey in, and then I'll have a talk with the guests. We must keep up the morale."

They looked at the guests. Tea had been served to them, very nicely, too, on little individual tables spread with pink linen cloths; they sat there in the light of the oil lamps, in the stifling heat, displaying the most admirable morale.

"I think I can give them a little air," said Mr. Fernandez. "Well! If you can get Mrs. Barley in shape to see the superintendent...? And while you're up there, you might look in on Mrs. Fish and Mrs. Boucher—see if they're all right."

They moved forward together, he stopped at the desk to speak to the clerk, and she went on to the stairs. She met the doctor coming down with the hurricane lantern, nimble as a grasshopper.

"Cheerio!" he said waving his hand.

Cheerio yourself, and see how you like it, thought Miss Peterson. I think I'll start at the top and work my way down. I'll see Mrs. Boucher first. And I'll never climb these stairs again. She was so tired, and hot, her legs ached, her temples throbbed, there was a feeling of pressure against her ear drums. The wind was still roaring by, and it seemed to her that the building shook from it. I hate these stairs, she thought, climbing up and up and up.

She knocked at Mrs. Boucher's door. "Come in!" said the old lady. And it was like entering a different world. A wonderful coziness prevailed; in her thin black dressing gown, the old lady sat at the little writing table with a shaded lamp on it, a tea-tray stood on a table; there were photographs in frames, and there was a big yellow cat lying in the armchair.

"I came to see if you wanted anything," said Miss Peterson.

"You shouldn't have come all the way up for that," said the old lady. "You look tired, child. Sit down and rest. Taffy, get out of that chair!"

The cat looked up at her, and closed one luminous green eye, and didn't stir.

Miss Peterson picked him up, and sat down with him on her knees. The old lady glanced at her, and then went on writing her letter. This happened to be exactly what Miss Peterson needed. She stroked the cat with her fine expert hand, and she thought about things. It was the first chance she had had, the first moment of peace and quiet. There's too much monkey-business going on here, she thought. Things I don't like. For instance....

She thought about the things she didn't like, and she began to get a steadier view. With a sigh, she rose and put the cat back on the cushion.

"This was a nice little visit," she said.

"Come again!" said the old lady. "You're welcome at any time."

Miss Peterson returned to that eternal staircase, and went down feeling much rested. She counted the landings; she opened the door on the second landing, and went to Mrs. Fish's room. No coziness here; it was curiously untidy, and Mrs. Fish herself, still lying on the bed, looked wilted.

"How is the toothache, Mrs. Fish?" Miss Peterson asked.

"It's almost gone, thanks to you," said Mrs. Fish. "Do you know, the last time I had a toothache was in Guatemala in the jungle, and an old Indian woman cured it, by magic."

"That's very interesting," said Miss Peterson.

"I had a good many strange experiences, traveling around with my husband," said Mrs. Fish in her flat tired voice. "We went to Nicaragua, Venezuela, Brazil, Peru, Chile. Jungles, swamps, mountains.... I've had fevers. I've been bitten by poisonous insects. It was all very picturesque."

"It must have been," said Miss Peterson, trying to imagine Mrs. Fish in a jungle.

"My husband was very adventurous," Mrs. Fish went on, and turned her head a little to look at that photograph of the Devil. "Quite out of the ordinary. I told you he was murdered, didn't I?"

"Yes, you did."

"I'm looking for his murderer," said Mrs. Fish. "That's really why I'm here."

"Here?" Miss Peterson repeated, startled. "But do you think he's here?"

"If he isn't here now, he's coming," said Mrs. Fish. "I've been looking for him a long, long time."

Miss Peterson looked down at the pale, limp little woman with a sort of dismay. It's not human, she thought, to say a thing like that, without any expression at all. It's crazy.

"But—do you know who the murderer is?" she asked.

"Yes—I do," said Mrs. Fish, still looking at the photograph.

"Have you told the police?"

"You see," Mrs. Fish explained, "I've spent so much time in places where there weren't any policemen, that I've got into the way of attending to things for myself."

"But this—" said Miss Peterson, "this isn't a thing you can attend to yourself."

Mrs. Fish said nothing to that.

She's out of her mind, Miss Peterson thought, and in a very dangerous way. Or if she isn't out of her mind, it's still worse. It's—ghastly.

"I'm sure the police here are very efficient," she said. "If you have any private information, Mrs. Fish, do take it to the police. It's always a mistake to try to handle things like that alone."

"No," said Mrs. Fish.

It was a rare thing for Miss Peterson to be at a loss, or at all irresolute. But she was now. Shall I try to draw her out? she asked herself. Shall I try to find out who she thinks is the murderer? And how she expects to 'attend' to things when she finds him? Or is this all just fantastic nonsense?

Mrs. Fish turned her eyes away from the photograph, and looked up at Miss Peterson.

"Is there any news?" she asked, with the first spark of interest she had shown.

"But—what sort of news?"

"Has anything happened?" asked Mrs. Fish. "Any accident?"

Well, there's a dead man on this floor, thought Miss Peterson. A murdered man, if that means anything to you.

"I mean anything about ships," said Mrs. Fish.

"I haven't heard anything about ships," said Miss Peterson.

She had to get out of here. The heat, the pressure against her ear drums, the sound of this flat voice, had suddenly become too much. She had to get away.

"I'll be back—" she began, when suddenly the lights came on; the chandelier and the bedside lamp in dazzling brilliance.

"Would you mind turning off that top light, please?" said Mrs. Fish closing her eyes.

Miss Peterson snapped off the switch, and went, closing the door after her. If the current's on, the elevator will be running, she thought, and I'm going to ride down to the next floor to see Mrs. Barley. Because I'm sick and tired of those stairs.

It was nice to see the corridor lighted. She rang for the elevator and waited, and it was very agreeable to hear it coming. The door rattled open; there was the boy in his uniform. Miss Peterson looked at him.

"You're one of the boys who carried Mrs. Boucher upstairs, aren't you?" she said.

"Yes, mistress. My name Howard, mistress."

"What was it you saw, Howard?" she asked.

"I do not understand, mistress."

"Was it a ghost?" she asked. "I was there on the stairs myself, behind you, and I thought I felt something."

"It was the Devil we see, mistress," he answered. "Oh, it was bad!"

"I've never seen the Devil," she said. "How did he look?"

"Oh, he was tall, mistress, tall as a tree, and he wear a white robe shining with fire. It was bad."

"A white robe? I didn't think the Devil wore white."

"He look anyhow he want, mistress. He can—"

The bell rang below, and a little red light showed in the car. Miss Peterson stepped into it, the door closed, the gate closed, and they started down. And then, out went the lights, the car stopped.

"Oh, Gawd!" moaned Howard. "What coming now?"

The Devil, probably, thought Miss Peterson, leaning against the wall of the car. Howard and the other boy saw the Devil, and Mrs. Fish has a photograph of him.... And here I am, shut up in a little box, hanging in the air.... All right! Let him come. I'm *tired*.

VI

She turned on her flashlight to confront Howard. His face was a mask of anguish.

"Death in the house, mistress," he said. "Devil come to fetch he own."

He knows about the dead man then, thought Miss Peterson. Probably they all know by this time; and possibly they knew before we did. The Devil in a white robe, shining with fire.... I'd like to know what it was they saw—who they saw.

"We cannot get out, mistress. Door will not open until we level with the floor."

"Mr. Fernandez will get us out," said she.

She was perfectly sure of that. She had complete confidence in Fernandez in all such matters. Combined with a very definite distrust of him in other matters. He would certainly get you out of an elevator that was stuck; he would, she thought, be the right man to have beside you in an earthquake, or a flood, or any such peril; he was resourceful, energetic and audacious.

But he would not forget his own interests. He'd save your life, in danger, she thought, but if anyone threatened his life, or his money, or his prestige, he'd.... Well, what? What is he capable of? He did his best to make sure that poor kid went to jail, and he knew as well as I that she wasn't guilty. What else would he do? What else has he done?

Sabe dios! she said to herself with a sigh, leaning her broad shoulders against the wall. I'm tired. I don't seem to feel very well—but I think that's because I'm hungry. If I could have some dinner now, and a cup of coffee—a little cup of Brazilian coffee, very sweet....

"Devil can go where he like, mistress," said Howard, in a miserable, hollow voice. "He can pass through the air."

"He can't come here," she said, almost mechanically, because it was second nature to her to reassure people. "I have a charm."

"Charm too strong for Mister Devil?" he cried.

"That's it," said she; and he laughed.

"Mister Losee, he don't believe us see the Devil," he said, and laughed again. "Maybe some day Mister Losee meet him, heself."

The lights came on, and the car began to descend, slowly, as if floating. Miss Peterson got out at the second floor, and went along to Mrs. Barley's room. She knocked, but there was no answer; she knocked louder, very loudly. But still there was no answer.

I don't like my job, she thought, going into the corridor and ringing for the elevator. The lights were still on, and that was something. Up came the elevator, and Howard opened the door. "Will you get me a passkey?" she asked, and stood waiting, unhappy about Mrs. Barley. She's a damned nuisance, she thought. I want to get to my room and take a bath, and then I want my dinner. She waited and waited in the bright, airless corridor with a floor of some dark-red composition. The wind still blew and the rain still rattled against the boarded windows at the end of the hall, but no longer with ferocity.

Oh, hurry up! she said within herself to Howard; but it was a long time before she heard the elevator start upward; it stopped, the door rattled again, and young Jeffrey stepped out.

"Lock yourself out?" he asked cheerfully.

"No. It's for one of the other rooms," she said, and held out her hand for the key.

"I'll open the door for you."

"No, thanks," she said. "If you'll just let me have the key for a moment."

"That's against the law," he said. "It's a Fernandez statute that I'm never to give the passkey to anybody. Ever."

"It's only Mrs. Barley's door," she said.

"If you wouldn't mind advice from an old hand," he said. "I think Mrs. Barley'd better be let alone for a while."

"I know," said Miss Peterson. "But she can't be. The superintendent will want to see her."

"He did see her, didn't he?"

"Let's get on with it," Miss Peterson suggested, gently; and he went along the hall and unlocked a door. "Thank you!" said Miss Peterson, wanting him to go. But he stood with his back against the open door, looking into the room where the candle had burned down very low in the glass shade.

"Suppose I open the shutters?" said Jeffrey. "Our Mr. Fernandez is ordering all of them on this side of the house opened."

"Well, all right, thanks!" said Miss Peterson reluctantly, for her instinct was to protect the wretched Mrs. Barley from the blithe and mocking gaze of Alfred Jeffrey. As he crossed the room, she turned on the bedside lamp and blew out the candle. Mrs. Barley still lay there, flushed and disheveled; she still snored. Miss Peterson bent to pick up the bottle of gin from the floor; she put it away in a bureau drawer. Then she picked up a lacy white cotton sweater that lay on the floor by the bed, and something fell out of it with a thud. It was a small automatic.

She dropped the sweater back on top of it, and glanced toward Jeffrey who stood by the window. And she found him looking at her. The little gun was covered now, but she couldn't tell whether or not he had seen it. In any case it must not be touched. She sat down in a chair and waited until he got the heavy shutters unfastened; the blessed fresh air came in, and the loud pounding of the surf and the hiss of the falling rain.

"Thanks," she said. "And will you please send somebody up with a pot of coffee, good and strong, and hot?"

"With pleasure," he said. But still he didn't go. "Poor old Barley..." he said, looking at her. "A victim."

"Of what?" asked Miss Peterson.

"Of Fate, very likely," said Jeffrey. "She has a past, you know. She used to have a little hotel of her own, doing very well, so I've heard. But one night, when she'd had a little drop of something to comfort her, she accidentally set the place on fire. It burned to the ground with a frightful loss of life."

"How frightful?" asked Miss Peterson.

"Thousands," he said. "A holocaust of cockroaches."

"I see!" said Miss Peterson. "Will you ask them to send the coffee as soon as possible, please?"

"I don't think you like me," said Jeffrey.

"Give me time," said she.

He went away then, and Miss Peterson set to work to do what she could for Mrs. Barley. She bathed her face and her wrists with cold water; she kept on speaking to her by name, with a quiet insistence. "Mrs. Barley, try to answer me, will you? Mrs. Barley? Mrs. Barley? Mrs. Barley."

"Yes...?" said Mrs. Barley, thickly, without opening her eyes.

"Mrs. Barley. I'm Miss Peterson. The storm is passing, Mrs. Barley. If you'll sit up, you'll feel the breeze. *That's* the way!"

She helped Mrs. Barley to sit up and propped the pillows behind her. She waited a moment, then she said very quickly and clearly, "There's been a murder here."

She had hoped to shock Mrs. Barley out of her semi-stupor, but it didn't work.

"Yes..." Mrs. Barley said, trying to keep her heavy eyes open.

"The police want to ask you some questions." Tears began to trickle down Mrs. Barley's face; her long upper lip quivered piteously.

"The police...?" she said. "The police.... *I* know.... It all—it all happened before. The police.... They said—crimiley—crimiley...."

"That's all over," said Miss Peterson, bathing her face.

"Crimiley—negli..." said Mrs. Barley, struggling miserably. "*This* time tried.... Tried.... Saw him—throw a match—on floor.... I tried.... But banged the door—in me face."

"One of the servants?"

"Prowler."

"A prowler here?"

"Prowler," said Mrs. Barley, weeping. "I tried. Resplons... responsi...."

"You're *not* responsible," said Miss Peterson. "Don't cry, Mrs. Barley. Just take it easy."

"I saw him.... Dead as a doornail.... So I took... I took it...."

"The gun?"

"I took the glun.... Then I—then I—"

It was painful to witness this. Her mind was clearing a little; but her tongue, her lips were beyond her control, and her tears, too.

"You took away the gun?" said Miss Peterson.

"Flom—floor..." Mrs. Barley said, with a frantic effort. "Tel—floor—"

"Telephone?"

"Tele-flon—police...."

There was a knock at the door, and Mrs. Barley gave a cry.

"Don't worry," said Miss Peterson.

It was a colored boy with a pot of coffee and cup and saucer on a tray.

"Miss Wilmot ask if you will say farewell to she, mistress?" he said.

"Is she going now?"

"Yes, mistress."

She took the tray and set it down on the bedside table. "I'll be back in a moment," she said to Mrs. Barley. "In the meantime...." She poured a little coffee into the cup. "If you'd just sip this, you'll feel much better. I'll be back in a moment," she repeated.

She was sorry to leave Mrs. Barley just at this point, but there was no help for it. She rode down in the elevator with Howard, and came out into the lounge that was utterly transformed, pleasantly lit by little gold-shaded lamps, the electric fans all purring away, stirring the damp, fresh air. It was empty.

"Sup'intendent in Mr. Fernandez's office, mistress," Howard told her, and she hastened there. The office, too, was changed, with the window open and an emerald-shaded lamp glowing on the desk. The superintendent was there and Constable Cannon, and Mr. Fernandez, all standing, and Cecily standing among them. She turned quickly toward Miss Peterson, and in those clear, light eyes there was a strange look, of appeal, of dismay, of fear.

"Miss Wilmot asked to see you before she left," said the superintendent. "I granted this request."

"I only wanted to say good-by," said Cecily.

Miss Peterson held out her hand to the girl a little absently.

"Superintendent," she said, "I've just been talking to Mrs. Barley, the housekeeper. I think you'd be interested. She was the one who called up the police."

"She...?" said Mr. Fernandez, with a start.

"I thought you'd like to talk to her. Before Miss Wilmot—leaves," said Miss Peterson.

"Very good," said the superintendent. "Presently."

"She has a gun there, Superintendent," said Miss Peterson. "A little automatic. You'd like to see *that*, I'm sure."

"Quite!" said Losee. "Cannon, you'll stop here with Miss Wilmot. Miss Peterson, I'll ask you to come up with me. You needn't bother, Mr. Fernandez."

"No bother!" said Mr. Fernandez. "Mrs. Barley would talk more if I was there. She's used to me, you know."

"Quite!" said the superintendent. "But I shan't need to trouble you just now, Mr. Fernandez."

Ja, ja, ja, don Carlos! You lost *that* move, thought Miss Peterson. And maybe you'll lose the next one, too. Maybe Cecily won't go to jail at all. She glanced at him and smiled, a slow wide smile that showed her even white teeth, and he raised both hands a little in a graceful and somehow rather touching gesture.

He walked with them to the elevator, he bowed them into it. "Oh, the key!" cried Miss Peterson.

"Mrs. Barley is locked in her room?" asked the superintendent.

"Oh, no! It's to save her the trouble of getting up," Miss Peterson explained, and got out of the elevator and went to the desk. There was nobody there; and she rang the bell standing on the counter. Out came a colored boy through a door next to Mr. Fernandez's office.

"Superintendent Losee wants the passkey," she said, and the boy gave it to her. They arrived at last before Mrs. Barley's door, and Miss Peterson knocked. No answer.

"Superintendent," she said, "will it be all right if I go in first? To—" She paused. "To prepare her?" she asked in a low, earnest voice. "She might not be fully dressed...."

She knew that would embarrass him. "Quite!" he said, and she unlocked the door and entered.

For a moment she stood motionless, completely at a loss. Then she stepped back into the corridor.

"I'm afraid," she said, "that Mrs. Barley isn't so well."

"Pardon me!" said Losee, and went past her into the room. The coffee tray had been pushed aside, it was balanced half over the edge of the table, making room for the bottle of gin that stood there, uncorked. Mrs. Barley was asleep again.

"I shan't get any information from *this* quarter," said Losee, affronted.

"She was better when I left her," said Miss Peterson.

Losee said nothing to that; he looked around the room. "I'd like to see this gun you mentioned," he said, "if you please."

"But—it's gone!" said Miss Peterson.

He closed the door and set to work searching the room; in the wardrobe, in the drawers, under the chair cushion.

"Be good enough to look in the bed," he said, and Miss Peterson did; she felt under the pillows, under Mrs. Barley, everywhere.

"Superintendent," she said, "somebody's been in here."

"What grounds have you for stating that?"

"The gun is gone," she said, "and the gin has come out again. I put it away in a drawer."

"Mrs. Barley may have brought out this bottle herself," he said. "She may have thrown the gun out of the window."

"I don't think she was capable of that, Superintendent."

"Have you had medical training, madam?" he asked. And there could be no doubt about his attitude.

"No, I haven't, Superintendent," she answered. "But I've seen people in her condition before this. I don't believe she could have got up and found that bottle so quickly. And I don't believe she'd throw the gun out of the window. She wanted to keep it, for some reason."

"You might give me a brief account of your conversation with Mrs. Barley," he said.

"She told me she'd seen a stranger—what she called a prowler—in the hotel."

"Where? In what part of the hotel?"

"She didn't say."

"When?"

"She didn't say. But it must have been before the telephone went dead, because she said she telephoned the police."

"Why did she telephone the police?"

"I suppose she was alarmed."

"Did she state that she was alarmed?"

"She couldn't speak very clearly, Superintendent. But that seemed to me the natural explanation."

"Did she state that she notified the police without telling anyone in the hotel of the presence of this prowler?"

"We didn't talk very long, Superintendent. But what she did say seemed to me so important that I wanted to let you know at once. I ordered coffee for her. If she'd drunk that, I'm pretty sure she'd have been able to give you an account...."

"Quite!" he said. "Well, we'll have to wait until this good lady is able to speak for herself." He put the cap on the gin bottle, and stood looking down at Mrs. Barley.

"I think I'll ask Doctor Tinker to take a look at this good lady," he said.

"Quite!" said Miss Peterson.

VII

Left alone with Mrs. Barley, Miss Peterson sat down near the open window, and looked out into the darkness where the rain was falling softly. Somebody came in here, she thought. I suppose it could have been anybody. Mrs. Barley might possibly have been able to open the door if someone had knocked. But I don't think anybody knocked. I think somebody came in with a key. The key that belongs to this room, or a passkey. And I think it was Alfred Jeffrey. He has a passkey. He knew the gun was here. He saw where I put the bottle of gin. Well, the gun's gone, and the poor woman is thoroughly *hors de combat*, and Superintendent Losee has a pretty poor opinion of me.

There was a jaunty rat-ta-ta-tat on the door, and she opened it to admit the merry Doctor Tinker.

"What have we here?" he asked. "A spot of alcoholism?"

"I hope it's not serious," said Miss Peterson. "There doesn't seem to be so very much gone out of the bottle."

"Well, we'll see," he said. But he was looking at Miss Peterson instead of at Mrs. Barley. "Your first visit to Riquezas?" he asked.

"Yes, doctor," she answered, gentle as a dove.

"I hope you'll stay a long, long time," he said.

"Thank you, doctor."

"I've been to New York three or four times," he said. "American girls.... Oh boy!"

Miss Peterson looked absently past him and turned to Mrs. Barley. She saw his thin brows twitch and draw together as he took her pulse. He raised one of her eyelids, he got out his stethoscope and he listened for a long moment. When he straightened up he was no longer blithe.

"Is it serious?" asked Miss Peterson.

"Yes," he said briefly. "However...." He took up the telephone, he waited, he signaled impatiently. "Will you be good enough to go down and ask the superintendent to come up here please?" he said. "And will you call the hospital and tell them to send the ambulance at once? Thanks!"

Miss Peterson went quickly out of the room; she rang for the elevator and waited in the quiet corridor. Very much too quiet. Not long ago the prowler must have been moving through this corridor. And after him had come his killer. Mrs. Barley's killer, too?

The elevator was coming down; it stopped for her, and in it she found old Mrs. Boucher, in a long black crepe dress with a black velvet band around her neck. "*Good* evening!" she said, bowing her head majestically. "The storm has passed, and I *hope* things are running smoothly again."

"Oh, I think so," said Miss Peterson. Everything's all right, she thought, except that there's a dead man on the third floor, and Cecily's been arrested for killing him, and the housekeeper's in a bad state. Otherwise, everything's just dandy.

It was startling to hear gay music as the elevator stopped at the main floor; it was a *paso doble*. The lounge had altogether an unexpected air of festivity; they were all there, the middle-aged couple, old Mrs. Green, Mrs. Fish, and the Major; all dressed for the evening, too. A colored boy stood beside a big cabinet phonograph, holding a record in his hand, and Mr. Fernandez was moving about, light-footed and urbane, in white mess jacket and black tie.

Miss Peterson stood still, and he approached her. "Anything *else?*" he asked, and she told him while the *paso doble* went on. He listened to her with his head bent; his face was blank.

"Losee has gone," he said. "I'll ring him up. And I'll send immediately for the ambulance. In the meantime.... If you could dress in fifteen minutes, d'you think...? I'd appreciate it if you could go into the dining room with the guests."

He looked up at her, and his black eyes seemed opaque; the lines from his nostrils to his mouth looked deeper.

"I want to divert their attention," he said. "While that carrion is taken away." She did not like his words or his tone.

"I thought everyone would have to view the body," she said.

"The cook identified him," said Mr. Fernandez briefly. "Now... I don't want to hurry you, Miss Peterson, but if you'll be good enough to get ready...."

"The cook identified him?" she repeated. "Did he—?"

"*If* you please—" said he. "We can talk about this later."

"Certainly, Mr. Fernandez," she said.

She was downstairs again, well within the fifteen minutes, in a dark blue evening dress of dotted Swiss, with blue linen sandals; she went into the dining room, and the head waiter conducted her to a table, the worst table in the room, beside the screen that concealed the service door. Mr. Fernandez was not present.

It was a good dinner, and she ate steadily through all the courses. But she did not enjoy it. The hurricane had passed them by with no more than a last flick of the tail, yet that oppression she had felt last night on the ship still lay upon her, heavier than ever. She was nervous, as cats are nervous; when somebody coughed, she turned her blond head with a twitch. She had a feeling of things going on around her; invisible and ominous things, while she sat imprisoned here.

What's happened about Mrs. Barley? she thought. And did they find the gun...? So the cook identified the body, did he? Well, who was it? I'd like to know. I'd like to know about the Devil in a white robe shining with fire. And Cecily.... Shut up in a cell now? Mr. Fernandez could have stopped that. But he did all he could to make things worse.

She was very anxious to escape, to make some private inquiries. But before she had finished her dinner, the middle-aged couple came to her table, and asked her to make a fourth at bridge with them and the Major. This seemed too obviously part of her hostess duties to refuse, so she joined them in the lounge. It was not bridge they were after; it was inside information.

"Such a dreadful thing, isn't it?" said Mrs. Fredericks, the middle-aged lady. She was a bright-faced little soul in pince-nez, with a soft pink and white skin. "Fancy that tramp trying to murder poor Cecily!"

"Doesn't make sense to *me*," said her husband, square, solid, serious. "Mean to say if the police had believed that, they wouldn't have arrested the girl."

"Lot of fools," said the Major.

"No," said Mr. Fredericks. "No. I heard of Losee when he was in Ceylon. Did a very good job there. No. The probable explanation is, that the girl had a rendezvous with this fellow—brought him into the hotel—"

"That's an unwarrantable assumption on your part, sir!" said the Major, growing red.

"No," said Mr. Fredericks, still serious and equable. "It's sensible, that's all. In the first place, there aren't any tramps in an island like this. In the second place, if he *was* a tramp—as you call it—the last place he would go into would be a hotel. In the third place, *if* there'd been anything to support the girl's statement that she shot him in self-defense, she'd have been given the benefit of the doubt. They don't put a white woman in jail in a place like this unless it's unavoidable. No."

"You never heard of a policeman making a mistake?" the Major asked.

"Not often," said Mr. Fredericks. "No. I don't believe in this tramp theory. I'd be willing to wager anything you like, that the deceased came here for a purpose. A definite purpose."

"Good God!" said the Major. "Did you *see* this man, sir?"

"I did," said Mr. Fredericks. "I don't suggest that—if he had a rendezvous with the girl—it was necessarily connected with any love affair. He may have come to deliver a message. He may have come for the purpose of blackmailing her. Or someone else."

"Very well, sir!" said the Major, with triumph. "If your man came to blackmail the girl, you'll admit she was justified in shooting him."

"No," said the serious Mr. Fredericks. "Certainly not, though in considering the alleged identification of the deceased by the cook, Robert—"

"Why 'alleged?'"

"It's completely unsupported by any other evidence, or presumptive evidence," said Mr. Fredericks. "The cook, Robert, alleges that he saw deceased last night on the North Shore, sitting by the roadside. He further alleges that he entered into conversation with him, and that deceased said that his name was Elfie, and that he was a seaman who had come here as a stowaway on some ship."

"Very well, sir! Very well!" the Major demanded. "Why shouldn't this story be true?"

"Several reasons," said Mr. Fredericks. "I don't credit—"

"And, who are *you*, sir?" cried the Major.

There was a moment's silence.

"Oh.... Nobody in particular," said Mr. Fredericks, and wandered away. Miss Peterson looked after him with astonishment.

"Armchair strategist!" observed the Major, and went off himself.

"Well, we shan't have any bridge *this* evening," said Mrs. Fredericks with a cheerful little laugh. "I suppose I might as well fetch my book and read."

Mrs. Fish was reading a magazine with a lurid cover, a picture of a girl with large, crazy eyes and a sinister hand covering her mouth; old Mrs. Green was knitting, and old Mrs. Boucher was doing a cross-word puzzle. It seemed to Miss Peterson that they could now be left to their own devices while she went to inquire about Mrs. Barley.

She moved away toward the elevators, and as she was passing the desk, Alfred Jeffrey spoke to her.

"Miss Peterson," he said, "could you spare me five minutes?"

"Why, yes," she said. "I just want to see how Mrs. Barley's getting on, first."

"She's gone off in the ambulance," said Jeffrey. "She's going to die in the hospital. It is one of Mr. Fernandez's regulations that employees must not die on the premises. Anyone caught doing so, will be fined. Five hundred marks, lira, or kopecks."

"You have a cheerful disposition," Miss Peterson observed.

"It hides a breaking heart," he said. "Will you step into my parlor said the fly to the spider."

"I'm a spider?"

"I don't know what you are," he said. "But if you'll step in here...?"

He opened a door next to that of Mr. Fernandez's office, another office, smaller and hotter, and in every way inferior. "As a test—" he said, "will you take a drink with me?"

"A test of what?"

"I'm prohibited to touch alcohol while on duty. Reasonable enough, isn't it? I'm only on duty from eight a.m. to eleven or twelve at night. But I want a drink now. And if you'll take one with me, then I'll trust you. Then I'll know you're on our side."

"What side is that?" she asked.

"The Peepul. The workmen versus the Boss. I make a mean mint julep."

"A mint julep can be good," said Miss Peterson.

He went out of the little office and she sat down. I don't know... she thought. And I want to know. I'd be glad to have Jeffrey talk a lot. It might help me to make up my mind. About a lot of things. But the chief thing is, *shall* I tell Losee what Cecily actually said? That she killed the man in don Carlos' room. If I only knew why she changed her story.... *Did* she find the man there, and deny it later?

Or is there anything in Mr. Fredericks's theory of a rendezvous? Fredericks is another dark horse. An official manner, and an official mind. You can't mistake it. Blackmail…?

Jeffrey came in again, with two tall frosted glasses on a tray. All ready beforehand, thought Miss Peterson. He couldn't have made them so quickly. He sat down on the desk beside her, looking at her with his mocking smile.

"Here's to our alliance!" he said.

Miss Peterson took a sip, and it was a very, very powerful drink. Is that his idea? she thought. To get me talking?

"Are we going to be friends?" he asked.

"Who knows?" said she. "Friendship is a plant of slow growth—"

"As Confucius say."

His gaiety was nervous; he was wary.

"Well!" he said. "Cecily's gone. And Mrs. Barley's gone. That's—convenient, isn't it?"

He was working around to something. Wary, adroit, but nervous.

"Convenient?" she repeated.

"Only I'm sorry for Cecily," he said.

"She's young," said Miss Peterson. "She can get over things."

"If she's tried for murder, she won't get over it."

"I don't know about that," said Miss Peterson. "I've met at least two people who'd been tried for murder, and they'd recovered." She glanced sidelong at Jeffrey, and went on. "One was a woman, too. She'd been tried for poisoning her husband. It's quite a long story, but it's unusual. If you'd like to hear it…?"

"I should," he said. "Only, right now, I'm afraid I haven't very much time. Don't you like your drink, Miss Peterson?"

"Fine!" she said, and took another sip, a very little one, looking at him over the rim of the glass.

He wiped his forehead and the palms of his hands with a handkerchief, like an acrobat getting ready for some difficult feat. He was very nervous.

"I suppose you've known Mr. Fernandez a long time?" he said.

"Not *very* long," said she.

"Quite a lad, isn't he?"

"He seems a good businessman."

"Yes, he's all of that," said Alfred Jeffrey. "Is your drink too sweet, Miss Peterson? Do I have to call you 'Miss Peterson?'"

"Yes," she said amiably. "I'm conservative."

She was not sure that patience was a virtue, but she knew it was a most valuable asset, and she saw that she had more of it than Alfred Jeffrey.

"Suppose I told you that Mr. Fernandez is not what you think?" he said.

"Well, you couldn't," she said, reasonably. "Because you don't know what I think he is."

"I could tell you something," he said. "If you'll give me your word not to say where you got the information."

"I couldn't do that," she said looking up at him again. "You seem very nice, but after all I don't know you. I don't know Mr. Fernandez, or anybody else here. I'm a stranger. Only—" She took up the glass again. "I'm very discreet," she said. "I'm not in the habit of talking too much."

His brows twitched in a frown of impatience. But he had to get over that. "I'm only asking you not to say where you got this information," he said.

He waited, but no reassurance came. "All right!" he said. "I'll trust you anyhow. There's a picture on the wall of our Mr. Fernandez's sitting-room. A very, very sweet picture of a young girl all in white, with a dove on her wrist. I think it's called 'Innocence,' or maybe it's 'Purity.' If you shift that picture, you'll see something interesting behind it."

"A secret panel?" she asked.

"A bullet-hole," said he.

She said nothing.

"And it's a bullet-hole that wasn't there yesterday. The picture's been moved to hide it."

"*That's* dramatic!" said Miss Peterson.

"Cecily's gone off to jail," he said. "I understand she's 'confessed.' And our Mr. Fernandez let her go. He didn't bother to mention that bullet-hole to the police."

"Mr. Jeffrey," said Miss Peterson, "why don't *you* tell the police about it?"

He looked down at the floor.

"Well, y'see," he said, "it would be pretty awkward for me. There's absolutely no legitimate reason for me to have gone into his room with a passkey. It puts me in a bad light."

"Wouldn't it put *me* in a bad light?" she asked.

"I thought—" he said. "With Barley out of the picture, I thought it would be a very natural thing if you fluttered around, doing some housekeeping kind of supervising tomorrow. Looking at the rooms and what not. You could notice that a picture was crooked and you could go to straighten it, and you could make this dramatic discovery."

"Why?" she asked.

"Why?" he repeated, surprised. "But—I mean to say—you want the police to know, don't you?"

"Why?" she asked again.

He was badly taken aback. "Well," he said, "it might be important for Cecily, y'know."

"Oh! Then do you think she's innocent?" Miss Peterson asked.

"I know dam' well she's innocent!" he cried, losing all the mocking nonchalance. "And I know Fernandez is guilty as hell. He's—"

There was a knock at the door, and Mr. Fernandez entered, smiling.

"Oh! Here you are, Miss Peterson?" he said. "I've been looking for you. Sorry to disturb you, but I'd like to talk over some little business matters." He turned his head toward Jeffrey. "By the way," he said. "A curious thing happened. *Extremely* curious."

He and Jeffrey stood facing each other. And Miss Peterson suddenly thought of a bull fight she had seen, and the moment when the bull and the matador stood facing each other. Alfred Jeffrey might be the slim and wary matador, and Mr. Fernandez a fresh and vigorous bull, decorated with flowers. She remembered that, in the bull fight she had seen, the bull had killed the matador, as sometimes happens.

"I found this," said Mr. Fernandez, taking something out of his pocket. It was a passport, lying in his long narrow hand. Jeffrey rose, slowly, his eyes still fixed upon Mr. Fernandez. It seemed very hard for him to lower his gaze, to look at the passport. When he did look, his face grew white as paper; he reached back to rest one hand on the table.

"I found this," said Mr. Fernandez again. "Very curious, no?" He turned to Miss Peterson. "If you'll excuse us, dear lady?" he said, "A little business to discuss...." He held the door open for her as she went out.

VIII

She was very glad to get up to her own room.... She was tired, she was unhappy; that indefinable and leaden oppression still lay upon her. Bad enough things had happened already, but she felt that worse was coming.

Part of this heavy dread was pure superstition, and she knew it. But part of it was logic and common sense. Things *had* to happen as a result of the poor little bald man's death. Things had to happen as a result of Mrs. Barley's strange relapse. And more things had to happen to Cecily.

I like that girl, she thought, lying relaxed in a hot bath. I dare say she's a fool, but that's the kind of fool I like. She's not a muddled, panic-stricken fool. She's a definite, vigorous, crashing sort of fool. What she's doing is probably a disastrous mistake, but at least she's doing it on purpose. She could shoot a man if it were necessary; but not in the back. No....

Then who did it? *I* don't know. The Devil, probably. The Devil in a white robe shining with fire. And Mrs. Fish has a photograph of the Devil in her room. Only *she* says *her* Devil was murdered.... Mr. Fredericks and his rendezvous theory....

She gave a long sigh, and deliberately stopped thinking about all this. That was something she could do when she chose; just as she could sleep quietly and soundly when she got a chance. She came out of her bath, refreshed, in a pale-blue silk kimono with a delicate pattern of mauve wistaria; she sat down on the bed and brushed her long flaxen hair, yawning, and letting little pictures of charming scenes drift through her mind, the snow-capped Alps, and the Andes, and the ineffable peace of a Norwegian fjord; she made two smooth braids, and took from the chest of drawers a new jar of cold cream. She was unscrewing the top, when there was a knock at the door.

She got up and turned the key expecting to see a maid. But it was Mr. Fernandez.

"*Di-os!*" he murmured.

"Yes, Mr. Fernandez?"

"But you are so beautiful...."

"Nice of you to say so."

"Well..." he said with a sigh. "I came to ask if we could have a little chat. I know you're tired, but I'm afraid it's necessary."

"I'll be ready in five minutes. Where? In the sun-deck?"

"In my little suite, if you don't mind. If you'll take the elevator up, and ask the boy which door...."

She understood this. He wished her to come openly, publicly, and he was quite right. This was the way to avoid gossip.

"I'll be there in five minutes, Mr. Fernandez."

"Do you have to put up that *beautiful* hair?" he asked.

"I think so, don't you?" she said. "If I went up in the elevator like this...."

"Yes," he agreed with another sigh, and went off.

She dressed quickly, and pinned up her hair, and in a very short time she was knocking at Mr. Fernandez's door. His sitting room was remarkable; there was a sofa upholstered in pink brocade, pink silk lamp shades; on a table she observed a white china swan filled with rosebuds. The effect was almost girlish. But Mr. Fernandez had none of the Anglo-Saxon male's anxiety to have a 'man's' room. He took it for granted that his masculinity was well established; he did not feel that he needed any pipes, and leather armchairs, any dogs.

"Sit down, dear lady," he said.

She had excellent eyesight, and she had a chance for a quick look at all four walls. There was no picture of Innocence, or Purity, or of a young girl with a dove. And that, she thought, meant that Mr. Fernandez had overheard most or all of the conversation between Jeffrey and herself.

He opened the door into the corridor, so that anyone could see them, Miss Peterson on the pink sofa, he in a fancy armchair. Also they could see anyone getting out of the elevator. He offered her a cigarette; she declined but he lit one for himself and smoked for a brief moment in silence.

"Well, my dear lady," he said, "I'm going to lay all my cards on the table. I'm going to be completely frank."

Miss Peterson put on the right look for that; grave and attentive.

"I'm on the spot," he said, briefly.

"You mean—?"

"I mean," he said, "I've got my back to the wall. I'm fighting for my life."

"Your life?"

"Dear lady," he said, "I have plenty of enemies, only looking for a chance to pull me down. One of my enemies is Willie Losee."

She was struck by the incongruity of that stern man being called Willie, but she dismissed that as frivolous.

"That's too bad!" she said.

"It's very bad," he said. "But while there is life, there is hope, no? Anyhow I won't go down without a good struggle. Be sure of that. I've been in a tight corner before this, and I've come out of it. Just two things are necessary. Courage. And even one loyal friend."

"I'm sure you have lots of friends, Mr. Fernandez."

"Oh, yes," he said. "There are people who would do anything for me—anything at all. But, unfortunately they're very stupid. What I want is someone who is loyal *and* intelligent."

And that means me, thought Miss Peterson. Well, I'm afraid my stock of loyalty is not high just now.

"I'm putting all my cards on the table," he said again. "I've sunk a great deal of money in this hotel, and at this moment, I have commitments elsewhere."

He paused. "There are some very fine friends of mine engaged in a little enterprise in Venezuela. No sense in going into all the details; it's a business matter, but also a little political. Anyhow, I've lent a great deal of money there. So that, at the moment, I'm—financially embarrassed. Only until my hotel is on its feet. For that reason, I'm going to advance the date of my gala opening. I'm going to have it this Saturday night."

"*This* Saturday?"

"I've just telephoned a note to the newspapers, and Jeffrey's typing a little note to the guests. We ought to get a nice little crowd of local people, anyhow. Also, one of the Marquis boats will be in."

This is not my affair, Miss Peterson said to herself; and probably she looked like that.

"You're thinking of this unpleasantness this evening?" he said. "That's just the reason, dear lady. I've got to counteract that. There's nothing more important to a hotel than atmosphere. This thing that happened made a very bad atmosphere—gloomy. It's got to be counteracted, and at once."

"But... Mr. Fernandez, suppose Cecily is tried for this shooting?"

"Yes?" he said.

"Don't you think that might—" She paused. "That might put a crimp in the gala opening?"

"No," he said. "In the first place, I don't believe it will come to that. The police will investigate, and they'll find that there's no evidence at all against the girl except her own hysterical confession. She can't even tell a straight story about it."

"Her story was very much straighter—when we first heard it, wasn't it?" said Miss Peterson.

He lit another cigarette. "That tale about finding the man in my room?" he said. "That was impossible. I asked her not to repeat that to Losee unless she was certain; and when she thought it over, she was *not* certain."

Miss Peterson was slow to anger, but she was growing angry now.

"If Cecily *had* told Losee that," she said, "I don't imagine she'd be in jail now."

"Who d'you think would be in jail, then?"

"I don't know," she said. "But I'm sure Cecily didn't shoot that man in the back."

"*Bueno*. I'm sure of that myself," he said, coolly.

"And still you wouldn't lift a finger—?"

"My dear lady," he said. "I am—realistic. It won't kill that girl to spend a little time in prison. I've got other things to think about. Mrs. Barley is very ill, you know."

"It's serious?"

"Yes. She's in the hospital. Suicide without a doubt."

"Is it?" Miss Peterson asked.

"Without a doubt. She's been in a suicidal mood for a long time. There are people who can attest that. I have a very clear picture of what happened. The poor woman caught sight of this prowler. Very good. The storm had already upset her; she'd been drinking. She saw this prowler and she called up the police. Then she began brooding over her former experience with the police, when her little hotel burned down. You can understand that. She thinks, I'm going to be questioned by the police again. She is depressed, nervous; she can't face the police. So she takes a dose of poison."

"Oh! poison, was it?" asked Miss Peterson.

"Who knows?" asked Mr. Fernandez.

"I wonder where she got the poison."

"Maybe we'll never know that," said Mr. Fernandez. "Let's hope the police won't come to a wrong conclusion about *that.*"

"For example?"

She looked at him, and he looked back at her, and his face had that heavy look, his black eyes opaque, the lines from nostril to mouth very deep.

"You know the peccaries?" he said. "They can drag down a jaguar. I'll see to it that I'm not dragged down that way. I'll see to it that my hotel isn't ruined by slander and malice. I want to be frank with you. I know what Jeffrey said to you. I know *just* how he feels about me. I know how to keep him quiet. Do you know what I showed him? I'll tell you. It was a passport I picked up in the corridor. Certainly the passport of the man who was killed. Very good. D'you know what his name was? I'll tell you that also. This dead man's name was Alfred Jeffrey."

Miss Peterson looked up, startled.

"You'll have to tell the police."

"I don't 'have to,' my dear lady."

"Then—suppose I do?"

"You can't," he said. "*You* never saw it. All I've got to do is to deny I've got such a thing."

"You're taking a pretty serious chance, Mr. Fernandez, concealing evidence like that."

"I've taken a good many chances in my life, dear lady. I'll take more, to keep from being dragged down by the peccaries."

"Mr. Fernandez," she said, "why are you telling this—to me?"

"Because I hope you'll stand by me," he said.

"In deceiving the police? In breaking the law? In letting that girl suffer for something she didn't do?"

"The girl brought all this on herself. And in any case, she won't hang for it."

"And why do you think I'd take the risk of getting into trouble with the police?"

"For this reason," he said. "Because I think you like a jaguar better than a pack of peccaries."

She glanced away, more impressed than she wished him to know, for it was quite true that she preferred jaguars to peccaries.

"Cecily's not a peccary," she said.

"She's chosen to run with them," he said.

"It seems to me," she said, looking at him again, "that Cecily's been remarkably loyal to you, Mr. Fernandez."

"Oh! You think she did all this for me?" he asked with a smile. "Well, I'm afraid you're mistaken, dear lady."

"Then why?"

"I think I know," he said. "But there's one thing I'm very sure of. The motive was—not love."

"May I have a cigarette?" asked Miss Peterson, after a moment.

He sprang up with a somewhat exaggerated gallantry; he gave her one, and lit it for her.

"That rat of a clerk of mine won't talk any more about bullet-holes," he said, standing before her. "He wouldn't care at all for this second passport to come to light. It has a more recent photograph of Mister Alfred Jeffrey—somebody else. If anyone should happen to find this second passport around anywhere... well! Our fine Mr. Jeffrey would be in jail, half an hour after the police saw it. Then he'd be deported, and maybe he wouldn't like that."

"You take a very great deal for granted," said Miss Peterson. "You say you're laying all your cards on the table. Well, suppose I don't want to play your game?"

"I don't take it for granted that you'll play my game," he said, unsmiling. "I only *hope* you will."

He moved away and sat down in his chair again.

"I think the weather will be clear tomorrow," he said.

IX

Miss Peterson was seldom plagued by doubt or uncertainty. She had seen plenty of trouble and plenty of danger; but she had known almost always what she wanted to do, and meant to do. Now, however, she did not, and it upset her, so that she lay awake a good half hour.

I don't know about don Carlos, she said to herself. I honestly don't. I don't know what his limits are. I don't know what he has done, or what he's likely to do. He certainly did not put *all* his cards on the table. He'd never do that. He'd always have an ace up his sleeve. But, to a certain extent, he did trust me.

Well, I don't much like being trusted with illegal secrets. If I keep quiet about the possible bullet-hole, and about the dead man's passport, I'm an accessory after the fact. And after *what* fact? The man is dead; and Mrs. Barley is seriously ill.

Don Carlos had the means and the opportunity for both of these killings. It's easy to see what motive he could have had, too. He wants to save his precious hotel. The question is whether or not he's capable of cold-blooded murder. And it's a question I can't answer.

Maybe I'm a *fool*, she thought, turning restlessly in her bed. Perhaps the only sensible thing to do is to go to Losee and tell him everything. Everything. All that I've seen, which isn't much; and all that I've heard, which is plenty. Certainly that's the sensible course and the consequences are none of my business.

But suppose don Carlos hasn't done anything seriously wrong or criminal, and I help to ruin his hotel? I don't much care to be a peccary. And suppose my truth-telling makes things much worse for Cecily?

Fernandez said the motive wasn't love. Then what? Hate? Jealousy? What sort of hate could make a girl confess to a killing she hadn't done? Because she didn't kill that man. I'm certain of that. He was shot in the back. And it happened in Mr. Fernandez's room. Fernandez doesn't deny that there's a bullet-hole in the wall.

The rain had ceased, and the breeze was sweet and steady; she could see stars in the sky. We were lucky, she thought. But the words echoed in her mind. Lucky? Not the poor little bald man. Not Mrs. Barley. Not Cecily. The storm had passed, but it had left a trail of wreckage.

Oh, go to sleep! she said to herself, angrily. And, after a time, she did.

It was better in the morning with the sun up. The surf still ran high; standing at her window she saw the giant breakers smashing on the barrier reef, and, even broken, they came rolling up on the beach in a long indomitable tide. She rose, she put on a bathing suit and a terry robe, and went down on the sands. She went into the sea and had a swim. She was an excellent swimmer, but she kept close to the shore this morning, for this was unknown terrain. There might be an undertow, a swift current; a shark or a barracuda might have found a way through the reefs.

She came out and sat in the sun, and there was not a soul to be seen all up and down the beach. The gulls mewed, and screamed and swooped, and she saw timbers beginning to come in, big timbers that made her narrow her eyes to see them better. They were not good to see. Those rounded boards looked very like part of a small boat—a lifeboat....

"There was considerable damage done last night," said a voice behind her.

She glanced up at Superintendent Losee, but she did not move; she sat there in her neat, dark-blue suit and her black rubber cap, her hands clasped about her knees. He moved so that he stood before her, lean and grim in his white uniform and helmet.

"This case," he said, "puts me in mind of cases I've handled in India. Native cases."

"Oh, does it?" she said with polite attention.

"It does," he said. "The most extraordinary amount of evasion and downright perjury. I'm quite well aware, y'know, that I haven't had one single complete and honest statement from anyone involved."

"Oh, haven't you?" she said, considerably taken back.

"Not as yet," said he. "However...."

There was a silence.

"Is Mrs. Barley any better?" asked Miss Peterson.

"Mrs. Barley is dead," he answered; and the words were as hard as bullets. Miss Peterson was not given to sentimentality, she could pretend to no personal emotion for Mrs. Barley. Yet it shocked her to hear this, in the sweet sunny morning. It gave a sudden reality to what had been a nightmare. She was silent, remembering Mrs. Barley in her dim, untidy room, struggling to speak, to get in touch with the last human creature she was ever to recognize.

"Do you think she was murdered?" she asked with the sledge-hammer directness she sometimes used.

"I do," said he.

"It was a brutal thing," said Miss Peterson.

"Murder generally is," said the superintendent.

They were both silent again. The sun was getting too hot for the blond and fair-skinned Miss Peterson; she rose. "I think I'll go in and dress," she said.

"Quite," said he. "And by the way...."

"Yes, Superintendent?"

"Would you care to visit Miss Wilmot?" he asked.

"Why, yes."

"I think it might be a good idea," he said. "Can you be ready in half an hour?"

Miss Peterson dressed quickly but carefully in a black linen dress with a white collar. Then she hastened down to the dining room and ordered a substantial breakfast. It was still early; the room was deserted, and she was glad of that.

She was finishing the last drop of coffee when Losee appeared in the doorway; she rose at once.

"Exactly on time," he observed, and she thought she saw a faint flicker of approval in his stern little eyes.

He had a small car outside which he drove himself; he set off very slowly.

"The coroner's inquest will be held this afternoon at two-thirty," he said. "You may be summoned, Miss Peterson."

They drove past a banana plantation, and the leaves of the plants were torn into rags; they passed fields where the cane lay beaten flat, there was a little house with a great palm tree athwart it; there were queer things strewn about, a white-painted door with a brass knob lay by the roadside, a chintz curtain was caught on a hedge. Yet the sky was an unclouded blue and the sea beyond the fields was a burning sapphire; all that violence, all that noise and fury were utterly gone. Two lives had gone with it, as swiftly and as completely.

"You mentioned getting a lawyer for the young woman," said Losee. "She refuses to see a lawyer. I propose—if you're still interested in her—I propose that you advise her to tell the truth."

"It's a great responsibility, to give advice, Superintendent."

"Even advice to tell the truth?"

"I think so, Superintendent."

"I questioned the young woman last night," he said. "Her answers were highly evasive and inconsistent. If she goes before the coroner's court with her present statement, the consequences will be most serious for her."

"But won't the consequences be serious, whatever she says or does now?"

"I'll see the Commissioner," he said. "With his consent, we haven't charged the young woman—as yet. Because her statement makes a charge of manslaughter or justifiable homicide impossible. The only charge possible—in view of her statement—is murder."

"Still," said Miss Peterson, warily, "I shouldn't think there'd be much chance of a conviction."

"A jury always attaches an exaggerated importance to a confession. What's more, the young woman makes an unfavorable impression. She's defiant, and reckless, and obviously lying; she insists she shot deceased while facing him. The fact is established that he was shot in the back; but there are other discrepancies. I hope you can persuade her to make a complete and truthful statement."

Well, I don't know about that, thought Miss Peterson. And aloud: "She could retract her confession entirely, couldn't she, and plead not guilty?"

"She'll have to plead not guilty, if she's charged with murder," he said. "But if she wants to enter a plea of homicide in self-defense, she'll have to make a truthful and intelligible statement. And there's very little time."

"She's got to have a lawyer."

"She'll be assigned one by the court, if the coroner's jury finds her guilty." He was silent for a time, still driving very slowly. "I'm going to give you a free hand, Miss Peterson," he said. "I'm going to give you half an hour alone with the young woman. You can take my word for it there'll be no eavesdroppers." He gave a bleak smile. "No secret panels, or dictaphones," he said. "Your talk will be absolutely private."

"But you'll expect me to give you a report of it?"

"Not at all," he said. "I only hope you can persuade the young woman to tell the truth, that's all."

He turned the car up a side road where four brand-new bungalows stood, each in its garden with a wall. He stopped before the first of these; the wooden gate was blown half off its hinges, and a leafy bough lay in the path, but otherwise it was all neat and tranquil.

"But is this the jail?" Miss Peterson asked.

"With the Commissioner's approval, the young woman is detained in the custody of my sister and myself," he said. "Only temporarily, of course. After the inquest, you understand—"

"Yes, Superintendent.... Will you let me send for a hairdresser?"

"A hairdresser?" he repeated with a look of distaste.

"You know how things are," said Miss Peterson in an earnest and confidential tone. "It'll make a difference, if she has a hairdresser before she goes into court. If it *could* be arranged— If I could just stop and see a hairdresser and tell him what to bring along...?"

He thought that over, and then turned the car and drove her into the little town; he waited with exemplary patience while she waked up a hairdresser and gave directions. They drove back to the bungalow and as they turned the corner, the sound of Brahms's *Hungarian Dance Number Three* came to them, played very brilliantly upon a piano badly out of tune.

"Good God!" said Losee.

A colored maid opened the door for them, and they entered a neat and cheerful little sitting room that seemed to rock with that music. Cecily sat at the piano in her black dress; she went on playing until the superintendent touched her on the shoulder.

"This won't do," he said.

"Is it against the law to play the piano?" Cecily demanded.

"At this hour of the morning it is," said he. "Here's Miss Peterson, very kindly come to visit you."

The girl was very pale; she looked tired and half-ill, her strange, light eyes fierce and hostile.

"I haven't anything to say," she answered.

"Half an hour," said he, and withdrew, closing the door.

"Will you have a cigarette?" asked Miss Peterson, sitting down and lighting one for herself.

"Well.... Thank you!" said Cecily.

"You're lucky," Miss Peterson resumed, "I thought I'd find you in a cell."

"I'd rather be in a cell," said Cecily.

"You don't know what cells are like," said Miss Peterson. "I visited a woman in jail, once, in Bahia. Well, here we are, all by ourselves. Nobody's listening."

"I don't believe that," said Cecily.

"Please do," said Miss Peterson. "And please believe that I'm here out of friendliness, and for no other reason."

"People aren't like that," said Cecily, blowing smoke through her narrow nostrils. "*Nobody* does things simply to help somebody else. It's everybody for himself. That's life."

"The law of the jungle?" Miss Peterson asked.

"That's it," said Cecily.

"I've never lived in a jungle," said Miss Peterson. "I seem to have come across a lot of very decent people. I've even seen people die to save somebody else. I've seen that more than once."

"Possibly," said Cecily. "In an emergency."

The precious time was going. But it was necessary to be patient with the wild gazelle, to lure it within reach.

"Of course," she said, "I think artists are privileged people."

That worked. She noticed the girl's start, and her air of frowning attention.

"Most people don't agree with that," she said.

"Oh, I think so. The Major, for instance, was so much impressed by your playing. And the superintendent—"

"Him?" said Cecily. "He's the most absolutely narrow, bigoted blockhead.... And his sister's nothing but a doormat for him. Last night he kept on asking me questions until I was almost frantic. You don't know what it's like, to be asked the same questions, over and over, and *over*. He was just trying to mix me up, and trap me."

"He will trap you," said Miss Peterson. "That's his job, and he's good at it."

"All right. Let him," said Cecily.

"I suppose you're counting on being acquitted?"

"Well, I certainly don't expect to be hanged," said Cecily.

"That could happen, though," said Miss Peterson. "But even at the very best, you'll be shown up as a most awful little liar."

"That doesn't worry me."

"And of course you'll be deported."

"*Deported?*" Cecily cried.

This, at last was the right word. "Oh, yes," said Miss Peterson. "That goes without saying. You'll be deported, turned out of the place on any ship they choose."

"I—don't want to be deported."

"I don't blame you," said Miss Peterson. "It's pretty humiliating."

The girl sat on the piano stool, holding the cigarette in her thin fingers, and staring at the floor.

"But, if they try me, and I'm acquitted...?"

Miss Peterson shook her head. "There'd still be all those false and misleading statements," she said. "And you're antagonizing people, too. Why do you do that? It's so stupid."

"I don't care, that's why," said Cecily. She frowned, she closed her eyes tight; when she opened them the black lashes were wet. "Look here!" she said. "If I give you some information, will you promise I won't be deported?"

"I can't promise anything."

There was a silence.

"If I—change my statement, will that superintendent promise?"

"I don't know," said Miss Peterson. "I just think it will be better for you if you tell the truth."

There was a long silence.

"I didn't realize how complicated the dam' thing was going to get," said Cecily, unsteadily. "It's hard now.... How do I know that pigheaded martinet will believe me if I tell the truth?"

"The truth is generally pretty convincing," said Miss Peterson.

There was a knock at the door, and an amiable face looked in. "The hairdresser is here," she said.

"Oh, thank you!" said Miss Peterson. "If she'll wait a few minutes, please."

The amiable face withdrew and the door was closed.

"Hairdresser?" Cecily said, frowning.

"For you," said Miss Peterson.

"I don't want a hairdresser."

"If you've got the sense that God gave geese," said Miss Peterson, "you'll let her get that black henna out of your hair—"

"No!"

"And you'll go into court, all natural and gentle, and you'll be polite, and you'll tell the truth. There isn't much time left."

"No!"

"Then I'll go," said Miss Peterson. "I've got other things to think about. There's Mrs. Barley's funeral—"

"Funeral? But what—?"

"Didn't you know how ill she was?"

"I didn't see her yesterday. She didn't like me, you know."

"Well, she's dead," said Miss Peterson, rising. "And I'll have a lot to do. I wish you luck. You'll need it."

"Wait!" said Cecily, and added, "If you please, Miss Peterson."

"Karen."

"Karen," the girl repeated, docilely.

They stood facing each other, and Miss Peterson had a curious feeling that was almost panic. I don't know whether I want to hear... she thought.

"I didn't shoot that man," said Cecily. "He was dead when I found him. I just fired a shot at nothing. That's the truth. All the rest of it is a lie. There wasn't any struggle. I just found him, lying there dead."

"Lying where?" asked Miss Peterson.

Cecily was a long time answering.

"I don't remember," she said, curtly. "But I didn't shoot him. I'm willing to tell the superintendent so."

Miss Peterson stood motionless. Oh, don Carlos! she thought. I'm a little sorry for you....

X

Miss Peterson went out into the hall, and in the little dining room opposite she saw the amiable Miss Losee talking to the hairdresser, a woman with a strangely radiant pink face, and an elaborate arrangement of white curls.

"If I could see the Superintendent...?" she said.

"Oh, certainly!" said the pleasant Miss Losee, jumping up. She went out of the room, and Miss Peterson heard her clear voice:

"William, Miss Peterson's ready for you."

He came out into the hall promptly, and he looked somehow different, perhaps because he was carrying a pipe in his hand, or perhaps because he was in his own house, which often changes people.

"I think Miss Wilmot has something to tell you," she said.

He looked at her, and then he smiled; a very unpleasant smile she thought, crafty.

"Quite," he said.

"Shall I wait?"

"Oh, no, thanks!" he said. "My sister will drive you back to the hotel. Thanks very much."

She lingered, hating to go, and knowing how futile it was to stay.

"Thanks very much," said he again, and she went away.

Miss Losee chatted pleasantly all the way back. She was a fresh, brisk woman of thirty-five or so in a brown print dress; she went all over the world, where her brother went, and in all places she tried to have tea at four o'clock, and some sort of pet, animal or bird. She talked about some of them.

The Hotel Fernandez was looking very attractive, dazzling white, with the beach and the blue sea visible behind it, the drive before it lined with palms, the tables set out on the lawn under the striped umbrellas, chair's with bright cushions on the terrace. I'm sorry for don Carlos—in a way, thought Miss Peterson.

"Thank you so much, Miss Losee," she said.

"Oh, it was pleasant to have such a nice little talk," said Miss Losee; and off she drove.

The lounge was empty, except for the *soi-disant* Alfred Jeffrey behind the desk. He glanced up at her with his rueful smile.

"I saw you go off with the superintendent," he said. "I thought you were being arrested."

"Not yet," said Miss Peterson, moving away.

"Cecily...?" he said with a sort of jerk. "Did you—is there any news about her?"

"Well... I saw her," said Miss Peterson. "She seems to be all right."

"Any message for me?" he asked, again with an obvious effort.

"I'm sorry, no," she answered.

He leaned over the counter and lowered his voice.

"Did you mention the bullet-hole to Losee?" he asked.

Miss Peterson looked at him thoughtfully.

"It might help Cecily," he said.

"I don't exactly see how," said Miss Peterson.

"At least, it might help our Mr. Fernandez—" he said, "into jail."

"Is that what you want?" she asked.

"Yes. If I can't see him in hell," said Alfred Jeffrey, softly.

"I'd advise you to be careful," said Miss Peterson, and went toward the elevator.

Howard seemed pleased to see her. "Mawning, mistress!" he said. "Mis' Fish she ask to see you; and Mis' Boucher she ask to see you."

"I might go up and see Mrs. Boucher now," said Miss Peterson, for she had taken a liking to that purposeful old lady. It would be a relief, she thought, to see somebody so pleasingly without emotions.

The old lady was still in bed, with a breakfast tray beside her; in a lacy white knitted bed-jacket, her hair neat, she sat propped up straight with pillows, and she was writing letters on a board.

"Good morning!" she said. "And what's this nonsense I hear about Mrs. Barley?"

"She was taken ill—"

"And what's the name of this illness if you please?" the old lady demanded.

"I don't quite know...."

"Don't you? Well, maybe I do," said the old lady. "Poor soul. And it's a sin and a shame for a *young* man to aid and abet an unfortunate woman, old enough to be his mother."

"How is that?" asked Miss Peterson, sitting down on the arm of a chair.

"That young Jeffrey brought her liquor," said Mrs. Boucher. "I saw him myself, a week or so ago, when I was down on that floor. I saw him with my own eyes opening her door with his key, and taking in a big bottle of gin. A sin and a shame."

"Yes," Miss Peterson agreed.

"Tell me, child! How *is* that poor Barley woman?"

"I'm afraid it's very serious."

"Do you mean that she is dead?" asked the old lady, gravely.

"I'm sorry...."

There was a little silence.

"Well! I shall go to her funeral," said Mrs. Boucher. "And I shall send flowers. She had that dreadful weakness, but she was a good woman. And she was absolutely loyal to Fernandez. Which is more than I'd care to say of that young Jeffrey. Poor woman...!"

Miss Peterson rose.

"Let me know in good time about the funeral, child," said the old lady. "And send someone to take away this tray."

Miss Peterson decided to walk down those stairs again; because she wanted a few minutes by herself. She wanted to think about that young man who was not Alfred Jeffrey taking liquor to Mrs. Barley. Mrs. Barley, who was absolutely loyal to Mr. Fernandez, and who had wanted very much to tell something....

The staircase was perfectly normal today, close, and with a dank and moldy smell, but in no way sinister. She sat down on a step and lit a cigarette. I'll have to see Mrs. Fish in a moment. And Mr. Fernandez. And everybody else. I'll have to go to the inquest. But first, I'll have a smoke.

I believe Cecily's told the truth at last. But I never did believe she'd killed the man. Killed the real, genuine Alfred Jeffrey. The logical one to have killed him is the bogus Alfred Jeffrey. But why in Mr. Fernandez's room? And if he was killed there by accident, why try to hush it up?

Then how did deceased get down to the third floor? Maybe he wasn't killed in Mr. Fernandez's room. The bullet-hole might easily have been made by Cecily when she shot 'at nothing.' But that means she found the dead man there.

And Mrs. Barley.... That's what sticks in my throat. It's not nice to shoot a poor little bald man in the back—but maybe he was a prowler, and up to no good. But Mrs. Barley.... That was brutal. That was horrible. I'd like to know who did that.

The bogus Alfred Jeffrey? Or Mr. Fernandez? Or somebody else? I hope it was somebody else. What about psychology? Would Jeffrey or Fernandez be capable of murdering Mrs. Barley? God knows. And nobody but God does know anything much about psychology. When you wander around the world, you see the most unlikely people, doing the most unbelievable things.... *Tout comprendre, c'est tout pardonner....* But I'm only human, and very fallible. I could never comprehend murdering Mrs. Barley, and never pardon it.

She crushed out the cigarette with her heel. Well, nobody's asked me to comprehend all and pardon all. I've got a job to do. Shall I see Mrs. Fish first, or go to headquarters for my orders?

She thought a moment, and then she decided upon seeing Mr. Fernandez first. Because, after all, she thought, it's a bit upsetting for a hotel to have two murders. Bound to make extra work. She rang for the elevator, and asked Howard where Mr. Fernandez was to be found.

"Was in the kitchen, mistress. I send a boy to find him."

That proved to be unnecessary, for Mr. Fernandez was in the lounge talking to Mr. and Mrs. Fredericks. Fresh as a daisy he looked, in one of his immaculate white suits, a blue handkerchief in the breast pocket, a blue shirt, blue flower in his buttonhole. He came toward Miss Peterson walking lightly and easily in his white shoes.

"If you'll step into my office, please..." he said. "We'll have to talk things over, eh?" He sat down on the edge of the desk. "Well here we are! A pretty kettle of fish. Two inquests—"

"Two?"

"Oh, yes! An inquest on Mrs. Barley's death this afternoon, after the other one. Then tomorrow morning, Mrs. Barley's funeral. Very sad. But—*así es la vida*.... After that, we'll have to get ready for Saturday."

"You're not *still* thinking of that gala opening, are you?"

He smiled. "Dear lady," he said, "I need that gala opening more than ever. And I shall have it."

"When you've just had two murders in the hotel?"

"Before the day is over," he said, "I hope there'll be an end to this talk about murder. Mrs. Barley's death—very good. She was an alcoholic, poor woman, and she drank some sort of medicine, without knowing what she was doing. As for the man who was found shot, very good again. Cecily shot him in self-defense."

"Suppose—" said Miss Peterson, slowly, "suppose she denies that?"

"I *hope* she won't," he said. "For her own sake."

"How's that?"

"Miss Peterson," he said, with a sort of formality, "when I am attacked, I know how to defend myself. That girl made her statement of her own free will. She could have kept quiet, and not been involved. But that she wouldn't do. She talked herself into jail; and that's the best place for her just now."

"Mr. Fernandez, when I'm called as a witness at the inquest, I may be asked what Cecily first said to you and me."

"Yes?"

"Perhaps you've forgotten? She told us the dead man was lying in your room."

"You'll tell that to the coroner?"

"I think I will," she said.

He was silent for a moment, standing before her looking at the floor.

"I'm sorry," he said at last, glancing up. "I hoped you would be my ally. But you must do as you please, dear lady."

He crossed the room and held open the door for her. She rose, slowly, with a curious reluctance; as she passed him she looked at him; their eyes met.

"I'm rather sorry myself," she said, and went out, past the desk toward the elevator.

"My God!" she heard Mr. Fernandez say, and turning, she saw Cecily standing in the entrance to the lounge.

Cecily with pale-gold hair that miraculously transformed her. Her aquamarine eyes no longer looked strange, when the level brows were light. She looked younger, she looked ethereal.

"Good gracious!" said old Mrs. Green from her corner. "What in the world have you been doing? Peroxide, I suppose."

"No. This is the way I really am," said Cecily.

Mr. Fernandez beckoned to her, and she crossed the lounge to his office. Miss Peterson retraced her steps and joined them. He closed the door, and stood looking at the girl with his heavy black brows raised, and his jaw thrust out.

"So here you are, eh?" he said.

"Superintendent Losee let me go," she said. "I told him the truth."

She spoke with the same unsmiling bluntness, but the effect was wholly different now. She seemed now like a deadly serious child.

"The truth..." Mr. Fernandez repeated. His, dark face was a little pale, but he smiled, showing all his fine white teeth; he shrugged his shoulders.

"I told him the man was dead when I found him," said Cecily. "I *didn't* say where I found him. I told you I wouldn't, and I won't."

Mr. Fernandez began to laugh.

"What's the joke?" Cecily demanded.

"I'm laughing at myself," he said, and held out his hand. "Welcome home!"

Cecily took the outstretched hand promptly.

"You didn't break your neck to help *me*," she said.

"My dear girl, I had to think of my hotel and myself."

"Yes," she said.

She accepted that as entirely normal and right, and she bore him no grudge. I believe she admires him for it, Miss Peterson thought. She likes him for being so beautifully and primitively selfish. She's still standing by him, still loyal.

He took the blue flower out of his buttonhole, and put it in her pale hair, fastening it deftly above one temple with a hairpin. "Charming!" he said.

"Is it?" said Cecily, doubtfully.

"*Hasta luego!*" said he, gaily, and went off.

"Cecily," said Miss Peterson at once, "did the superintendent just let you go? No strings?"

"No. He believed me," said Cecily.

"He must have asked you why you said you killed the man. Why you fired a shot at nothing."

"He didn't ask me that," said Cecily. "If he had, I wouldn't have told him."

"Tell me, won't you?"

"I *can't!*" Cecily answered. "I'm sorry. You've been awfully nice; but that's something I can't even talk about."

"Listen, Cecily! There's a lot of monkey-business going on. You're in danger."

"Of what?"

"Of being sent to prison—seriously."

"The superintendent believed me. Honestly he did."

"He wouldn't turn you loose that way, unless he had a reason."

"Well, the reason was that he believed me. He knows I didn't kill the man."

"What are you going to say at the inquest?"

"Say? Just what I told you. That the man was dead when I found him, and I picked up a gun I saw there and fired a shot at nothing."

"Was it your gun? Your automatic?"

The girl's level brows drew together.

"Of course not," she said, "I never had a gun."

"You'll have to get a lawyer," said Miss Peterson. "And you'll have to get one quick. Before that inquest."

"But why?"

"Because Losee hadn't finished with you. Things are going to happen. Bad things."

The wild gazelle was alarmed. And must be kept alarmed, and alert.

"I'll help you to find a lawyer. In the meantime, don't talk to anybody; and *don't* for heaven's sake, make any promises to tell things, or not to tell things. You're—"

"Still here?" said Mr. Fernandez, coming back. "I think we should drink a little toast, eh? To celebrate Cecily's return."

"Oh, thanks!" said Miss Peterson, "but I've got to go and see Mrs. Fish. She's been asking for me."

"Just drink a toast," said Mr. Fernandez. "To whatever you like. To the winner, eh?"

Cecily glanced sidelong at him, a little wary. And looking at the little fair thing with a blue flower over her temple, Miss Peterson felt worried. She downed her drink quickly.

"If you'll excuse me...?" she said, and left them.

She went to the elevator quickly, so that nobody in the lounge should catch her. I'd like a bit more time alone, she thought. I certainly can't say I'm overworked. In fact, I don't know what my duties are, if any. But I do have to talk such a lot, and that's something I've never cared for much. I'll never be a hostess again, that's one sure thing.

She rode up to the third floor, and knocked at Mrs. Fish's door.

"Come in," said the flat, tired voice.

She was lying on her bed, all dressed; and she looked, to the neat and orderly Miss Peterson, like a rag bag, in a thin black dress over a white slip, and clumsy white sandals, and her dark hair streaming out from the bun on the nape of her neck.

"I do wish you'd give me some more of that medicine you gave me yesterday," she said. "I feel so wretched, and my tooth aches again."

"Don't you think you'd better see a dentist?"

"I'm too nervous," said Mrs. Fish.

Miss Peterson went downstairs to her room, and prepared another dose of aspirin and bicarbonate of soda tinged with a cough drop and brought it up to Mrs. Fish.

"I do wish you'd stay and have an early lunch up here with me," said Mrs.

Fish. "I do feel so nervous and miserable."

"I'd like to, Mrs. Fish, but there's so much to be done."

"Well, have a cup of tea with me while I eat, then."

Miss Peterson preferred coffee. She ordered a cup for herself when she telephoned room service for a light lunch for Mrs. Fish.

"The food's quite good here," said Mrs. Fish. "It's quite a nice hotel. I'd enjoy myself if I wasn't so worried."

"You must try not to worry, Mrs. Fish."

"Do you think you could possibly rub my head a little? Here, on the right side?"

Miss Peterson rubbed Mrs. Fish's head and neck in expert fashion, and the limp Mrs. Fish grew limper still, lying relaxed with her eyes closed until her lunch came.

"I'm better," she said. "Only I had such nightmares, all night long. Can you interpret dreams?"

"I'm afraid I can't," said Miss Peterson, pouring herself a cup of coffee.

"I dreamed that I was trying to get away from somebody, and I was sinking in a quicksand. Do you think it *means* anything?"

"No, I don't, Mrs. Fish," said Miss Peterson.

"Every time I've had that dream before, something dreadful has happened," said Mrs. Fish.

"If you could get out in the sun and fresh air, Mrs. Fish...."

"Maybe that would help," said Mrs. Fish. "But would you mind opening that right-hand little drawer, Miss Peterson, and getting out a big, brown envelope?"

Miss Peterson looked in the drawer that was filled with a jumble of stockings, earrings, old letters, necklaces, scarves. It was marvelous that anyone could make such disorder in a few hours.

"I don't see any big envelope here, Mrs. Fish."

"Then maybe it's in the other drawer, Miss Peterson."

It was. A large manila envelope, and addressed in pencil to Miss Peterson.

"I'd like you to keep that, please," said Mrs. Fish. "In case anything happens to me."

"You mustn't think of things like that, Mrs. Fish."

"Was there anything in that medicine you gave me that could make me feel queer, Miss Peterson?"

"Nothing at all. You're tired, Mrs. Fish. You must take a little rest, and then go out in the fresh air."

"The air doesn't seem very fresh, does it?"

"I'll turn on the fan."

"Oh, no, thank you. I think I'll take a little nap, Miss Peterson. You always help me so.... Don't forget the envelope."

Miss Peterson rang for the elevator, and Howard had a message for her from the woman in charge of the linen room. The linen room was on the second floor;

she went there, and she was overwhelmed with a torrent of questions. About the outgoing laundry, about a bale of Turkish toweling to be made up into bath towels, about curtains, about some new soap. These were matters she knew little or nothing about, but it was clear that Mrs. Barley's death had caused a minor panic, and she did the best she could.

"You girls understand these things," she said. "We'll have to work things out together."

She talked to a seamstress, to a worried maid; she talked and talked, and at last she left them calmer. Then she went along the corridor, and around the corner to her own room. She ordered lunch sent up there because she was sick and tired of talking. And because she felt curiously drowsy.

I'll rest a few minutes, she thought, because I want to be fit for that inquest in case I'm summoned. I'll rest, but I won't lie down. I'll just sit here comfortably, and smoke a cigarette. The cigarette tastes a little funny.... I'll turn on the fan. For a moment. It's very stuffy in here. I'm very sleepy; but I'm not going to go to sleep.

If you feel dizzy, bend forward with your head between your knees. If you feel drowsy—*get up.*

Get up and walk. Order black coffee.... This is.... *Get up!*

Sinking in a quicksand...? Get up! Get up! Move. Order black coffee.... Please send me up some black coffee.... But that's no good—unless you get to the telephone. Nobody hears you. You're sinking.... *Please....*

XI

A squeak and a rattle, and *down* comes the sail.... But there's no breeze, she thought. It's so hot.... She was bathed in sweat, her hair was damp on her forehead, her eyelids were glued together. So unbearably hot....

Then there was a soft whirr, and the breeze came against her face, and she sighed.

"My dear lady.... Are you better?"

"It's—you?" she said, with difficulty, because her tongue felt thick.

"I have some hot coffee here...."

Hot coffee—from morning till night, she thought. Mrs. Barley had hot coffee.... I had hot coffee in Mrs. Fish's room.... I'm sick and tired of hot coffee.

The pillows were moving, relentlessly pushing up her heavy head. She got her eyes open and looked up at Mr. Fernandez in the dim light. He was holding a cup to her lips.

"No..." she said.

"Doctor Tinker said—"

"No, thank you."

The overwhelming drowsiness was lifting, and she wanted it to stay. She wanted to go to sleep again and not struggle. But something was running around in her brain. Get up.... Get up.... The jalousies were closed, but through them she saw a fiery glare of sun. And that wasn't *right*....

"Please!" said Mr. Fernandez, kneeling beside her and holding the cup to her lips.

"No!" she said.

Through the cracks in the blind, the sun blazed like fire, and that was wrong. But why?

"*What time is it?*" she asked, suddenly.

"It's—let me see—four twenty," said Mr. Fernandez.

Everything fell into place immediately. She looked straight into his face.

"I've been sleeping a long time," she said slowly.

"A very long time," he agreed. "I was worried. I called you on the telephone before I went to the inquest. No answer. I came up and knocked at the door. No answer. Doctor Tinker was here and I unlocked the door for him. And he said you had taken a little too much of your medicine."

"What medicine?"

He stood up and went to the chest of drawers: he picked up a little bottle and brought it to her. It bore the label of a chemist in Port-of-Spain, and written on it was Miss K. Peterson. Dose one teaspoonful when needed. Doctor scribble, scribble, scribble. It was paregoric.

"Tinker said you'd obviously taken a bit too much. Not serious, he said, but enough to make you sleep. And as Losee said your evidence wasn't essential...."

"Yes.... I see..." said Miss Peterson, thoughtfully. "Then everything is just dandy."

"Would it annoy you if I smoke?" he asked.

"Not at all. I'd like a cigarette myself, please."

He lit one for her, and then he sat down near the window with the fiery streaks of the sun through the blinds behind his dark head, like some infernal halo. Curiously quiet, he was, no trace of his usual exuberance.

"And the inquest?" she asked.

"Nothing," he answered. "Nothing at all. My cook identified the dead man—"

"Your cook is an employee very obliging, it seems," said Miss Peterson in Spanish.

"*Cómo no?*" said he. "Well, the police asked for a week's delay. It was granted."

"What about Cecily?"

"About her—nothing at all."

"Her confession wasn't brought up?"

"No. She stood up there, very honest, very straightforward, and she said she had found the body in an empty room. The coroner asked her some little questions, not very many. She said she did not know which room. And that was all."

"So she's still defending you?"

"You mean by not telling Losee where she found this dead man?"

"Do you admit it?" she asked quickly.

He laughed. "You want to trap me? You are like that Portia of Shakespeare." He pronounced it 'Por-ti-a,' and it was the first time she had heard him mispronounce a word in English. "I do admit it—only to you. I also admit that I took him out of there. He was a small man, and I," said Mr. Fernandez, with superb candor, "I am extremely strong. I first put on my white raincoat in case there should be any—I don't want to upset you, but in such a case there might be—bloodstains, you know."

"Oh!" she said, "then you're the one the boys saw. You were carrying a torch I suppose, and the light shone on your white rubber coat."

"Those fools!" he said with a sigh. "If they hadn't seen me and made such a row, I'd have carried the man downstairs, to the side door, and he'd have been found *outside* my hotel. I didn't know, of course, about the telephone call to the police."

"Then you're the Devil," she said musingly.

"Dear lady," said he, "it's your privilege to say so. Personally I think what I did, or rather, what I tried to do, was simply good business. I hoped to get the man out of the hotel. I hoped to persuade that confounded girl to keep it quiet. Then the police would have found the man outside, they would have thought he was simply some sailor, killed in a brawl, and there would have been no scandal in my hotel. As I told you, I'm realistic."

Yes, she thought, it certainly doesn't show too much sentimentality, to be able to carry a dead man in your arms, with the intention of dumping him out in the rain.

"And letting Cecily go to jail..." she said, half to herself.

"Letting her?" he cried. *"Dios de mi alma!* What did I have to do with that?"

"You must have asked her to tell a lie for you. About finding the man in your room."

"I admit it. I did ask her. And why not? Everything she said was a lie: why not one more, eh?"

"If she did that for you, don Carlos, you might have said even one little word to save her."

"'Save' is a very big word," he said. "She was in no danger at all. A little inconvenience, no more. Losee could be trusted to see to that. If there had been any danger, I should, naturally, have thrown all other considerations to the wind." He flung out his hands, his fingers spread open, to show everything being thrown away. "I am not an animal, without humanity."

"You said you were a jaguar...."

"Dear lady," he said quietly, "I have lost your good will. That's my misfortune. Well... there's one more misfortune I have to worry about. One of my guests has disappeared."

"Who?"

"Mrs. Fish," he answered. "Losee came here to ask her some little questions. Well, she wasn't in her room. She's not anywhere in the hotel. He thinks that's very strange. I supposed that maybe she'd gone out for a walk, and he looked at me—"

He gave an excellent imitation of Losee's unwinking, steely regard. "So he asked me questions about Mrs. Fish. Ah ha! She came on the boat with you? Quite! You knew her in Trinidad? No? Quite! He'd like to accuse me of strangling Mrs. Fish, but he can't find any corpse."

"How long has she been gone?"

He shrugged his shoulders. "I don't know," he answered. "It can't be very long, she had lunch here. To be frank, I'm not interested. I don't see anything strange in Mrs. Fish going out and staying out even for a whole day. She may have gone for a drive—for a walk—shopping; she may be having a nice cup of tea somewhere at this moment. But Losee has been looking for some new way to get at me, and he's using this for a pretext. He sent two men to search Mrs. Fish's room. All right! They searched. They found—nothing at all. But he says that if she isn't back by dinnertime, he'll question all the other guests. And that—Well! That finishes me."

Miss Peterson leaned back, staring at the wall before her.

"We have this prowler shot in the hotel," he resumed. "All right. That's an accident. We have Mrs. Barley dying. All right again. She's only an employee of the hotel, and everybody knows about her little weakness. *But*—only let

Losee put it into their heads that there is some mysterious danger for the guests, and they'll leave. The rumor will go all over the island. It will travel to other islands. It will reach all the way to New York." He drew his forefinger across his throat.

There was a long silence. Miss Peterson was thinking intently.

"Well," he said, "I hope Mrs. Fish will come back by seven o'clock. That's the deadline. Is there anything I can do for you, dear lady?"

"No, thanks," she said, slowly.

"I suppose you wouldn't care for a cocktail with me at six o'clock?"

"May I let you know?"

"Certainly!" he said. "I'll be in my little office then."

He stood still for a moment, and they looked at each other. I don't know, thought Miss Peterson. I honestly don't know what to make of you, don Carlos.... Maybe I think you're a jaguar, and I'm sorry for you. Maybe I've misjudged you....

The door closed after him, and for a time she lay quiet, still thinking intently. Then she got up and looked at herself in the mirror, with distaste. Her black linen dress and the white collar were rumpled, her hair was disheveled, she looked pale and forlorn.

She took a cold shower, and put on her pale-blue kimono, and then she took up the envelope Mrs. Fish had given her; she sat down at the window looking at it.

Mrs. Fish thought something bad was going to happen to her. Maybe if I tell the superintendent that at once, he can stop it, whatever it is. But he must be searching for her anyhow. He must have some information and some suspicion.

Queer? It's queerer than anyone knows. Paregoric. Paregoric has opium in it. Poison. Mrs. Barley was poisoned, and she died. And was I meant to die? That's a nasty thought. It sends shivers up and down your spine.

It makes you feel very lonely, to think that somebody wants to kill you. I am very lonely here. No friends except don Carlos. And what do I know about him? Nothing. He asked me to marry him. Bueno! He may be a Bluebeard for all I know, murdering women right and left.

But just the same, I can't believe he wanted to murder me. Vanity, I dare say. Taken in by his hand-kissing and his 'dear lady' and his Latin technique. I ought to know better. I ought to find the superintendent and tell him everything. All about the bullet-hole, and the passport, and the paregoric. And about Mrs. Fish. Above all about Mrs. Fish. I'm worried about her.

I have a right to be worried about her. She thought something might happen to her. Things happened to the little bald man, and to Mrs. Barley. Even to me. Losee gave don Carlos until dinnertime. Seven o'clock is the deadline. I don't like the word. Suppose it is a deadline—for Mrs. Fish?

She looked at the envelope with a frown and then she raised the little metal tab that fastened it, and opened it. There was a folded legal-looking document inside, and a smaller envelope, addressed to Miss Peterson.

> Dear Miss Peterson:
> I came down to Riquezas to look for Harold Cartaret who murdered
> my husband. I had a detective in New York looking for him, and he
> learned, from a sailor, that Harold Cartaret had come here to this ho-
> tel. He must be using an assumed name, so that I shall have to manage
> a private talk with every man here, one by one, because I don't know
> what he looks like, or his age, either.
> I have had such nightmares lately that I felt quite nervous. So that if
> anything should happen to me, please take care of my will, which is en-
> closed. You are the only person here I feel I can trust.
>   Sincerely yours,
>   Ella Perch (registered here as Ella Fish.)

Miss Peterson went to the telephone. "Order, please?" said the blithe voice
of the *soi-disant* Alfred Jeffrey. "Can you get Mr. Fernandez for me?" she said,
and in a moment Mr. Fernandez's voice spoke. "I must see you, Mr. Fernandez," she said. "Will you be in your office in five minutes?"

"At your service, dear lady," he said.

She put on a black chiffon dinner dress, and she was knocking at the door of
his office in something a little less than five minutes. He opened it with a
flourish and a bow.

"Dear lady, you are exquisite in black," he said.

"Thank you!" she said. "Will you shut the door, please, Mr. Fernandez. I was
sitting with Mrs. Fish while she had her lunch—"

"Wait!" he interrupted. "Did you eat with her?"

"No. I only had coffee. But that's not—"

"You drank coffee with her? In her room?"

"Yes," she said, looking at him with a faint frown.

"My God! I wish I'd known that," he said. "I found out that you didn't go
to the dining room for lunch. I couldn't think where you'd had anything.... Who
brought the lunch, and the coffee?"

"Let's go into that later," she said. "Because this is important. Mrs. Fish gave
me an envelope. She told me to open it if anything happened to her."

"And you think something has happened to her?"

"You'd better read the note," she said, and handed it to him.

She watched him read it; his head, with the thick dark hair bushed out behind
the ears, moved from side to side. He looked alert. Then he looked crafty, with
his jaw outthrust, his eyes turned sideways. Then he gave a wide and brilliant
smile.

"We'll have our own little court," he said. "I'll ask some questions myself."
He crossed the room and opened the door.

"Jeffrey! Just a moment, please."

Alfred Jeffrey came promptly, and at the sight of Miss Peterson, he smiled his rueful mocking smile.

"Sit down!" said Mr. Fernandez.

"Oh, thanks!" said Jeffrey. "But I'd rather stand."

"Suit yourself, my dear Harold Cartaret," said Mr. Fernandez.

He sat down then, collapsed, pallid, the collar of his white jacket standing out behind his neck as if he were a Pierrot dangling on a string.

"You don't feel well, eh?" asked Mr. Fernandez.

"Finish it," said the other. "I quit."

XII

"You can't quit," said Mr. Fernandez. "No. You've got a lot to go through with before you've finished."

"All right. Get the police, and start it."

Mr. Fernandez was silent, sitting on the edge of the desk, one ankle on his knee, an intent look on his face. What's he thinking about? Miss Peterson wondered. How much does he know? And how much is just improvising? He didn't know this lad was Harold Cartaret. It was a shot in the dark, but it turned out to be a bull's-eye. And now he's going to take advantage of it in some way.

She looked at Harold Cartaret, slouched in his chair, his legs stretched out before him, and she had a sudden impulse to warn him. But Mr. Fernandez was speaking.

"Believe me," he said, "I'd have sent for the police without bothering to give you any notice, my dear Harold Cartaret, if it hadn't been for Cecily."

"*She's* got nothing to do with this."

"She's in it up to the neck," said Mr. Fernandez, and repeated with a sort of humming sound. "Up to the nnnnneck."

"That's a lie!" said Harold Cartaret.

"I think we'll call her—"

"No!" said Cartaret.

Mr. Fernandez pressed the buzzer under his desk, and Cartaret stood up; his hair was ruffled up in back, his coat collar stood out from his neck, he had a dazed and a defiant look. He lit a cigarette for himself as Mr. Fernandez opened the door to a knock.

"Ask Miss Wilmot to come here," he said and closed the door.

What's he up to? Miss Peterson thought. Did he know anything about the Mrs. Perch-Harold Cartaret affair, before I showed him the note? Or is it a bluff?

There was another knock at the door, and Cecily came in; the new blond Cecily with the blue flower in her hair.

"Sit down!" said Mr. Fernandez. "We're going to have a very curious conversation." His look of abstraction had vanished; he was confident now. "Allow me to present—Mr. Harold Cartaret!" he said, with a gesture toward his clerk.

"What's *this* mean?" asked Cecily.

"That's his name," said Mr. Fernandez.

She glanced at Cartaret and frowned. "Is anything the matter?" she asked.

"He's headed for the gallows," said Mr. Fernandez.

"Shut up!" said Cartaret.

"What does this *mean?*" Cecily demanded, standing squarely before Cartaret.

"Whatever it means, it's none of your business," said Cartaret.

"Sit down! Sit down!" urged Mr. Fernandez; but she turned toward Miss Peterson.

"What's it all about?" she asked.

"I think Mr. Fernandez is going to explain," said Miss Peterson. "You'd better listen, and *not talk.*" She looked at Cartaret when she said that; but he was slouched in the chair again, staring at nothing.

"I'm a businessman," said Mr. Fernandez. "Not sentimental. I'm thinking of my hotel; and for that reason I'm willing to make concessions. Personally, I shouldn't be too much upset to see Mr. Harold Cartaret hang—"

"Hang for what?" Cecily asked.

"There's only one thing they hang you for," said Mr. Fernandez. "Murder. Willful murder."

She stared at Cartaret, waiting for him to say something; but he was silent.

"He'll be hanged for the murder of Mr. Perch—"

"Excuse me," said Cartaret. "Captain Perch."

"Alfred," said Cecily incredulously, "is that true?"

"I don't feel like talking," said Cartaret.

"I assure you it's perfectly true," said Mr. Fernandez. Watching them both. Feeling his way. "This man I picked up on the beach in Havana—gave a job to—trusted—"

"My benefactor!" said Cartaret. "I kiss the hem of your garment." He was trying to speak with his old mocking lightness, but it was poorly done.

"A wanton murder," said Mr. Fernandez, with a quick, sidelong glance at Cartaret. "Then, in a panic, he stole a passport and escaped."

"I wasn't in a panic," said Cartaret.

"*Alfred!*" said Cecily. "Haven't you anything to say?"

"Nope," he said, "except that I wasn't in a panic, and that I'm not suffering from remorse for choking the late Captain Perch."

Now you've done it, you idiot, thought Miss Peterson. Now you've given yourself away completely.

"You—choked a man to death?" said Cecily, incredulously.

"That's what I did," said Cartaret. "He advertised in the newspaper for an 'amateur' sailor seeking adventure. That appealed to me. I was out of a job, and I'd had rather a row with my father; so I wrote for an interview."

He was making his explanation for, and to Cecily; they looked straight at each other with a curious air of defiance.

"Perch said it was going to be just a sort of leisurely pleasure cruise. He got me to sign articles, just as a matter of form, he *said.* But it turned out to be a trading voyage, and I turned out to be his personal steward. And he turned out to be—the damnedest swine.... He knocked me around once too often. He kicked me, that last time, and it—irritated me."

"Oh, you mean it was just a fight?" said Cecily with a sigh of relief. "That's not murder."

"Well," said Mr. Fernandez, "the police will call it murder. You choke a man and leave him dead. You steal a passport and run away. That's quite good enough for the police."

"He can tell the truth," said Cecily. "He can tell them how Captain Perch treated him."

"No..." said Mr. Fernandez. "No. No good. You're in a spot, Cartaret. You know that, I guess?"

"I do," said Cartaret, with a stiff grin.

"You haven't a chance," said Mr. Fernandez. "You stole a passport from Alfred Jeffrey, and the man who was killed here in my hotel was Alfred Jeffrey. All right! You couldn't ask for a better motive. We'll suppose that I send for Losee. I tell him I've found the dead man's passport—somewhere. He looks at the passport. What!" He put on a look of stern amazement; he was now being Superintendent Losee. "The dead man was Alfred Jeffrey? Very well then, who is this other man? And then of course the cat is out of the bag. You'll certainly be charged with this second murder, too. Fine motive. Perfect opportunity. You have a passkey. You can get in and out of any room. And that's the end of you."

"Possibly," said Cartaret, with great nonchalance.

"Unless..." said Mr. Fernandez, slowly, "unless I save you."

"Oh, you want to bargain?" asked Cartaret.

"I don't need to bargain," said Mr. Fernandez. "I'll state my terms. This murder of Captain Perch doesn't interest me at all. I'm thinking of my hotel; and I want the shooting that happened here to be cleared up in a way that won't disturb my guests. All this investigating is annoying to them. Bad for my business. *Bueno!* Of course, Cecily, I understood at once why you made that confession."

"You couldn't," she said.

"You did it," he said, "to shield Mr. Harold Cartaret."

"Shield him from what?" she demanded with a sort of scornful indignation.

"My dear young lady," he said, "I assure you I know very well what goes on in my hotel. I know about those little midnight strolls you took with our friend Mr. Harold Cartaret. Very good! I suggest that during those little strolls, Mr. Harold Cartaret told you something about his difficulties—"

"Well, he didn't!" said Cecily.

"Then you discovered it. By intuition. You knew he was in trouble, didn't you?"

"In a way," she admitted.

"*Bueno!* Then when this shooting occurred in the hotel, you thought at once that he was involved. Confess now, didn't you?"

"No," she said with her startling bluntness. "When I first saw the man in your room, I thought *you'd* shot him."

"Ha...!" said Mr. Fernandez, taken aback. "Then your confession was not made for love?"

"Love?" said Cecily, as if the word astounded her. "I don't love anybody. You needn't smile like that. It's true!"

"Then why were you so anxious to stay in my hotel, even in the powder room?" Mr. Fernandez asked, still smiling like that.

"Very well, I'll tell you," said Cecily. There was a hot color in her cheeks now: she was angrier, more upset by being accused of love than by the charge of homicide. "I'm trying to build up a career for myself. My people wouldn't help me a bit. My father didn't *want* me to be successful. He wanted me to stay home and play for the family. My teacher was all ready to arrange a recital for me in New York. My father absolutely refused to put up the money for it. So I left. I went to a travel agency, and I got a ticket for the first ship that was leaving."

"Do your parents know where you are?" asked Miss Peterson.

"No," said Cecily. "But I gave one of the cruise passengers a letter to post for me in New York, to tell them I was all right. Because as soon as I got here, I *knew* this was the right place for me. I knew an exotic background would do a lot for me, and it's been good for me to get away from home. I made up my mind I wouldn't go home until I'd got into the newspapers. And when I saw that man lying there—Well, it seemed like a wonderful opportunity."

"And that's how a dead body impresses you?" said Cartaret, thoughtfully. "As a wonderful opportunity.... I see!"

The fine color drained away, and she was pale again. But still defiant.

"Yes," she said. "That's how I feel. I thought it was a chance to get into the newspapers. I wanted to get the most sensational publicity I possibly could. So I picked up the gun and fired it at the wall. That's why I told the police the story. Not for *love.*"

In contrast to her passionate energy, the two men seemed sadly deflated. Cartaret turned away from her and picked up the baby alligator constable; Mr. Fernandez stared at the floor. They were dismayed, even shocked at this denial of love by anyone so young and so pretty.

Mr. Fernandez recovered himself. "*Bueno!*" he said. "Now you have a chance to get more publicity. Tell Losee you made that confession to shield Cartaret."

"I won't!" she said. "I'm not going to do anything to injure him. I sort of like him."

"It won't hurt him," said Mr. Fernandez. "Here are my terms. Cartatet will write a confession that he shot Alfred Jeffrey. Wait! When you've done this, Cartaret, I'll get you out of the island to Venezuela. I have friends there. If you're not a fool, you can keep away from the police until the whole thing's forgotten. Cecily can tell the police she confessed to protect you—"

"Very neat!" said Cartaret, with a kind of gaiety. "You ferreted out this Captain Perch affair, I don't know how—and you've used it now to—" He paused, and moistened his lips. "You needn't have told Cecily," he said, a little unsteadily.

"I told her because I thought she'd be glad to help you."

"Well, I am," said Cecily.

Cartaret shook his head. "No need," he said. "I'm not writing any confessions. If they get me for this Captain Perch affair, very well." He looked at Mr. Fernandez. "They'll get *you* for the other killing," he said. "I know how you bribed the cook to identify that fellow. Complete lie that was, from beginning to end. Robert had never set eyes on him before."

They looked at each other, those two men, with undisguised hostility.

"Very well!" said Mr. Fernandez. "Then go to hell—your own way."

He opened the door and went out, and Cecily began to cry.

"Why are you crying?" asked Cartaret, coldly.

"I'm not—a monster!" she said with a sob. "I don't want you to be hanged."

"I think you're a monster," he said. "I've thought so for a long time. All this ought to be just dandy for your career. I hope you've kept those two notes I put under your door at different times. They'll be valuable later on. You can get them printed in any newspaper, easily. Love Letters of Condemned—"

"Shut up!" said Cecily.

"I won't," said Cartaret.

Miss Peterson went out, closing the door behind her.

XIII

She almost ran into Losee, who was standing facing the door of the office, stiff and immobile.

"Do you happen to know where Mr. Fernandez is?" he asked.

"He was here a moment ago—"

"Quite!" said he. "But I'd like very much to know where he is at the present moment."

His tone was ominous, and, very unreasonably, she resented that. She felt an impulse to make light of Mr. Fernandez's absence.

"He can't have gone very far," she observed.

"Possibly not," said Losee. "The point is, however, that I'd like to see him."

Miss Peterson was silent for a moment.

"Has Mrs. Fish come back, Superintendent?" she asked.

"She has not," he said.

"Then," said Miss Peterson, "I have something to tell you."

It was going to be like an avalanche; the first word she spoke would start it. She would have to tell him about Mrs. Fish-Perch's letter, and then, down would come the great, roaring landslide of justice, retribution and death. Death for Harold Cartaret, and Heaven knew what for Mr. Fernandez.

"Yes?" said the superintendent.

Mr. Fredericks was approaching them.

"We'd better go somewhere else," she said. "It's rather long."

"Quite," said he. "Suppose we—"

"Superintendent," said Mr. Fredericks, "may I have a word with you?"

"Presently, sir," said Losee.

"The matter brooks no delay, Superintendent," said Mr. Fredericks. "I understand that Mrs. Fish is missing; and I have some very important information to give you about her."

"I'll be at your service in a few moments, sir," said Losee. "But—"

"I'll be glad to wait, Superintendent," said Miss Peterson, courteously, "if Mr. Fredericks has important information."

"That's very kind of you, Miss Peterson," said Mr. Fredericks. "I'll try not to be long-winded."

Losee compressed his already very thin mouth into a wide straight line, and unexpectedly, two dimples appeared in his leathery cheeks. He was deliberating. "Very good, sir!" he said. "*If* Miss Peterson's willing to wait...."

She went off on a little private hunt for Mr. Fernandez. It's getting late, she thought. The sun's going down. Getting near the deadline. She went up to his suite, and knocked, in vain. She went downstairs again and sent for Howard.

"Do you know where Mr. Fernandez went, Howard?" she asked.

"Mistress, I do not know," he answered. "I seek him everywhere. It must be he went out, mistress, but he did not say any word."

"Let me know as soon as he comes in, please," she said.

This worried her. This was no time for Mr. Fernandez to be absent. She went into the lounge and chatted with old Mrs. Boucher for an interminable time; then she went into the sun-deck and rang the bell and Moses, the head boy came.

"Has Mr. Fernandez come back yet?" she asked.

"Mistress, he has not," said Moses. "Policeman came to see he; and we seek him. But he is not here."

"I suppose he just stepped out..." said Miss Peterson.

"Mistress, he never do *so*," said Moses. "When he go out, he tell me every time, when he coming back. Every time, mistress."

"Let me know when he comes in, Moses, will you?" she said.

She was more than worried now. She went up again to his suite; she knocked again without the least hope of an answer. He was gone; and Mrs. Fish was gone.

At seven o'clock she went into the dining room; she smiled as she passed old Mrs. Boucher, and old Mrs. Green and the Major; she sat down at her own little table. It will be in the newspapers tomorrow, she thought. That'll be the end of the hotel, and the end of all don Carlos' princeliness. He said there were plenty of people wanting to pull him down. Peccaries. Well, I'm afraid they've got the jaguar treed now.

I'm sorry. I'm sorrier than I'd have expected. I wish I didn't have to run with the peccaries. I'm not going to say any more than I must. I'll tell Losee about the letter from Mrs. Fish-Perch, and that's all.

And not tell him about Cartaret and the passport? Just tell him Mrs. Perch is looking for her husband's murderer; and not tell him the murderer's here? No. It can't be like that. I've got to tell the whole thing. And I'll be the one to hang Cartaret, and bring the whole avalanche down on don Carlos.

I've protected don Carlos before. Did he think I'd do it again this time? Did he count on that? After I heard him with my own ears blackmailing Cartaret? Yet here I sit; feeling sorry for him.

Ah, well! she said to herself. I've never pretended to be reasonable. Who'd really try to be in a world with such unreasonable things as hurricanes and earthquakes and wars? I like cats, and I hate mice. I like blue, and I don't like green. *Así es la vida.*

It's dark night now, and where is don Carlos? There's one thing certain. If he's trying to get away, he has some plan. He's a smart guy, and maybe he will get away....

She sat alone at her little table and tried to enjoy her dinner. But the absence of Mr. Fernandez was almost a palpable thing; without his exuberant, alert presence, the hotel seemed horribly empty. There was no one in charge. I'd even be glad to see Losee, she thought.

She never hurried over eating, or over anything else if it was not necessary; she enjoyed a dessert of boiled custard with a meringue of egg-whites and guava jelly, well chilled; she drank her coffee, and then she went out into the lounge.

The Major was walking on the terrace; she saw his pompous form pass back and forth before the lighted windows. The other guests sat in the lounge; and how tranquil, how innocent they looked! With a murderer behind the desk, a few feet away from them....

She went past the elevators and looked into the powder room. Very elegant it was; gray and rose, and on a little Empire sofa sat Cecily in her black and white uniform.

"I really don't think you need to stay here, Cecily," said Miss Peterson.

"I want to," said Cecily. "This is what I'm getting paid for."

Miss Peterson, tall and nonchalant, leaned against the doorway for a while. But there was nothing to say and presently she moved away.

I suppose I'd better go and do some more reassuring until Losee's ready for me, she thought, making her way toward the lounge. But she was stopped by Mr. Fredericks.

"Would you care to take a little stroll?" he asked.

He was upset. His voice was perfectly steady, his appearance in no way changed, yet somehow his agitation was plain.

"I'd like to," she answered, "but I have to see Superintendent Losee—"

"He's gone," said Mr. Fredericks. "Called away. He'll be back presently, of course. But—we'd have time for a little stroll, if it suits you."

It did suit her, and they went out on the terrace, where the Major still patrolled alone; they went down the steps along the drive toward the beach.

"I'm sorry to say this," Mr. Fredericks began, "but Losee is not the man for this job. He's—impervious. Typical official mind. I have a good many friends throughout the islands in positions of authority, and I shall feel obliged to let them know that my suggestions have been ignored."

"Oh, have they?" said Miss Peterson with an air of sympathy.

"Completely ignored," he said. "I've done a great deal of work on this case, and I've come to certain conclusions—based on my experience and my knowledge. I've presented these conclusions to Losee—and he brushes them aside as negligible."

"I see!" she said.

"I want my conclusions on record," he went on. "It's not that I'm interested in receiving any credit. It's more a matter of exposing the incompetence of the police under the direction of Losee. And you, of course, are the obvious person to address in the matter."

"Obvious?" she repeated.

"Who else is there?" he asked. "I've told my wife, naturally, but she might be considered biased. There's no one else in the hotel one would consider confiding in for a moment. But I can count on you to confirm my statement, later."

I'm tired of being counted on, she thought. I'm worried and—rather unhappy, and not sure about anything. It's a mistake to count on me. I might do anything....

"I attended the inquest on the man found dead in the hotel," Mr. Fredericks continued. "And it was obvious then, that someone was being shielded. The girl Cecily was permitted to withdraw her confession without any adequate examination. I sent the coroner a note, respectfully suggesting that the girl had had a rendezvous with the dead man. My note was ignored. The whole inquest was a farce. And tomorrow's inquest on the unfortunate Mrs. Barley is likely to be just as futile. I managed to elicit from Tinker that she was poisoned—"

"Doctor Tinker told you?" she asked surprised.

"Well.... We'll say I elicited the information. I have an introduction to Tinker, you know, from a person of considerable influence asking him to give me any assistance he can. Very well. To make a long story short, I laid all my information, and the logical deduction I had made from it, before Losee. And he brushed it aside. I want my conclusions on record, Miss Peterson."

"I see!" said Miss Peterson, again.

"You'll remember that I mentioned before the possibility that the girl Cecily had had a rendezvous with the dead man. I had—even at that time—a fairly shrewd idea of the object of such a meeting; and now I have no further doubts. The man was a purveyor of drugs."

They had come to the hard, damp sand at the edge of the sea; they walked slowly, side by side under the sky powdered with stars, with a mild and steady wind blowing across the water.

"This hotel," said Mr. Fredericks, "is the headquarters of a drug ring."

Miss Peterson turned her head but she could not see his face in the dark.

"Have you—managed to get any evidence?" she asked.

"Not yet," he said. "My conclusions are deductions, so far. It's for Losee to produce the evidence. Mrs. Barley was undoubtedly a drug addict—"

"I don't think so, Mr. Fredericks."

"I'm afraid it's true, Miss Peterson. And there is another addict here. Someone who came here for the sole purpose of procuring a supply of some drug—probably opium."

"Who's that?" she asked.

There was a row-boat pulled up on the beach, a little ahead of them; she looked forward to reaching that and sitting down.

"You haven't noticed?" he said. "It's this Mrs. Fish. Undoubtedly a drug addict."

No, thought Miss Peterson, but she said nothing aloud. Let him go on.

"She came here in order to procure this drug," he went on. "And the girl Cecily is the intermediary between the purveyors and the head of the ring, who, naturally, tried to remain incognito. This arrangement has probably been working smoothly for some time. And then—something went wrong. I believe

I know what it was. Shortly before the storm the other day, a schooner put in here—a schooner called the *Hesiod*. She anchored out in the roadstead, and some time previous to, or during the storm, she disappeared. It seems to me certain that the dead man was from the *Hesiod*."

"Let's sit down," said Miss Peterson, and she did sit down on the gunwale of the boat, while Mr. Fredericks stood before her.

"This is my reconstruction," he said. "This man learned in some way that the schooner had gone and left him here. He became panic-stricken—possibly he has a police record as a drug purveyor. He desired protection from the head of the drug ring. He demanded that he be concealed in the hotel. The head of the ring—whom we can call X, for convenience, was unwilling to take such a risk and shot him. Mrs. Barley, no doubt, knew the dead man. She may have secured drugs from him in the past. She would have been able to identify him—and she was also put out of the way."

"Have you a cigarette, Mr. Fredericks?" asked Miss Peterson.

He gave her one and lit it for her.

"X by this time has gone too far to withdraw. It's absolutely necessary for him to commit another murder. He has got to get rid of the other addict who might betray him. He has got to silence Mrs. Fish. And Mrs. Fish has disappeared."

He waited a moment. "You follow me, Miss Peterson?"

"Yes..." she said, overwhelmed by this extraordinary recital.

"Very well," he said. "X has murdered Mrs. Fish. Do you know *now*, Miss Peterson, who X is?"

"No," she said.

"Mr. Fernandez," said he.

That was the name she had expected.

"I've put the case before Losee," he said. "I told him that Fernandez had either killed or would kill Mrs. Fish, and would then make his escape by way of some schooner, or even some launch previously concealed in one of the rocky inlets on the South shore. I proposed offering a reward for Fernandez. But he brushed aside the whole thing."

"Mr. Fredericks," she said, "are you—connected with the police?"

"I have connections with the police, yes," he answered. "It may surprise you to know that my name is T. Myron Fredericks."

"Is that...?"

"My fourteenth book has just been published," he said. "Perhaps you've seen the reviews? *Death Under Glass*. I've written stories with very varied backgrounds; in India, China, Mexico, and so on. I've always had good introductions, and I've always—until now—met with courtesy and co-operation from the police."

"Have you solved other cases?"

"Well, no," he answered, reluctantly. "But I've never happened to come into actual contact with a murder case before. However, I've made a study of criminology, and of police methods. My mind is trained along those lines."

He struck a match and held it cupped in his hands against the steady breeze. He held it, and let it drop on the sand.

"Oh—God!" he said in a low voice.

"What's the matter, Mr. Fredericks?"

"She's here..." he said.

"Who? Who's where?"

"Mrs. Fish," he said. "In the row-boat."

Miss Peterson sprang to her feet. He struck another match, but he dropped it. He and held out his jacket to protect it. Miss Peterson looked down.

Mrs. Fish was lying huddled in the boat, with her long black hair loose, and her eyes wide open.

XIV

"Don't touch her!" cried Mr. Fredericks. "Wait until the police—"

"I've got to see..." said Miss Peterson. She knelt on the sand and groped in the dark; she found a wrist, very thin and very cold. She could feel no pulse.

"Dead?" asked Mr. Fredericks, very low.

"I think so," Miss Peterson answered, rising.

"Then," he said, "my case is proved."

She heard him, but without understanding. It was as if the shock of this discovery had broken her mind up into the tiny bright prisms of a kaleidoscope; thoughts were twinkling in her head, but they made no sense. The sea, she thought, was coming closer, with a strange quiet rushing sound; she was suddenly afraid it would lap up the row-boat and take it away. She turned toward the hotel.

"My case is proved now," Mr. Fredericks said again.

"Oh, no it isn't!" she said.

"You think not?" he said, keeping at her side. "After all I've told you? After I *told* you Mrs. Fish would inevitably be murdered?"

"No," she said, going faster and faster, with her long-limbed effortless step. "I don't believe Mr. Fernandez is a murderer. Or a drug peddler. Or a swindler, or a thief."

"Why don't you believe it?" he cried.

Why? she asked herself. I just don't, that's all. The more things he's accused of, the more faith I have in him.

"If he's innocent," said Mr. Fredericks, his voice unsteady with emotion, and with the rapid pace, "then why has he run away?"

"He hasn't," she said.

"Then, where *is* he?"

"I don't know," she said. He's certainly gone, but you don't have to be guilty of a crime to go away for a while. Maybe Mrs. Fish wasn't murdered at all. Maybe it was just an accident. Maybe she isn't even dead. I must hurry and get help. I must hurry....

"You'll bear witness to what I said," Mr. Fredericks insisted. "You'll remember that I foretold this murder."

"Yes, I will," she said, to keep him quiet. It was such an immense distance to the hotel that stood there like an enchanted castle with lighted windows....

Somebody was coming toward them. "Miss Peterson?" called a man's voice.

"Oh, Superintendent Losee!" she answered, stopping short with a long sigh of relief. "I wanted you."

"Quite," he said.

"Mrs. Fish..." she said. "She's in that row-boat, and I'm afraid she's dead."

He spoke over his shoulder to one of the two dark figures that followed him. "Get Doctor Tinker," he said, and advanced toward Miss Peterson. "Ha, Mr. Fredericks," he said. "I see...! I'd like an account, if you please, of this discovery."

"I'd just been telling Miss Peterson my solution," said Mr. Fredericks. "I've just told her that Mrs. Fish would inevitably be murdered. Then, as I struck a match to light a cigarette, I saw the body lying in the bottom of the boat."

"Did you touch the body, or in any way disturb it?"

"I felt her pulse," Miss Peterson said.

"That's justifiable," said Losee.

He reached the boat and turned the bright beam of a flashlight into it. He sat down on the gunwale and stared down intently. "Sergeant!" he said, and one of his shadows came to his side. "Make a note of the position," he said. "Make a sketch."

"Yes, sir!" said a deep, gentle voice.

Then there was a silence, with only the steady murmur of the sea.

"No oars," Losee observed. "High tide was at six-forty."

"But it's coming in now," said Miss Peterson.

"Going out," said Losee. "What was the reason for your coming here?"

"We were merely taking a stroll," Mr. Fredericks answered.

"Who suggested a stroll?"

"I did. I wanted to tell Miss Peterson—"

"Quite. Who suggested strolling in this particular direction?"

"Nobody. I don't think we mentioned it. We just happened to come this way."

"Finished, Sergeant? Good! Now we'll lift the body out. You needn't stay, Miss Peterson."

But she couldn't make up her mind to turn her back on Mrs. Fish-Perch. She couldn't go away and leave her alone with the two policemen. Mr. Fredericks lingered, too. It was easy to lift Mrs. Fish; she was very light. They laid her on the sand, and two flashlights focused upon her now. This is death, Miss Peterson thought. Not a hard death.

They turned her over on her face, and the back of her sheer black dress was wet between the shoulders.

"Miss Peterson," said Losee, "d'you feel able to assist? Get this dress off?"

He held Mrs. Fish up, and Miss Peterson got her arms out of the sleeves, and stripped the dress off her shoulders.

"Yes..." said Losee.

The clear ray of light was fixed upon the deep puncture in the back on the left side. "Knife wound," he said meditating. "Yes...."

He laid Mrs. Fish back gently; he pulled up the dress, he took out a handkerchief and covered her staring, astonished face. "We'll wait here for the doctor—" he began.

"Have you found Fernandez yet?" asked Mr. Fredericks.

"No. No, we haven't," said Losee. He seemed in a curiously mild mood now, standing straight and quiet, with Mrs. Fish lying at his feet. "I followed your suggestion, sir. Your suggestion that the dead man had come from the schooner *Hesiod*. She returned here late this afternoon, and I've just been on board. Everything in order. Nobody missing."

"Did you search the schooner?"

"Why, no sir, I didn't," said Losee. "American registry—and I had no authority."

"Then you don't know whether or not there were drugs on board?"

"That's a fact, sir. I don't," said Losee.

"And you refuse to take any steps?"

"I'm taking steps, Mr. Fredericks," said Losee.

"Your steps are too slow," said Mr. Fredericks. "If you'd listened to me, sir, this innocent woman would not be lying dead at your feet."

"She'd have been in jail," said Losee.

"What do you mean?"

"A warrant has been issued," said Losee, again in that meditative tone.

"For what?"

"Charging Mrs. Fish—"

"Charging her with *what?*"

"Accessory before and after the fact. In the case of the man found shot in the hotel. Also in the death by poison of Mrs. Barley."

"This woman? You denounce this woman?"

"You ought to be able to write a very nice story about this, Mr. Fredericks," said Losee. "And you'd have a great advantage over me. *You'd* be able to put in a motive; and that's what I can't do. I've got a fairly good idea of *what*; only I don't see any *why*. And a jury always wants a motive. Curious thing, that. You can present a watertight case—and if there isn't a good strong motive, the jury won't convict."

He seemed to be talking to himself in the dark, and neither Mr. Fredericks nor Miss Peterson interrupted him.

"A jury is always instructed to bring in a verdict based upon the facts," he went on. "But they don't. They want the motive. Even in a suicide case. And the trouble is, that the motive for suicide, and sometimes for murder, is often— inadequate.... Queer reasons people have, sometimes, for killing. Very queer."

"I'd be interested to hear the case you've built up against this unfortunate woman," said Mr. Fredericks. "I'd like to hear how you deduce her guilt."

"Well, I don't do much deducing," said the superintendent. "I collect all the facts I can; and sometimes if I'm lucky, they mean something. In this case.... In the course of interrogating the servants, I came across a very significant fact." He paused. "I found out that Mrs. Fish, within an hour of her arrival at the hotel, had sent for Mrs. Barley and had talked to her for some time." He paused again. "Mrs. Barley's passkey has not been found," he said. "There are several possible explanations for that. One: she lost or mislaid the key. Two: the key was stolen from her. Three: she lent the key to someone. Very well. My interest now being directed toward Mrs. Fish, I questioned the chambermaid who looked after her room, and I learned that she had a case or bag entirely filled with bottles."

"Drugs!" said Mr. Fredericks.

"Purveyors of drugs don't carry their wares in bottles, sir. I managed to get a look at this case, and I found in it several bromides, and a good number of standard remedies for indigestion and so on. And a preparation containing a certain narcotic poison. After Doctor Tinker had given it as his opinion that Mrs. Barley was suffering from the effects of a poison of this kind, I wanted to see Mrs. Fish."

"Well..." said Mr. Fredericks, in a sulky, disappointed tone.

"If Mrs. Fish was in the possession of a passkey," said Losee, "and if she also had this narcotic in a considerable quantity, she had the means and the opportunity to commit this murder. When I later found among her papers an American permit to carry a gun, I felt we were making progress. We proceeded along those lines. We found an excellent set of Mrs. Fish's fingerprints on the bottle of gin in Mrs. Barley's room. As well as a set of yours, Miss Peterson. But you admitted being in the room, and Mrs. Fish did not."

He waited, but nobody spoke. "A most peculiar piece of information came from two of the maids. Mrs. Fish had spoken to these girls separately, but their accounts corroborated each other. They remembered what she had said, because she had alarmed them both. She asked these girls if there were any zombies on the island. This is a superstition confined chiefly, I believe, to Haiti. Anyhow it doesn't obtain here. She explained to them that a zombie was a person who had died—generally by murder—and was forced to work as a slave after death. She told them that she had seen zombies, and knew them to exist. And she said to both of them, that nothing done by a zombie could be called a crime."

"It may have been a joke," said Miss Peterson, uncertainly.

"I differ from you," said Mr. Fredericks. "I should call it a very subtle line of defense, prepared in advance." He stopped and looked along the beach, to a group of figures advancing with flashlights. "But the question before us now is: who killed Mrs. Fish?"

"Quite," said Losee.

"And I believe I can give you the answer. I can't see that my theory has been at all invalidated by yours. I still maintain that what we have here is a drug ring—a murder ring if you like, and as head and chief of it is Fernandez."

There was a silence.

"Very well!" he said. "I predicted the death of this unfortunate woman. I'll tell you, here and now, who the next victim will inevitably be. It will be this young lady standing here. Miss Peterson."

"You think Mr. Fernandez would—" she began.

"Yes!" he almost shouted. "And when it's too late, the authorities will real-ize—"

"Hello! Hello! Hello!" said Doctor Tinker's merry voice. "More work for me, eh? Well, let's see...."

"There's no need to wait," said the superintendent, with significance, and Miss Peterson moved away. Mr. Fredericks went along with her.

"You too," he said. "I suppose you also will hold to the official point of view—the 'ostrich' point of view. *Three* deaths, three murders aren't enough to disturb the official complacency."

"Why do you think that Mr. Fernandez should want to kill me?" she asked, plaintively.

She heard him sigh in the dark.

"Let's suppose that Losee's right," he said. "I think it's very far from likely, but let's assume that Mrs. Fish shot the man, and poisoned Mrs. Barley. Then let's consider what Mrs. Fish said on two occasions to two maids. I refer to the zombie statement. A zombie is a slave without volition. We can assume she was trying to justify her acts, trying to protect herself by hinting that she acted un-der orders from somebody else. That somebody else was the head of the drug ring—Fernandez. She committed these murders—if she did commit them—at his command and for his benefit. He then found it convenient to destroy his tool."

"But I'm not a tool."

"Possibly not," he said. "But I overheard a strange remark, Miss Peterson. I was passing through the lounge this evening, when the door of Mr. Fernandez's private office opened a little, and I heard that young Jeffrey say to someone in-side: 'Well, Karen of the Golden Hair will finish don Carlos, all right.' I did-n't need that observation to complete my knowledge, Miss Peterson. *I know who you are.*"

"Well, who am I?" she asked anxiously. "I mean, who do you think I am?"

"I knew, directly you arrived, calling yourself a 'hostess.' My wife and I both saw that you had no knowledge of a hostess's duties, and you were, obvi-ously, not the type at all. No. You came here at the instigation of the British Gov-ernment, to make inquiries."

"Oh!" she said, and let it go.

"I don't expect you to admit it," said Mr. Fredericks.

So I'm the golden-haired spy, she thought. All right. I just can't cope with this. I'm tired. I'm going to bed. And I hope I won't think about Mrs. Fish. Jeffrey—or Cartaret killed her. And if Losee doesn't find that out for himself very soon, I'll have to tell him. I hope he finds it out for himself. I like justice and fair play and all those nice things. I haven't much use for Cartaret. Yet I hope I don't have to be the one who sends him to the gallows.

They were approaching the terrace now.

"You can count on me and my wife for the fullest co-operation, Miss Peterson," said Mr. Fredericks. "I only urge you to be careful."

"Yes, thank you, I will be," she answered, glad to get away from him, longing for the quiet of her room. But on the way to the elevator, Moses stopped her.

"Boy here, mistress. Got a letter for you. Wouldn't give that letter up 'cepting into your hands, mistress."

"All right, bring him along!"

"Could not do so, mistress. He a small boy from the bush, mistress. Look like a scarecrow."

"Where is he?"

"In the kitchen, mistress. I send he up the back stairs to your room."

"Yes," she said, and got into the elevator.

It's going to be a note from don Carlos, she thought. She propped open the door and sat down in a chair facing it, to wait. The whistling frogs were loud tonight, and the sea was loud. And there's Mrs. Fish lying out there, dead....

The little black boy came, noiseless on his bare feet; he wore a tattered pink and white striped pyjama jacket over a pair of filthy white duck shorts.

"For you, mistress," he said, holding out an envelope covered with dirty finger marks.

"Who gave it to you?" she asked.

"Sailor man, mistress, on the wharf."

"What was his name?"

"Never see him before, mistress. He say, give this letter Mistress Peterson in the new hotel in she own hands."

She took a sixpence from her purse, and he thanked her and ran padding away. She closed the door, and sat down again, and with reluctance tore open the envelope. For she had a feeling that nothing good could happen; that this letter could bring only bad news.

Dear Miss Peterson:

Please treat this in the *strictest confidence*. By a very strange chance I have run across an old friend who is ready to buy my hotel, lock, stock, and barrel. Because of circumstances which you know, I shall be glad to sell.

My friend has also agreed to give Alfred Jeffrey a very decent job in his large hotel in Montevideo. This is an excellent opportunity for Jeffrey, and I, as you know, will be glad to see him leave Riquezas. Will you please see Jeffrey at once and give him his instructions. Tell him to get the private ledger from the safe, and also the analysis charts I had made in New York. Tell him to bring them to Bowfin Cove at eleven to-night, where a launch will pick him up. He has so little sense that perhaps you had better point out to him that he must be careful to get away unobserved by the police. If he is discovered I shall certainly not lift a finger to help him. As soon as this deal is concluded, I shall be with you again.

Then it's true, she thought. Don Carlos is making a getaway. I'm sorry.... He's selling out. I suppose he had to, but I'm sorry. She lit a cigarette, and read the letter again. And this time she noticed the signature.

Carlos Embustero Fernandez y Carter.

Embustero...! she cried, half aloud. He had signed himself 'embustero'—liar: to warn her. That meant he had written under duress. That meant that he was in danger.

XV

What about telling Losee? she asked herself, and answered, no. Mr. Fernandez might be in danger somewhere, but Losee was very clearly another danger. I'll have to tell about Cartaret in the course of time, she thought. But it can wait. It doesn't matter very much when he's caught and tried and hanged. The first thing is to find don Carlos.

She lay on her bed and smoked a cigarette, her long slender body relaxed, her mind working lucidly. She rose and telephoned to the desk, and asked Cartaret to send Moses up to her. He came promptly, very smart in his uniform, very eager.

"Come in and close the door," she said. "Mr. Fernandez trusts you, doesn't he, Moses?"

"Cert'ny does, mistress. Cert'ny does."

"Where's Bowfin Cove, Moses?"

"It's not too far, mistress."

"Could you get there in a row-boat?"

"Oh yes, mistress."

"How long would it take to row there?"

"Half an hour, mistress."

"Can you borrow a row-boat, Moses?"

"I can, mistress."

"Nobody must know about this," she said. "You understand that? Nobody at all!"

"I understand, mistress."

"I want you to go close to Bowfin Cove, and wait in some place where you won't be seen until a launch comes. When the launch leaves, I want you to find out where it goes."

"Row-boat slower than launch, mistress."

"I know. But if you use a motor it would be heard."

"I will use a sail, mistress."

"All right, as long as you can do it alone."

"Take my brother, mistress. He secret and faithful as me."

"All right," she said. "Ten shillings. And ten more if you can follow the launch. And let me know as soon as you get back—unless there's someone with me."

There probably will be someone with me, she thought, and sighed. Losee will go on, and on and on. That's his job, of course. And in the end, he'll find out who killed Mrs. Fish. He'd know now, if he knew about the Alfred Jeffrey passport and Mrs. Fish-Perch's will. It's funny how much everybody has to depend upon being told things. Losee's no fool. But he isn't interested in Cartaret because nobody's told him anything.

Losee, who knew nothing about the Perch aspect, had been steadily on the trail of Mrs. Fish. With everyone concerned either lying to him, or withholding vitally important information, he had still gone ahead in the right direction. And he would, no doubt, continue.

Mr. Fredericks was wrong about everything, she thought. Well, suppose I'm wrong, too. I believe that Cartaret killed Mrs. Fish-Perch. Suppose he didn't? She stubbed out her cigarette, and stretched out limp and flat. I think I'll go to sleep until somebody comes, she thought, and turned out the bedside lamp.

Mrs. Fish's white face and wide eyes and long black hair came before her closed eyes. But she contemplated it quietly until it vanished. Then the little bald man swam up from the depths and dissolved. And then Mrs. Barley.

Mrs. Barley's image stayed longest, because her death was most disturbing to Miss Peterson. But after a time, she too had gone. And last of these images was the Devil. Mrs. Fish-Perch's devilish husband. The Devil shining with fire.... Mrs. Fish believed in zombies.... You could see them in Haiti, people said; a blank-eyed, silent gang risen from their graves, going along the road in a cloud of dust under the burning sun.

"I don't believe—in it," she said with an effort. A judge in a white wig was looking at her sternly, and when she looked straight at him, she saw that he was an alligator. That frightened her, but she was not going to let him know it. "I don't believe in zombies," she said, quietly. "It's just a trick. It's—theatrical.... They just want publicity." "They're knocking," said the judge; and she heard them knock. *"You can't keep them out!"* he said with a crescent smile, from one ear to the other.

She was very much afraid of that gang of zombies knocking at the door.... Some door.... What door...? She opened her eyes and turned on the lamp—and somebody was knocking at her door. She got up and opened it, and Moses stood there.

"Launch from the schooner, mistress," he said, very low. "Know she, soon as I see she. But we go after, mistress, till she go alongside the schooner."

"What schooner?"

"Schooner *Hesiod*, mistress."

She glanced at her watch. Nearly one. "What's going on in the hotel, Moses?"

"Isn't nothing going on, mistress. Policeman, he sitting in the lounge, another policeman, he sit in the kitchen, and he drink coffee like he victim of the famine of Egypt."

"Superintendent Losee is there?"

"No, mistress. Everybody gone to bed, except those 'foresaid policemen."

"Has anyone...? Did the police take anyone away?"

"No, mistress. It cannot be so. How they think to catch Mr. Devil?"

"Do you think the Devil did all of this, Moses?"

"Must be so, mistress," he said earnestly. "He raise up a great storm and darkness for his evil work."

"Why should he pick out this hotel?" she asked, reasonably.

"Must be that there is someone bad here, Mistress."

"Who would that be, I wonder?" she said.

But Moses had no more to say. He took the pound note with earnest thanks, and went away; and Miss Peterson undressed and got into bed. So don Carlos is on board the *Hesiod*, she thought. Against his will? Losee said that he'd been on board, but he said, too, that he hadn't searched the vessel. Mr. Fernandez might have been there all the time. Of course, he may be hiding on board, keeping away from that warrant, arranging a getaway. But there's that note....

He signed it *'embustero,'* to warn me. That means—that *has* to mean, he couldn't write what he wanted. He said he wanted Alfred Jeffrey to go out there—but he sent the note to me. All right! I know why. It's because he's counting on me *again*. He keeps on and on, counting on me, and trusting me. Telling me secrets. I don't want to be counted on. I want to tell Losee the whole thing now—before I get into serious trouble for not telling it. I want to be *done* with all this.

She felt so angry that she flounced in the bed. I'm concealing important information from the police, she thought. If I have the sense that God gave geese, I'll go to Losee first thing in the morning and tell him everything. If he arrests Fernandez, very well. He'll be set free if he's innocent; and if he's guilty of anything he deserves to be in jail. The whole thing is perfectly simple and straightforward. Once Losee knows the facts he'll question Cartaret, and this last murder will be cleared up. It's my duty under the law. It's my duty to society. To myself.

If I *do* go out to that schooner, she thought, I'll take plenty of precautions. I'll go in broad daylight, and I'll take my gun. *If* I go. Moses can take me, she thought. I'll think up a story for Losee. I'll say I think there's a cousin of mine on board. He ran away from home, and he's working under an assumed name. I'll recognize him, of course. His poor mother in Minnesota is in such a state....

It won't be hard, and it won't be dangerous. Not in broad daylight with Moses along. But it's the last thing I'll do for Mr. Fernandez. I'm going to tell him straight that he's got to stop counting on me. I have too much common sense to do things like this.

Like Napoleon, she told herself at what hour to wake. Six o'clock, she said to her subconscious mind, and went to sleep. Only she waked at five.

She took as long as she could about bathing and dressing, and when she went downstairs one of the cooks was in the kitchen, and there was fresh coffee made.

"Is Moses anywhere around?" she asked.

"He here, mistress," said the cook. "I send him with your coffee on the terrace."

"You don't seem to get much time off," said Miss Peterson when Moses brought the tray.

"I'm the head boy, mistress," he said. "And now Mr. Fernandez gone, Mis' Barley gone, they's plenty to do."

"Can you get a boat again?" she asked. "A motor boat, this time."

"I can, mistress."

"Can you run an engine?"

"I can, mistress."

"I'd like to start as soon as possible," she said. "And—is there any quiet place we could start from?"

"Unobsahved, mistress? Can leave from the marsh. Boat there now, mistress. We can go when you wish."

"I'll just eat my breakfast," she said, and this time she hurried over it. Because she very much preferred going without seeing Superintendent Losee. There was a policeman in the lounge, but he had only said good morning. There might be other policemen around, and they might stop her. But she hoped not.

She went upstairs for a hat, and returned to Moses, who now wore a khaki helmet.

"We be more unobsahved this way, mistress," he said, and led the way round the building to a path that went to the garage. Behind the garage was a clump of bamboo, delicate against the pure blue sky; they went by that and skirted a wall, and came out upon a road.

A group of laborers came along, barefoot in the dust, wearing tattered straw hats and carrying machetes. "Morning to you, mistress," they all said; and she returned the greeting. They turned the corner, and before them was a mangrove swamp, evil-smelling and gloomy. Moses knew the way; she followed in his footsteps until they reached a tidal inlet where a small launch was tied to a mangrove root. It was very, very quiet here; the noise of the engine sounded outrageous, banging and spitting like a machine gun. Moses wiped off the seat carefully, and she got in, and off they went through the inlet to the open sea.

"I want to go to the *Hesiod*," she said.

"Yes, mistress," said Moses.

The launch ducked up and down merrily through the quiet sea; the freshness of the early morning was still in the breeze; they headed away from the town, and there was nothing before them but sky and water.

"Is she moored far out, Moses?"

"I do not know if she shift her mooring in the night, mistress. Last night she was lying off the South Shore."

"Have you heard anything about the *Hesiod*, Moses?"

"From America, mistress."

"Coming here to trade?"

"I do not know that, mistress."

"Do you know anyone who's talked to any of the crew? Anyone who's been on board?"

"No, mistress."

The little boat went dancing across the water that was blue as sapphire; it was a beautiful morning. Only it was lonely. Where are the gulls? Miss Peterson thought. There were not even any clouds in the blue sky; it was empty. She turned her head to look back at Riquezas, and the vista was suddenly unfamiliar: a black rock covered with verdure; no houses, no roads.

It's broad daylight, she thought. I've got Moses with me, and I've got my gun in my bag. We're in full view of the shore, and there are sure to be other boats around. I didn't leave word where I was going, because I didn't want anyone coming after me. And because it wasn't necessary. When I go on board Moses will be waiting for me.

And who told me to trust Moses?

She looked at him, and his thin face was ineffably melancholy beneath the helmet. Why did he have that look of bitter grief? Did he know something? Something that had happened—or something that was going to happen? A premonition...?

Don't be such an idiot! she told herself. And then she thought she had already committed a prodigious folly, to come here out in the middle of the sea with Moses. Perhaps he wasn't going to the *Hesiod* at all. Perhaps there was no *Hesiod*. Perhaps she and Moses and the boat would disappear; never be heard of again.

This young lady is inevitably the next victim. That was what Mr. Fredericks had said. Mr. Fredericks had been wrong about everything—or hadn't he? What if he had been right, and Mr. Fernandez was all he said? Chief of a drug ring? Chief of a murder ring? What if that note had been cunningly and subtly designed for just this purpose? To entice her into—what?

"Moses," she said. "I've changed my mind. We'll go back."

"Yes, mistress," he said in his soft voice, and immediately swung the boat round in a wide arc.

"No, I haven't, after all," she said, ashamed of herself. "The *Hesiod* can't be much farther off."

He swung the boat back again.

"I wonder why there aren't any gulls," she said, with a great desire for conversation.

"They do congregate sometimes, mistress. Got their own island where they go."

"Have you been to their island?"

"Oh, I could not go there, mistress. Some gulls live there, big as buzzards. Man set he foot on their island, they pick he eyes out, pick he bones clean."

"Quite," said Miss Peterson. Dear Superintendent Losee! I hope you're smart enough to figure out where I've gone....

"*Hesiod* there, mistress."

They had rounded a rocky point, and now she saw a schooner at anchor; a weather-beaten wooden hull with bare masts, and flying over it was a flock of gulls, screaming and swooping.

"Moses," she said, "if I go on board, you must wait for me."

"Yes, mistress."

I'm trusting completely in you—and I don't know anything about you. I thought I was being sensible and practical, going in broad daylight with a gun. And it was—a crazy thing to do....

Nobody on deck. Nobody in the whole sunny world but Moses and herself.

"You might give them a hail, Moses."

"*Hesiod* aho-ooy...!" cried Moses, in a wail like a lost soul.

"Ahoy 'ere!" shouted a hearty voice, and a man came to the rail, a big, blond young fellow, dressed only in blue trousers rolled up to his knees.

"I have a message for Mr. Fernandez," Miss Peterson called back.

He shook his blond head.

"Ay call de skipper," he said, and vanished below. Moses brought the boat closely alongside the schooner, just below the rope ladder. "You'll wait for me, Moses?" she said again.

"Oh yes, mistress!" he said.

The big, blond young fellow came back and leaned over the rail.

"De skipper ask your name," he said.

"Miss Peterson," she answered, and on impulse, repeated it with a Swedish pronunciation. He grinned from ear to ear and went away again, and when he returned, he spoke to her in Swedish.

"If the young lady will come on board...?"

He started to go down the rope ladder, but Miss Peterson needed no assistance. She caught the ladder at the right moment, and began to mount nimbly. He retired before her and gave her a hand as she reached the rail.

"If the young lady will go forward...?" he said, looking at her with a bold and artless admiration.

She smiled at him, her slow and gentle smile that showed her teeth as white as milk, and he slapped his hand against his forehead as if overcome. Then he went along the narrow deck and she followed him. He stood aside to let her pass, and then left her before a closed door in the deck house.

She knocked. "*Come* in!" cried a sharp voice. She opened the door. And there was the Devil. There was the murdered Captain Perch with his black beard and his glittering eyes.

XVI

Only she had not known he was so big. Enormous. And he wore a black silk kimono, neatly belted around his waist, and reaching to the calves of his bare legs.

"How do you do, Miss Peterson?" he said in a cultured voice.

"How do you do?" said she.

This couldn't be true, and the sooner she stopped believing it, the better.

"Sit down, Miss Peterson," he said.

He had a very cozy little cabin; she saw white ruffled curtains at the ports, and there was a pink and blue rug on the deck, and a patchwork quilt on the bunk.

"Won't you sit down?" he said, giving a slight push to the only chair, a wicker one with a chintz cushion.

She realized that she must immediately stop believing in this.

"I'm afraid I don't know your name, Captain," she said, politely.

"Oh, I'm sorry!" he said. "Norman Perch, at your service, *mademoiselle.*"

She sat down then. Very well! she said to herself. It's perfectly simple. Mrs. Perch thought he was dead, and he isn't. She said he'd been murdered; but she was mistaken. That's all.

"Will you have something to drink, Miss Peterson?"

"No thanks, Captain."

"Coffee?"

"No, thanks."

"Will you smoke, Miss Peterson?"

"Thank you. Yes."

On a table he had a red lacquer box with a scene painted on it in gold; the lid slid back in grooves, and he held it out to her; she took a cigarette, and he held a match for her, bending forward from his great height. She drew deeply on the cigarette.... And stubbed it out on the ash-tray.

"You don't care for that brand, Miss Peterson?"

"I'm afraid not, Captain."

"I'm very sorry," he said. "They were given to me. I don't smoke, myself, so I'm not a judge."

Once before, Miss Peterson had been given a 'reefer,' and that time had thrown it into a river as if it were a snake. Marijuana.... That's bad medicine. A drug ring?

"Do I understand that you have a message for Mr. Fernandez?" Captain Perch asked, courteously.

"If you please," she said. "A rich American has offered to buy the hotel, and he wants an answer at once, by cable."

"That's very interesting, isn't it?" said he.

"Well, interesting to Mr. Fernandez," she said, pleasantly. "May I see him, please?"

"Oh, did you think he was here, on board?" asked Captain Perch, smiling, his lips very red above the black beard. "That's too bad. But I expect to be in communication with him later on, and I'll give him any message you like."

"If you would tell me where I can find Mr. Fernandez?"

"Well..." said Captain Perch, "I happen to know that he's waiting for his clerk—the one they call Alfred Jeffrey. I happen to know he's waiting very anxiously, for Jeffrey to come on board."

"I'm here, instead," she said.

"It's an honor and a pleasure to have such a charming lady on board," said he. "But I'm afraid we must have Jeffrey."

She was silent for a moment, thinking. Harold Cartaret choked you to death, she thought. And Mrs. Perch said you were dead. So that you really can't be here. Only, there's certainly *somebody* here, sitting on the bunk, somebody very big with a black beard and red lips and bright eyes.... If he's the one Cartaret choked, he can't like Cartaret very much.

No.... That's what it all means. He wants to get Cartaret here, for some devil's reason.

"I hope you'll urge Jeffrey to come," said Captain Perch.

"Why?" she asked bluntly.

"Why? Because Mr. Fernandez is so *very* anxious to see him," Captain Perch answered.

It was pretty clear now that don Carlos was being held as a hostage, until Cartaret came, and of course Cartaret wasn't coming.

"I'm expecting Superintendent Losee—" she said; and Captain Perch laughed.

"Oh, no!" he said. "I had a visit from him yesterday, and he found everything in order. He's not coming back, Miss Peterson."

"He'll come again if I'm not on shore in half an hour."

Captain Perch smiled.

"He's not coming back, Miss Peterson. I'm an American citizen. My papers are all in order. I'm ready to sail. There's nothing to bring the British police here." He looked at his watch. "I'll wait an hour for Jeffrey," he said, "and then I think sail."

"But—do you think Jeffrey's coming?"

"Yes," he said.

"You've sent him another message?"

"No," he said. "I think you're going to send your boatman back to fetch him."

"I'm afraid not, Captain Perch."

"Well, it's up to you," he said with another smile. "We can sit here and chat a while, and then as soon as you've gone, we'll sail. I wanted to see Jeffrey; but if I can't, I can't."

"Is Mr. Fernandez on board?" she asked, trying that quick, direct attack again.

"I don't know," said Captain Perch.

"Don't know?"

"I shouldn't be surprised to hear that he's jumped overboard," said Captain Perch. "The last time I saw him he was so thirsty." He looked at his watch again. "As the day gets hotter and hotter, he'll get more and more thirsty. That is, *if* he's still there."

"May I see him?" she asked.

"What's the point?" he asked. "It wouldn't be pleasant for you. Especially as you're responsible."

He signed it 'embustero,' she thought. That meant not to believe him. So he can't be—so very thirsty. He can't be so very bad. He certainly wouldn't suffer very much for the sake of Harold Cartaret. Or for anybody else. He's—realistic.

But she wanted to be sure.

"Before I send for Cartaret," she said, "I'd like to see Mr. Fernandez."

"I really advise against it," he said, "but if you insist.... This way please."

He kicked off his rope sandals and walked barefoot before her out of the cabin, and down the companion that led to the little saloon. It was bright and airy, gay with chintz, and Mr. Fernandez was sitting there in an armchair facing the door. His hands were tied behind his back, and there was a strip of adhesive tape across his mouth. On a small table before him was a carafe of water and a glass.

He looked up as she entered, and his black eyes were strangely liquid and soft, the black lashes like rags. Sweat was pouring down his face, his black hair was plastered across his forehead, his linen coat was buttoned and the collar turned up. He sat there, looking up at her with those extraordinary, beautiful, terrible eyes.

His anguish seemed to vibrate in the cabin like the echo of a scream. It shook her so that she could hardly stand; she leaned against the bulkhead.

"Don Carlos...!" she said.

He tried to rise, twisting his shoulders, and at last he got on his feet, still looking and looking at her.

"He can have a nice tall glass of water—with ice in it," said Captain Perch. "As soon as Cartaret comes on board."

"Captain Perch!" she cried. "Let him go!"

"I want Cartaret here," he said. "If I can't have him, Fernandez will have to be his substitute."

"Mr. Fernandez has nothing to do with that. Let him go...."

"Your Mr. Fernandez had Cartaret and my wife both under his roof. Those two people. That damned witch thought I was dead, and I wanted her to think so. I had the news spread all over Cuba that Cartaret had finished me off. I didn't want her to bother me any more. The last cruise she took with me, she lost her precious jewelry, and some other little things. She was a damned, vindictive woman and I wanted to keep an eye on her. A friend of mine in New York told me she was coming down here, so I came along to see what she was up to."

He paused. "Damn' vindictive," he said, with a sort of sadness. "I sent poor Jeffrey ashore to check up. He knew her, of course. He'd been on that last cruise as steward. Well, he never came back. I sent Nils ashore to find out, and she told him to row her out here. She came. She had the effrontery to come here, on *my* schooner, and she told me she'd shot poor Jeffrey. Unbelievable! She told me she had come here looking for Cartaret, whom she'd never seen. And do you know why? Out of gratitude! She said she was willing to spend any amount of money to find the man who'd murdered me."

Miss Peterson moved a little, and put her hands behind her back. She was opening her raffia purse.

"Drop it!" said Captain Perch, sharply.

But she got the clasp open, and the automatic in her hand. Before she could bring her hand out, Perch had reached out one long leg, and hooked her ankles; he took her off her guard and she fell full length on the deck with a crash that stunned her.

She got up slowly on her hands and knees, still dizzy, and he had the gun, tossing it up idly, and catching it.

"You—you can't get away with this," she said, helping herself to her feet with the aid of a chair.

"Why not?" he said. "I'll just sail away. I'll leave the schooner somewhere, and buy another. Who's going to run all over the Seven Seas looking for me? Or for Fernandez? He came on board of his own accord. Curiosity—that was his undoing."

"Your wife's body has been found," Miss Peterson said. And she felt, she knew, that everything she said was wrong, stupid, utterly useless.

"Who cares?" said Perch, with indifference. "She told me she shot Jeffrey, and then she poisoned some poor old woman who'd found her gun where she'd hidden it in her own room. Fantastic, isn't it? Poisoning the poor old woman simply to get her gun back. And then—she told me to my face that *I* was responsible. She told me that I'd made a zombie out of her, and that she wasn't to blame for anything."

"And you—killed her?"

"Naturally I'm not going to admit *that*," he said, indignantly. "I simply say it doesn't *matter* what happened to that woman. She hated me. You never saw anyone as eaten up with hatred. That's a thing I can't understand. I've never hated anyone in my life."

With a dreadful effort, Miss Peterson turned her head toward Mr. Fernandez. He stood there with his bound hands, and his taped mouth, his broad chest rising and falling, the sweat running down his face, trying to tell her something with his eyes.

"If you don't—hate anybody..." she said, "then—don't bother about

Cartaret. Just—let Mr. Fernandez go. Just sail away. We'll go ashore. You'll never see us again."

"I don't want Cartaret here because I hate him," Captain Perch explained, tossing the automatic up again. "It's simply because my wife told me she'd made a will leaving most of her money to him; and if he isn't around, I'm her legal heir, d'you see? I've been very hard up lately. I'm what you might call a gentleman adventurer, and I have ups and downs.... I need that money. Are you going to send for him?"

"Will you let Mr. Fernandez speak to me?"

"No," he answered. "Your time's getting very short. I can't hang around here forever...."

My God! she cried to herself. I *can't* do that.... Tell Cartaret to come here— to be killed.... I can't do it.... She looked again at Mr. Fernandez. How long had he been without water? How long must his torment last?

"You can go when you like," said Perch.

It was not a problem at all. It had nothing to do with right and wrong. It was impossible, that was all. She couldn't leave him here like this. If she could save Cartaret, she would. If not, he would have to die.

"But how do I know that you'll keep your word?" she said. "Suppose I do get Cartaret here; and then—?"

Mr. Fernandez lurched heavily against her. She thought that he was dizzy, ill, dying perhaps. She put her arm around his shoulders to steady him, but he pushed her away, shaking his head, looking and looking at her.

"Oh, please let him speak!" she cried.

"No," said Captain Perch. "And you don't have to worry about my keeping my word. Why shouldn't I? *I* don't go around killing people for no reason whatever. I don't care what happens to Fernandez once I get Cartaret on board. I don't care in the least what tale you tell the police on shore, either. I can get away easily. And I can come back to claim my dear wife's money with a perfect alibi. I'm not a *fool*. I don't kill people for *fun*. But if Cartaret doesn't come—I'll close the door on Fernandez, and leave him here."

If I could find that Swede, thought Miss Peterson. Suppose I run out and call? Moses would hear me, too.

And Captain Perch would probably shoot her. Or the Swede wouldn't come.... There must be other people on board, she thought. They couldn't let don Carlos die like this.

But he was here like this; and no one had come to his aid. She looked at him, and his black brows twitched; a horrible sound came from his lips.

"All right!" she said. "I'll—"

He came lurching against her again, so heavily that she stumbled.

"Will you let him write, then?" she said. "Just let one hand free—just for a moment?"

"Oh, all right, if you'll be quick about it," said Captain Perch. "Nils!" he shouted, and the blond young Swede came to the door.

"Untie his hands," said Perch. "Hold his left hand behind his back."

"For the love of God—" Miss Peterson began in Swedish.

"None of that, now!" said Captain Perch; and Nils gave her a good-humored apologetic smile, and did as he was bid.

She felt herself in a world where nobody was human. Not Captain Perch, not Nils, not Mr. Fernandez. There was no use speaking in human language. Nobody would answer.

Captain Perch laid a pencil and a piece of paper on the table. But Mr. Fernandez's arm hung limp at his side.

"Go on and write! Write!" said Perch. "I'm not going to wait forever."

He raised his arm a little, but it fell. He must have been tied up a long time.... A long time.... He bent his arm, and stretched it out; he took up the pencil in his cramped fingers, and wrote in a big scrawl.

"No. I will not."

"Will not what?" she cried.

He dropped the pencil, and she picked it up for him.

"Not—to live," he wrote slowly. "This expense. *Que no venga él. No.*"

"Tie him up again," said Captain Perch. "Well, Miss Peterson?"

The tears stopped. The sense of urgency and fear and horror left her. She looked at Mr. Fernandez. Don't let him come, he had written. I don't want to live at the cost of another man's life.

"*Sí, sí,* don Carlos," she said gently and steadily.

Mr. Fernandez raised his black brows, and leaned back in the chair as well as his bound hands allowed him.

"All right!" said Captain Perch; and when she did not move, he took Miss Peterson by the arm. She looked back over her shoulder.

"You are a man, don Carlos," she said, in his own tongue. "I shall never forget you."

XVII

"Moses," she said, "get back to town as fast as you can. It's urgent."
But she knew they could not be fast enough.

She was going away, leaving don Carlos to his fate.

She thought his choice had been right. She thought it was practical. She thought it was foolish to keep your life at the price of your self-respect. It was of no value to you. Only when she thought of him sitting in that cabin....

"Mistress, you weep?"

"I think so, Moses."

"Launch coming, mistress."

The police? she thought. Oh, if it only would be Losee. If only he's followed me! But it was only a little boat with an outboard motor, and only one figure in it. The two boats were approaching each other; in the glare of the sun she could see a man in a white suit, and a gray felt hat.

"Mister Jeffrey, mistress."

"Stop!" cried Miss Peterson in her strong, steady voice. "Stop!"

The tiny boat swerved and came rushing toward them, and Moses slowed down and waited, with a look of melancholy calm.

"Whither away?" called Cartaret, gaily.

"Captain Perch is on the *Hesiod*," said Miss Peterson.

"He's dead," said Cartaret, staring at her.

"No, he's not!" she said. "He's there, on board."

The two boats were rocking side by side; Cartaret stared and stared at her.

"He's got don Carlos there. He's killing him."

"Too bad," said Cartaret. "I found his note in your room. I apologize for snooping, but I was looking for my passport—the bogus one, you know. I thought it might be in your keeping. When I found the note, I felt I was being done out of a good job, so I came along. But if Captain Perch is there, it's no place for me."

"It's not," she agreed. "The idea was to get you on board and kill you. And you'd be dead by this time, if don Carlos hadn't saved you."

"Sorry," he said, "but I can't see don Carlos saving me at any trouble to himself."

"He signed that note to me so that I'd know not to send you," she said, looking squarely at him. "He's dying now, because he wouldn't send another note to get you on board."

"Oh, my dear, good Miss Peterson!" Cartaret protested. "You're not trying to make me believe that our Mr. Fernandez is laying down his life for me?"

"That's it," she said. "Not for love of you, but for something I don't think you'd understand. He won't buy his life at the cost of somebody else's. Anybody else's...."

The brim of Cartaret's hat was turned down, and in its shadow, his thin young face looked hard and fierce.

"You're mistaken," he said. "Fernandez isn't like that."

"He's dying for you," said Miss Peterson. "And you're not worth it. Moses, let's get on."

The launch shivered and leaped forward. And Cartaret's tiny boat headed out again, toward the *Hesiod*.

"Don't!" Miss Peterson shouted after him. "Oh, you fool!"

For a moment, she who was so definite, was completely without decision. If he goes, she thought, don Carlos can get away. But her mind rejected that hope. The Devil wouldn't let don Carlos go now. Not alive. If Cartaret went on board he too would be killed; and for nothing.

"Moses," she said, "we'll have to follow him."

Without a sound, Moses turned the launch in a wide circle. The *Hesiod* was under way, moving very slowly, and the tiny boat was rushing toward it through the sapphire sea, leaving a creamy wake that glittered in the sun.

"Come back!" Miss Peterson called with all her strength.

But on the tiny boat sped. The launch could make much better speed, but before they could overtake it, he had hailed the *Hesiod*.

"*Hesiod* ahoy!"

Nils leaned over the rail, his blond eyebrows raised, his lips pursed as if to whistle.

"Tell the captain I'm here," said Cartaret. "Throw a line, Nils."

He caught the rope and the schooner towed him along. Then her engine stopped, and he caught hold of the rope ladder.

"*Don't!*" cried Miss Peterson.

"It's fate," said another voice, and there was the Devil looking down at her, smiling. "It's obviously Cartaret's destiny to come back here—to me."

Cartaret's boat was adrift now, and he stood on the rope ladder looking up, his head thrown back.

"*Come* on! *Come* on!" said Captain Perch, and bringing up his hand he posed a heavy revolver negligently on the rail. "I'm waiting."

Cartaret laughed. Cartaret, hanging to a rope ladder with the sea behind him, and the Devil facing him, laughed. It was pure bravado, but it was superb.

"Look here, Captain Perch," said Miss Peterson. "You can't get away with this. I'll go to the police."

"Go right ahead!" said he. "You've no idea what I've got away with in my time."

Cartaret climbed over the rail and stood on the deck. Facing that tremendous man, he looked so very slight, so young, so horribly defenseless.

"Let Fernandez go ashore with Miss Peterson," he said, "and you and I can talk things over."

"Nils," said the Captain, "tell Hook to start the engine."

"No!" cried Miss Peterson. "No!"

But Nils had gone off to give the order.

"*Good*-by, Miss Peterson!" called Captain Perch, looking down at her.

That was his mistake. The instant he turned his head, Cartaret sprang at him like a cat, and caught him round the neck. But the Captain's arms were free, he reached the revolver behind him. Cartaret caught his wrist; they were engaged in a strange struggle in which they did not seem to move.

"Moses! Go alongside!" said Miss Peterson.

"No, mistress."

"You must! We've got to go—"

"No, mistress."

Cartaret fell with a crash, and Perch on top of him; the revolver went off with a sharp crack. Miss Peterson in the launch below could see nothing.

"Harold!" she called. "Harold!"

Then they were up again, facing each other. Captain Perch began to walk backward, leisurely, with the revolver aimed steadily at Cartaret. Aimed low, Miss Peterson noticed, to cause the ghastly death of an abdominal wound.

And Mr. Fernandez was coming along the deck behind him, hands tied behind his back, his mouth taped. He walked slowly and noiselessly, lurching from side to side like a stricken animal. He came on, walked straight into Perch with an impact that almost overbalanced him.

As Perch turned his head, Cartaret sprang at him again and seized his wrist in both hands, forced that mighty arm that held the gun aloft. Captain Perch smiled down at his slender, young adversary, and began slowly to lower his arm. The gun came level with Cartaret's head.

Then Mr. Fernandez tripped the Devil up; Perch stumbled forward, as Cartaret let go, his elbow struck the rail, the gun jerked upward and went off, and the bullet went through his throat. He fell with a crash.

Everything was very quiet now. Miss Peterson sat in the launch which seemed to swoop up and up to the sky, and drop and drop.... She was trying to stop falling, when Cartaret climbed over the rail on to the ladder, and after him came Mr. Fernandez, his hands free now, but his mouth still taped. Cartaret helped him down and without any order, Moses took the launch alongside.

Nils was leaning over the rail again, innocent and gay. "You send de cops?" he said. "I tell dem, hey? Dey pay us, hey?"

Nobody answered him. The two men got into the launch and sat down, and Moses steered toward the shore. Mr. Fernandez was pulling with a dogged savagery at the adhesive tape; he got the end loose, and he ripped it off, leaving his lips bleeding. He took out of his pocket a handkerchief of dark purple silk, and pressed it against his mouth for a moment.

"A perfectly clear case," he said thickly through his swollen lips. "Three witnesses, Cartaret. Perch shot himself. No difficulty."

"He called it fate," said Cartaret, with a poor attempt at a smile. "It must have been my fate—not to kill Captain Perch. It's just as well. I don't really like killing."

"Miss Peterson, I think we needn't bring up that note Mrs. Perch wrote you?" said Mr. Fernandez.

"No," she said, and was silent for a time. She knew it was difficult and painful for him to talk. But she couldn't help asking him a question.

"Why did you go out to that schooner?"

"To look for Mrs. Perch," he answered, with an effort. "As soon as I saw that name on her note, I remembered the butcher had spoken to me of a Captain Perch, who had ordered chickens sent out to his schooner. I wanted to find that woman. I was afraid that Losee would make *more* trouble for me if she disappeared. So I went out there by myself in one of my launches. Captain Perch had it scuttled...." He pressed the handkerchief to his mouth again. "Has she come back?" he asked.

Miss Peterson told him, and he listened in silence.

"It's an ill wind..." he said presently. "I took a little glance at that will she left with you, dear lady. She leaves sixty thousand dollars to Harold Cartaret. 'For his kindness to me,' she said."

"Sixty... Sixty thousand...?" said Cartaret.

He collapsed quietly on to the bottom of the launch, and they left him so. His head was in the shadow of the seat, and Miss Peterson took his hat and gave it to Mr. Fernandez.

"Thank you, dear lady," he said, putting it on. He looked down at Cartaret. "Love..." he remarked gravely. "He's been in love from the very first day with that little wild-cat. But I suppose when he believed he had a murder charge hanging over him, he didn't want to say anything. Well, I wish him luck. He disliked me very much—but that's understandable, no? I had the upper hand, knowing he had a false passport. He didn't like that! Also I think he was somewhat jealous. Without any reason, of course."

"Don Carlos," she said. "You are magnificent."

"I?" he said, casting down his eyes, with an outrageously false modesty. "Oh, no.... Very ordinary."

"Magnificent!" she repeated.

"If you think so," he said, "then it was worth enduring that little unpleasantness, dear lady. Now this is the...." He glanced at Moses who was looking straight before him. "Dear lady," he said, lowering his voice, "in a moment like this, everything is revealed. You know, without any doubt, how you feel. You know your own heart. Dear lady, do you know now...?"

She looked at him with tears in her eyes.

"Don Carlos, you honor me," she said in Spanish. "I feel the highest respect and esteem for you, but—"

"Dear lady," he said, his bruised mouth making a wry little smile, "if you please.... That's sufficient. I understand all about 'respect' and 'esteem.' Well, better than nothing, eh?"

How much she liked his responsiveness, his quick practical acceptance of a situation! How immeasurably happy she was to see him here alive and well! And how impossible to consider becoming Mrs. Fernandez....

He lit a cigarette for her and one for himself; he inhaled deeply.

"You'll forgive me for breaking our agreement?" he asked. "It won't happen again. You'll stay?"

"I'll be glad to stay."

"We'll have plenty to do," he said, "for the gala opening on Saturday."

"What!" she cried.

Cartaret stirred and opened his eyes, and they helped him up on the seat; Mr. Fernandez put his hat back on his head.

"I was just speaking," Mr. Fernandez said, "of the gala opening on Saturday."

Cartaret stared at him with dazed, unfocused eyes.

"I'm going to let Cecily play at the gala," said Mr. Fernandez. "She shall give a little recital—a little concert."

They were in sight of the town now, making for the jetty.

"But—" said Miss Peterson. "Mrs. Barley...?"

"Regrettable," said Mr. Fernandez.

"And Jeffrey," she said. "And Mrs. Perch. I don't see how you can have your gala, don Carlos."

"It's more necessary than ever," he said. "I have three people—important people—coming from Trinidad by plane. The northbound Marquis boat will be in, and I've sent a radio inviting the officers and passengers. I've already invited the chief people here on the island...."

"But Losee? But the police?"

"They'll have to ask us some questions. Very well. We'll answer them. We're all entirely blameless."

"But won't it seem a little—?"

"Dear lady," he said, "the hotel business is like the theater. No matter what happens—" He paused. "The show must go on!" he said with energy.

"It will," said Miss Peterson.

THE END

The Obstinate
Murderer
by Elisabeth Sanxay Holding

To Frank E. Blackwell

I

Van Cleef sat in the hotel bar, alone and at peace. It was eleven o'clock on a June morning; the sun was bright gold behind the venetian blinds; the little bar was dark and cool; the sound of traffic in the street outside was too familiar for him to notice. He lit another cigarette and turned his head to signal the bartender. The man wasn't there.

That did not matter. At noon, or a little before, fellows he knew would begin coming in, and he would have drinks with someone. With anyone. He moved over to a leather divan in a corner and stretched out his long legs; in this dim light he looked boyish, lean and powerfully-built and nonchalant. But when he struck a match, the little flame showed the lines about his good-humoured mouth and his tired eyes; his fair hair was growing thin at the temples. It had taken him forty years to become what he was.

"Another Scotch, Mr. Van Cleef?" asked the bartender, suddenly appearing beside him.

"Okay!" said Van Cleef. After the first couple of drinks in the morning, which were badly needed to pull himself together, he was no longer impatient, but he refused no suggestions.

"Going away over the week-end, Mr. Van Cleef?"

"Couldn't say," answered Van Cleef. For that, too, depended on other people's suggestions. It was Friday now; if someone got after him, he would pack a bag and go—somewhere. If he were not got after, he would do nothing.

"Beginning to feel like summer," the bartender observed. "What is it, boy?"

"Telephone for Mr. Van Cleef," said the bell-boy, and Van Cleef got up, and went leisurely out into the lobby, and into a booth.

"Mr. Van Cleef?" said a familiar enough voice.

"Emilia..." he said. "Hello, my dear girl. How's everything with you?"

"Arthur, I've got to *see* you!"

He glanced around him, as if the booth had become a trap. "Certainly, my dear girl! Why not come in to dinner—lunch—?"

"I can't," she said. "Can't you come out here, Arthur? It's very serious.... Arthur, I'm being blackmailed!"

"What!" he cried. "But—Yes, of course. Yes, I'll come, Emilia...."

"At once, Arthur?"

"Oh, yes!" he said. "Certainly, my dear girl."

Hanging up the receiver, he went immediately to the bar; it seemed providential that there was a drink standing on the little table waiting for him.

"Blackmail," he said to himself. "Extraordinary girl....What put that into her head, I wonder?"

Sipping his drink, he fell into a reverie, melancholy and resigned; a voice spoke his name so gently that it scarcely disturbed him.

"Mr. Van Cleef!"

He looked up, to see a boy standing beside him, an extraordinarily handsome boy, slim, almost slight in build, with a dark narrow face, brilliant with life.

"I'm Russell Blackman," he said. Said it with a curious eagerness; as he stood there, hat in hand, he had the look of one imploring a favour.

"Sorry..." said Van Cleef, with an apologetic grimace.

"Don't you remember me?" said the boy. "You knew my Aunt Hilda—"

"Yes," said Van Cleef, sitting up straight. "Yes. Sit down, Russell. Have a drink?"

"Thanks," said Russell. "Just ginger ale, please."

"Ginger ale, and another Scotch," said Van Cleef, without looking at the waiter beside him; he was staring before him. "Yes," he said. "I remember your Aunt Hilda."

"Then don't you remember *me?* When they realized how ill she was, they sent me off to board at the day-school I went to. It was in the Easter holidays; nobody else there. It was the first time I'd been away from home, and it was hell. I didn't know what to do with myself. I felt—forgotten. And then you came, in your car. You brought me a steamer-basket full of cakes and chocolates and fruit, with a big silver gauze bow on the handle."

Van Cleef glanced sidelong at him.

"Ten years ago..." he said.

"Yes. I was eight then."

"And you've remembered, all this while?"

"I don't forget much," said Russell.

Van Cleef shifted his big shoulders, so that he could look more easily at the boy.

"When my aunt died, you came again," said Russell. "You drove me home and you talked to me."

"I remember. You were a queer little kid. Excited—"

"I was a freak," said Russell, with a sudden, almost spasmodic smile.

"I don't know.... Just a queer kid. Found you walking up and down in a big, overgrown garden like a jungle—pouring rain—arms folded behind you like a little Napoleon...."

"I was a freak," said Russell again. "They took me out of school that year. I went ahead too fast. I had tutors at home, and there was a great effort to get me interested in sports. I went in for swimming and tennis, and got all the junior cups. And still I was ready for college before I was fourteen. My people sent me abroad with a fine, wholesome young man for a tutor. We climbed mountains. We made walking tours with knapsacks. He did his best; it wasn't his fault that I picked up three languages."

"Bitter...?"

"Not any more," said Russell. "I've got past that."

"Have you?" said Van Cleef, looking at him with his tired eyes narrowed.

"Once you accept the fact that you're a freak," Russell went on, "there's considerable stimulation in finding that you're entirely alone."

"No family?"

"Mother and father, a sister, a brother, uncles, aunts, cousins, and so on. But they've let me go now. I get an allowance of four hundred a month—"

"That's a hell of a lot, at eighteen."

"My parents feel guilty because they don't like me," said Russell. "It eases their conscience to give me plenty of money. And I have no vices. I don't even smoke."

"What do you do?"

"Nothing."

"College?"

"I tried it, for a month. But I wasn't what you'd call popular, either with my fellow students or the professors."

"Where d'you live?"

"Here," said Russell. "I just moved in to-day. As soon as the home ties were broken, I started looking for *you*. And when I found you here, I took a room."

Van Cleef took up his glass, and stared at it.

"Mistake..." he said.

"How?"

Van Cleef smiled, his curiously gentle smile.

"Ten years..." he said. "People change, in ten years."

"You haven't changed," said Russell.

"My God!" said Van Cleef, setting down the glass. He looked at Russell, and the boy's black eyes met his steadily.

"I've got my car here, Mr. Van Cleef. What about driving out to the country for lunch?"

"Oh! The country?" said Van Cleef, with a start. "I've got to go out to Blackhaven for the week-end."

"I'll drive you out."

"Good enough!" said Van Cleef, rising. "I'll go up and pack a bag."

"Can I help you?"

That smile came over Van Cleef's lined face again, half rueful, infinitely good-humoured.

"No.... No, thanks," he said. "Can do."

"What time will you be ready?" Russell asked, but the other had already turned away; he crossed the lobby with his loose-jointed stride, his broad shoulders a little bent; he got into the elevator and went up to the top floor. He had a suite there; the sitting-room was in perfect order, shades drawn half-way down, furniture stiffly arranged, a room as impersonal as it had been when he had come into it two years ago. Nothing belonging to him except a few books on shelves built into a corner, and a radio.

The chambermaid was in the bedroom.

"Don't mind me, Nelly," he said. "I've got to pack. Happen to see a bag around?"

She was stout and middle-aged, and competent; she knew Mr. Van Cleef's ways. She found the bag for him, and, in a persuasive fashion, she got it packed for him.

"Don't bother, Nelly!" he kept saying, and she kept answering, "No, sir," while she opened the bureau drawers, got out clean shirts, pyjamas, socks, underclothes, handkerchiefs. A very neat gentleman, Mr. Van Cleef was, and all his things were of the best. Very neat; no trouble at all, and so very kind....

"I hope you have a good time, sir," said Nelly.

But somehow she didn't think he would. Somehow, he looked sort of sad, so neat in his dark blue suit and his well-polished brown shoes, standing there and looking at himself in the mirror.

"Hilda..." he said to himself. "My God.... Ten years.... So damned long.... Yet, in another way, so damned short.... Like one day.... I must be indestructible.... Asbestos lining.... Only not the soul. Poor little dried-up soul, rattling around inside somewhere.... Come in! Come in!"

A bell-boy took his bag, and they descended together. Van Cleef looked into the bar; Russell was not there.

"I'll wait a bit," he said to the bell-boy, and sat down on a sofa in the lounge. "Queer kid, this Russell," he thought. "Hard to say whether he needs a kick in the pants, or a little kindness.... Hilda wouldn't like him. Very intolerant girl. But she had every right to be. She was an angel, and angels don't have to put up with anything. Such a fierce little angel.... 'That's that!'.... She wouldn't like me, any more.... She never liked me, much. Just loved me."

"Ready?" asked Russell.

"Ready, aye, ready!" said Van Cleef, and they went out into the brilliant sunshine. "That's a good car," said Van Cleef, stopping to examine the roadster. "A very good car."

"They don't come any better," said Russell.

The boy was a master driver, but arrogant.

"It seems to me you're one of these roadhogs," said Van Cleef. "You worried the good lady in the Ford."

"I don't cultivate consideration for others," said Russell.

"Kiddish."

"No. It's biologic."

"Meaning you're the superior animal? Well, no.... I don't think so."

"Superior in cunning," said Russell.

"Q.E.D.," said Van Cleef.

They got out of the city traffic, on to a parkway; the indicator showed fifty, sixty, seventy, eighty.

"Too fast for you?" asked Russell.

"No," Van Cleef answered, agreeably. "If it's a traffic cop, you'll be the one to pay or go to jail. And if we both break our necks, there won't be many mourners, eh?"

"The question is, if death is worth dying. It may be the great experience—the big thrill. But suppose it isn't? Suppose it's—nothing?"

"More kiddishness."

Russell slowed down the car.

"I wish to God you'd talk to me," he said, unsteadily. "I've been waiting ten years to get back to you. I've been thinking of you, all that time, as the only human being I've ever met."

"What d'you mean? *Must* be plenty of human beings—"

"No! You don't even know what I mean."

"I don't. I'm sorry," said Van Cleef, disturbed. "I don't."

"Let it go," said Russell. "I can't explain."

But Van Cleef was troubled now, with a dim oppression of guilt.

"Failed him, some way," he thought. "Thing is, what did he expect? What was I, ten years ago? Someone different? Probably. I'm sorry," he said, aloud. "Look here! Suppose we stop for a bite of lunch? There's a decent-looking place."

Without a word, the boy turned into the drive-way of an inn, and Van Cleef looked at him anxiously. His profile was extraordinarily fine, subtle in modelling, intelligent, but so very young. The smooth olive cheek had a downy look; the line of the jaw was still rounded.

"May be mistaken about himself," thought Van Cleef. "Certainly he's not average, but he may not be as wonderful as he thinks he is. We'll hope not."

They found a table on the glass-enclosed veranda of the inn, and the waiter came to them with an enormous menu.

"Always wonder at these things," said Van Cleef. "They couldn't have all these items ready, could they? Duck, chicken, turkey, lobster, crab, sole, nine vegetables. . . But also they couldn't get 'em ready in time, if anyone ordered them...."

Russell spoke to the waiter, in a foreign tongue; the waiter's face lit up; they talked volubly.

"He recommends the broiled lobster," said Russell.

"I'll trust him. But in the matter of drinks—tell him bring along a bottle of Scotch. Unopened."

The waiter went off, and Van Cleef lit a cigarette, leaning back in his chair; he gazed thoughtfully out across the lawn; he did not look at Russell, he asked no questions.

"Do you know any Greek?" asked Russell, presently.

"No. Oh, no...."

There was a long silence; the waiter came with a bottle of whisky, and opened it; he spoke in his own language to Russell, but got only a brief answer.

"You're not going to encourage me in showing off," said Russell. "Quite right."

Van Cleef glanced at him, and sighed. Then that smile came over his face. "That was the idea," he said.

"Why?" Russell demanded vehemently. "For God's sake, why be so grudging? I don't expect you to like me, but why do you feel it's necessary to belittle me? If it were anyone but me, you'd have asked what language I was speaking, and how I learned it, and so on. But because it's me, it's irritating."

Van Cleef poured himself a drink.

"Well.... D'you have to be like this?" he asked, with anxiety.

"Yes, I do. I thought you'd understand."

There was another silence.

"What are your plans?" asked Van Cleef.

"I haven't any."

"What are you going to do with yourself?"

"I could be a doctor," said Russell. "I could be a chemist. I could be a zoologist, a lawyer. I could be a financier. There are plenty of careers open to me. I don't want any of them. I'm trying to find—something to want."

"It's possible to live without wanting anything much," said Van Cleef. "I do, y'know. But at your age, maybe it's not possible."

"Is that your advice? Renounce ambition, stop wanting anything—"

"I'm not giving advice. I'm talking, that's all."

There was a flicker of uneasiness in the boy's black eyes. "I think I see the motive behind it—" he began.

"If you do," said Van Cleef, "you're a damn fool. There's no motive. I'm talking to you as one human being to another. I thought that was what you wanted. But you can't take it. No. What you're looking for is reassurance. I haven't any to give. I don't know what life's all about. I can't tell you what you ought to do. I won't admonish you. I won't praise you. In fact, putting it frankly, I'm getting tired of talking about you."

The waiter set the broiled lobster before them; he glanced at Russell, but got not a word.

"I'm pretty sick of thinking about me," said Russell. "You're not afflicted like that. You don't think about yourself, do you?"

"No..." said Van Cleef, half to himself. "Can't. I'm a sort of ghost...."

He was tired, with the hopeless fatigue of a ghost. Nowhere to rest....

"If you'll keep on talking to me..." said Russell. "If you can put up with me...."

He spoke humbly, miserably; he was asking most urgently for something most desperately needed. And Van Cleef, the ghost, refused no one. He admitted all claims.

"Sure!" he said, and smiled.

II

"What's the street in Blackhaven?" Russell asked.

"Oh.... Big house, just off the Shore road. I'll tell you when to turn."

"Are you going to stay there long?"

"Couldn't say," Van Cleef answered, with resignation.

"Isn't it a week-end party?"

"Not a party. No. Y'see, the place used to belong to a friend of mine. Bill Swan. He died, two years ago, and his widow had this idea of running it as a boarding-house. Guest-house, she calls it. *Not* a good idea."

"Look here! I might stay there, too," said Russell. "My car might be useful to you. I could run you anywhere you wanted."

"I never go anywhere," said Van Cleef, dismayed. "It's—there wouldn't be anything there for you. No young people."

"I'm not looking for 'young people'; I'd like to stay. Unless you don't want me."

"To tell you the truth," said Van Cleef, "this is what you might call a personal visit; see what I mean?"

"All right..." said Russell, with a faint smile.

"Well.... Damn you," thought Van Cleef, looking at him. "This won't do.... Altogether too sudden.... It's—what?—half-past two. Eleven o'clock this morning, this boy drops out of the sky. Doesn't live anywhere; hasn't any plans. Simply goes where I go. Won't do."

He was determined not to accept this preposterous responsibility. But he could, of course, be decent; he could be what the boy called a "human being."

"D'you like the country?" he asked.

"Oh, I love it!" said Russell. "The green grass and the blue sky, and the birds...."

This was heavy-handed irony; too clumsy to be annoying. "He's a pest," thought Van Cleef. "But you've got to make allowances for his age.... Hilda was—let's see—twenty-three when she died.... Didn't seem so young to me then, because I was young, myself.... Next turn to the left!"

They turned off into a side road lined with fields, and before them rose Bill Swan's house; a long, flat-roofed rectangle of grey brick, faced with white, a two-tiered veranda with iron railing surrounding it, a little like a cage. The wide lawn before it was neglected; there were weeds in the driveway; the house had somewhat the look of a child's creation, set down at random. Russell stopped the car before the door.

"Good-bye," he said.

"Come along in."

"You're tired of my company."

"Mistake, to talk like that," said Van Cleef. "Don't challenge people. Take it for granted that they're more or less agreeable. Come along in."

He pressed the bell, and promptly enough a coloured boy in a white jacket opened the door.

"How are you, Harly?" asked Van Cleef, seriously.

"Thank you, sir. Very well, sir," Harly answered, with equal seriousness. "I trust I see you well, sir?"

"Never better. Will you tell Mrs. Swan—" He stopped, at the sound of a step, and there she was, coming down the stairs, in all her incredible beauty.

She wore a black dress with a high collar and a little bow under one ear, incredibly chic, incredibly slight; her lips had the half-petulant, half-wistful curves of a true Cupid's bow; her brows were arched high above her heavy-lidded dark eyes; her curly dark hair was cut perfectly to the shape of her little head.

"Aa-rthur!" she said, stopping, with one delicate hand on the banister rail.

"Hello, my dear girl!" he said; he smiled, but not she. "Emilia, this is Russell Blackman—"

"How *nice!*" she said.

She gave the boy both her hands, but, in spite of that gesture, and her fervent tone, there was no warmth in her. She looked at him, and it was obvious that she did not see him; some intense preoccupation made her lovely face blank.

"Do come in!" she said, and led the way across the wide, square hall, her high heels clicking prettily, into a large square drawing-room furnished in a cold and conventionally handsome fashion. She sat down on a little Empire sofa, and her smoothly-fitting black dress fell into graceful folds. The black bow under one ear gave her a coquettish look; the Cupid's bow mouth was formed in an eternal smile; only her eyes betrayed her.

"Will you ring, Aa-rthur?" she said. "We'll have tea."

"No, no. Don't bother."

"It's quite ready, Arthur. I'm sure Mr. Blackman...?"

Russell looked at Van Cleef, asking permission.

"Thanks," said Van Cleef.

There was a silence, which he made no attempt to break.

"No," he said to himself. "They're both too dramatic. I can't cope with 'em."

"I have only four people here now, Arthur," she said, at last. "Major Bramwell, and Annie and Harry Downes, and Lizzy Carroll—"

"I like Lizzy," he said.

"Oh, yes. They're all out now, except the Major. You won't mind if he joins us?"

"Why should I?"

Harly brought in a tea service and set it on a small table before the sofa; as he left the room, a man entered, a big man with short white hair and angry little blue eyes in a ruddy, heavy-jowled face. He stopped short, almost as if he dug his feet into the carpet, and stood straight as a ramrod glaring.

"Carlo," said Emilia, "this is Mr. Van Cleef. Major Bramwell. And Mr. Blackman."

He gave a curt nod, and sat down on the sofa beside her.

"Another one," thought Van Cleef. "Poor girl."

She poured the tea and Russell became attentive, stood beside her, with an air of polite alertness. And she looked at him as she looked at any man, with the dainty smile of a Valentine.

"Because she can't help it," Van Cleef thought. "Doesn't mean anything. She's The Lady, and she treats us all as Gentlemen, which we aren't. She should have had a knight, poor girl, and what she got was Bill Swan, roaring around...."

The Major addressed himself to Russell.

"Well, young man!" he said. "Having a summer vacation?"

"Yes, sir," said Russell, in a modest tone.

"That your car out there? I suppose that's your idea of exercise—tearing around the country in a high-powered car."

"I'm very fond of walking," Russell said. "Only, it's hard to find anyone else who likes it."

"I wonder what you call 'walking,'" said the Major. "Four or five miles, along a smooth road."

"The best I ever did was twenty miles in one day, in Germany," said Russell, still modest, almost shy.

"Germany, eh?" said the Major. "Ever been in Switzerland? I had a curious experience there—"

"Arthur..." said Emilia. "I'd like to show you Regina's letter...."

The three men rose as she did, and Van Cleef followed her out into the square hall. She hesitated there, looking lost; then she led him to the dining-room. He lagged behind her, looking at the five small tables set up there, each with a white cloth and a little vase of flowers; he remembered how it had used to be in Bill Swan's day; the massive table, the sideboard with a fine display of silver....

Emilia looked back over her shoulder, and he moved to her side.

"Arthur," she said, "there's a horrible girl, trying to blackmail me."

"Sit down, and let's hear...."

She laid her hand on his arm.

"You're not taking it seriously! It's very serious for me, Arthur. This girl has somehow got hold of Annie Downes, and Annie invites her here—into my own house. It's— I can't tell Annie not to."

"D'you mean this girl has tried to get money from you, Emilia?"

"Not yet. But I know it's coming."

"See here, my dear girl.... Nothing she can blackmail you about."

"She can make up things."

"My dear girl!" he protested.

He had expected something wildly unreasonable; it wasn't possible to black-mail someone who had nothing at all. But this was sheer fantasy.

"Arthur, it's true!" she said.

"Sit down, Emilia."

"Arthur, she's putting ideas into Annie's head, horrible ideas—"

"Annie's told you?"

"No. But I can see."

He felt so tired. Tired of Emilia and her troubles. She had sent for him before and he always came, but the other troubles could be settled by a cheque; some bill that had grown like a snowball, a stern notice about taxes or assessments. The cheques were called loans; she wrote them down in one of her extraordi-nary books.... "When I get this place on its feet..." she always said, anxious and unhappy.

"She tries," he thought. "Does the best she can. It's too much for her, that's all."

He was ashamed to feel tired.

"Just put it plainly for me, my dear girl," he said. "I don't quite get it, d'you see? You say this girl's trying to blackmail you. Any—facts?"

She glanced at him, and then away.

"No," she answered. And that answer, unprecedentedly direct and simple coming from her, made an almost startling impression upon him.

"I think she's lying," he said to himself. "Not like her, to lie. She's truthful—too truthful for her own good, as a rule. Must be something here...." He spoke without looking at her.

"I might have a talk with Annie, find out what the girl's been saying—"

"Annie wouldn't tell you. She's very secretive. No.... I thought—if you could persuade the girl to go away...."

"Mean pay her something? No, my dear girl; that's a bad thing to start. If she's causing you any trouble, we'll find a way to stop it. What's her name?"

"Dulac," she answered. "Blanche Dulac. She works in that stationer's shop, opposite the railway station. Somehow she's scraped an acquaintance with Annie, and she's got Annie to bring her here to lunch. And—Annie's changed, very much."

"Still and all, my dear girl, that's hardly blackmail."

"No.... Perhaps it's not.... But I don't like her, Arthur! I don't want her here."

"Tell Annie—"

"That wouldn't do any good. You know how obstinate Annie is. Arthur, I don't *like* that girl!"

He lit a cigarette, still taking care not to look at her.

"Any definite reason for not liking her?"

And again she gave that answer—No!—that was so much too prompt and too clear, coming from her. Now he looked at her, and her dark eyes were unfathomable to him.

"It's really the change in Annie," she added. "And—it's something in the atmosphere.... I don't like to ask you to lend me any more, Arthur, but if that girl could be persuaded to go away—"

Her head was turned aside, so that the black bow was against the smooth curve of her pale cheek; her long lashes were down; she looked coquettish, charming, and completely baffling.

"That was how poor old Bill felt," he thought. "Damned artificial, he called her. It made him miserable, and so he made *her* miserable...."

"Aa-rthur..." she said, plaintively.

"Thinking things over, my dear girl," he said, hastily. "Give me a little more time, will, you? They seem—complicated."

"Shall we go back now and have our tea?"

"Good idea!"

They were crossing the lounge, side by side, when Harly came, to summon Emilia to the telephone, and Van Cleef went on alone to the drawing-room. Russell was standing by the window, looking out; the Major sat by the tea-table, his hands on his knees; at sight of Van Cleef, he rose quickly, with a sort of quiver, like a spring uncoiling.

"I note that you have a bag with you, sir," he said. "If you contemplated an extended stay here, I have to tell you it is *not convenient.*"

"Afraid I don't get you..." said Van Cleef, apologetically.

"I say it is *not convenient*, sir."

"Mean for me?"

"I do not. I mean it's not convenient for Mrs. Swan to—to receive you at this time."

"Oh, I see!" said Van Cleef, still apologetic. He struck a match for a cigarette and sat down on the sofa, his long legs stretched out, one hand in his trousers pocket.

"Do you intend to leave, sir, or do you not?" demanded the Major.

"Well, see here.... Let's not make an issue of it just now," Van Cleef suggested.

"You can't put me off this way, sir!" said the Major, and he was shouting now. "I ask you to leave this house immediately!"

"Perhaps you'd *better*, Arthur," murmured Emilia's voice at his side. "You could come back some other day...."

He rose politely, took his hand out of his pocket, and stood looking down at her.

"Well, no..." he said. "Sorry, but I think not."

There was a complete silence.

"Russell," said Van Cleef, "if you'll be good enough to drive me down to the village.... I'll leave my bag here, Emilia. I'll be back in good time for dinner."

He waited, but he got no answer; he smiled, vaguely, and went out of the room.

III

"I want a drink," said Van Cleef, simply, as he got into the car.

"All right. I'll keep an eye out for a bar," said Russell. "Which way is the village?"

"Left, along the boulevard."

"What d'you think of the Major?"

"Don't want to think of him at all," said Van Cleef.

"I wonder what it is he's so much afraid of...."

"Afraid?"

"It was pretty obvious, wasn't it? He wanted to get you out of the house—"

"Probably he didn't like me," said Van Cleef. "That can happen."

"He was panicked."

"I may even do that to people."

Russell turned the car into the wide, smooth boulevard.

"Something's going to happen there," he said.

"Psychic?" asked Van Cleef.

The boy's dark face flushed.

"No. Just a half-baked young fool. Just a damn nuisance—"

"Y'know," said Van Cleef, "in a way, you *are* a damn nuisance, being so sensitive. If you feel like talking, talk. If you've noticed things, if you've got any ideas, go ahead."

Russell didn't answer for some time.

"Geoffrey Blackman is a second cousin of mine," he said, presently.

"Never heard of him."

"He's considered one of the leading psychologists in the country. In the world. He's let me do some studying with him, attend some of his clinics. He's interested in me."

"Well, there you are!" said Van Cleef, pleased. "Fellow's a prominent man, and he's interested in you. There's a career for you."

"The only trouble is, that he hates me."

"O God! I suppose you can't help being that way. Why d'you think he hates you?"

"He admits it," said Russell, smiling. "We've talked it over; we've analysed the situation. He's fifty, and he can't stand my being eighteen. He says he's going to watch my career with great interest, but he never wants to set eyes on me again."

"Must be plenty of other psychologists, if that's what interests you."

"Criminal psychology. I'd like to be a super-detective, one of the scientific kind."

"I see! Nice work, if you can get it."

"Very nice work," Russell agreed. "It combines all the things that interest me—chemistry, medicine, psychology—and action."

"Hey! There's a bar!" said Van Cleef, and Russell backed the car, and turned into the drive before an imitation Swiss chalet. Incredibly loud music came out at them; a patron had dropped a coin into an apparatus that started a gramophone; the stamping beat of a rhumba filled the place.

"Straight Scotch," said Van Cleef to the waiter, and lit a cigarette, leaning back in his chair and watching Russell. The boy's fine dark brows twitched, his mouth tightened; he pushed back his chair.

"Sit down," said Van Cleef.

"I'm going to stop that damned filthy row—"

"Sit down! Can't be done. The fellow's paid his money; he has a right to his music."

Russell sat down, and the terrific music ended. But up got that client again, dropped in another coin, and this time it was worse; a monster voice bellowed the chorus of a song. Van Cleef finished his drink and rose; they got into the car again.

"If I ever make a fortune, or inherit one," said Russell, "I'm going to use the money to found an Anti-Music League."

"Mean Anti-Noise, don't you?"

"No. If you have money, you can keep away from noise. What I'd like to do, is to bar the mob, the *canaille*, from hearing music. I'd spend my fortune to keep Mozart off the radio. There'd be no gramophone records. I'd make it cost fifty dollars to hear an hour of Bach."

"Aristocratic," Van Cleef observed. "Ancient regime."

"How d'you know it's not new? It's possible that we've finished forever with the theory of democracy. It was never anything but a theory, and it grows more and more impossible as human breeding grows more chaotic. Superior men are becoming fewer, and they'll have to become more ruthless."

"Looking around the modern world," said Van Cleef, "the ruthless men don't seem biologically superior to me."

The boy glanced at him with a faint frown, and Van Cleef smiled broadly.

"What's so amusing?" Russell demanded.

"You underrate your fellow-creatures," Van Cleef answered. "Mustn't do that, when you become a super-sleuth. I'd like to see you, when you come up against the criminal Master-Mind."

"I'd like to come up against a criminal with intelligence," Russell said, thoughtfully. "I comb the daily news, looking for one, but I never find any."

"Some pretty slick financial crooks."

"That doesn't interest me. I don't think it's criminal to take money away from fools. There's only one crime that has colour and charm."

"Murder."

"Murder," Russell repeated. "To meet up with a really subtle murderer, to study him, catch up with him, step by step.... There can't be any other experience in life to equal a man-hunt."

"Poor devil!" thought Van Cleef. "I'm afraid his nastiness is genuine. Not a pose. May outgrow it, of course. But you can see why nobody likes him.... And the more nobody likes him, the nastier he grows. Naturally.... Love thy neighbour as thyself.... But what if you don't love yourself?"

"This seems to be the village," said Russell.

"Right. Stop at that stationer's, will you? I'll be out in a minute. Or—tell you what. There's a liquor store around the corner. Might get me a couple of bottles of Scotch, will you?"

He got out of the car, in his headlong, lurching way, big shoulders stooped.

"We'll take a look at the blackmailing girl," he said to himself. "Very original idea, to blackmail someone who hasn't got a red cent...."

It was a very small shop, windowless; it would have been dark but for the setting sun that streamed in through the doorway and filled it with a dusty glory.

"Yes?" asked the girl behind the counter.

A young girl in a white dress. A slim girl with brown hair and grey eyes and a beautiful, generous mouth.

"What cigarettes do you recommend?" he asked.

"Well, I don't know..." she said, earnestly. "I guess it's a matter of taste."

"Suppose I haven't any taste?"

"Well, do you like Turkish or Virginia?"

"Have you any Havana cigarettes?"

"I'm sorry...."

"Any Russian?"

"I'm sorry. But there wouldn't be any demand for them in a little place like this." Suddenly she smiled, a grin so wide that it gave her the look of a kitten, all mouth and eyes. "I guess you come from New York," she said.

"Right! But how did you guess it?"

"I can almost always tell," she said, with a certain nonchalance. "Of course, lots of people stop in here; this street's a by-pass. I have a wonderful chance to study types. I bet that if I ever do get to New York—"

"Never been there?" he interrupted, surprised.

"Nope," she said, briefly.

"It's under two hours by train."

She said nothing to that. She was not smiling now; she looked almost stern.

"Anyhow," she said, after a moment, "it's not particularly important. I mean, you can learn just as much about life and human nature in a village as in a city. Look at the Brontës, for instance."

"Like to read?"

"Well, of course. Who doesn't?"

"I don't," he said. "I can't."

Her clear eyes rested thoughtfully on his face.

"You're—" she began, and stopped suddenly, with a hot colour rising in her cheeks.

"I'm what? Please say whatever it was."

"No. It was—nothing."

"Y'know," he said, "I wander all over looking for someone to tell me what I am. Who I am."

"I couldn't tell you that," she said, with gentleness.

"You've got that feminine intuition," he said. "Nothing like it. You looked at me, and you got some sort of impression. It would *help* me, if you'd say it."

"I just thought—you weren't happy," she said.

He was curiously impressed, by the words and by the tone.

"Is anyone happy?" he asked.

"Lots of people."

"You?"

"I'm just beginning to be happy," she said. "I mean, when you're too young, you're waiting to be happy—waiting for life to begin. I'm just realizing that life isn't around the corner. It's *now.*"

He took cigarettes out of his pocket and lit one, in an absent-minded way.

"I have an inferiority complex," he observed.

"I think an inferiority complex is—a beautiful thing," said she, with a sort of vehemence. "I don't see why it's supposed to be wrong. It's—well—it means having a humble and a contrite heart, doesn't it?"

He was silent for a long time.

"D'you mind—" he said. "Is your name—are you Miss Dulac?"

"Yes. Blanche Dulac. Why?"

"I'm paying a little visit at Mrs. Swan's—"

"Oh! Mrs. Swan!" she said, and the tone was unmistakable. She had no liking for Emilia.

"You're a friend of Mrs. Downes, aren't you?" he asked.

"Well, not exactly a friend," she said. "Mrs. Downes has been rather nice to me—in a way."

"She doesn't like Annie Downes, either," he thought.

"Thing is—" he began, when Russell entered the shop He looked at the girl, and she looked at him, and it was, thought Van Cleef, the way two strange children look at each other, with curiosity, and interest, and faint hostility.

"Buying supplies?" asked Russell.

"I can't make up my mind," said Van Cleef.

"I've done your little errand for you...."

"Thanks."

There was a silence; Van Cleef leaned against the counter, smoking, gazing at nothing.

"Shall I go away, and come back in an hour or two?" asked Russell.

Van Cleef turned to the girl.

"I'd like a dozen packs of cigarettes; all different," he said.

She smiled at him, a different smile this time; there was look of anxiety in her face. She wrapped up the package for him and handed it to him.

"I hope you'll come in again," she said, earnestly.

"Thank you," he said, taking off his hat. He kept it in his hand as he went out to the car.

"You're interested in women, aren't you?" said Russell.

"After all, such a lot of 'em around..." said Van Cleef. "It would be a bit hard not to notice 'em."

"But you like them."

"And you don't?"

"I don't."

"Unrequited love making you bitter?"

"I'm not bad-looking. I'm not stupid. And I have money. I could have a pretty wide choice—if I wanted."

"Sorry you don't smoke," said Van Cleef.

"Why?"

"If you did, maybe you wouldn't talk so much," said Van Cleef. He watched the dark flush that rose in the boy's face, saw the sullen thrust of his lip, and he was surprised by his own sense of satisfaction.

"Won't do," he thought. "This must be what happens to him all the time. He arouses in his fellow-creatures a passionate yearning to give him a kick in the pants. He knows it, and he can't help it. Kicks are very helpful, to some young people. Not to him. I don't want to, but maybe he's been sent by destiny.... Anyhow, here he is.... Thing is, I sit around with all the doors and windows open, and people get in. They don't know it's an empty house.... If you let them in, you've got to be affable...."

He sighed, and looked at the sky for inspiration. The sun was going down, in a quiet and melancholy fashion; the car turned into the drive, and Emilia's house rose before them, neat and stark against the blank sky; the two-tiered balconies on each side looked, thought Van Cleef, like a cage supporting an unfinished structure.

"Are you going to defy the Major, and stay?" asked Russell.

"Oh.... I think so...."

"He's a pathological case—"

"Aren't we all?"

"He's dangerous," said Russell.

"Don't agree with you."

"You're making a mistake," said Russell, curtly. "I wish you'd listen to me, and get away from here."

"What's the danger?" asked Van Cleef, with resignation.

"If I told you, you wouldn't believe me."

"No," said Van Cleef. "No.... I'm afraid I shouldn't."

"Then, if you don't object too much," said Russell, "I'll stay, too."

IV

He rang the bell, and the door was opened promptly by a grey-haired lady with a pince-nez.

"Arthur!" she exclaimed. "Emilia told me you'd come. I *thought* I heard a car...."

"Van Cleef!" said a man's voice behind her.

These were the Downeses. When he had first met them, or where, or how, Van Cleef had no recollection; he knew only that for fifteen years he had been meeting them—everywhere. He would go to a dinner party, and the Downeses would be there; they appeared at cocktail parties; they could be seen in restaurants, at plays; once he had met them in London, again in Paris, and it had been entirely natural.

"Maybe they're an hallucination," he thought. "Maybe nobody else sees them. I turn my head, and there they are." They were, as always, extremely pleased to see him. Mrs. Downes had things to tell him about mutual friends.

"Have you heard," she said, "that Alicia is going to marry again?"

"The man's a cousin of Wellington, the writer," said Downes. "Were you with us when we met him in Paris, Van Cleef?"

"I don't know," Van Cleef answered, and that was true. "Maybe I was with them in Paris," he thought. "Or I wonder.... Is it 'them,' or 'it'? Mean to say, are they actually two people, or different aspects of one Downes?"

Except for the fact that they both wore pince-nez, they were not physically alike. Harry Downes was a plump and elegant little man; Annie Downes was thin and untidy; the resemblance lay in their nebulousness.

"Woolly," thought Van Cleef. "Like clouds—or sheep."

They were not interesting; when he did not see them, he never thought of them, yet, for some reason, he was always pleased to see them.

"Are you stopping here long, Arthur?" Mrs. Downes asked, and he noticed that she was staring past him at Russell.

"This is Russell Blackman," he said.

"Blackman..." Mrs. Downes repeated, with an anxious frown. "Are you related to the Maryland Blackman?"

"I don't know," said Russell.

"You don't know?" she said, taken aback. "But surely.... I met a Miss *Grace* Blackman in Egypt.... She was from Maryland."

"My people live in Boston," said Russell. "I don't know where they came from."

Nothing could have affronted Mrs. Downes more than this.

"That's very peculiar," she said.

"We know a good many people in Boston," said Mr. Downes.

"I don't," said Russell.

This was more than Annie Downes could endure. He was undermining the foundations of society.

"Very eccentric…" she said. "Tell me, Arthur, have you heard anything of the Telfairs lately? They seem to have disappeared off the face of the earth."

"I did hear a rumour—" Downes began, when Emilia entered.

"I've told Harly to make cocktails," she said, with her sweet Valentine's smile. "Do you want to go up to your room first, Arthur?"

He was silent for a moment.

"Can you put Russell up for the night?" he asked.

Because he felt sorry for the boy, standing there ignored.

"Oh, yes!" she said. "Harly will take up your bags—"

"I'm sorry, but I've come without anything," said Russell. "If there's time, I'll drive down to the village and get a toothbrush, and so on."

He spoke nicely to Emilia, and she smiled nicely at him.

"There's an hour before dinner," she said.

No one spoke until the boy had gone out of the room.

"Who *is* he, Arthur?" asked Mrs. Downes.

"I used to know his people. Very decent."

"I suppose," said Mrs. Downes, "that his rudeness is a pose. So many young people…."

"He's very handsome," said Emilia.

"Theatrical," said Mrs. Downes.

"Well!" said a new voice.

"My Lizzy!" said Van Cleef.

Miss Carroll held out both her hands, not smiling, looking at him with her cold blue eyes; a neat, spare little red-haired woman, pale, sharp-featured, supremely composed. Her fingers closed tightly on his big hands; then she let him go. Harly entered with a tray.

"Will you have a cocktail, Lizzy?" asked Emilia, ingratiatingly. "In honour of Arthur's visit?"

"I will not, thanks."

She lay down and took out a cigarette, and Van Cleef lit for her. With an oddly youthful limberness she swung one knee over the other; very sporting, she looked, in a tailored blue silk blouse and a grey skirt.

"I've had a Mozart programme, for an hour and a half, on my radio," she said. "And that nonsensical Bramwell was bubbling around in his room all the time, muttering. He's insane."

"He doesn't like music," said Emilia.

"Then why does he stay in his room?"

"His work—"

"His work!" said Miss Carroll. "What does he think he's doing?"

"But he's told you, Lizzy. He's writing his reminiscences."

"Impossible. He's never done anything, and he's incapable of inventing anything."

"He has a medal," said Emilia, in her apologetic way, and Miss Carroll laughed.

"Change him to another room, my poor darling," she said. "Before one of us murders the other."

"If you're ready, Arthur...."

Van Cleef followed Emilia out of the room and up the stairs; as they reached the top, he leaned forward and took her hand.

"My dear girl.... I know a fellow who wants to buy a—a guest-house—"

"No, you don't, Arthur."

"If I can find someone to buy it—?"

She shook her head, and went on, holding his hand and drawing him after her. The room was familiar to Van Cleef; he had occupied it in Bill Swan's day; only now it was a little shabby, and a little dusty.

"I'll put that boy in the next room, and you can share the bath. Is that all right, Arthur?"

"That's all right, Emilia."

"You'll come down in a moment, for a cocktail, won't you, Arthur?"

"Oh, yes!" he said, and she left him.

He sat down in an arm-chair by the open window and lit a cigarette. "A blackmailer?" he said to himself. "Not that girl. Honest, and gentle. Good. Good, without any complications. I wish I was good. And young. Or maybe I wish I were dead. That's possible—" He stretched, and sighed. "But probably I wish I had a drink," he thought. "What did my protégé do with the whisky?"

It might still be in the car, in which case he couldn't very well go down and get it. He did not like cocktails; he did not want to join the group in the drawing-room. He closed his eyes, and went to sleep.

"Excuse me, sir. Excuse me, sir," said a soft and sorrowful voice from an immense distance, over and over again. "Excuse me, sir. Excuse me, sir—"

"My fault!" said Van Cleef, and opened his eyes. The room was dark; he couldn't see....

"Excuse me, sir...."

"Oh, Harly, is it? Yes?"

"The madam says, sir, shall she wait dinner for the young gentleman?"

"What young gentleman? Oh, yes.... No, don't wait. Turn on a light, will you, Harly? Thanks...."

The thin and melancholy Harly, soft-footed as a ghost, withdrew, and Van Cleef stepped out on to the balcony outside the window, to shake off his drowsy fatigue. At this side of the house the lawn sloped downward toward a coppice of young trees, and he saw something moving there. His sight was excellent; he moved forward toward the railing of the balcony; it was too low to lean over, but narrowing his eyes, he could see now that it was a man moving among the trees; a small nimble man. He reached the wall that bordered the highway and climbed over it; there was a street light there, and for an instant it shone upon him, showed a dark face and a fierce white moustache, beneath a soft hat worn at a rakish angle. Then he vanished into the shadows.

"Very good conspirator," thought Van Cleef. "*Is* there something afoot here? Emilia and her talk about blackmail... Major and his fury.... And now this little guy...."

He re-entered the room, to wash and get ready for dinner.

"Thing is," he thought, "Emilia makes things happen. She doesn't do anything. Things happen to her. She was on a ship that foundered. And there was Bill.... Drama...."

When he got downstairs, everyone was in the dining-room; the Downeses and Lizzy Carroll at one small table; the Major alone at another; Emilia sat at a table laid for three.

"Sorry to be late, Emilia."

"It doesn't matter, Arthur."

Each table had a vase of flowers and two green candles in silver holders; the china was fine Spode, but the plated ware was cheap and clumsy, and the cloth coarse. Harly, all alone, waited deftly upon everyone, setting before them the most minute servings of food.

"Emilia doesn't give a damn about eating!" Bill Swan had said once.

"Poetic," Van Cleef had suggested.

"Neurotic!" Swan had said. "It's unnatural. By God, you could give her a dish of that stuff—those dried roses—what d'you call it?—that potpourri, and she wouldn't care. She's not *human.*"

"Poor old Bill..." thought Van Cleef. "You take a fellow like me.... I never did know what I wanted. Maybe I got it, and didn't recognize it. But Bill Swan knew exactly what he wanted, and he never could get it. He wanted to be a sort of feudal lord, benevolent, but supreme—"

"You're very quiet, Arthur."

"Sorry, my dear girl—"

"What happened to that boy?"

"I don't know. Quite natural for him to disappear. Came suddenly from nowhere, y'know."

"I like him," she said. "I wish I had a son as handsome as that."

"Lord!" thought Van Cleef, glancing at her charming face. "I suppose you're—you must be forty, or close to it. It's hard to believe...."

"*There* he is!" she said, and raised her hand, in a gay little salute to the boy who stood in the doorway. He crossed the room and sat down at the table with them.

"I'm sorry to be so late, but I couldn't find anything in the village, and I drove on, to Bainville."

Harly set a cup of bouillon before him, and presently took it away, untasted; brought a tiny ramekin of fish au gratin. Like Emilia, Russell seemed completely indifferent to food.

"Excited about something," thought Van Cleef. "What is there that could excite him, I wonder?"

The Major was the first to leave the dining-room, and he went directly upstairs. The Downeses went into the drawing-room; Miss Carroll went out on the veranda; and Van Cleef would have followed her, if Russell had not stopped him, with a hand on his arm.

"I've got something to tell you," he said. "Will you come upstairs?"

They entered Van Cleef's room, and Russell closed the door, and leaned against it.

"It was sheer luck," he said, his dark face alight. "I just happened to go into the chemist's in Bainville.... A woman came in and asked for a box of sleeping-tablets, one of the barbital preparations, and the chemist said he wouldn't give it to her without a doctor's prescription. After she'd gone I got talking to him. He told me that two years ago there'd been a death from an overdose of those same tablets, and he'd had to go into court and produce the prescription."

Van Cleef sat on the edge of a table, looking at the boy.

"The label he'd put on the box said, 'One as required,' and the coroner's jury gave a verdict of accidental death."

"Yes, I know."

"You know who it was—"

"Yes. Bill Swan."

"The chemist was very discreet but I gathered—"

"Yes," Van Cleef interrupted. "You gathered an earful of brutish gossip. I'm a friend of Emilia's. I was Bill Swan's friend. I heard all that. It's what happens in a tribe of savages. Everybody whispering 'poison—poison....' Forget it."

"There's one aspect you may not have considered—"

"Forget it!" said Van Cleef, and there was no good humour in his face now. "And if you speak of it, or even hint of it again while you're under this roof, I'll take pleasure in kicking you out."

"You misunderstand me," said Russell, with a faint smile. "I didn't hear a word of suspicion against the person you're obviously defending."

"Then—" Van Cleef began, but thought better of it. "Forget it!" he said. "All of it." He rose and crossed the room; Russell moved aside to let him open the door, and he went slowly down the stairs. He found Emilia and Lizzy Carroll on the veranda, silent in the dark; he sat with them, smoking.

"I wonder if poor Emilia ever knew?" he thought. "Probably not. She was stunned by Bill's death—in a daze, for weeks. Wouldn't have noticed anything, and no one would have been likely to tell her. No. Probably never entered her head that any groups of friends were running around, saying *of course* they didn't believe poor dear Emilia had poisoned her dreadful husband."

It was a cool night, with a light wind that moved the white clouds across the starry sky; it was quiet, only insects chirping in the grass, and the trees rustling. "I don't like peace and quiet," thought Van Cleef. "Makes me restless.... I'd like to have heard what that infernal Wonderchild was going to say, but it won't do to encourage him. Ever, in any way. Let the past bury its dead.... Everybody'd be glad to let it, if it would, only it doesn't.... That girl.... That Blanche.... I'll have to talk to Annie Downes about her. Set Emilia's mind at rest. That girl...."

That girl, who had spoken to him like a friend, yet was remote from him as if she lived in another era. She was beginning, opening a window upon a fresh, cool morning, and he was smothered with the dust of defeat. What had defeated him? He didn't know....

"What's that?" he said, sitting forward.

Someone was running across the hall. The house door opened, and someone ran out, stood in the dark, breathing fast.

"Who is it?" cried Emilia.

They were all standing, waiting for an answer. And the answer came in Mrs. Downes's tremulous voice. "Harry—doesn't feel well."

"Oh! I'm so sorry!" said Emilia. "Shall I call Doctor Robinson?"

"No.... Harry doesn't want a doctor. He thought—we thought—if Miss Carroll would just take a look at him—"

"Me?" said Miss Carroll. "*I'm* not a doctor."

"You're so—practical..." said Mrs. Downes.

"I'm certainly too practical to meddle with—" she began, but Mrs. Downes interrupted.

"Oh, do please hurry!" she cried, with a sob.

"Don't be hysterical!" said Miss Carroll. "I'll go and see Downes, but *I* can't do anything."

The door closed behind them.

"Aa-rthur.... Do you think I'd better go, too?"

"No," he answered, reassuringly. "They'll let you know if there's anything.... Probably nothing serious."

"Annie's changed so.... She's so hostile towards me.... I'm—" She paused. "Arthur.... Sometimes I'm *afraid* of Annie."

"My dear girl!" he protested.

"It's true! She's.... There's something vindictive and dreadful about Annie Downes."

"Any definite examples?"

"Little things," she said. "Little things she's said and done. Ever since she first brought that hateful girl here."

He lit another cigarette.

"I stopped in to see the girl this afternoon," he said. "Didn't tell her my name. Just wanted to see.... Emilia, you're wrong about her."

She said nothing to that.

"Only a kid," he went on. "Honest sort of kid."

"I asked you here to help me. I didn't—invent all this. Arthur, that girl will ruin me!"

"With gossip?" he said.

He heard her skirt rustle in the dark.

"There's something behind the gossip," she said, with a straightforwardness very unusual in her.

"Care to tell me?"

"No," she answered, and after a long silence, "I—sometimes I've felt quite sure—that you knew."

He wished now that he could see her face. Because her voice seemed unfamiliar; not the voice that belonged to the piquant and elegant little doll. It made him uneasy. More than uneasy....

"*You* knew—how things were," she said. "You knew how desperately unhappy Bill made me.... It was—too much...."

"My God!" he thought. "She can't mean.... Shall I make her say plainly what she means? But if it's that.... And if it's once said.... I don't know. I don't know whether it's better to let her go on, or not. It's—"

The door opened again, and closed smartly.

"That boy you brought, Arthur—" said Miss Carroll. "He's looking after Downes. He's giving him medicine—God know what—and Downes is swallowing it."

"What's wrong with him?" asked Van Cleef.

"Well..." she said, with deliberate hesitation, "he and his wife both call it indigestion."

"Not uncommon," said Van Cleef.

"If I had the sort of indigestion Downes has," said Miss Carroll, "I shouldn't be satisfied with a doctor. I'd call in the police."

V

They were perfectly silent and still there in the dark, all three of them.

"I'll go and see him," said Emilia.

"Don't," said Miss Carroll. "He's in pain. You won't like it, Emilia."

Their voices, disembodied in the darkness, were charged with infinite significance; it was as if they were moving stealthily around each other, looking for an opportunity for a rapier thrust.

"No..." said Van Cleef to himself. It was the protest of his body and his soul against an enormous responsibility; he was not adequate, he *couldn't* take charge. "I want a drink," he thought, aware of a familiar feeling, a sort of internal fluttering; the hand holding his cigarette was unsteady.

"If the man dies—" said Miss Carroll.

"Pull up your socks," Van Cleef told himself, and rose. "I'll go up..." he said. "Leave it to me, my dear girl."

"Arthur!"

"Leave it to me," he repeated, and groped for her hand, found it cold as ice. "Lizzy," he said, "better come along."

Miss Carroll entered the house with him; the light in the lounge dazzled him for a moment, so that she looked pale and fierce, her sandy hair had a coppery glint.

"No use upsetting the poor girl," he said.

"I'm sorry," said Miss Carroll. "Sometimes I forget that Emilia's peace of mind is the most important thing on earth. But Harry Downes doesn't forget it."

"What's the meaning of that, Lizzy?"

"I went in there," she said. "He was in agony. The only thing he said to me was, 'Tell Emilia not to worry!'"

"Humane."

"I hope Annie appreciates his humaneness," said she.

"I don't think I like women, Lizzy," he said, and turned towards the stairs. "Tempest in a teacup," he said to himself. "I hope to God it is."

The door of the Downes's room was open; he stopped on the threshold, profoundly disturbed by the scene. A small lamp on the bedside table cast a bright circle of light upon the figure of Downes, in vest and trousers, lying on his back with his eyes closed. Russell was bending over him, fingers on his wrist, a look of intense concentration on his fine dark face that made it noble. Annie Downes sat in a wicker armchair with her hands clasped in her lap; the light caught her glasses and made them glisten. It was not easy to break that silence.

"How is it going?" asked Van Cleef.

Russell, still bending over the prostrate figure, glanced up under his level black brows.

"I'm giving him a sedative," he said.

"D'you know what you're doing?"

"Yes. He'll be all right when he wakes."

Van Cleef came a few steps nearer, looking at Downes. Without his pince-nez, without a trace of his healthy colour, he looked strange. Very strange.

"We'll call a doctor," he said.

"It's not necessary," said Russell.

"Still and all, we'll have a doctor."

"No, we won't," said Annie Downes, in a flat voice. "If you call a doctor, I won't let him see Harry. You have no authority."

"Look here, Annie.... If anything—"

"If anything goes wrong, I'm responsible," she said, and rose. "I'm going to go to bed in one of the empty rooms."

"I'm sorry," said Russell, "but Mr. Downes can't be left alone."

"Get someone else," said she. "I'm tired. I've got to rest. Good night!"

She went past Van Cleef, out of the room; her face had no expression except a sort of primness.

"You can't read faces," thought Van Cleef. "Some of 'em don't say anything...." He turned again to Downes, whose face, very dreadfully, said nothing. "I'll now cut the Gordian knot, with common sense," he said aloud. "I'll get hold of a doctor—"

"You'd better have the facts first," said Russell, sitting down on the bed beside the motionless figure. "The man was poisoned with arsenic."

"Says you."

"All right. Get your doctor. Maybe it's an attempt at suicide, in which case they can arrest Downes. I've got the bottle here."

"What bottle?"

"Thermos bottle," said Russell. "It seems it's always left on the hall table downstairs, with a hot cereal drink for Downes. For his insomnia. He didn't take all of it."

"How the hell do you know there's arsenic in it?"

Russell got up, stood very straight and tense.

"I found this man suffering from arsenic poisoning," he said. "I found an empty cup beside him. I saved his life. Because I happen to know the symptoms, and the antidote."

"Happened to have the antidote handy?"

"Would you care to come into my room for a minute?"

"No, I don't think so."

"All right!" said Russell. "I've finished. Nothing more for me to do until I have to give my evidence in court."

"Why d'you want me to go to your room?"

"I have something to show you."

"Can't leave this poor devil alone."

"It won't matter for ten minutes. We'll lock the door on the outside."

Van Cleef did that, and dropped the key into his pocket. They went along the corridor to a door at the end; Russell stepped in and switched on the light. A pleasant tranquil room, with a smooth white bed, and on the open flap of a little writing-desk lay a thin black kitten, stiff as a board, it teeth showing in a monstrous grin.

Van Cleef stood motionless, struggling against something horrible, against fury, was it, or nausea, or something else?

"What's the idea?" he asked.

"I was making an experiment," Russell answered, looking squarely at him.

"Killed this—little beast?"

"Yes. I wanted to make some observations."

Van Cleef turned his back on the boy, and lit a cigarette "Pack up your experiments, and what not, and get out will you?" he said.

"All right!" Russell said. "You'd better listen to me first though. Someone tried to murder Downes to-night, and someone succeeded in murdering Swan, two years ago."

"Pull yourself together!" thought Van Cleef. "This is serious. You can't just kick the boy out and forget it. Suppose he talks to somebody else?"

"I've covered up the 'experiment,'" said Russell, behind him. "Sorry I offended your finer feelings. Personally, I'm not sentimental about animals."

"Skip that. You were saying—"

"Do you want to hear? If you don't, we can skip all of it. I don't give one little damn about justice. To me this is an interesting problem, and nothing more. I'm willing to shut up about it, forever, if you like."

"I do want you to shut up," thought Van Cleef. "But that won't do." He sat down on the arm of a chair, still with his back to the desk. "Let's hear about all the murders," he said.

"This boy Harly was in the house when Swan died," said Russell. "I had a talk with him after dinner. He saw Swan an hour or so before he died, and he saw him ten minutes after he died. He remembers all the details."

"He gave his evidence at the inquest."

"Not about the cup."

"What cup?"

"The cup that wasn't there," said Russell.

Van Cleef drew on his cigarette, surprised, even alarmed by the emotion that stirred him. For a long time he had taken his own equability for granted; he didn't get angry, or even irritated.

"I'll buy it," he said, presently. "Let's hear the Adventure of the Cup That Wasn't There."

"When I was talking to the chemist in Bainville, he said one thing that impressed me," Russell went on. "He happened to mention that Swan died at six in the evening."

"Is that an especially sinister time to die?"

"It's rather an unusual time to die from an overdose of sleeping medicine, isn't it?"

"I see your point. Go on."

"I got Harly talking."

"Cleverly, without arousing any suspicion in his mind, and so on?"

"You're right," said Russell. "I told him I'd gone to buy some sleeping medicine for myself, and that the chemist had told me Swan died from a dose of the same thing. I said I was nervous about taking the stuff now. I asked him if Swan had taken a hot drink with it."

"Why did you ask him that?"

"Random shot. I'd asked other questions that drew blank, but this one was good. He said that when he last saw Swan, there was an empty cup and saucer beside him. He was sure of it, because he wanted to take them away, and Swan said no. When he brought up the doctor, there was no cup."

"And you, and you alone were able to get this information out of him."

"No. He says he told the family lawyer."

"Ah-ha! So Perrson was in the conspiracy, too.... Perrson tell Harly not to mention the fatal cup?"

"The lawyer told him it was of no importance."

"But you know better."

"I'm sick of this!" cried Russell, with startling violence. "These people are friends of yours. I was doing this for you. And all you do is sneer at me.... My God! I believe you *hate* me!"

"I believe I do," thought Van Cleef, with a sense of shock.

He didn't like that, he didn't approve of hatred; he felt unhappy, and wholly confused. He was silent, staring at the floor for a time; then he looked up at the boy with an uneasy smile.

"Sorry!" he said.

"For what?"

"Hell!" said Van Cleef with a sigh. "I dunno.... Anyhow, suppose we drop the sleuthing?"

"You want me to drop it?" Russell asked, looking at him with narrowed eyes and a faint smile. "Now? After what's happened to Downes?"

"Better be getting back to Downes now.... We can see what he has to say when he recovers. Mean to say, if *he's* satisfied...."

"All right!" said Russell. "It's up to you."

He went past Van Cleef, out of the room, without another word, or a glance.

"I need a drink," thought Van Cleef. As he rose, he was obliged to glance towards the desk where the kitten lay, covered with a clean white linen handkerchief. "I need a drink. I don't like this—any of this."

He went into the hall towards his own room, wanting a drink very badly.

Quite suddenly the boy's last words came back to him. "It's up to you."
"Up to me?" he asked himself. "Can't see it."
Two bottles of Scotch stood on the chest of drawers. He opened one of them.
"Thing is, if it's up to me.... Better keep a clear head...."
He didn't take a drink. He went out into the hall again, and he saw Lizzy Carroll sitting in Downes's room, wearing a flannel dressing-gown, and reading a book. She glanced up at the sound of his step, and looked at him sharply and sternly. With reluctance he went down the stairs in search of Emilia, to give her what reassurance he could. He did not find her in the house, and he thought, with another sigh, that she might still be on the veranda, alone, in the dark, thinking—Heaven knew what. He opened the house door.

"Get rid of the man!" Major Bramwell was saying, in a high, unsteady voice. "I tell you, Emilia, he's dangerous! He's an irresponsible—*sot.*"

Van Cleef closed the door softly and went directly upstairs, and poured himself a drink.

"Sot, is it?" he said to himself. "Unpleasant word...."

He hated the smell of whisky, hated the taste of it; the first sip made him shudder. But it helped. Pulled him together, cleared his mind. When he had swallowed that drink, he sighed, leaned back, relaxed, lit a cigarette.

"I'm committing the supreme psychological sin," he thought. "Refusing to face facts. I don't like Russell's notions, therefore I refuse to consider them. Won't do. I'm alone now. I don't have to be on the defensive. How does the set-up really look? Downes is taken sick. That's a fact. Lizzy Carroll thinks it queer. That's not a fact; that's a notion. Russell says it's arsenic, and that he's got a sample of it. That may be a fact, or it may be a notion. It ought to be tested, anyhow."

He poured out another drink.

"Anyhow," he repeated to himself. "Nothing so bad as rumour, gossip. I don't know whether Emilia ever knew what people were whispering, two years ago.... But here it is, cropping up again.... All right! By God, I know she didn't poison Bill! How do I know it? How does anyone know that his friends aren't assassins, thieves, blackguards? I've seen her, observed her for eight years. She's not a murderer. The poisoning of Bill Swan is very definitely a notion of Russell's. No evidence then, and no evidence now. If Downes has been poisoned, it's an isolated incident. Nothing to do with Bill Swan. Who'd want to poison Downes? Nobody. Who could have poisoned him? Anybody. The thermos bottle was on the table in the hall. Anybody could have put arsenic into it. What is arsenic? A powder? A pill? A liquid? Can anybody buy it? Russell bought some sort of poison. That little cad...."

He swallowed the rest of the drink, and put away the bottle.

"When you come to think of it, that's a damn queer coincidence.... Russell went out before dinner, in his lighthearted, boyish way, to buy a spot of poison. And after dinner, Downes got a dose. Maybe Downes was just another experiment.... Russell's story is, that he saved Downes's life. He doesn't impress me as the life-saving type. I'm prejudiced. I admit it. I think Russell's probably Satan. All right! How can I find out? How can I find out anything, about anything? Go to the police? With what? Downes and his missus won't back me up. They wouldn't have a doctor. *That's* queer. Does it mean suicide? This bores me. Like the way those detective johnnies in books recapitulate. They do it aloud, though, with a Watson to check up. They use numbers, or letters. Or both. One—A: Has anything really happened at all? One—B: If so, what? Two—A: If not, why not, and who is responsible?"

He rose and stood looking out of the window, and suddenly he remembered the man with the white moustache.

"Who the hell was that?" he thought. "He was certainly what they call skulking, or prowling.... May have been simply an outside burglar. Thrown in to make things harder. Or—"

Something else came back to him.

"I'd forgotten what brought me here. Emilia's blackmail case... I'd forgotten—that girl.... That Blanche...." Sorrow came over him in an overwhelming tide; a dreadful sense of loss. He brought the bottle of whisky back to the table and opened it again.

"Such an honest kid.... So kind.... 'I just thought you weren't happy.'... You're right, my dear little kid.... Not happy.... Sots aren't—very happy...."

VI

It was early when Van Cleef awoke; he never slept long. He got up immediately, as was his habit, filled with a familiar restlessness. He went into the bathroom and took a cold shower; he had just stepped out of the tub, when the other door opened, and Russell stood there, in shirt and trousers, bare-foot, his black hair disordered, his eyes heavy.

"I'm sorry," he said, sombrely.

"All right!"

"I was a bit beyond myself," Russell went on. "But I'd had a shot of morphine."

"What?"

"Oh, I'm not an addict, if that's what you're thinking," said Russell, with a frown. "I don't take the stuff once in six months. I needed it yesterday."

"Sick?"

"I've never been ill in my life. It's something else. It's a depression—a feeling of inadequacy and failure.... Maybe you can understand."

Their eyes met for an instant; Van Cleef looked away, went on drying himself with a flimsy Turkish towel.

"Can't be anything but a random shot," he thought. "Boy can't *know* how I feel...."

He stretched out the towel, to dry his broad shoulders, and it came in two; he looked at it in surprise.

"I didn't kill the cat," said Russell.

"You said it was an experiment."

"I found it in the road, run over. I brought it in and gave it a morphia injection."

"How about the rest of it? About saving Downes's life?"

"That stands."

"Very interesting. Very curious. I mean your having antidotes all ready."

"I didn't. I found what I needed in Downes's own room. He has two shelves in a closet, packed solid with drugs. Either he or his wife must be a first-class hypochondriac."

"So, in the end we have this. That Downes had a stomach-ache and you gave him something, and he got over it."

"Downes was poisoned," said Russell.

"If *he* doesn't mind, or his wife doesn't mind.... Going to get dressed now."

Van Cleef went back into his own room, closing the bathroom door on Russell.

"Pleased to hear he didn't kill the little beast," he said to himself. "But still and all.... You get the impression that he *would* do things like that...."

He dressed with care, as he always did; he paid fabulous sums for his suits, his shoes, for everything; he was fastidious to the point of fussiness. Not from vanity; it was an article in his queer, confused code, that a man must look decent. When he was ready, he went downstairs, and into the dining-room, and he was glad to see no one there except Miss Carroll.

"How's my Lizzy?" he asked.

"I don't know, Arthur. I sat up with that idiot Downes all night. I suppose I dozed in my chair, but it didn't seem that way."

"How's he doing?"

"He slept all night, and he seems perfectly well this morning. Annie's making some sort of hot drink for him. Arthur—I don't like it!"

He sat down at the table opposite her, and Harly came to his side.

"What would you wish, sir?"

"Oh.... Coffee..." he answered. "Just coffee, thanks...." He waited until the boy had gone. "You're tired, Lizzy."

"Arthur," she said, and her tart voice had an undertone of sadness, "you'd like to turn life off, like a tap. Make it stop. It worries you to hear it keep on running. But it doesn't stop. There's no use pretending there's nothing wrong here. You can run away from it, if you like, of course—"

"What's wrong, then?"

"Emilia," she said. "Poor darling! She's a *femme fatale*, without even knowing it. It's rather like seeing a child with a machinegun; not a very bright child, either.... That idiot Downes was talking about her in his sleep.... 'You can trust me, Emilia.... I'll never tell. You can trust me never to tell any one!'"

Van Cleef frowned miserably.

"What would that mean, d'you think?"

"I've no idea. But if he has a secret, Annie certainly knows. Knows, I mean, that he's concealing something. She's been married to him for some thirty years. If he's infatuated with Emilia, Annie must know it. And it couldn't please her much."

"Let's have everything in words of one syllable. All plain."

"I think Annie poisoned him," she said.

"My dear girl!"

"That's what I think. And I think he'd have died, if your Russell hadn't been so clever."

Harly brought a cup and saucer, and a pot of coffee; he waited a moment, and then withdrew.

"It's hard," said Van Cleef. "Extraordinarily hard to see Annie Downes in that light."

"Not at all. She's fading. Growing old; she hasn't a penny of her own; she has nothing, no position, no occupation except her husband. If she saw—or thought she saw him turning to another, younger woman—"

"Logical thing would be to try and remove the woman."

"Maybe she will," said Miss Carroll.

"Mean you think—there's more to come?"

She was silent for a time. She was neat as a pin, in a fresh white shirt and a tweed skirt, her red hair in a smooth knot; her pale, sharp-featured face was composed, but there was some shadow upon it....

"I had premonitions, last night," she said, presently. "I don't believe in them—but at the same time, I do believe in them. Especially at four o'clock in the morning."

"Premonitions of what?"

"Just horror, Arthur."

"All right!" he said. "Let's break the spell—bust up the whole thing. You help me. We'll get Emilia to give up the guest-house—persuade her to take a trip—"

"Good morning!" said Bramwell's voice, beside them. "Boy!" he shouted, and Harly came running.

"I'll back you up, Arthur, to the best of my ability," said Miss Carroll, "but—"

The rest of the words were drowned by the Major's bellow.

"Damn you, boy! Trying to be impudent?"

"No, sir!" said Harly, in extreme distress.

"You are impudent! You know damn well that I don't eat this muck—"

"Don't make such a noise," said Miss Carroll. "Can't you go outdoors to have your fits?"

He rose, and he was shaking, his blue eyes blazing.

"Madam!"

"Sir!" said Miss Carroll, unperturbed. "You're being ridiculous."

"I'm being persecuted!" he said. "But I know how to defend myself, and I intend to do it!"

Russell slipped quietly into the chair beside Van Cleef; at sight of him, the Major fell silent, and in a moment sat down again.

"What will you have, sir?" the anxious Harly asked Russell.

"Everything you've got," said Russell. "I'm hungry."

"That's right!" said Miss Carroll, with an air of indulgence that surprised Van Cleef. "Did you go in to see Downes? How was his pulse?"

Russell answered; she asked more questions. They were serious, friendly, professional, like a doctor and a nurse. It was extraordinary, thought Van Cleef, and rather touching, the way the boy responded to her amiability. Perhaps it was something more than touching, to be alight with pleasure for so small a benefaction....

Emilia came into the room, and the Major, Van Cleef and Russell all rose.

"Oh, please sit down!" she said, earnestly. "I just came to see if everything was quite all right?"

Her dark hair grew in a point on her forehead; what they call a widow's peak, he thought; her dark brows were so arched as to look artificial. It suited her, to look artificial. She was wearing a black skirt, and a ruffled white blouse; she was a charming imitation of a boarding-house mistress, with boarders who rose as she entered.

"What's real in her?" he thought. "Does she love anyone, or hate anyone? Is she happy, or unhappy?"

She smiled at him, looking straight into his eyes, as if there were no one else. She always had done that to him, to Bill, to everyone. Maybe she didn't realize how fervent a look it was; and maybe she did.

"When you've finished, Aa-rthur," she said, "would you like to look at the flowers?"

"Finished now," he said. "If you'll excuse me, Lizzy...."

He followed Emilia across the hall, and through the drawing-room to what Bill had called "the conservatory"; it was little more than a large bay-window, shut off by glass doors covered by curtains. He hated to look at the place now. Bill had had a gardener, and a rather ostentatious collection of brilliant flowers, but now it was lamentable, pots of earth dried into dust, with stalks standing up in them, dead dry vines nailed against the walls; the spring sun was dimmed by the dusty windows, the air smelt of dust.

"There..." she said, resting her delicate hand on the edge of a wooden box where three pansies were still alive. "They're quite sweet, aren't they?"

"Oh, very!" he said, and waited.

"Arthur..." she said, "*now* you know what I mean, don't you?"

"Sorry, my dear girl..." he protested, anxiously.

"Oh, Arthur! Surely you see now what that girl has done?"

"No. Sorry, but I can't."

"She's set Annie against me so completely.... She's put this horrible, absurd idea into Annie's head." She paused, touching the velvety petal of a pansy with her forefinger. "This idea of poison," she said in a low tone, her eyes downcast. "For that to come up *again*.... It's too much...."

"Nothing's come up, my dear girl."

"If you could make her go away, Arthur!" she cried. "If you'd only believe me, that *she's* the cause of all this...."

"Emilia, look at it reasonably, my dear girl. What motive could she have for trying to stir up trouble? Thing is, you're tired, and a bit overwrought. No, listen, please! I'm sure this fellow I spoke about would buy the house—"

"You, too?" she said, still with her eyes downcast. "This is my home. You agree that I've got to go—to be driven out by the cruelest slander?" At last she looked up at him, "This is my home. I love it. *Must* I be driven out—by Blanche?"

"Not by Blanche. Couldn't be. There's no sense in it."

"I wish she was dead!"

That cry was the more shocking because her face didn't change, that heart-shaped Valentine face with the arched brows, with Cupid's bow mouth.

"You don't wish that, Emilia," Van Cleef said, briefly.

"No. Of course not," said she, turning away. "I only wish she'd live somewhere else...."

"Last night you said—you mentioned—that there was—something behind this gossip.... We're old friends. Mean to say, perhaps if we talked more frankly—"

"There's vindictiveness behind it," said she. "That's all. Malice and vindictiveness. Not one word of truth." She opened the glass door into the drawingroom. "But people can be destroyed by lies," she said, and went out.

Van Cleef looked at his watch.

"Too early..." he said to himself. Because he had a rule; no drink before eleven. He couldn't remember when he had adopted the rule, or why, but it was somehow of great importance. He had nearly two hours to wait, two hours of this vague restlessness. He went upstairs to the open door of the Downes's room, and it was, for some reason, relief to see Mrs. Downes in there, knitting.

"How's the patient?" he asked.

"I'm better, thanks, Van Cleef," Downes answered gravely, "but I'm still shaky. I'll have to be careful, very careful of my diet, for some time to come."

"Any sinister meaning?" thought Van Cleef.

Downes did not look sinister, or even very ill; his face was a little sallow, but he lay back on a mound of pillows with a comfortable air.

"I have a nervous stomach," he continued. "In a way, that's bad, but in another way it is good. My digestion is very easily upset, but, on the other hand, sufficient rest will almost always restore it."

Quietly and earnestly he described his digestive processes, as they seemed to him.

"Harry had an attack exactly like this when we were in Cairo," said Mrs. Downes. "The doctor there—he was a Pole—a wonderful man... he said—"

Leaning against the doorway Van Cleef kept an attentive expression, without listening to a word.

"Cosy scene," he thought. "Leave well enough alone? Question is.... Too damn many questions—and who am I, to answer them? Only one definite idea in the brain; to wit, that Blanche is not a scandalmonger, not vindictive, not anything but a nice kid. *She* could be talked to. She alone."

For half an hour he displayed a vaguely polite interest in Downes's digestion, and then he crossed the hall to his own room. Harly was dusting the lampshade; the bed was made, everything in order.

"Housemaid gone?"

"Yes, sir. Just me left, sir."

Van Cleef closed the door, and poured himself a drink.

"Only ten o'clock," he thought. "This is the beginning of the end. A sot.... Well...." He swallowed the drink, and recorked the bottle; he went in search of Russell, and found him in his bedroom sitting at a desk and writing. "Busy?"

"Nothing important," Russell answered, with a sidelong glance.

"Wants to be asked," thought Van Cleef, and did ask, "A spot of science?"

"No. I was making a psychological analysis of the people in the house for my own amusement."

"Too much!" said Van Cleef, half to himself. "Well, the thing is, if you can spare the time, want to drive me to the village?"

Russell answered fluently in a foreign language.

"Meaning *con amore?*" said Van Cleef, with a sigh. "All right, let's go."

It was good, he thought, to get away from that house; he lit a cigarette and slouched down in the roadster.

"Where do you want to go?" the boy asked.

"Stationer's."

"She's a pretty girl," said Russell, with a half-smile. "I wish you luck."

"Let it go!" Van Cleef told himself. "He's like that, and forever will be."

The main street was busy this morning, cheerful in the clear sun. Russell stopped the car at a corner.

"Shall I wait?" he asked. "Or come back?"

"Neither," said Van Cleef. "Thanks for the buggy ride, and adieu."

A young fellow in overalls was leaning on the counter, talking to Blanche, both speaking quietly, earnestly. Van Cleef stood unnoticed just inside the doorway of the dim little shop.

"Well, so long, Babe!" said the young man, presently. "Be seeing you!"

"Be seeing you!" she answered absently, and stared after him with a small frown. When Van Cleef came into her line of vision, she looked at him in the same way, not surprised, not pleased; simply accepting him. "Hello!" she said.

He liked that reception more than anything; it seemed to him more friendly than a smile, more welcoming than a handclasp. "Hello!" he answered. "I was wondering—" He moved away as someone else entered, stood inspecting the three shelves of books beneath a sign, "Lending Library," until behind him he heard a fierce, hissing whisper in French.

"How much hast thou received?"

"*Rien,*" answered Blanche, nonchalantly. "*C'est tout-à-fait fini, ça.*"

Van Cleef wanted a look at the customer, he turned his head. He saw a short man with a fierce white moustache, and a somewhat theatrical wide-brimmed, black felt hat. It was the man he had seen moving among the trees last night. There was no more conversation; the man with the moustache went briskly out of the shop, with a straight and soldierly bearing.

"Rather unusual type," said Van Cleef.

"That's my father," she said.

"French?"

"He was born in France, but he's lived here for ages. He's a night-watchman at the hat factory."

He lit a cigarette and stared at it.

"Emilia asked me to look into this," he thought. "That's why I'm here. Emilia says this girl is making trouble for her, and I've been denying it. Why? Because I like her. I like her so well that I'm not afraid to ask questions."

"Would you like to sit down?" she asked.

"Thing is, can you get out of here?"

"Well, how do you mean?" she asked.

"Could we take a walk or a drive?"

"You mean now?" she asked. "Right now?"

"That was the idea."

She thought it over for a moment.

"I guess so," she said. "If I can get hold of Mrs. Klein."

She was accepting this, too, without comment; she disappeared through a door in the back of the shop and he heard her running upstairs; she was down again, promptly.

"It's all right," she said. "I can have an hour."

They walked out of the shop; that was all there was to it.

"Is Mrs. Klein the boss?" he asked.

"Boss's wife."

"Are they nice to work for?"

"Yes," she said. "But, you see, I started in the right way. I told Mr. Klein, before I took the job, that I wanted to be a human being. I said I was willing to accept a nine-hour day, but that if I wanted to take time off, I could do it, and make it up another time. And without giving any reasons, either. I specially said that. Sometimes I haven't any reason; I mean, not a reason I could explain. I just feel like—not going to work."

"Not a very interesting job, is it?"

"No, it's not," she admitted. "Would you like to see the nice houses? If you do, we turn left here."

"Don't care too much for the nice houses, do you? My idea was, we might take a taxi, and go somewhere for lunch."

"It's pretty early..." she paused. "Thanks! I'd like that."

They crossed the street to the railway station, and got into a taxi.

"Is there a restaurant?" he asked.

"Well, there's Franchi's," she said. "They say the food is good, but it's sort of disreputable."

"Any other place?"

"I'd *like* to go to Franchi's," she said, "if *you* don't mind."

"Maybe your father wouldn't like it."

"He never interferes with me," she said. "He's brought me up to be independent. That's one of his theories."

She leaned back in the corner of the cab, looking out of the window, and Van Cleef looked at her; at her straight little nose, her short upper lip, and the quiet vigour there was about her. Clear features, clear skin, clear voice; all definite, he thought.... Then she turned her head, and her grey eyes had that look of gentleness again.

"Mr. Van Cleef.... If you've got something on our mind.... If there's anything I can do...."

He felt a sudden sharp desire to be definite, himself. But he could not be. There was an unhappy confusion in his mind about Emilia; there was his confirmed habit of vagueness. For so long a time he had managed not to judge, not to criticize, not to care; for too long a time. Blanche was waiting for an answer, and he could not give one.

"I need a drink," he thought.

"Is it something about Mrs. Swan?" she asked.

He looked at her, and a sort of anguish filled him; because he could not answer, could not be honest and clear.

"I need a drink," he said aloud.

He saw her eyes fill with tears, and he was amazed.

"Sorry..." he said.

She smiled, uncertainly, and turned away her head, looked out of the window; they said nothing more until they reached the sort of disreputable Franchi's, a road-house like a hundred others.

"Might wait," he said to the taxi driver.

They mounted the steps to the glass-enclosed veranda; no one there, nothing ready, chairs were piled one upon another; a swarthy man with a black moustache came hastening out, with an anxious deference. The menu, he said, was not quite ready, but they could have anything, anything they wished, chicken.... Very nice chickens....

"Cocktail?" Van Cleef asked the girl.

"Yes, thanks!" she answered.

"What kind?"

"I don't care," she said. He ordered a Martini for her, and a Scotch for himself; they sat down at a table and waited; a waiter came and spread a cloth on it, brought the drinks.

She took a sip of hers and set it down.

"Mr. Van Cleef.... Is there anything you want to ask me?"

He swallowed his drink, and held up his glass to show the waiter.

"It's hard to get at..." he said. "Emilia—Mrs. Swan, y'know.... Feel like telling me your point of view about her?"

"I don't know what I think—now," she said. "I've been trying to make up my mind.... Before I'd met her, I believed what I'd heard, but now I don't know...."

There was a pause.

"What had you heard?" he asked.

"My father says she's a murderess," said Blanche.

VII

It was a shock to hear that word, and it was a relief.

"Dangerous thing to say," he observed.

"He's never said it to anyone but me. He came home one day, and asked me to take a walk. There was something so queer about him.... We went past the Swans' house, just as Mr. Swan's funeral was coming out. Father stood here with his hat off. Mrs. Swan came by in a car, all in black with a veil over her face, and Father said: 'That woman is a murderess.' I didn't say anything then; I couldn't. But a few days later I asked him about it; I asked him if he was sure. And he said yes. I asked him why he didn't tell the police, and he said: 'It's too late. They couldn't do anything. But she'll pay for it, in the end.'"

"You're a bit matter-of-fact about it," said Van Cleef.

"I try to be," she said. "I can't tell you how I hate anything—melodramatic. I want to be—" She paused. "I want to be quiet about things."

"Yes..." he said.

"You see," she went on, "I've been brought up in a sort of melodrama. Father's the most upright, honourable man; he is very kind, and generous to people, really, but his ideas are so—so violent. Ever since I can remember, he's been talking about a class war, about enemies, about the day of reckoning. He sent me to a queer little school where we heard that sort of talk all the time. I never liked it. I don't want to hate anyone. I couldn't hate Mrs. Swan."

"Do you think your father hates her?"

"I know he does. He said so."

The waiter brought the fried chicken, excellently cooked, but he felt no appetite.

"You don't?" he said. "You've been seeing a lot of her, lately.... Been visiting Annie Downes...."

"I'm glad to be able to talk about this," she said, slowly. "It's been worrying me—" She raised her eyes to his face. "It's—queer!" she said. "I don't understand it. I don't like it."

"How did it begin?"

"Mrs. Downes came into the shop one day to buy a magazine, and got talking. She seemed—just friendly. When she asked me to come and see her, I was glad to go. I was curious to see Mrs. Swan. And I'd never been in a house like that. But when I got there... I didn't like it."

"Any special reason?"

"I guess there's always a reason for those—feelings," she said, soberly. "Even if you're not conscious of it. I've tried to think it out, but I haven't grasped it yet."

"What sort of 'feeling'?"

She considered that, and he watched her with an indefinable pleasure, a sort of delight in that sobriety. She wanted to say exactly what she meant.

"I think Mrs. Downes is using me for something," she said. "I've been there three times, but I'm not going again."

"What does she talk about?"

"Nothing. Just about knitting, or books or things like that."

"You can't think of anything out of the way that she's ever said?"

"There's never been anything. We just sit there in the drawing-room and— chat, that's the word for it. Once I had lunch with her and Mr. Downes, and he was queerer than she. He didn't talk at all."

The waiter brought two little biscuit tortonis.

"I love this!" she said. "But what time is it, Mr. Van Cleef? Twelve-fifteen? I'm sorry, but I'll have to get back."

"Didn't like your cocktail?" he asked.

"No, thank you," she said, and he saw a faint colour rise in her cheeks.

They got back into the taxi again, set off towards the village.

"Shan't see her again," thought Van Cleef. "No reason for seeing her. She's not conspiring against Emilia. She's all right. How do I know? I do know. I'd go into court and swear…. This is a good and honest child."

He got out with her in front of the shop.

"Good-bye," he said. "And thanks."

"I'll see you again, won't I?"

"Oh, sure to!" he said.

There was something on her mind; he could see that; she stood in the sunny street, her eyes downcast. Presently, she looked up at him.

"Mr. Van Cleef!" she said. "I—won't you *please*—look after your health?"

"What?" he said, startled. Then he understood her. "I see…" he said. "Thanks, dear."

On the way back to the house, he thought about that.

"Means alcohol," he thought. "'Take care of my 'health,' so I can go on and on—nowhere…. No. Something's broken. Mainspring?"

They were still at lunch when he entered the house, and he went quickly and quietly up to his own room.

"Something wrong about Annie Downes," he thought. "Blanche felt it. Well, suppose she did try to poison Harry? Where do we go from here? And Papa Dulac calls Emilia a murderess…. And Lizzy Carroll thinks it was a case for the police. And Russell 'knows.' Russell knows everything. I have only one idea, but it is a sound one. Emilia's got to give up this place, go somewhere else. Annie and Harry can settle their differences elsewhere…."

He stayed shut in his room, because he did not want to talk. But he had nothing to read, nothing to do; he walked up and down, smoking, thinking; and disgusted, bored with his thoughts.

"What was Papa Dulac doing here? Emilia's afraid of Blanche. Why? Maybe no reason. She's not a reasonable creature…. Downes…. Maybe he doesn't think he's been poisoned, or maybe he doesn't mind. Or maybe he's afraid to mention it."

There was a knock at the door.

"It's Russell!"

"This is my silent hour," said Van Cleef. "Meditating."

"I'd like to speak to you."

"I'll have to resist the temptation."

"It's important."

Van Cleef opened the door, and the boy entered.

"I've had that cereal drink analysed," he said. "There was arsenic in it."

"You have a one-track mind."

Russell stood looking straight at him.

"Of course," he said, "if you don't want this cleared up, that's all right with me. I don't give a damn whether or not all these people poison one another. I'll drop it if you like. I thought that very likely you had all the fine old traditions of justice, and truth, and so on."

"Drop it!" said Van Cleef. "Find another diversion, more suitable to your age. There's a Country Club here. Emilia's a member. Tell her you'd like to play tennis there this afternoon."

"What about going back to New York?"

"Good idea!" said Van Cleef. "Nothing much here for you."

"I mean, going together."

"No. I can't, just now."

"You prefer to stay here until there's another attempt at murder? Possibly successful the next time."

"Yes," said Van Cleef, with a great sigh.

"You won't take it seriously?"

"I won't take it at all," said Van Cleef. "Rather leave it. There's nothing to worry about, and anyhow, I'm not good at worrying. Let me have peace."

"You've come to the wrong place for 'peace,'" said Russell, and went out.

Later in the afternoon, Van Cleef was obliged to agree with that. A door was opened, and slammed shut; someone was knocking; he looked out, and it was Major Bramwell, knocking at a door across the hall. Lizzy Carroll opened it.

"May I request you, madam," he said "to—*move* that radio?"

"Don't bother me!" she said. "I've just got a very good programme—"

"You—your instrument is placed directly against the wall of my room, causing a—vibration—"

"Change your room. Emilia suggested it—"

"I won't!" he cried. "I won't! I came here first—"

"You're unbelievably childish," she said, looking at him in a sort of scornful wonder. "And you're a nuisance. I'm going back to listen to my programme, and if you knock on the wall again, you'll be sorry."

"You're—you're *insane!*" he cried. "You take an insane pleasure in torment-

ing people. I know very well who's responsible for the persecution I've been sub-
jected to. Persecution—"

Miss Carroll retired into her room and closed the door; he stood there, scarlet with rage.

"Might take a walk..." Van Cleef suggested. "Exercise—"

"You're insolent, sir!"

He came nearer to Van Cleef, his blue eyes glaring. And with a sigh, Van Cleef,
too, closed his door.

"Don't like quarrels," he said to himself.

After a few moments, he went in search of Emilia; for he was determined now
to make her abandon her enterprise.

"Never lived in a boarding-house before," he thought. "But still I'm sure the
atmosphere here isn't the usual thing. Too much gossip, so on. Emilia's fault,
maybe. Poor girl doesn't know how to cope with people—with anything."

He walked about the house, looking for her, and found her at last in the
kitchen; Harly was buttering and slicing bread, and she was supervising this.

"*Very* thin, Harly."

"Yes, madam."

She smiled at Van Cleef, but she was not, he thought, pleased to see him.

"We'll be having tea in a few moments, Arthur."

"Could we have tea alone?"

She went through the swing-door into the pantry before she answered.

"I can't do things like that, Arthur. It hurts other people's feelings."

"Meaning Bramwell?"

"Well, yes," she admitted. "He's very sensitive."

"Too sensitive. My dear girl, the whole set-up is wrong. Impossible—"

"He's fond of me," she said. "And nobody else is. Nobody else in the world."

Her charming face was incapable of expressing sorrow, even her voice was no
more than plaintive.

"I'm fond of you."

"Not very," she said. "You're *kind* to me, and that's quite different." There
was a pile of clean, folded napkins on the shelf; she took them up, one by one,
and made another pile of them. "I'm so lonely..." she said, in a low voice. "I'm
so lonely...."

"You needn't be, my dear girl. You won't be, if you get away from here. Come
to live in town. Different type of life. Friends."

"I have no friends, Arthur."

"That's nonsense, my dear girl. You have any number of friends. I hope I'm
one of them."

"There's no one really fond of me but Carlo," she said.

"Even if we admit that, my dear girl, what of it?"

"I can't live without love," she said.

That stopped him for a moment.

"I see," he said presently. "However, you can still come to live in town. Little apartment. Ask your friends to dinner—tea."

"What could I live on?"

"This fellow I told you about will buy the house—"

"I can't give up this house—my—home...."

"But, my dear girl.... This guest-house idea isn't pleasant for you, and it's not profitable."

"It's the only way I can keep my home."

"Home is where the heart is," he said in desperation.

She saw nothing out-of-the way in that.

"My heart is here, Arthur," she said. "Where Bill and I lived—together. I know Bill would want me to live here."

"If you feel like that," he said, "at least you'd better change your guests, my dear girl. Get rid of all of them. We'll find new ones—strangers, this time. Mistake, having friends."

"They're not friends. Not one of them, except Carlo."

"Will you do this?" he asked. "Will you tell the others—all except Carlo, if it has to be that way—that you're going to close the house for a while?"

"Let me think it over, Arthur."

"Don't!" he urged. "Tell them this evening. Get them out, and we'll make a fresh start."

"Please, Arthur, let me think it over."

"Until this evening."

"Yes," she said. "I'll think carefully, Arthur, and I'll tell you this evening."

"Promise?"

"I promise," she said. "Now, here's Harly with the tea. You'll join us—"

"No, thanks!" he said, and then changed his mind. "Better have another look at them," he thought. "Especially Annie."

He was surprised to see Downes in the drawing-room. "I thought it would do me good," Downes explained. "Lying in bed is weakening."

They all assembled. Mrs. Downes, Miss Carroll, the Major, even Russell; and it was a scene of harmonious politeness. Russell sat on the floor beside Miss Carroll, and they talked in low tones, paying no attention to anyone else. Annie and Harry Downes sat, one on each side of Van Cleef, talking as they always talked, about little restaurants in Paris, London, Venice, telling bits of news about people he knew or didn't know. The Major sat on the sofa beside Emilia, and was attentive and deferential to her.

"When are you going abroad again, Arthur?" asked Mrs. Downes.

"I don't know," he answered, and he thought, "Never. Why travel just to meet the Downeses somewhere else? I'm better off at home. Home, I said to Emilia, is where the heart is. How true! How do you think of these things, Mr. Van Cleef? Blanche calls me Mr. Van Cleef.... It wouldn't bore her to travel. She'd be happy. She's alive, said please take care of your health.... Meaning, can't you lay off the whisky? I wish I had a drink now."

"Mr. Van Cleef!"

It was Major Bramwell standing before him. Van Cleef rose, frowning uneasily beneath the steady glare of those blue eyes.

"Is he going to fly at me?" he thought. "Embarrassing.... Shall I have to knock him down?"

"Mr. Van Cleef! Will you take a drink with me, sir?"

"What's this?" thought Van Cleef.

"I have a small private stock of liquor," the Major went on. "I imported it myself. If you'll do me the honour—"

"Thanks!" said Van Cleef. "Thanks very much!"

"I propose that we go into the conservatory," said the Major.

No one else seemed surprised, or even interested in this invitation; the Major led the way across the drawing-room and opened the glass door into the dusty little wilderness. He closed the door, and even the curtains that covered the glass, Van Cleef noted, were dusty and somehow brittle-looking, like scorched paper.

"I've told the boy to bring both cognac and Scotch," said the Major. "Good quality.... Cigar, sir?"

"Thanks, but I'll stick to cigarettes."

The Major sat down at the bamboo table and cut off the end of a cigar.

"The—er—*amende honorable*," he observed.

"I see," said Van Cleef. Harly came in then, with glasses, two bottles, and a siphon of soda.

"Which do you prefer, sir?" asked the Major.

"Scotch, any day," Van Cleef answered.

"Personally, I prefer cognac. I—er—I'm glad to have this opportunity, sir, to—express my regret for a certain attitude towards you, which was entirely due to a misunderstanding. I apologize."

"Very good of you. Here's wishing you luck!"

They drank.

"What d'you think of the whisky?" asked the Major.

"Oh, excellent!" Van Cleef answered.

The Major began to relate some of his experiences in the Philippines, and Van Cleef sat in unhappy silence; the stories were dusty, stale, melancholy, like the room in which they sat. There was no air....

"Another drink, Van Cleef? Come, come! I insist!"

"No, thanks," said Van Cleef.

He felt sick. Very sick. He sat still while a ghastly nausea came over him like a tide, ebbed, came back; the world swooped up and down, sweat broke out on him, his breath came fast. He was blind now; he could not see the Major, could only hear his voice, very far away.

"Dying...?" he thought.

VIII

"Are you feeling better?" she kept on asking. "Are you feeling better now?" She kept on asking it, a hundred, a thousand, a million times, so that, to put an end to it, he came back from somewhere and said, "Yes."

"Drink this, Arthur," she said. "Drink this...." She put her arm under his neck, bending his head forward, and pain shot between his eyes like a knife-thrust.

"Please!" he said.

The rim of a glass touched his teeth. He swallowed what was offered, and she let him lie back again, and have that headache. There was nothing left in the world but that headache, and nausea. He didn't go to sleep; he went spinning round and round in a blackness where little lights whirled.

"Are you feeling better, Arthur?"

He knew now that it was Emilia, miles away.

"Yes," he told her.

"Try to drink this, Arthur...."

It was coffee; the smell of it was sickening.

"Rather—rest, thanks..." he said.

"Just drink this first, Arthur."

He could see her face now, enormous, sorrowful black eyes that grew wider and wider until he was lost in them. Again his head was raised, again with that savage thrust of pain, again he drank to be let alone. But he was getting better. The hot, black coffee was driving out the cold nausea.

"Take one more cup, Arthur...."

She wore a long, pale blue robe, her black hair was loose about her face, she had a cup in one hand, and, he thought, a candle in the other. Coming towards him down an endless corridor, with a candle and a cup of poison.

"Poison...?" he said.

"No. It's coffee, Arthur."

"The dagger, or the bowl..." he said anxiously. He didn't quite understand that; but it was important.

"Please, Arthur, drink it!"

Not a candle; it was a shaded lamp behind her. He drank what she gave him, because he must. Her little fingers clasped his wrist, cold fingers. The wind that blew in at the open window was cold; it was good to breathe.

"Are you better?"

"I'd like a cigarette," he said.

She gave him one, and held a match for him. It made him feel sick and dizzy for a moment, but are you getting better, Arthur, getting better....

"What happened to me?" he asked.

"It's all over now," she said. "Just rest, and you'll feel all right in a little while."

"No," he said, and began remembering. The dusty conservatory, the Major's voice going on and on.... The sun had been shining then, outside the dusty glass, and now it was night....

"What happened, Emilia?"

"It doesn't matter, Arthur, dear...."

"Sorry.... Does matter..." he said. "What happened?"

"Aa-rthur, dear.... Nobody knows, except Carlo and myself, and we'll never mention it."

It was difficult and unpleasant, to think with such a headache.

"Won't mention what?" he asked.

"What happened. It was an accident. We both understand—"

"It wasn't an accident," he said. "Someone gave me something."

"Arthur, *don't* say that!" she cried. "It's dreadful!"

The thinking was going better now.

"My dear girl," he said, "I've been quite uncomfortable.... I don't like it."

"You didn't realize...."

"Realize what?"

"I've seen Bill like this, often enough," she said.

"You're not trying to say I was drunk, are you?"

"Arthur dear, we both know you didn't realize—"

"I had one drink," he said. "A small one, too."

She said nothing.

"Another cigarette, please," he said. "What time is it? Eleven.... Look here, my dear girl, I had *one drink*."

"All right, Arthur," she said, with her dainty little smile.

"Does Bramwell say that I had more?"

"I—it doesn't matter in the least, dear."

"I want to see Bramwell. Now."

"He's gone to bed."

"He can get up then."

"Please, Arthur, don't make a scene! It's quite bad enough—"

"I think so. Mind going away for a while? I want to get up."

"Arthur, *please* don't try to see Carlo! He was as kind and nice as possible, getting you up here, without anyone seeing, except Harly.... He understands perfectly."

"Emilia, did he tell you I was drunk?"

"He didn't need to tell me," she said, curtly.

"I'll tell you now that I've been poisoned."

"It hasn't done you much harm," she said, in the same curt tone, a tone he had never before heard her use.

"Still and all, I don't like it," he said. "I don't seem to feel resigned."

"To-morrow morning you'll realize—" she began.

"Sorry, but I'm not going to wait," he said. "Mind leaving me while I get up?"

She turned away, crossed the room; she took the key out of the lock and, closing the door after her, locked it on the outside.

"*Bien alors!*" he said aloud.

When he got out of bed, it was bad, extremely bad. But anger sustained him. He hadn't felt anger for years; he had forgotten what it was like, what warmth, what energy it gave. He had been undressed, and put into pyjamas by someone; he didn't bother about a dressing-gown; in bare feet, he went into the bathroom and knocked at the door that led to Russell's room.

The boy opened the door promptly.

"What's the matter?" he demanded. "You look like hell."

"Yes. I want to get out through your room."

Russell asked no questions, attempted no interference. Van Cleef went past him and out into the corridor; he knocked at Bramwell's door. He waited; no answer, he knocked again, louder, and the next door opened and Lizzy Carroll came out. For a moment she did not speak, only looked at him, with her thin lips compressed, and pity in her eyes.

"You'd better get back to bed, Arthur," she said in a whisper.

"I have to see Bramwell—"

"Come!" she said, firmly, and took his arm.

He yielded, let her lead him across the corridor, unlock his door, enter with him. He could think of nothing to say that would sound in any way convincing. "Go to bed, and to sleep, Arthur," she said.

"Lizzy," he said, "I *haven't* been drinking."

"Arthur," she said, with a great compassion, "it's been a good many years since you could say that truthfully."

"I had just one drink this afternoon. This is—something else."

"I have some sleeping-tablets," she said. "They're quite harmless. I'll get you one."

"You don't believe me, Lizzy?"

She regarded him, still with her lips compressed into a thin line.

"No," she said, after a pause. "Get a good night's sleep, Arthur. We can talk things over in the morning. I'll get you a tablet—"

"No, thanks, Lizzy."

"You'd better, Arthur. You don't want to go wandering around the house like this."

"I shan't wander any more, Lizzy."

He lit a cigarette, and she frowned.

"That's dangerous," she said. "Suppose you were to fall asleep?"

"I shan't."

She looked so small and neat, in her flannel dressing-gown, with her red hair in two braids; she looked so anxious and unhappy.... He laid his hand on her shoulder.

"Don't worry, Lizzy," he said. "I shan't wander, or set the house on fire. Or have D.T.s."

She reached up and kissed his cheek. He was astonished, greatly touched; he put his arm about her shoulders and hugged her.

"Good night, dear!" he said.

"Good night, Arthur!"

He stood staring at the closed door.

"It's—worse than you'd think..." he said to himself. "You get in the habit of being believed. Sort of shock, not to be."

He went into the bathroom again; the door into Russell's room stood open and he saw the boy, sitting facing him, in his shirt-sleeves, relaxed, sombre.

"What's wrong with you?" Russell asked.

"What d'you think?" asked Van Cleef.

"Take a look in the mirror," said Russell.

"No...."

"When you didn't come down to dinner, I made enquiries," said Russell. "It was all very mysterious. You had indigestion. Mrs. Swan was with you. I came to the door and asked if I could see you. She said you were asleep; but I could hear you muttering. I told her I knew a little about medicine; I pretty well begged her to let me in. But she wouldn't. I waited in here, with the door a little open—and when she went out for a moment, I got in to see you."

Van Cleef went to the window and looked out; the stars were bright and clear in the sky.

"I gave you an antidote," said Russell. "If I hadn't, you'd be dead now."

"Not dead," said Van Cleef. "I think I'll get a spot of sleep, now."

"Do you understand what I've just told you?" cried Russell, springing to his feet. "You were poisoned!"

There was a fierce, blazing look in his dark eyes, an imperious ring in his voice, and it was intolerable; it was like hearing someone shriek.

"'Night!" said Van Cleef.

"Are you going to let the murderer—"

Van Cleef went through the bathroom, into his own room, and locked the door; he sat down on the bed, his hands clasped loosely between his knees.

"No!" he said to himself. "No!"

It was a revulsion almost physical; it was as if he had witnessed a scene of disgusting violence. Then in a little while, he began to think.

"I was going to make it worse.... God! Going to drag out Bramwell, and accuse him.... Yell at him.... Standing out there in pyjamas and bare feet—banging on the door.... I know how I looked to Lizzy."

He got up and went over to the mirror that hung over the chest of drawers; he stood there and looked at himself. His eyes were narrowed, lined at the corners; his face was haggard, pallid; his short, fair hair was wildly ruffled.

"Yes," he said to himself, "that's what I look like—to everyone. That's what I am. Take care of your health, Mr. Van Cleef.... Don't get murdered. You're too valuable." He leaned forward, to look more closely at himself. "Wish you were dead," he said.

His knees felt weak, his head still ached, he still felt sick.

"But it's not much more than a supreme hangover," he thought. "I've felt almost as bad as this, without poison. The murderer is the Major? Rather crude. He's not very bright, but even he.... Harly brought in the two bottles. They'd both been opened before; I noticed that. Then we have to assume that the Major planned it all in advance, and that he was reasonably sure I'd take whisky, instead of cognac. Why did he—Well, never mind about motives. He may be jealous. He may be a homicidal maniac. Tried to kill Downes, too. Extremely amateurish work. His victims don't die. But that's because Russell always saves their lives. Russell...."

He sat down and lit a cigarette, and observed that he had one, freshly lighted, lying in an ashtray.

"He knows all about poisons, and antidotes, and everything else..." he thought. "He had the opportunity, along with everyone else in the house. And he's more suitable. Far more suitable. The poisonings begin when he arrives—"

Had they? He remembered what Blanche had told him. Her father called Emilia a murderess.

"What must I do?" he thought. "Suppose I go to the police, and tell them I've been poisoned? Emilia, and Lizzy, probably Harly, and probably Bramwell would swear I was drunk. Then I'd say that, the night before, Downes was poisoned, and he and his wife both deny it. I then go on to say I've heard that Bill Swan was poisoned. At that point, they either kick me out, or lock me up in a padded cell. What must I do?"

For it was clear to him now that he must do something. It was his responsibility. He didn't know why it should be, but he had to acknowledge it.

"I won't be working along with Russell," he thought. "That's very definite. In fact—he's got to go. To-morrow. I think I'm sorry for him; but just the same, he goes. I wonder if there are any of these private detectives? Like in a book.... Quiet, gentlemanly young fellow.... I bring him here as a friend of mine.... Only, where do I find him? And if I did find one of those, and he did get the truth—would I like it? If it's Emilia.... Even if it's Annie Downes, gone queer.... What I want isn't to punish the malefactor. I want to put a stop to this. Downes and I are none the worse. If I can make sure there won't be any more attempts...."

He could think of no possible approach; the whole thing was impossibly difficult, and distressing, and he wanted to be rid of it. He had had no private problems for a long time, a very long time; other people appealed to him, often enough, and he assisted them with money, and with his advice, always vague, yet curiously apt. But he hadn't been worried; he had forgotten how to be worried.

"I want to be let alone..." he thought, irritably. "I can't turn sleuth at this time of life."

He got into bed and turned out the light. Through the window he could see the stars in the sky, very clear and bright. "You'd have been dead," Russell had told him.

"Not very important," he said to himself.

When he closed his eyes, he had a sudden vision of Blanche, standing in the sun. And such regret came to him, such grief, for his youth, his love, for all that was gone....

"I want a drink!" he cried in his heart.

But he did not take one. He lay still, and let that black and bitter tide wash over him, until it was exhausted, and he slept.

The morning was bad. But he had had plenty of bad mornings, and they always passed. He bathed; he shaved with an unsteady hand, he went downstairs, and found no one about except Harly, laying the tables. He watched Harly for a few moments; slim, neat and deft, still a boy. He couldn't actually be a boy; he must be middle-aged, but there was nothing to show that.

"How about Harly?" thought Van Cleef. "He could poison people. And if I keep steadfastly to the homicidal idea, he's as good as anyone. The maniac simplifies things. No bother about motives."

Harly caught sight of him then.

"Breakfast, sir?"

"Thanks. Was it you who got me to bed last night, Harly?"

"Yes, sir." Harly was eagerly respectful, as usual; he did not seem at all embarrassed by the question; he stood as if waiting for more.

"That whisky of Major Bramwell's didn't seem to agree with me," Van Cleef went on, tentatively. "Only had one drink, as I remember."

"Yes, sir. Wasn't but one drink gone from the bottle."

"Unusual.... I'd like to have a look at that bottle, Harly."

"Major took the bottles up to his own room, sir."

"Where did you get them from yesterday?"

"Major's room, sir."

"Brought them straight to the conservatory?"

"No, sir. Major told me to bring them down before tea; I left them on the sideboard in here, sir, till he'd be ready for them."

"Did you—did the Major ever give you a drink?"

"I'm a teetotaller, sir."

"I don't think it was good whisky."

"No, sir," said Harly.

"Does he mean anything by that?" thought Van Cleef. There was nothing to be read in Harly's face, or in his tone, but he still had an air of waiting alertly. He decided to go on. "Night before last," he said, "I saw a man lurking around the place."

"Yes, sir."

"I thought he might be one of these fellows who sell liquor. They say they've bought it from a ship's steward, something like that, sell it cheap. I wonder if the Major gets his liquor from someone like that?"

"Didn't come to see the Major, sir. Came to see Mr. Downes."

"And did he see Mr. Downes?"

"Yes, sir."

"Did he get into the house?"

"Just into the kitchen, sir. There they had words."

"What words?"

"Didn't say much, sir. Man knocked at the door and gave me an envelope, told me to give it to Mr. Downes. So I took it upstairs—"

"Leave the man alone in the kitchen while you went upstairs?"

"No, sir. Left him outside the back door."

"He could have come in?"

"Yes, sir. I gave the envelope to Mr. Downes, and Mr. Downes, he came downstairs, and he went out to speak to the man. And he came sort of rushing in, and the man after him and pushed Mr. Downes against the wall. Then he saw me in the pantry, and he cursed and went out."

"Mr. Downes say anything?"

"Yes, sir. Mr. Downes said that the man must have been drinking."

"Did you get that impression?"

"No, sir."

"Did you know the man?"

"Yes, sir," said Harly.

"What did you think about the whole thing, Harly?"

"Didn't think, sir," said Harly.

This was somewhat disconcerting.

"Know anything about the man, Harly?"

"Know his name, sir, and where he works."

"You didn't think it was—even interesting, for him to shove Mr. Downes around?"

"Didn't think about it, sir. I have a lot of work to do now, sir, with the cook gone. Too busy to think."

"I suppose you told Mrs. Swan, of course."

"No, sir. I never told anybody but *you*, sir."

The emphasis on the pronoun puzzled Van Cleef.

"Why me?" he asked.

"Remember you from the old days, sir, when you used to come visiting Mr. Swan. Seemed like you were the right one to tell, sir."

"Ever see the man here before, Harly?"

"Yes, sir. Saw him on the balcony, upstairs."

"What?" said Van Cleef, startled.

"Yes, sir. Was a Sunday afternoon, and most everybody was out. I went around that side of the house—"

"Which side?"

"East, sir. And I saw him climbing down off'n the balcony."

"What did you do?"

"Didn't do anything, sir.".

"Didn't tell anyone?"

"I told Mrs. Swan, sir, when she came back from the tea-party she was at."

"What did she say?"

"Didn't say anything, sir."

There was a muffled sort of knocking.

"Excuse me, sir, but that's the boy with the eggs," said Harly. "I'll have your breakfast ready in ten minutes, sir."

Van Cleef turned back into the lounge, opened the door, and stepped out on the veranda. It was a sweet morning, fresh and cool.

"It's one thing to get information," he thought, "and it's another thing to have any idea what it means. Dulac the murderer? I'd prefer him not to be, for strictly personal reasons. Blanche wouldn't like it. Seven-thirty.... I suppose she's up now. Maybe this is one of the days when she'll want to be a human being, and not go to work...."

He lit a cigarette, and sighed.

"Next step is to inspect the premises," he thought. "Never occurred to me that you could climb down from that balcony. Climb up, too? That would make it more complicated.... I can't suspect Russell wholeheartedly any more. He couldn't very well have had anything to do with Dulac or the balcony, and Dulac shoving Downes around. And Swan...."

There was dew on the grass, and the sun made it glitter. He had seen hundreds of summer mornings, but never, he thought, one so lovely. He turned the corner of the house; a gravel path ran along the side of the veranda and on the opposite side of the path was a rock garden planted by Bill. Like all the things he had left behind, it had turned to dust; there was nothing planted there, only weeds, and the struggling survivors of hardy plants.

And there was something else there this morning. There was a small brown figure, lying on the rocks, flat as a leaf. He ran to it and turned it over.

"*Lizzy!*" he cried.

She was never going to answer anyone again.

IX

Her face was not disfigured; there was only one small cut on her cheek that had bled a little. She looked composed and quiet, almost amused, her eyes closed, her brown flannel dressing-gown belted neatly about her waist. Her hand was cold, but not stiff.

"Lizzy..." he said. "My dear girl...."

She looked so *little*.... He rose from his knees beside her, and stood looking down at her for a time. The sun shone in her face, he covered it with his handkerchief. Then he went to the back door, and entered the kitchen. Harly was at the stove.

"Harly," he said, "telephone for whatever doctor comes here. And send for the police. There's been an accident to Miss Carroll."

Harly stared at him with his mouth open, suddenly become stupid, idiotic.

"Telephone—" Van Cleef began.

"Yes, sir!" said Harly, becoming alert again.

Van Cleef went back to Lizzy Carroll.

"How long has she been alone?" he thought. "I was talking to Harly—I was so near.... When did this happen to her?"

Then he thought with a shock, *"How* did this happen to her?"

He looked up at the balcony, and he saw that part of the iron railing had carried away; all of it was eaten with rust. "Leaned against it and fell?" he asked himself.

It didn't matter much, now. She was gone, and in his heart was the feeling that she had gone too soon, before she was ready.

"Enjoyed life," he thought. "Knew how to live. I wish she could have known I wasn't drunk last night.... But she was still my friend...."

The breeze stirred the hem of her nightdress beneath the dressing-gown; her feet were bare; narrow little feet.

"Oh, God! I'm sorry!" he said to her.

He took out a cigarette, but he did not light it.

"She wouldn't like me to smoke," he thought. "She'd say: 'I did think you'd have enough self-control not to smoke beside my dead body.'"

Harly came out to him; stopped with a very hasty glance at Miss Carroll.

"Dr. Robinson is coming, sir, and the police. Shall I tell Mrs. Swan?"

"I wouldn't know..." said Van Cleef, frowning. He felt that perhaps he should be the one to tell Emilia, but he was not going to leave Lizzy Carroll lying out here alone. "She'd hate it," he thought. Harly was waiting. "Better tell her, Harly," he said, and Harly went.

Van Cleef stood in the path, a lonely sentinel, hands in his pockets, his head bent, his big shoulders hunched, so lost in his meditations upon this friend that he did not hear a car come up the drive, did not notice the appearance of a man until a voice spoke:

"I'm Doctor Robinson."

A jaunty fellow, Doctor Robinson was, neat and slim, with a little toothbrush moustache, and a bow tie; youngish, with bright brown eyes.

"Name's Van Cleef. An old friend of Miss Carroll's."

The doctor knelt beside Miss Carroll, and Van Cleef strolled off a little way down the path. He waited until he heard the doctor's step behind him.

"D'you know how this happened, Mr. Van Cleef?" he asked, with a pleasant smile.

"No," said Van Cleef, resenting that smile.

A door banged, someone came running down the steps of the veranda. Emilia came running round the corner of the house. She wore a green linen blouse with long sleeves, a pleated black skirt; she ran daintily in her high-heeled pumps.

"Doctor *Robinson!*" she cried, and caught his sleeve. "It's suicide!"

"Emilia!" said Van Cleef, aghast.

"It's suicide!" she repeated, looking fervently into the doctor's face. And he continued smiling pleasantly. They were incredible.

"Of course, if you have any information, Mrs. Swan, the police—"

"Do the police have to come?"

"I'm afraid so."

"I—saw her do it...."

"Emilia," said Van Cleef, again, "come into the house."

"I want to tell Doctor Robinson first—"

"No."

"I *must*, Arthur! It's important! I saw poor Lizzy—"

The doctor looked at Van Cleef, still with that unfading smile, but his bright eyes were serious.

"I think it would be advisable to go into the house, Mrs. Swan," he said. "The police will be—occupied here...." Still smiling, he took her hand from his sleeve, and laid it upon Van Cleef's arm, as if making him a present. "And, y'see, your evidence will be of vital importance, Mrs. Swan. Miss Carroll was not killed by the fall."

"Not."

"No, oh, no!" he said.

"Then what?"

"There'll he an enquiry," he said, "And—" he paused, "I'd be inclined to say that Miss Carroll has been lying here for some time," he said. "An hour—possibly longer." He obviously intended that she should get that clear in her mind. "*At least* an hour," he said.

"Come on, Emilia!" said Van Cleef.

She walked by his side to the front of the house.

"Where, Arthur?" she asked.

"Conservatory," he answered, and they went in there; he closed the door. "Emilia, don't tell that story to the police."

"What story, Arthur?"

"Don't say you saw Lizzy commit suicide."

"I—I thought I did," she said, faintly.

"Where were you when 'you thought you did'? Where could you be, to see the balcony outside her room?"

"Arthur!" she cried. "Please... I—only thought it would be better—"

"For whom?"

"For—everyone. It's so horrible—when the police come.... Everything—the most private things—all dragged out...." She stood with her hand on the back of a chair, her lashes lowered. "I'm sure, Lizzy herself wouldn't like—all that publicity...."

"Nothing to worry about in Lizzy's private life," Van Cleef said, briefly. And all the time he was thinking: "She never looked at Lizzy. Never even turned her head. Not once."

"Arthur, she was older than she admitted. She was forty-two. I *know* that."

He looked away from her.

"Arthur.... Please!"

"I'm sorry," he said. "I can't understand you."

"Oh, please don't say that!" she cried, with such anguish that he was startled.

"I don't. I can't," he said.

"I thought *you* did. I never know how to explain things. I never have."

"Explain?"

"I'm—fighting for my life!" she said.

"Emilia!"

"I am! I am!"

"But how? What do you—" The doorbell rang. "Don't tell that story to the police!" he said, in haste. "For God's sake, don't tell them any lies. You'll make it worse for yourself."

"I couldn't. I wish I was dead."

"Sergeant Warren is here, madam."

"Show him in," said Van Cleef, before she could speak. Sergeant Warren entered, a stout man, bald, with an ivory-coloured face of severe calm.

"Mrs. Swan?" he said. "Like to ask you a few questions, madam." He glanced at Van Cleef.

"I'm the one who found the—found Miss Carroll."

"That so?" said the Sergeant, raising his almost invisible eyebrows. "Then maybe you'll give me a little information.... Name—occupation—no occupation?—age—address.... Did you note the posture of the body, Mr. Van leef? Did you move, or in any way disturb— Were you acquainted with the deceased?"

"Yes, I've known her for years."

"When did you last see deceased?"

"Last night—about eleven."

"What was the occasion?"

"I wasn't felling well, and Miss Carroll asked if she could do anything for me."

"What impression did you get about Miss Carroll? Was she cheerful, for instance?"

"Yes," he answered, curtly, "Miss Carroll was just as usual."

"She wasn't in unusually high spirits, for instance?"

"She was not."

"You state you've known deceased for years. Did you ever have reason to think she was addicted to the use of any drug, or drugs?"

"I'd take an oath that she was not."

"How is that? Did you ever discuss the subject with her? Ever hear her mention any drug, or drugs?"

Then Van Cleef remembered that she had offered him a sleeping-tablet; quite harmless, she had said. The Sergeant was waiting for an answer, but he took his time.

"No!" he said, at last. "Nobody who knew Miss Carroll would think for a moment that she was addicted to drugs; she was a woman of courage and—highest character."

The Sergeant wrote something in a notebook; Van Cleef wondered if he were writing that Lizzy had been a woman of courage, and the highest character. He glanced up.

"This may be important," he explained. "It may be that you were the last to see the deceased alive." He asked a few more questions, then he turned to Emilia. Her name? Her age? Thirty-seven. Occupation?

"I take paying guests," she answered, and Van Cleef wondered if the Sergeant wrote that down verbatim.

Had she known deceased long? Yes, for years. Ten years at least. When had she last seen deceased? A little after dinner, last night. Had Miss Carroll seemed to her in good spirits?

"No," said Emilia, "she was very much depressed. She said she had a bad headache. I asked her if she wanted some aspirin, and she said she had something better than that."

"Say what it was she had?"

"No. She was always very nervous, and highly-strung."

"Would you say she was subject to fits of depression?"

"Yes."

"Did she, to your knowledge, have any financial, or other worries?"

"I know she was worried about *something.*"

Van Cleef turned his back, lit a cigarette, and looked out through the dusty panes.

"Fighting for her life?" he thought. "And this is the way she's 'fighting'....
Against a dead woman." At the first moment of silence, he turned to the Sergeant. "There'll be an autopsy, won't there?"

"Yes. Now, Mrs. Swan, can you give the name or names of deceased's near-
est relatives?"

"She didn't have anyone, much," Emilia answered. "She always said she liked
the friends she picked out better than the relatives that had been picked out for
her. I can give you the names—"

"I was an old friend," said Van Cleef. "I'll look after the arrangements. I'll get
in touch with her lawyer, Ross. Know him well. Finished with me?"

"For the moment. There'll be an inquest. We'll notify you."

"Au revoir!" said Van Cleef, and went off across the drawing-room, to the hall.
He saw Annie Downes in the dining-room, alone.

"Arthur!" she said, raising her voice. He went to her table, and she patted the
chair next to her. "Sit down with me?" she said. "Harry went back to bed when
he heard.... Any sort of shock gives him this dreadful nervous indigestion."

"Not—bad, is he?" asked Van Cleef.

"Oh, no! Harly's taking him a tray. If he rests, he's always better. Isn't it a sad
thing? Poor Lizzy!"

"Very dangerous, that balcony," said Van Cleef, glancing sidelong at her.
"Railing's crumbling away."

"Do you think the fall killed her?" asked Mrs. Downes.

"What else?"

"I thought that perhaps she had one of her heart attacks.... She suffered so horribly with them. Angina, you know."

"I didn't know."

"I was with her once, when she had one. I remember there was some sort of
capsule she told me to break and hold under her nose. I was very thankful that
Harry wasn't there. He can't stand the sight of suffering."

Harly brought their breakfast; Van Cleef drank black coffee.

"There'll be an autopsy," he thought. "The police will find out the truth. Not
my job, thank God!"

He had no theory as to how Lizzy Carroll had died; he made no attempt to
form one, he did not want to form one. The thing that mattered was, that she
shouldn't be slandered.

"Too early to catch Ross," he thought, looking at his watch. He went upstairs
with Mrs. Downes; she went to see her ailing Harry, and Van Cleef went into
his own room. The bed was not yet made; the place had somehow a debauched
look in the morning sun; two unemptied ash-trays, two bottles of whisky on the
chest of drawers.

"I need a drink," he thought. He took up the open bottle and stared at it, and
set it down; with a sigh that lifted the leaden oppression from his heart, he
thought of Blanche. It seemed to him that everyone else was old, sad, timid; and

only she was young and honest, and brave. It was a good world, if she were alive in it. "Suppose Mr. Van Cleef did 'take care of his health'?" he asked himself. "He was a sick man last night, but here he is alive. What are you going to do about being alive, Mr. Van Cleef?"

There was a knock at the door. "Come in!" he said, and in came Russell. He had forgotten Russell, and it was no pleasure to be reminded of him.

"Better go home," he suggested. "Mean to say there's plenty of trouble here for Mrs. Swan. The fewer people in the house, the better."

Russell sat down on the unmade bed.

"There's more trouble on the way," he said.

"You think."

"I know," said Russell.

He looked sulky and miserable; and Van Cleef felt sorry for him.

"Look here!" he said, with a somewhat anxious smile. "I've been a bit short-tempered with you. Sorry. You've tried to be helpful. Only—I wish you would-n't be. I—Miss Carroll was a friend of mine. It's upsetting.... The rest of it does-n't interest me at the moment."

"It certainly doesn't interest me," said Russell. "It's turned out to be so damned obvious. But I was afraid you'd be unhappy if any more of your friends got murdered."

"There haven't been any murders. Hold on! Let me finish! I'll admit that someone gave me something unpleasant, and apparently to Downes, too. Whether with intent to kill or not, I don't know, and neither do you. I'm not making light of the situation. It's ugly. I'm going to put it to an end in the only possible way, and that is, by breaking up the group here."

"That will be too late. There's a killer loose here," said Russell.

"Meaning a fiend who's going to go on poisoning people? No. Sorry. That doesn't click. I feel I'd recognize a fiend if I met him."

"You've met the killer."

"Potential killer, maybe. As I pointed out, nobody knows whether or not Downes and myself were meant to die."

"Miss Carroll's dead."

"She's dead. And the police will look after that."

"I've just been talking to Doctor Robinson. He knows my uncle, and for that reason he was indulgent to my boyish curiosity. There's going to be an autopsy. But no analyses."

"No analyses.... Oh, I see what you mean."

"They'll find exactly what Robinson intends to find; a diseased condition of the heart. He treated Miss Carroll for that. He was almost ready to give a cer-tificate without a post-mortem, when Mrs. Swan began talking about sui-cide."

"I see what you're getting at, of course. Forget it."

"She was murdered," said Russell.

"*Will* have someone murdered, won't you? No.... Forget it. Go back to town now.... I'll see you there in a few days, when this is over."

"My God!" cried Russell. "Isn't there *anything* I can do? I know that woman was murdered, and I know how she was murdered. I tried to tell that grinning fool of a doctor. I'm trying to tell you. But nobody—"

Van Cleef rose, and laid his hand on the boy's shoulder.

"Take it easy!" he said, with a sort of gentleness. "Mistake to think everyone else is a fool. Dangerous mistake. Go home, and leave this to the doctor and the police."

The boy sat motionless, a blank look on his face. Van Cleef withdrew his hand and lit a cigarette.

"Oh, get out!" he cried in his heart.

The boy rose.

"I've tried to tell you," he said. "I've tried to warn you. There's been one murder done, and there's going to be another." He paused. "Unless you'll listen to me," he said.

"Look here!" said Van Cleef. "You're getting a bit pathological. Mean to say, it's bad, it's dangerous, to be the one person on earth who's always right. I'll have a word with Doctor Robinson, and if there's anything amiss in Miss Carroll's death, he'll find it out. Not your headache. Hop into your car, and drive home."

"Home?" said Russell with a smile. "All right! I'll go. You can enjoy the next murder in peace."

X

Harly came in to make the bed and Van Cleef stood aside, watching him. Harly didn't look at him, and did not talk, would not suddenly begin to talk. "Too much talking," thought Van Cleef. "I'm going to stay shut up here until it's time to ring up Ross. Then I'll have a word with Robinson. Then I'll have a drink." He moved aside for the carpet-sweeper Harly was pushing. "Suppose I never took another drink? Would I go to pieces, or would I turn into something else? What else? Nothing probably. Probably too late."

Harly dropped the carpet-sweeper against the wall, and hastened out of the room; a telephone bell was ringing.

"Lot more talking to be done," thought Van Cleef. "I'll have to talk Emilia into closing this house. I don't feel like talking to her, ever again. Or seeing her."

"Telephone for you, sir," said Harly.

"Where's the telephone?"

"In the lounge, sir."

The Major was sitting in the lounge, reading a newspaper; he looked over it with his usual glare.

"Good morning, sir!" he said, challengingly. "I hear that imputations have been made—"

"Sorry!" said Van Cleef, and took up the receiver. "Hello!"

"Mr. Van Cleef?"

"None other," he said.

Strange, to hear *her* voice.

"Could I possibly see you?"

"Anything wrong, Blanche?" he said, alarmed.

"Yes," she said.

"I'll come," he said, and hung up the receiver.

"Arthur," said Mrs. Downes, "I must speak to you."

She was standing beside him with her knitting in her hand, a faintly annoyed look on her mild face.

"Got to run along to the village just now," he said, apologetically. "But I'll be back—"

"I must speak to you *before* you see Blanche," said she, in a low voice. "It's important."

"All right!" he said. "I'll be back in a moment."

"I'll meet you in the conservatory," said she.

He ran upstairs to Russell's room, found the boy there reading a pamphlet.

"Care to drive me down to the village in ten minutes?" he asked.

"Yes," Russell answered sullenly, and Van Cleef ran down the stairs again, and went to the conservatory, that spot, he thought, destined for unwelcome confidences.

"Annie's a dark horse," he thought. "Or is it a dark sheep?"

He had absolutely no curiosity as to what she might say, no interest. And he was not worried about Blanche, not disturbed; only impatient and strangely elated.

"Thought of me when something went wrong," he said to himself.

Annie Downes was sitting in a wicker chair, her eyes upon her swift-moving knitting needles.

"I happened to hear you say 'Blanche,'" she said. "I wondered if you knew?"

"Knew what?"

"I only found out, a little while ago," she went on. "But it seems that poor Lizzy knew, and I *imagine* the Major knows."

"Don't get you, Annie."

"About Blanche," she said. "Do you know who she is, Arthur?"

"No...."

"She's Bill Swan's child," said Mrs. Downes.

"Is that a rumour?"

"No, it's a fact. When I found out, I talked it over with poor Lizzy. *She'd* known from the beginning, but she and I didn't see it in the same light."

"How did Lizzy know?"

"She was here when the mother—Mrs. Dulac died. There was a frightful scene, she said. Dulac came, threatening to shoot Bill, and so on. He said his wife had been murdered."

"Like everybody else..." said Van Cleef.

"What's that, Arthur?"

"Sorry! Nothing.... How did you find out about this, Annie?"

"I can't tell you that, Arthur. But as soon as I did find out, I looked up the child. I asked her here, I talked to her. It's an outrage!"

"What is?"

Her eyes looked cold behind her glasses.

"She's a charming child—Bill's own daughter—and simply abandoned in poverty, and misery—"

"Hardly—"

"That Dulac is a workman of some sort! The child's had no education, no advantages. She doesn't even know the truth about herself."

"Better off, not knowing."

"Arthur, how can you say that? Is it better for her to think she's the daughter of a common workman, instead of Bill Swan's daughter?"

"Very much better."

"You're like Lizzy," she said. "That's what Lizzy said. But I don't agree. In Norway, or is it Sweden...?"

"Couldn't say."

"Well, in some country like that, they have a law.... There's no such thing as an illegitimate child. That's only just. It's not a child's fault."

"Did you tell Blanche?" he asked.

"No, I haven't. I *wanted* to tell her, and I think she has a *right* to know; but to be frank, Arthur, I didn't dare to tell her. I was afraid for my life."

"Annie!" he protested.

"Arthur," she said, leaning forward, "you don't *know* that woman! There's nothing she'd stop at, to gain her ends. Nothing! She wouldn't let Bill do anything for his child—"

"How do you know?"

"I do know. She wouldn't let Bill do anything. And she deliberately disregarded Bill's *dying* wishes."

"Annie, how do you know all this?"

"I can't tell you. But it's *all* true. With his dying breath, Bill asked Emilia to look after Blanche. And she promised that she *would*. She's—infamous!"

"No!"

"Arthur Van Cleef," she said, "you're a fool!"

She folded her arms and looked at him, exactly like a severe school teacher. "You're a fool!" she repeated. "You, and Major Bramwell, both of you...."

He was silent for a moment.

"Annie.... I've been thinking quite a bit, lately.... Whole set-up is bad.... Why don't you and Downes clear out, at once?"

She began to cry. She rose, letting her knitting fall to the floor; she stepped on it as she opened the door.

"I wish," she said, "I wish the house—would burn down—with her in it!" The door closed after her.

"So that's it?" he said to himself.

It seemed to him obvious that what so troubled Annie Downes was not his folly, and not Bramwell's.

"Must be Harry," he thought. "Is Emilia a Circe? Can't see it...."

He sat down, wanting and needing a few moments to think.

"It could be true about Blanche," he thought. "I wish it wasn't. I wish, anyhow, that she'd never have to know. Papa Dulac hasn't done badly by her. Better maybe than Bill ever would have done.... Rather fine thing for Papa Dulac to do. Bring up another man's child. Bring her up to be the honest, darling kid she is...."

"It's fifteen minutes," said Russell, opening the door. "I thought you'd want to be reminded."

"Yes, thanks. *Allons!*"

"Where?"

"Leave me at the railway station, will you? I have some telegrams to send." Russell smiled.

"All right! I'll wait for you—in the stationer's," he said, and said it with malice.

"On second thoughts," said Van Cleef, evenly, "I'll stop at the stationer's first. I want to speak to Blanche."

"She has a nice French sense of finance," Russell observed.

"Meaning—?"

"I called on her yesterday. And she asked me how much money you had; and if you were in love with anyone."

Van Cleef waited before he spoke.

"Well..." he said. "You're going home to-day; and after this, I won't have to believe in your existence."

"You're right. You can kick me back into limbo. You can hate me. I'm used to it. And, by God! This is the last time I'll ever try to—" He stopped, with a gasp like a sob. "Ever try to make a friend. I can't do it. I've tried—with you—"

"Why do you always spoil everything—?" Van Cleef began, half-angry, and wholly distressed.

"Because that's the way I'm made," said Russell, fiercely. "I have to 'spoil everything.' When I found you again, I thought I'd be different. But I thought *you'd* be different, too. I thought you'd be the one human creature I could be honest with, and I was honest. I gave myself away, completely. I told you my faults. And you hate me for them, like everyone else."

"I don't hate you!" cried Van Cleef, exasperated. "You're a pest, that's all. You say things you know damn well I won't like, and when don't like them, you call it 'hate.' You—you goad me. That's the word for it."

"A pest..." said Russell. "I'm not a fool, though. I've found out, without any help from anyone, what's happened in that house. I did it on your account, because the people are friends of yours. You won't believe me, and you won't listen to me. You've simply kicked me out."

It was bad, altogether bad, thought Van Cleef, to feel as he did towards the boy. If it wasn't hate, it was something very like it.

"About that," he said. "It's in the hands of the police, now. They'll find out whatever's essential."

"I don't think so," said Russell. "There's one essential fact that's been obvious all the time, yet no one's noticed it. Miss Carroll was an intelligent woman, and she didn't notice it. You haven't noticed it. I don't think the police will notice it. A beautiful case of persecution mania."

"What?" asked Van Cleef, sharply.

"Someone with well-developed delusions of persecution. Anyone who knows even the rudiments of psychology, knows the dangers of those delusions."

"You mean.... Who's got these delusions?"

"Bramwell," said Russell.

Van Cleef considered this, with interest, and a vast relief.

"Persecution?" he said, presently.

"You've heard him, and seen him. What grievance he had against Downes, I don't know—although I can guess it. But your offence is plain enough."

"Yes," said Van Cleef; but Russell was not to be stopped. "He's jealous of you, of course. I imagine he was jealous of Downes. As for Miss Carroll it was her radio—"

"No. That won't do. Too trivial."

"He's not sane," said Russell. "He was convinced that she was deliberately annoying him. She wasn't any too gentle with him, either."

"You think he killed her?"

"I do. His room is next to hers. All he had to do was step out on the balcony, to reach her room."

"Walks in through the window, and offers her a dose of poison."

"It's not difficult to think of something more reasonable than that. How about her being asleep, with a glass or a jug of water beside her?"

"Don't care much for that. She has her own bathroom. Most people will get fresh water, instead of taking what has been standing beside them."

"You'll admit it's possible, though."

"All right. For the sake of argument, Bramwell puts poison in a glass of water, and she drinks it. Dies immediately."

"No. From what I was able to observe, I'd say she's been given an overdose of some barbital preparation. She probably died in her sleep."

"I hope so..." said Van Cleef, half to himself. "I hope so...." He frowned, and glanced up. "What's your idea about the fall from the balcony?"

"He wasn't sure she was dead. And he intended to make sure."

"Threw her off?"

"That seems obvious."

"No...." Van Cleef said. "I don't seem to care for the details.... But this persecution mania thing might be looked into."

"I agree with you," said Russell, with a half-smile. "Just as well to look into it—before there's another killing."

"You'd better take your theory to the police."

"No."

"If you think the fellow's dangerous—"

"It's my duty," said Russell. "My duty to go to the police, and be sneered at. When my 'theory' is proved to be fact, I'll get no credit. I'm a half-baked young fool, with too much money and not enough work."

"I'll tell the police, then."

"Tell them what? There's no evidence, yet. They'll be civil to you, and that's all. There's only one thing you can do. You can tell Doctor Robinson you want analyses made, to determine the presence of poison. He'll do it for you."

"I'll think it over."

"Better not think too long."

"Next chapter entitled: 'The Killer Strikes Again.' Maybe.... I'll think it over."

"You don't accept my theory?"

"Don't know. I've got to think. But I'll keep an eye on the Major. Don't worry. I'll see that you get credit—if you're right. You can tool back to the city with an easy mind."

"Do you object very much, if I stay one more night?"

"I do! I do!" thought Van Cleef. "Mustn't be arbitrary, though. Who do you think is the next candidate for the Major's attention?" he asked, aloud.

"I couldn't say. He's in a condition in which any sort of fancied grievance will do."

"May not find any grievance for days, weeks...."

"He'll find one immediately. You've got to remember that the man's a homicidal maniac. He's killed once, and got away with it. He'll try again, probably to-night."

"We'll keep an eye on him," said Van Cleef.

"You're not taking it too seriously, are you?"

"I told you I wanted to think it over," said Van Cleef, with a kind of sternness. "There's something—"

"What 'something'?"

Something in the background of Van Cleef's mind that eluded him. Something he couldn't remember, or perhaps couldn't understand, just yet. He wanted to be left in peace for a while.... But they were in the village, now, and the thought of Blanche came, and blotted out everything else.

"She wouldn't ask me to come, unless it were important. She's a self-reliant kid.... Has she found out—what Annie told me? No, she wouldn't send for me for that. She'd—I don't know how she'd take that. But I think it would hurt. No matter how sensible, and modern, and what not she is; that would hurt.... I don't like her to be hurt...."

"Want me to wait?" asked Russell.

"D'you mind?"

"I haven't anything to do," said Russell. He parked the car beside the railway station, settled down comfortably behind the wheel, and Van Cleef crossed the street to the dim little shop.

She was standing before the shelves of that very modest "Lending Library," rearranging the books; in a sleeveless dress of dark green linen she looked tall and slight, cool as a dryad. At the sound of his step, she turned her head.

"Oh!" she said, unsmiling. "Do you want to take a book out, Mr. Van Cleef?"

"Thanks, yes," he said, approaching the shelves.

"This is a good one," she said, and pressed something into his hand. "You'll like to read this, after you get home. That'll be a dollar deposit, and twenty-five cents for each book, which you may keep out for one week."

He put his hand into his pocket to take out his bill-fold, and to put in the paper she had given him. Maybe there was someone watching. Or maybe she was making a mystery out of nothing. Whatever it was, he was more than willing to play up to her.

"I understand the terms," he said. "Thanks for recommending a book."

He smiled, but not she; her grey eyes were troubled, he thought she was pale; he thought, with alarm, that she was very unhappy.

"I'm a quick reader," he said. "I'll probably bring the book back to-morrow."

"There's more to it than you think," she said. Someone else came in to buy cigarettes. "Good-bye!" she said to Van Cleef, and he went out into the street.

"I'll send my telegram," he said to Russell. "Shan't be long."

There was nobody in the waiting-room, even the ticket office was closed. He took out the paper she had handed to him, opened it, and an enclosure fell out. He snatched it up in haste.

Dear Mr. Van Cleef: was written on nice blue paper, in a clear, small hand, *I got the enclosed note, this morning. Please take it seriously. There isn't time to think over this. I can only write what comes into my head. I am afraid you don't care what happens to you, but I care, terribly. If that makes any difference, please look after yourself. God bless you.*

Your friend,
Blanche.

He had not known that he could feel so keen a pain. His heart had been numb so long.... He put her letter into his pocket, and looked at the enclosure. It was made of letters and words cut from a newspaper, and pasted to make a message. "Do not trust V.C. If he continues seeing you he will be killed."

He put that into his pocket, too, and went into the telegraph office. This was for Russell's benefit only; he sent an entirely superfluous telegram to his hotel. "Returning in a few days will notify." Then he went into a telephone booth to call up Ross, his lawyer and Miss Carroll's; in his halting fashion, he gave an account of what had happened.

"Cause of death isn't determined yet," he said. "Better come out, don't you think?"

Hanging up the receiver, he thought for a while.

"Police?" he asked himself, and presently answered himself. "Not yet."

XI

"Any other errands?" asked Russell.

"None."

"Want to stop somewhere for a drink?"

"No drink just now."

No drink would serve him now, he thought. He could not get back into the shadow of vagueness; he had been stabbed into life, and he had to endure it.

"You'll see the doctor, won't you?"

"The doctor?" he replied, frowning. "Why? Nothing wrong—"

"About getting the analyses made," said Russell, impatiently; and Van Cleef answered him with equal impatience:

"I said I wanted to think it over. Give me a little peace, can't you?"

Russell turned sulky then, and began to drive faster and faster. The indicator showed seventy-five.

"Slow down!" said Van Cleef.

Russell laughed and went on, swerving round a corner, and there was a furniture van before them, looking like a house. Van Cleef had a glimpse of the driver's face, stupid with fear; the car swerved sideways across the road, splintered through a fence into a garden. The van driver stopped to yell curses at the boy; backing the car out on the road, Russell called back an insult of startling obscenity, and was off again.

"Sorry I frightened you," he said, glancing at Van Cleef, his dark face alive and joyous.

"Have you ever been caught?" asked Van Cleef, slowly.

"No. Only chased. That's magnificent!"

"Never had to pay, yet, for anything, have you?"

"Never."

"Some day you'll get a bill," said Van Cleef; and Russell laughed again.

They were silent for a time.

"If I'd been killed," Van Cleef thought, "she'd have been sorry.... Who sent her that note? Was it Bramwell? How could it be Bramwell? How would he know that I was interested in Blanche? Easy. Someone could have told him. But why should he object? If he's jealous of me on Emilia's account, he'd be pleased.... Doesn't make sense, for him to have sent it. But suppose he's so crazy that nothing he does makes sense? No.... If he was as bad as that, I'd have noticed it. Emilia would have noticed it. Everyone would have noticed it. If a lawyer, or a doctor asked me questions— Did you notice anything remarkably peculiar in Bramwell's behaviour? Sure he's peculiar, but not more than most people. I've met much queerer birds. He impressed me as a pompous, cantankerous old ass, of which there are plenty. Maniac? Homicidal maniac? There's only Russell's word for that."

He glanced at Russell, and found his face serene and happy.

"Thing is, that Russell's theory is the only one that fits. There *can't* be any other one person in the house who'd have it in for Downes and myself and Lizzy. How about three separate murderers? Or how about no murderers, and no murder? That's the crux of the whole thing. If Lizzy was poisoned, then there's a case. I'll have to see Doctor Robinson. I'll ring him up later, when I'm alone."

He frowned, surprised at himself. "There you are!" he thought. "It's the boy's own idea, but I don't want to admit I'm even considering it. This must be what we call human nature.... Petty. Very low." He sighed. "We might stop and see Doctor Robinson," he observed.

"Do we know where he lives?"

"We make enquiries."

They asked a postman, and got directions; they drove to the doctor's house, but he was out; his wife wrote down a message, asking him to ring up Van Cleef.

"I'll tell Ross," Van Cleef thought. "Trained legal mind.... Never believes anything.... His business, to give advice. How does he feel, when it turns out to be wrong? A bit sheepish?"

They turned into the drive, and the sight of the house brought his drifting thoughts into focus.

"Where's Lizzy?" he thought. "Poor little thing...."

Harly opened the door for them, and as they entered, Van Cleef thought that the very air had changed; this house in which no one was young had always been quiet, but now it was hushed. Russell ran up the stairs, and Van Cleef, at a loss, wandered into the drawing-room. Nobody there. Where were they all? What were they doing?

"Van Cleef!" said Bramwell's voice. "I'd like a few words with you."

He had put on a black tie; his blue eyes still glared in his ruddy face, but he had a subdued voice.

"Oh, yes...!" Van Cleef said.

"Perhaps you'll take a drink with me?"

"Thanks, no..." Van Cleef answered, surprised. This was, surely, the most naïve poisoner ever known.

"I propose that we walk in the grounds," said the Major. "I have a certain communication to make...."

This, thought Van Cleef, was a unique opportunity to study the Major; the only drawback was his own sense of inadequacy for making such a study. They went out of the house and on to the lawn, where they began to pace, side by side, Van Cleef tall, loose-jointed, hands in his pockets, the Major straight and stiff.

"In this crisis," said the Major, "I feel—very much alone, Van Cleef."

Van Cleef glanced sidelong at him, still more surprised.

"We are, comparatively speaking, strangers," the Major went on. "But there's the—er—freemasonry that exists among men of the world...." He paused a moment. "You, as a man of the world, will be able to understand my—er—point of view.... A cigar?" He lit one for himself. "I've had a talk with Emilia," he said. "I was able to persuade her to withdraw her unfortunate—her most unfortunate remarks to Robinson and the Sergeant. I must say they both understood the—er—conditions that prompted her. Hysterical...."

"I don't quite follow...."

"Emilia retracted what she had said relative to Miss Carroll's death being suicidal. I—reasoned with her. I endeavoured to point out the—the injustice of this. Injustice to a woman for whom, in spite of certain differences of opinion, I had, and have, a profound respect," said the Major. "I am absolutely certain that Miss Carroll would never, in any circumstances, have taken her own life."

"Then you think the thing was—"

"An accident. Absolutely. Doctor Robinson fully agrees. Our reconstruction of the tragedy is this. Miss Carroll suffered one of her heart attacks and either went out upon the balcony or was already there when attacked. The attack proved fatal; she fell against the railing, which gave way."

"Doctor agrees with that?"

"Entirely! There is no alternative explanation. It was certainly not suicide, and it was certainly not murder."

"Why 'certainly'?"

"Who'd murder Miss Carroll?" asked the Major. "And how? Her door was locked on the inside. Nobody could have entered her room by the window except myself or Emilia, and you will agree that no sane person would suspect either of us. No. It's unquestionably an accident."

"Is this the cunning of a madman?" thought Van Cleef.

"Emilia's conduct is easy to understand," said the Major, "and—for us, at least—easy to condone. She's never recovered from the ordeal of—er—Swan's death, and she was panic-stricken at the thought of a recurrence of those monstrous suspicions. A highly-strung, intensely sensitive nature.... Not—er—logical."

"I'm not so sure about that," thought Van Cleef. "Has her own kind of logic, maybe."

"The problem now," said the Major, "is to prevent Downes from making his—his outrageous confession."

"Confession?"

"He wants to tell the police!" cried the Major. "Most disgusting cowardice.... He says he'd prefer to go to jail and be done with it. My God, sir! I could cheerfully shoot that—scoundrel!"

They had stopped walking; Van Cleef looked at the other in stupefaction.

"You're amazed," said the Major. "I don't wonder, sir. You're, of course, acquainted with all the circumstances of that deplorable affair, and you know as well as I do that Emilia can't be considered *morally* responsible for what she did.

She was overwrought. She's—impulsive. But the fact remains, that she's *legally* responsible, and if that scoundrel does go to the police with his story, she can be charged with criminal conspiracy. It's possible—it's even probable—that she might be sent to prison. He's got to be stopped!"

"Let's go over it, point by point," said Van Cleef. "Let's see exactly what there is against Emilia...."

"But it's, unfortunately, only too plain," said the Major. "She's never attempted to deny that she destroyed Swan's will. You and I understand her temperament, but in a court of law.... I've thought and thought over it.... It's my belief that the only defense would be to prove she had been temporarily insane."

"Ha!" said Van Cleef, as if he had had a blow in the midriff.

"It's not pleasant," the Major agreed. "But there's a good deal of truth in it. When the poor girl saw that will—when she learned for the first time about that illegitimate daughter of Swan's, it undoubtedly threw her off balance. You can picture it.... There's her husband lying dead. Terrific shock to her. She comes across the will in his desk, acknowledging this girl, bequeathing her a share in his estate.... It's nothing short of a calamity that she turned to that scoundrel Downes at that moment."

"Might be established that she'd acted under his influence," said Van Cleef, carefully.

"Not while Annie Downes is able to speak," said the Major. "She, of course, is going to assert exactly the opposite opinion. Going to declare that Downes was led astray by Emilia. It's been—ghastly—to watch that woman ferreting out the truth. I don't know what put her on the track. Probably Downes himself, with some unpardonable stupidity. Anyhow, she's got the whole story now, and, upon my word, I believe she'd gladly see her husband go to prison if Emilia could suffer, too!"

"Fact that Swan didn't leave any estate might be an extenuating circumstance," Van Cleef suggested.

"I'm afraid not. It's a very serious matter, to destroy a will. If Downes is allowed to confess.... My God! I—the possibility nearly drives me mad!"

"Are you mad?" thought Van Cleef.

"When I think of Emilia... in the dock... Emilia in prison..." said the Major, unsteadily, "I tell you frankly, sir, I could shoot that cowardly scoundrel who's responsible."

"That wouldn't help."

"It would," said the Major. "If Downes were out of the way, the thing would never come to light."

"What about Annie Downes?"

"She hasn't any evidence. Any statement she might make could be discredited as the slander of a jealous woman. And there's nothing to fear from Dulac, of course."

"You trust him?"

"Completely! In fact, it was he who warned me about Annie Downes. Came here to talk it over with me. Told me she'd taken up with the girl. He threatened Downes, too."

"With what?"

"With physical violence," said the Major. "Dulac, of course, knows nothing about the will. His only concern is to protect the girl from the disgrace of having the truth made public. He was alarmed when Annie Downes began asking her here."

They began walking again, silent for a time.

"Downes must be restrained," said the Major.

"Yes..." Van Cleef said, absently. There was so very much to think of now....

"We're both men of the world," the Major continued. "I can speak to you with candour. We both know that poor Emilia had no criminal intent, and that her action has had no detrimental effect upon anyone. Swan had left the house to Emilia, anyhow. The money he left to his daughter didn't exist. He'd squandered everything. But the legal criminality is undeniable. Downes has got to be restrained. And I see only one way to accomplish it."

"And what's that?"

"I tried this morning to buy him off," said Bramwell. "I'm by no means a rich man, but I'd have given him all I had. He refused. He's entirely in the—grip of his wife, and her one idea is to make Emilia suffer. Talks about 'conscience' and 'atonement.' The one idea she has is *vengeance*. I think that Downes was undoubtedly somewhat infatuated with Emilia. But she didn't know it. She never knows that." He was silent for a time. "And now, because of a vindictive woman's jealousy, she's in danger of—of utter ruin. It cannot be!"

"What d'you propose?"

"This was my idea," said the Major, in a half-apologetic tone. "I have no car, and if I hired one, it might seem suspicious. But this car of yours could be used in a perfectly natural way."

"Not mine, y'know. Belongs to Russell."

"It does? However, you came here in it. You could borrow it, in a perfectly natural way. You can ask Downes to come with you, on some pretext, and you meet me at some designated spot. The whole episode could be given the appearance of a hold-up, by motor-bandits."

"But—" said Van Cleef, in stupefaction.

"You're a man of the world!" cried the Major, desperately earnest. "We can arrange this between us. I can fire a shot or two at the car, afterwards."

"After—shooting Downes?"

"Exactly. You, of course, will claim to have been robbed. We can 'plant'—I believe that's the word—'plant' some of your possessions in a thicket—some place where the police will find them, as if dropped by the bandits in their flight. You'll say that Downes was killed, resisting the bandits."

"Needs quite a bit of thinking over..." said Van Cleef.

"Unfortunately, we have no time," said the Major. "It will have to be done at once, before Downes has an opportunity to go to the police. It ought to be done before lunch."

"No!" Van Cleef said to himself. "I'm insane myself. He can't possibly be saying what I imagine he's saying. That we've got to murder Downes before lunch.... He.... No! *Look* at him! Ordinary, matter-of-fact man—smoking a cigar...."

"I don't want to hurry you—" said the Major, courteously. "But there's no time to spare."

"There might be a—better way out," said Van Cleef. "I mean to say—I don't quite like your plan."

"I dare say I'm old-fashioned," said the Major. "But it's my code, and always will be. I'd have no compunction whatever in shooting down any man who attempted to ruin a woman's reputation. Shooting him down like a dog!"

"My God!" thought Van Cleef. "I don't know.... I don't know anything.... Only that I've got to stop this...."

"Have you an alternative plan of action, sir?" the Major demanded.

"Working one out," Van Cleef answered. "Just wait a bit...."

They walked up and down, side by side. Anyone in the house could see them; perhaps Downes and his wife were looking at them. Two men of the world, discussing the murder of Harry Downes.... Ought to be done before lunch....

"I'll see Downes," said Van Cleef, abruptly.

"I've already seen him—"

"We'll give him one more chance," said Van Cleef, firmly. "I'll let you know at once...."

"I have little or no hope that you'll succeed," said the Major.

He remained, walking up and down the lawn, while Van Cleef went towards the house, with a purposeful air, and a stunned mind.

"See Downes..." he thought. "Offer him a bribe, to shut up? Suppose it's all a huge lie—an invention of Bramwell's? But he means business, all right. He's quite ready to shoot Downes 'like a dog.' Whatever else is true, that's clear. The man's dangerous. I don't know whether or not he's insane. But he's dangerous. So what do I do about it? Go to the police? Then they hear this story about the will that was destroyed. If it's true, it's bad for Emilia. Damn bad. And it easily could be true.... She could have done that. She could go to jail for it. If I don't tell the police, then what? Shall I tell Robinson? He looks ethical. If he hears this will story, he probably wouldn't shut up...."

The front door was unlocked; he stepped into the hall, in a furtive, quiet way; he wanted to hide somewhere for a little time, while he thought. The drawing-room was empty; he went in there, and closed the door.

"One thing at a time," he told himself. "Chief thing now is, to keep Bramwell from shooting Downes. Apparently I'll have to do without the help of the police, or the medical profession. Can't get him locked up in jail or in an asylum,

without bad consequences to Emilia. I've also got to keep Downes from con-
fessing—if he really intends to, and if there's anything to confess."

He struck a match to light one of his eternal cigarettes, and his hand was shaking.

"Nervous," he thought, surprised. "I need a drink. No, Mr. Van Cleef, you
need a clear head, for the next few hours.... Only you haven't got one." A foot-
step in the hall made him jump. And an idea came to him. He opened the door
and went out into the hall, and there was Emilia.

"Hello!" he said, with a cheerful smile, and went past her, up the stairs, went
to the Downes's room and knocked at the door. Annie Downes opened it.

"Like to speak to Harry..." he said.

"He's dozing," she answered, in a whisper. "Lizzy's accident upset him—"

"It's urgent," said Van Cleef, loudly, and Downes spoke: "Come in, Arthur!
Come in!"

He was lying on the bed, in a dressing-gown, and he looked just as usual.

"They all do," thought Van Cleef. "All the time! If they'd ever register anything.... Annie," he said, aloud, "if you don't mind, I want to speak to Harry
alone."

"All right, Arthur!" she said, with an amiability he found suspicious. She
picked up her knitting and went out.

"About Swan's will..." Van Cleef began.

Downes closed his eyes, in a look of suffering.

"Horrible..." he said. "If ever a man was punished for a moment's folly—"

"New development," said Van Cleef, very low, standing close to the bed. "The
idea is, for you to come at once to see this fellow—"

"What fellow?" asked Downes, opening his eyes.

"Weatherby," said Van Cleef, without the slightest hesitation. "He's got
hold of what he claims is *another* will—later one."

Downes put on his glasses and sat up.

"He wants us—you and me—to take a look at it—see if we can identify Bill's
writing. It's a holograph will, y'see. All his own hand."

"I don't understand this, Van Cleef. Who's this Weatherby, and where did he
get hold of this document?"

"It's very mysterious," said Van Cleef. "Personally, I think he stole it. But if
we think it's valid, Downes, we can buy from him—at a price. This will makes
no mention of anyone except Emilia, and, of course, it invalidates any former
will. Or wills," he added, to make it more legal.

"I don't quite see—" Downes began.

"I'll explain, more fully," said Van Cleef. "But the great thing is haste. We
must get in touch with Weatherby at once, before he—"

"Before what?"

All Van Cleef's inventiveness suddenly failed; for a moment he was speech-
less.

"You're a man of the world, Downes," he said, at last. "You'll understand, as soon as you meet him. But we've got to start at once. And the thing's got to be kept secret, for the moment. Better tell Annie the Chief of Police has sent for us, to answer some confidential questions."

"She won't believe that. I'll have to tell her the truth, Van Cleef."

"Impossible! I've given my word—"

"Van Cleef..." said Downes, unsteadily, "I can't get away from Annie without a very satisfactory explanation.... She's extremely intuitive. She—guesses things."

"We'll take her along, then," said Van Cleef, suddenly. "Explain to her, while you're dressing. I'll have a car here in ten minutes."

He went out of the room, closing the door behind him; he took out his handkerchief and wiped his forehead; he descended the stairs to the lounge and rang up a garage, to order a car. As he hung up the receiver, the Major spoke, at his shoulder.

"I see..." he said, very low. "Where shall I meet you, Van Cleef?"

"I'll handle this alone," said Van Cleef.

XII

The car came up the drive and stopped before the house, and someone sitting on the veranda in the dark rose.

"Is that you, Van Cleef, by any chance?" asked a man's voice.

"Oh! Ross! Yes! Here I am!" answered Van Cleef. He handed a bill to the driver, and got a startled "Thank you!" in return; he mounted the steps. "So you're here, Ross!" he said.

"Naturally!" said Ross. "I told you this morning on the telephone that I'd come as early in the afternoon as possible. I've been here for over two hours."

"*Two hours?*" Van Cleef repeated, as if shocked. "Sorry."

"No one could tell me where you'd gone, or why. Or when you were likely to return. I was entirely at a loss."

"Sorry," Van Cleef repeated. "Suppose we go inside—" Because he wanted to look at Ross, with the old hope of learning something from his face.

"As you please," said Ross. "I'm obliged to stop here for dinner now, although I had an engagement."

He was offended, and he looked offended; a thin and distinguished man with a high-bridged nose and black hair turning grey. He kept on:

"I understand that you particularly wanted to see me, Mr. Van Cleef. Otherwise I'd have gone back to town as soon as I'd seen the police here, and made the necessary arrangements. I certainly understood, from your telephone conversation—"

"Very sorry, Ross. What about a drink?"

"I could do with one," said Ross.

They were shut into Van Cleef's room, and there would have to be an explanation.

"How much shall I tell Ross?" Van Cleef asked himself, as he poured out two drinks. "Water? How much? Well.... Here we are!"

They sipped their drinks in silence.

"The doctor who'd been attending Lizzy— Doctor—"

"Robinson."

"Doctor Robinson came here. He said you'd left a message at his house this morning that you wanted to see him."

"How much shall I tell him?" thought Van Cleef again, glancing again at that distinguished and disagreeable face. "That part of it, anyhow.... I do want to see him," he said, aloud. "I wanted to ask him to—make a rather particular point of looking for any trace of poison."

"Someone's already been after him about that," said Ross, with what seemed to Van Cleef an inhuman indifference.

"What did Robinson say?"

"He's sending the organs to an analyst. He's the coroner's physician here, and he's more or less obliged to do so."

"You don't seem much bothered about the possibility of Lizzy's having been poisoned."

"I don't regard it as a possibility. I've seen this happen dozens of times before. In the shock of a sudden death, some hysterical friend or relative or servant will start talking about poison. The doctor assured me there was no superficial evidence of any poison. There's no imaginable motive for anyone's wishing to poison Lizzy. There's absolutely no reason to suspect poisoning. The only result of this hysteria is that the inquest will be delayed and the state will be put to unnecessary expense."

"Who spoke to Robinson about poison?"

"The house-boy. He had some garbled tale about your having been poisoned as well."

Van Cleef took another sip at his drink, and it occurred to him, suddenly, that for the first time in years it tasted good. It occurred to him that he had not particularly wanted it; that at seven o'clock he was having the first drink of the day....

"I can take it, or leave it..." he said to himself. "Maybe.... But there are more weighty matters at the moment.... How much shall I tell him?"

"What put the idea of poisoning into *your* mind?" asked Ross.

"I was probably hysterical," Van Cleef answered.

Ross glanced at him; their eyes met, and it was not a friendly glance.

"If you had, or have, any basis for suspicion, you would, of course, inform the police?"

"Of course," Van Cleef answered, and added to himself, "When I'm damn good and ready."

"Sergeant Warren was also here, asking for you," Ross went on. "He was very much annoyed that you and the Downses had all disappeared, without notifying him."

"Didn't disappear. Here I am."

"I advise you to telephone him, to say that you've returned, and to tell him where he can reach Downes."

"What does he want to reach Downes for?"

"He may be wanted at the inquest."

"Well, you said the inquest would be delayed. Downes will turn up."

"Van Cleef," said Ross, "you've put me in an embarrassing and humiliating position. You ask me to come here, to meet you, and discuss Lizzy's affairs. I come, and you've disappeared, without leaving any message for me."

"You'd have had to come, though, in any case, wouldn't you? She was your client."

"That's not to the point. You're also a client of mine. And you are not showing the necessary confidence in me. You are concealing things from me, Van

Cleef."

"I'm not being a client at the moment, if you know what I mean," said Van Cleef, apologetically.

"You mean, I take it, that you do not want me to represent your interests in this case."

"If it is a case."

"Van Cleef.... As a friend of Lizzy Carroll's, have you any information which should be given to me?"

"I don't know," said Van Cleef. "That's a fact. I don't know whether what I've got is 'information' or not. But I'll know better to-morrow."

"You're willing to assume the responsibility of withholding what may be important information?"

"Another drink, Ross?"

"Thank you."

Van Cleef stood with the bottle in his hand.

"Can I do without another drink? Excellent!" he thought.

"I advise you, however, to notify the police immediately as to Downes's whereabouts."

Van Cleef stared at him, his face tense and stiff with the effort not to laugh.

"Very likely it's not funny, anyhow," he told himself. He tried not to picture Annie and Harry Downes.... They were at the moment sitting in a room he had engaged for them in his New York hotel; they were waiting for a telephone message from "Weatherby." "It may be late," Van Cleef had warned them. "Lot of complications.... If the call's delayed—you could have dinner sent up.... You could turn in, and sleep for a bit, if the call was—very much delayed...."

It had taken a great deal of persuasion to get them there, and a great deal of ingenuity. Mrs. Downes clung to the idea that her husband should confess his guilt to the police. She had strange quasi-legal arguments for this; the courts, she said, are always lenient toward people who *volunteer* information. It was much better, she held, to explain the whole thing to the police before they found it out for themselves. "And now, of course, with the police in the house, investigating about poor Lizzy, they're sure to find out," she had said.

"Shouldn't say sure, by any means," Van Cleef had protested.

But she wanted to believe that. She was trying to disguise, even from herself, her bitter desire to see Emilia disgraced.

"I'm *sure,*" she kept saying, "that if Harry tells the police now, there'll be no unpleasantness. Everyone will understand that Emilia wasn't herself." And when that hadn't worked: "I do think," she had said, "that it's a dreadful injustice to Blanche. Bill wanted to acknowledge her. She really has a right to know who she is."

Van Cleef felt that he had done well. He had talked to Annie alone; he too had been legal; he had assured her that Downes would lose all civil rights.

"What does that mean?" she had asked.

His explanation had been vague, but alarming. He had also talked about what prison would do to Harry Downes's health, and he had assured her that a confession would inevitably mean prison. He had made an impression on her, and a night to think it over, a night without the sight of Emilia, would deepen the impression. But his chief object had been to gain time. He had had to get Downes away from the Major and his gun; he had had to get both the Downeses away from the police, before they could talk.

What he now had to do was to work over the Major, convince him that Downes was no longer a menace to Emilia, to pacify him.

"I think it can be done," he said to himself. "He's not what you'd call clever. But he's not crazy. His idea for killing Downes wasn't crazy. It was stupid. Brutal, if you like. But not insane. It simply looked to him like the one way to protect Emilia. If Downes and myself were poisoned, he didn't do it. That's not the way he'd take."

If there was a poisoner, who was it? He had thought that over all the way home in the hired car. He ruled out the Major, and Lizzy Carroll, and, that done, he could make out a good enough case against everyone else in the house. Downes was his favourite. Downes had tried to commit suicide, and, failing in that, had tried to kill Van Cleef, because he was Emilia's friend. After Downes then Emilia, Russell, Harly, and Dulac, in that order.

"It's a psychological grading," he thought. "It'll do, for the time being. And if the doctors find that Lizzy wasn't poisoned, that's the finish. I'll get Emilia away from here, scatter this crew, and that's the finish. Important thing is, to keep everything quiet until we know about poor Lizzy."

No use thinking beyond that now. And no use thinking too much about the warning Blanche had got.

"Might be some boy-friend of hers," he thought. "Someone entirely outside the rest of it."

She must have boy-friends. She must have a life of which he knew nothing, never would know anything. He hoped she wouldn't have to know about Bill Swan. He hoped nothing would hurt her, much. She was too honest and too kind not to be hurt at all, but he hoped it would never be much....

"I shan't be seeing her again," he thought. "Only makes trouble for her."

Ross cleared his throat.

"There were two or three reporters here," he said. "I gave them a brief statement. I said Miss Carroll had fallen from the balcony, during a heart attack. I also sent a cable to her nephew in London, and to an old friend of hers in Mexico. There were only three people she wanted notified in case of her death. You were the third."

"I?" said Van Cleef, and was silent for a time. "We never saw much of each other," he said. "Never were intimate. Only—I liked her."

"Apparently she liked you," said Ross. He held up his glass and stared at it. "Mrs. Swan's attitude is—peculiar," he observed.

"Very highly-strung."

"Quite. The Sergeant and Doctor Robinson both told me she'd been insistent at first that the death was a suicide."

"Oh, yes! That's natural."

"Why is it natural?"

"Y'see," Van Cleef explained, "Emilia felt responsible for the condition of the balcony. Very sensitive about things like that."

"Hmm..." said Ross, glancing at him. "I'm also informed that she suggested Lizzy had been addicted to drugs."

"Same idea. Panic-stricken attempt to evade responsibility for the condition of the balcony."

"Scarcely admirable..." said Ross.

"She took it all back. It was nothing but an impulse—self-preservation...."

"Hmm..." said Ross, again. "Well, I'll be leaving after dinner, Van Cleef. We'd better discuss matters at once."

"Yes. Arrangements for the funeral—"

"Is that all you wanted to discuss?"

"That's all," said Van Cleef, sure now that he did not care to tell Ross about the Major, about Downes, above all, about Emilia.

"Who's the boy?" asked Ross, abruptly.

"Name of Russell Blackman. I used to know his people, years ago."

"What's he doing here?"

"Drove me out. Doesn't know what to do with himself."

"Van Cleef, if I were you, I'd get rid of him."

"Gets under your skin, doesn't he?" said Van Cleef, with a smile.

"I've met his type before," said Ross. "They're always potentially dangerous."

"What way?"

"I had a talk with him. Or I might better say, he had a talk with me. He has a well-marked delusion of persecution."

Van Cleef heard that with surprise, and a slow-dawning amusement.

"The biter bit," he thought. "Exactly what Russell said about the Major.... These amateur psychologists are all so positive. Warning you...."

"I'm not joking," said Ross, glancing at Van Cleef's face. "The boy is convinced that everyone's against him."

"Not a delusion, though," said Van Cleef. "It's a fact. Pretty well everyone is against him. That's the effect he has on people."

"The cause of—" A knock at the door interrupted Ross; it was Emilia, in a dress of dark purple wool, cut square at the base of her throat, with short puff sleeves; she was anxious, appealing, and altogether beautiful.

"Are you ready for dinner?" she asked. "Harly's rather late, I'm afraid...."

It was a strange dinner, almost macabre. Emilia had Ross and Van Cleef at the table with her; the Major sat alone at one small table, and Russell at another; nobody spoke to either of them.

"I wonder..." thought Van Cleef. "I wonder what's in Bramwell's mind, just now? Does he imagine I've done away with Downes—both the Downeses? Could he sit there, eating his dinner, if he believed that? If he'd done it himself, how would he behave? *Is* he sane, after all, to propose a murder in a perfectly matter-of-fact way? Or am I the morbid one? He saw the deed as a practical necessity, that's all...."

Emilia spoke to him; he turned towards her and engaged in conversation. But his attention wandered; he glanced again at those two who sat, each alone and disregarded, at his little table.

"*Both* having delusions?" he thought.

It was a cool and breezy night; the trees rustled incessantly, the curtain on the window near him stirred back and forth against the screen with a faint rasping sound. Harly moved about quietly.

"Ross doesn't like Emilia," Van Cleef thought. "Do I? Yes, I don't know why." Ross was speaking:

"Then if you'll excuse me, Mrs. Swan? I've ordered a taxi to take me to the train.... One or two matters to discuss with Van Cleef...."

They went up to Van Cleef's room again.

"The inquest will be held as soon as the reports of the autopsy are completed," said Ross. "Then I hope there'll be an end to this—" He paused. "This most unpleasant affair.... This unnecessary and most unpleasant affair...."

"Yes...."

"I advise you once more, Van Cleef, to get in touch with the Sergeant, in regard to Downes."

"Thanks."

"Any sort of unusual behaviour will, naturally, give colour to these preposterous and utterly unfounded rumours," said Ross, with a sudden irritability. "These rumours.... An insult against Miss Carroll's memory.... And utterly unfounded."

"You're worried," thought Van Cleef, with uneasiness. They had little more to say; in half an hour or so, Ross left, and Van Cleef remained in his room, disinclined to talk to anyone. "Rumours..." he thought. "Ever since I came out here, I've been listening to rumours... Blackmail—poisoning... delusions.... Is it all unfounded? I wish to God I knew. Almost anything would be better than this cloudiness.... Has there been any crime? Any murder?"

He sighed, and lit another cigarette, walked up and down his room. He thought of Lizzy Carroll, and he thought of Blanche; he thought of Emilia.

"I'll have to suggest that idea to her," he thought. "Idea that she was panic-stricken about the condition of the balcony. It's a good one for her."

He heard a shot. Loud, sharp, somewhere near him, somewhere inside the house. He stood as if stunned, until he heard running footsteps in the hall.

"It's happened..." he said, aloud. And felt that he had been waiting for this shattering sound, this open violence.

XIII

It was Harly who had gone running by; he was standing across the corridor now, outside the Major's door.

"I heard a shot, sir," he said, looking over his shoulder at Van Cleef.

"In there, d'you think? Knock...."

Harly knocked.

"Well?" answered Bramwell. Or someone imitating Bramwell, in a shaking, falsetto voice. "What d'you want?"

"Mind opening the door just a moment?" asked Van Cleef. And now Emilia was beside him, clutching his arm.

"I—I do mind!" said Bramwell. "Kindly let me alone...."

"Aa-rthur...."

"Hush!" he said to her. "Bramwell, just a moment—"

"Go to hell!" said the Major.

"Arthur.... Was that a shot?"

Russell had come out of his room; he stood leaning against his closed door, sullen and still.

"Bramwell," said Van Cleef. "Mrs. Swan's worried. Open the door, will you?"

"I won't. I'm—in bed. Get out, and let me alone, if you please!"

"Carlo! Are you all right?" she cried.

"Yes! Entirely all right! I want—to be *let alone!*" he shouted.

"Perhaps—" Van Cleef began, when Russell took a step forward.

"Look!" he said.

Van Cleef looked where he pointed; he saw the little thread of blood running from under Bramwell's door.

"Emilia," he said. "Go into your own room for a while, will you?"

"No..." she said. "I don't want—"

"Come, my dear girl," he interrupted, taking her by the elbow. He wanted to speak kindly, he wanted to feel kindly towards her, but there was in him only an exasperated impatience to get her out of the way.

"Please, Arthur.... I don't want—to stay alone...."

"Only for a few moments," he said. He tried to draw her forward, but she resisted. He could not drag her; there was no time to persuade her. "Russell," he said, "look after Mrs. Swan, will you?" He took her hand from his arm and raised his voice. "Open that door, Bramwell!"

No answer this time. Never any answer again, perhaps. He moved to the next door, the door of the room that had been Lizzy Carroll's; he tried it, and it was locked.

"We'll have to break in his door," he said to Harly.

Emilia was beside him again, clutching his arm again.

"Arthur, why? Arthur, what's happened?"

"Russell, can't you look after Mrs. Swan?" he shouted. "Harly, get an axe—"

"I have a key—for Lizzy's door, Arthur...."

"Good! Will you get it, please?"

"It's here," she said, and tried to open her purse with shaking fingers. She brought out a key at last, and dropped it; he picked it up.

"Wait—in my room—anywhere you like," he said. "Russell will stay with you."

But Russell did not say a word, did not move; he stood leaning against his door, sullen and still.

"Harly—look after Mrs. Swan," said Van Cleef, and unlocked Lizzy Carroll's door. The room was in blackness, with a strong, cool current of air blowing through it; he felt for the switch, and turned it, but no light came. The window made a pale square; he moved across the room towards it.

"Shot himself," he thought. "Why? Because he's mad? Shot himself—but maybe he's not dead...."

When he reached the window, the world outside seemed almost light; the unclouded sky was thick with stars. He saw the gap in the iron railing, saw the boards splintered and sagging. He set foot on it cautiously; when he got out there, he saw brilliant light shining from the Major's window. And he heard, or thought he heard, the sound of difficult breathing. He edged along, keeping close to the wall; he went very slowly, testing each step, and he was filled with a peculiar nervous fear completely new to him. He remembered the mare he used to ride, and how she had always balked at a wooden bridge, sometimes becoming unmanageable, sometimes consenting, stepping across the planks with a trembling, unsteady gait.

"Felt like this," he thought. "You think the thing'll give way under you.... I'm glad Lizzy—didn't know...."

He had got to the Major's window; he stepped upon the low sill with a sigh of relief. The room was brightly lit, by two lamps, and a chandelier in the ceiling, and lying near the door was a man. Not Bramwell. It was Dulac, shot through the head.

There was no need to touch him. No need to look at him again. He was dead, brutally dead, shattered. Van Cleef stared down at his own feet for a moment....

"Pull yourself together..." he said in his heart. "Where's Bramwell?"

He raised his head, as if someone else had asked him that question; he looked about the bright room, every corner of it visible. And he heard, or thought he heard, the sound of difficult breathing. It was not Dulac. It did not come from inside the room. So it had to be on the balcony. He stepped into the room.

"Bramwell must have a gun," he thought. "And he must be mad."

No one in the house now but himself, Russell, Harly, and Emilia. And

Bramwell crouched on the balcony, outside the bar of light from the window. He crossed the room to the door; and he had to move Dulac.... He unlocked the door, took out the key, opened it, and stepped into the corridor; he locked the door behind him.

"Aa-rthur!" cried Emilia. "Blood—on your *hands!*"

He caught her before she fell, lifted her and carried her into his room, where he laid her on the bed.

"Stay with Mrs. Swan, Harly," he said. "Lock the door on the inside. Lock the window, too."

Russell still stood there, motionless.

"Look here!" said Van Cleef. "There's been a murder. Dulac. Go down, will you, and call up the police."

"What are you going to do?"

"I'm pretty sure Bramwell's on the balcony. I'll go round there and see if he comes down."

"I'll do that," said Russell, and took a small automatic out of his hip pocket. He smiled, "I'll wait for the Major, and you can telephone."

"Better give me that," said Van Cleef.

Russell dropped the automatic into his pocket again.

"Give it to me," said Van Cleef.

"Why the hell should I?" cried Russell. "I won't—"

"Shut up and give it to me."

"I will not!"

Van Cleef thought for a moment, staring at the boy with a frown. Then he acted very quickly. He gave the boy a short right to the jaw that jerked his head back, caught his arm and pulled it up, and took the gun out of his pocket.

"Telephone to the police," he said, briefly, and turning away, ran down the stairs. The front door was unbolted; he opened it and stepped out on the veranda. It was a sweet, cool night, so quiet.

"Mad..." he thought. "Homicidal.... Likes to kill.... Did he kill Lizzy?"

Walking silently on the grass, he turned the corner of the house, and he saw a figure hanging to the edge of the balcony by its hands.

"Bramwell," he called, as quietly, as reasonably as he could.

The figure dropped to the ground and began to run towards a plantation of trees that stood on the lawn, a sharply-defined octagon of black. Van Cleef started after him, and stopped.

"He's got a gun, and he's mad. No use being a fool...."

He drew close to the house, in the shadow, and went forward cautiously. But he could not reach the trees without crossing a clear space; he stopped again; he could see nothing in the plantation, but he heard things stir, things rustle; he heard a twig snap.

"Bramwell!" he called persuasively. "Let's talk this over."

No answer. He heard a twig snap, a branch rustle as if thrust aside, and the sounds were farther from him now.

"I'll take a chance," he thought, and ran across the clear space, to the shelter of the trees. He listened, tense, alert, alive; it was a sort of exultation to be so alive. "If I could get up behind him..." he thought, listening for another sound. Very dark here among the trees, very still. He moved forward, listened, took another step. And heard that breathing. He grinned to himself, moving stealthily nearer.

"Where are you, Van Cleef?" called Russell's voice.

There was a scrambling, crashing sound, a swishing of leaves.

"He's off, down the lawn!" yelled Russell.

Van Cleef got out of the little wood, and then he saw Bramwell, big and square, charging over the grass towards the wall, with Russell after him. He ran after them; he was gaining on them; the boy wasn't much of a runner. The Major reached the wall and flung himself over it, clumsily, almost in front of a car that came round the corner. It stopped with a screech from the brakes.

"What the hell—!" cried the driver.

"We're after that man!" called Russell. "A murderer—"

"Someone up at Mrs. Swan's?"

"That's right!" said Russell.

The driver got out; he was standing in the road when Van Cleef joined them. Bramwell was nowhere in sight. Across the road there was a barn, a field with a white wooden fence, and in the background a little old farmhouse.

"Has to be in the barn," said Van Cleef.

They all three crossed the road together, and again it was Russell who sighted the quarry.

"He's got out! There he goes!"

There he went, running across the empty field, towards the house. Van Cleef was climbing the fence when the driver drew in his breath with a sort of hiss.

"Jeeze!"

The Major turned and started back towards them, and after him came a huge dog, loping silently in the starlight. The Major looked back over his shoulder, and seeing the dog so close, gave a yell. He made a desperate spurt forward; he stumbled and fell, and the dog was on him. Van Cleef heard that sound that has meant the extremity of terror to man since his beginning. A beast worrying his prey.

He got over the fence, and took aim; as the shot rang out, the dog leaped into the air, and came running at him. He fired again, and it dropped. Bramwell was on his feet again, running, bent over, not like a man any more. Like a beast, hunted by beasts.

"Bramwell!" cried Van Cleef. "For God's sake, man!"

A beast himself gone back ten thousand years in time, to have felt that atrocious exultation.

"Bramwell!"

He wanted some way to reach him, to reassure him. But Bramwell fell on his face and lay still.

The driver had an electric torch; Van Cleef turned the Major over, and the light shone on him.

"Got the throat half torn out of him..." said the driver, in a sort of awe. "You wouldn't think he could have kept going—"

A light sprang up in the farmhouse, a shaking old voice shouted from an upper window.

"What's all this?"

"It's me, Mr. Horton!" called the driver. "We caught this here murderer...."

"Van Cleef..." said Russell, putting a hand on his shoulder. Van Cleef shook him off.

"Got a telephone?" he called to the man at the window. "Then call Doctor Robinson, will you, and the police!"

"Van Cleef..." said Russell again, and leaned weakly against him. "I'm going to be sick...."

Van Cleef pushed him away, gently, absently, not interested. The boy was being sick, horribly sick; the driver was murmuring phrases of encouragement to him. But Van Cleef stood erect, beside the Major, waiting for him to die.

Not dead yet; the breath whistled in his torn throat. He lay there, in the dark, empty field, and wouldn't die. He had been hunted and harried; this was his last chance to escape, and he was not taking it. If he didn't go now, there would be worse things ahead of him.

"Let him go!" Van Cleef said to himself, in a sort of prayer. "He's had enough, poor devil...."

The wail of a siren startled him. It didn't seem possible that the police could come so soon. But perhaps he had lost track of time. Turning his head, he saw two cars come tearing along the road and stop; saw four or five dark figures jump out, come hastily towards him, with electric torches.

"Where's the man who was shot?" asked a serious young voice.

"Here!" he answered. "Not shot, though."

Two men were carrying a stretcher; the light of powerful torches shone on the prostrate man.

"God!" said the serious young voice. "This is...." He knelt beside Bramwell. "Funny..." he said. "When we got back from a call, there was this message. 'Man shot near Horton's barn....'"

Van Cleef moved aside, out of the radius of light.

"I see..." he said, after a moment. "I see...."

XIV

They put the man who wouldn't die on the stretcher; he wore a bandage like a very high collar that gave him a grotesquely formal look; they carried him off to the ambulance. "We'll go along up to the house now," said Sergeant Warren. "Get an account of all this."

"There's a—a—corpse in the house," said Russell, with a slight stammer.

"That so?" said the Sergeant, unmoved. "We'll take that up, when we get there." He stood, flanked by two policemen, obviously waiting, and Van Cleef touched the boy's arm. "Come on!" he said.

They set off across the field together, the Sergeant and the two policemen behind them.

"How are you feeling now?" asked Van Cleef.

"Fine!" Russell answered. "It was just the excitement...."

"Yes...." He lowered his voice. "This is the last chance we'll have, to talk alone."

"What d'you mean?"

"The last chance," he repeated. "Y'see, I *know*."

There was a silence.

"What do you think you know?" Russell asked, scornfully.

"I know who killed Lizzy Carroll, and Dulac, and Bramwell."

"Bramwell killed Miss Carroll and Dulac, and a dog killed him."

"No."

"You'll find that the police will agree with me."

"Wasn't thinking of the police, at the moment."

Again they were silent for a time; they reached the road where the police car stood, making a bright river of light that flowed over white dust, green grass, quiet trees.

"I ought to have seen, from the start..." said Van Cleef. "It's my fault...."

"Seen what? My little plan? Nobody could have seen through it. It's been foolproof."

"One error. One serious error. You telephoned the police that a man had been shot near the barn. Telephoned a bit too soon."

"That's easily covered. I didn't telephone myself. I made Harly do it. He said what I told him, but I can always deny that. I can say he got mixed up. Nobody'll take his word against *mine*."

"You're going to fight this?"

"There's nothing to fight," said Russell, with a light laugh. "There's absolutely nothing against me. Surmises and suspicions won't count. The case against Bramwell's perfect."

"I'd like to know about Lizzy," said Van Cleef.

"I'll tell you, then. You can't use it. I'm glad of a chance to tell you. I knew you were fond of her. She wasn't intended to die."

"Just to get indigestion, same as Downes and myself?"

"That was the idea. After she'd said good night to you, she was upset. She was sitting in her room, reading, with her door open, and two big pitchers of water on the floor beside her."

"Yes," Van Cleef said, half to himself. "Afraid I'd set the house on fire."

"She was glad to see me, and have a chat," said Russell. "When I suggested making tea, she was pleased. I went down into the kitchen and made it, and brought it up, all ready for her. What I gave her wouldn't have done any harm, if she hadn't had that cardiac condition. I didn't know anything about that, of course. We had our tea, very cosily, then I carried the tray downstairs. When I came back, she was dead."

"A—an easy way to go?"

"As easy as falling asleep. I was sorry, but I wanted to turn the accident to advantage. I decided that she had better be found on the balcony outside the Major's window. I was carrying her there, holding the railing to steady myself, when the damned thing began to crumble. I just saved myself, but I had to let her go. That pretty well spoiled the whole thing. I couldn't see how her death could be linked up with Bramwell."

"How would you have linked up the 'indigestion' with Bramwell?"

"Elementary, my dear Watson! She had a thermos jug of water there; she told me she made a habit of drinking—I forget how many glasses of water at night. Poison would have been found in the thermos jug. The Major's room was next to hers. The Major had suffered acutely from her radio, and from her tongue."

They were on the lawn now; there were lights in the house before them.

"About Bill Swan?"

"I don't know any more about Bill Swan's death than you do. That was just an artistic touch."

"Was Downes meant to die?"

"No. Downes was simply a demonstration. If you'd believed in him, it would have been the end."

"Not quite clear." Van Cleef slackened his pace; there was no sound behind him; he did not know how close the Sergeant and his two men might be, or how much they could hear, and he dared not look.

"I wanted to make you realize what I am!" said Russell steadily. "I hoped you'd take that episode at face value, hoped you'd believe I had the skill to save the man's life, and the brains to solve a mystery. If you had believed it, there'd have been no need to go on. You'd have accepted me as an equal. I shouldn't have needed to—" He paused. "To show off any more," he said, with a sigh.

"Show off..." Van Cleef repeated.

"That's what it amounts to," said Russell. "Ever since I was a kid, I've had it in my mind—that some day I'd make an impression on you. It's been easy to impress other people. But you were damned obstinate. Even when I gave you a dose yourself, you weren't convinced. So I had to go on. I had to make a first-class thriller out of it. I had to make a better case against Bramwell, for myself to solve."

"Was Dulac an accident?"

"No. He was carefully planned. He got a telephone message, asking him to see Bramwell at a certain time. He'd been to the house before, to see Downes; I found that out from Harly, and he was in a rage at Downes, I don't quite know why. Downes wanted to tell something that Dulac didn't want known. The voice on the telephone asked him to see Bramwell about 'the Downes affair' and asked him to come up by way of the balcony. He was one of those athletic old boys who like to show how nimble they are. He came, and he climbed up, and I was waiting. I gave it to him just as he reached the window."

They were close to the house now.

"If Bramwell hadn't played into your hands, you'd have been in a spot," said Van Cleef. "Curious way for him to behave."

"Not at all curious," said Russell. "Ten minutes before Dulac arrived, there was a note pushed under the Major's door. Typed. Signed, Emilia. Emilia wrote her gallant Major that Dulac was threatening her, and that she was going to have a final interview with him, and then flee. She asked the Major to meet her in Horton's barn at exactly half-past nine. I knew it was the sort of note to appeal to him. I knew he'd think that *she'd* shot Dulac, and he'd be delighted to assume the guilt."

"Still, the message to the police that Bramwell had been shot was a bit of a mistake...."

"Yes..." Russell admitted, reluctantly. "I did lose my head, a little. You see, if you hadn't taken my gun, he would have been shot. The whole thing was so vivid, in my mind.... Just as I'd planned it.... I'd seen Horton's dog, and made enquiries about it. When I led everyone to the barn, he'd try to escape by the back, and he'd meet the dog. And I'd shoot at the dog, but I'd hit Bramwell first, by mistake. I did lose my head, for a moment.... It's the only mistake I've made. And it's understandable enough.... The idea of a man-hunt had me pretty worked up."

They had reached the veranda steps.

"You sent that note to Blanche?"

"Yes. She makes me sick.... I could see you falling for that naïve, miller's-daughter stuff.... I wanted to stop it, if I could."

Now Van Cleef looked back, and the Sergeant and his men were only a few paces from them.

"Russell..." he said. "Do you want your gun—now?"

Not a sound from the house. The trees rustled in the light wind, an insect chirped briskly.

"You mean...?" said Russell.

"Yes. Last chance."

Everything so quiet....

"Come along, please," said the Sergeant.

"No!" cried the boy, "I'm not worrying. I'm all right."

They all went up the steps together, they entered the house, and, in the lighted hall, Van Cleef looked at Russell. His dark face had a slightly dazed look, a look of wonder that gave it a terrible innocence. The innocence of a very young devil, who had not tasted of the fruit of knowledge, but knew only evil. A devil, shut out of hell where he belonged, and set down in a world of human creatures who rejected him. They all rejected him, all.

The Sergeant looked on, like a calm idol, while those two faced each other with that long glance.

"Where's the body, Mr. Van Cleef?" he asked, at last.

"Upstairs. In Bramwell's room."

"I'll ask you and this boy to wait here in the hall while I take a look. Kelly, remain here."

"Yes, sir," said one of the policemen.

He was there, to hear all they might say. The last time, the last chance had gone.

"If I'd understood in time..." thought Van Cleef. "If I'd even tried to understand.... Lizzy might still be here. And Bramwell.... I didn't try.... *Mea culpa....*
Mea maxima culpa...."

XV

"I told you at the time," said Ross, "that the boy was dangerous. Delusion of persecution."

"I told you he was persecuted," said Van Cleef, with unusual energy. "You couldn't help persecuting him. Something about him that antagonized everyone."

"That, of course, was because of his defensive attitude. Convinced, as he was, that—"

"You don't know," Van Cleef interrupted. "Nobody knows."

"Any competent alienist knows."

"What does this bird say?"

"Von Felder? He says that even now, after only one interview with the boy, he's prepared to state definitely that he's a psychopathic personality."

"Meaning crazy?"

"Exactly. Definitely—and incurably—insane."

"What happens about it?"

"I doubt," said Ross, "if he'll ever be brought to trial. I think that in all probability there'll be a commission appointed to examine him, and declare him incompetent."

"And then what? Strait-jacket and padded cell?"

"Surely you know better than that," said Ross, annoyed. "You know that in a modern institution he'll get such treatment as his condition requires."

"Same thing," said Van Cleef. "He'll make baskets. Much better to hang him."

Ross said nothing to that; they sat facing each other in the drawing-room, both smoking, both irritated. Ross glanced at his watch.

"Mrs. Swan is taking all this very well. Very well indeed," he observed.

"Love," said Van Cleef.

This flippancy still further irritated Ross; he stirred restlessly. He repeated the offensive word.

"Love? For Bramwell?"

"Oh, yes!"

"He didn't impress me as a man of any particular intelligence or personality."

"He's got what it takes," said Van Cleef.

"He has extraordinary vitality," said Ross. "Doctor Robinson says that not one man in a thousand could have survived such an ordeal."

Van Cleef stopped listening to him. He had seen Bramwell that morning in the hospital, Bramwell with that bandage like a very high collar, his ruddy face grown pallid. He had obviously been in pain, and he could not speak, would not be able to speak for days, and never again much above a whisper. But his blue eyes still had that stupid and honest glance; he was still alive.

"He'll never understand what's happened to him," Van Cleef thought. "They'll talk to him about Russell's psychopathic personality and so on...."

Emilia had been sitting in the hospital room with him. Just sitting there, getting up now and then, to pat his pillow, smooth the bed, adjust the blind; and his eyes followed her with devotion.

"Possibly the one man on earth who'd never be exasperated by her," Van Cleef thought. "Poor girl! She'll marry him, and they'll be happy. She has this house, and he has his little income.... They'll both be able to forget. The balcony will be repaired, and they'll never, never see Lizzy standing there. They'll never stop outside the door of Bramwell's room because Dulac's lying there again. No ghosts.... Bill Swan's ghost never came back here. Emilia wouldn't encourage it."

He was waiting now, with Ross, for a little lunch offered them by Emilia; after that, they were going back to town together. A woman from the village had come to stay with Emilia in her empty house; only she and Harly would be left, of the eight who had been here twenty-four hours ago. Would she sit alone in the dining-room to-night...?

A car was coming up the drive.

"The police have been remarkably efficient in handling the newspaper men," said Ross, uneasily. "I hope—"

The doorbell rang.

"There'll be a great deal of publicity, though," he went on. "It can't be avoided. It's a remarkably sensational case."

"Front-page stuff."

"As you say, front-page stuff. And I'm afraid you'll figure in it, Van Cleef." He waited, but there was no reply, and a sort of remorse came over him. "You're looking rather seedy, Van Cleef."

"I feel seedy. That's because I *don't* need a drink."

Harly went along the hall to open the door.

"You can't—" Ross began, when Harry and Annie Downes came into the room. Van Cleef rose, with guilty alarm; he smiled at them. And they both smiled at him; they were just the same—the middle-aged couple with eyeglasses that he met everywhere....

"Annie, this is Mr. Ross, Lizzy's lawyer, and mine.... Downes, Mr. Ross...." Annie sat down and took off her gloves.

"I called up the house, and Harly told me..." she said, in a hushed voice. "So terrible.... I—we thought we ought to come back, to be with Emilia until it's all over...."

"Telephone, Mr. Ross, sir," said Harly, and Ross went out of the room. Van Cleef was left alone with the couple he had deluded; they must know now that they had been deluded.

"How did you make out?" he asked.

"Harry saw Mr. Weatherby, late last night," said Mrs. Downes. "And he was quite convinced that this other will is genuine."

"I see!" said Van Cleef. He could not help going on. "What did you think of Weatherby, Downes?"

"Oh.... A gentleman," said Downes.

"In every sense of the word," said Van Cleef.

"Yes," said Downes, gravely. "In every sense of the word."

"Does Annie believe that he really saw a Weatherby?" thought Van Cleef. "Or is she pretending, because she wants to drop the revenge motif? Or did I make a Weatherby materialize?"

"We stopped—" said Annie Downes, in a whisper, "we stopped to speak to poor little Blanche. We thought she ought to know the *truth*."

"You told her—"

"We felt that she ought to know, before Dulac's funeral," said Downes. "Ought to know he was not her father. Otherwise, it's making a mockery of—" He paused. "Of a—very solemn thing," he said.

"I'll be back," said Van Cleef.

He almost collided with Ross who was re-entering the room.

"I'll be back," he explained, and telephoned for a taxi; took up his hat, and walked down the drive to wait for it. Two policemen were stationed there; two photographers had cameras set up on tripods, and they got him as he passed.

"Millionaire Playboy leaving Murder House.... I may be followed.... All right! I'm buying cigarettes.... It was only right to tell her.... To knock her on the head.... To spoil all she can remember of her mother.... To undo all that Dulac tried to do...."

The cab came, and he got into it; he drove to the shop, but she was not there. "I might have known that," he thought.

A stout woman in a black wig was behind the counter. "Will you let me have Miss Dulac's address?" he asked.

"No, I won't," she said. "It's a sin and a shame the way you people bother her."

"I'm not from a newspaper. I'm a friend—"

"No, you're not!" said she.

"Will you ring her up and tell her Arthur Van Cleef wants to say good-bye?"

"She doesn't want to see anybody, poor child. With her father not in his grave yet."

"Will you just ask her?"

The woman looked at him with her little black eyes.

"All right! I'll *ask* her," she said. "Wait here."

She disappeared through the door at the back of the shop. A customer came in, and stared at Van Cleef, waited, rapped on the counter with a coin; then he grew angry, and walked out. It was a good ten minutes before the woman returned.

"You can go right up," she said, with a sort of gentleness. "She's staying here with us for a while."

He went up a dark and narrow flight of stairs to a crowded little sitting-room, hot in the noon sun. Blanche was standing, waiting for him. She had obviously been crying; her face was tear-stained and sad. But not tragic.

"I hoped you'd come," she said.

"Mrs. Downes said she'd—seen you...."

"Yes," she said, and turned away her head. With a strangely comprehensive glance, Van Cleef noticed the details of the room; an upright piano covered by a blue velvet scarf fringed with gold, a little rug before the hearth, with a St. Bernard dog woven in it; a round table with a marble top, upon which stood two bronze houris designed to serve as bookends, but idle now. A neat, clean room, smelling of cabbage....

"Mrs. Downes told me," she said.

"I'm sorry."

"Well, no..." she said. "I guess it's always better to know the truth. I—" Her voice grew unsteady; she stopped for a moment. "It doesn't—really make any difference," she said. "I'm going to keep on thinking of him—as my father.... And if *he* could—forgive mother—and go on liking me...."

He found nothing to say.

"You look terribly tired," she said.

"I haven't had a drink for a long time," he said, smiling.

"That's nothing," said she.

"I wanted a little praise...."

"You never *had* to drink," she said. "I mean, it was just psychological—"

"I don't think I believe in psychology."

"Oh!" she protested, shocked. Their eyes met.

"I mean," he explained, "I don't like psychology."

"I see!"

They were both embarrassed, ill at ease.

"I didn't—" he said. "I couldn't leave without saying good-bye."

"Well, but does it *have* to be good-bye?" she asked.

The question astounded him. He could think of a good many answers....

"Au revoir," she said, resolutely, and held out her hand. He took it, in a quick grasp, and let it go.

"Maybe you're right..." he said. "Au revoir!"

THE END

Elisabeth Sanxay Holding Bibliography (1889-1955)

NOVELS

Invincible Minnie (1920)
Rosaleen Among the Artists (1921)
Angelica (1921)
The Unlit Lamp (1922)
The Shoals of Honour (1926)
The Silk Purse (1928)
Miasma (1929)
Dark Power (1930)
The Death Wish (1934)
The Unfinished Crime (1935)
The Strange Crime in Bermuda (1937)
The Obstinate Murderer [aka No Harm Intended] (1938)
Who's Afraid [aka Trial by Murder] (1940)
The Girl Who Had to Die (1940)
Speak of the Devil [aka Hostess to Murder] (1941)
Killjoy [aka Murder is a Kill-Joy] (1941)
Lady Killer (1942)
The Old Battle-Ax (1943)
Net of Cobwebs (1945)
The Innocent Mrs. Duff (1946)
The Blank Wall (1947)
Miss Kelly (1947)
Too Many Bottles [aka The Party Was the Pay-Off] (1950)
The Virgin Huntress (1951)
Widow's Mite (1952)

STORIES

Patrick on the Mountain (The Smart Set, July 1920)
The Problem that Perplexed Nicholson (The Smart Set, Aug 1920)
Marie's View of It (The Century Magazine, Dec 1920)
Mollie: The Ideal Nurse (The Century Magazine, Jan 1921)

Angelica (Munsey's, May-Oct 1921)
The Married Man (Munsey's, Dec 1921)
The Foreign Woman (Munsey's, July 1922)
Hanging's Too Good for Him (Munsey's, Sept 1922)
Like a Leopard (Munsey's, Nov 1922)
Lost Luck (The Bookman, Dec 1922)
The Girl He Picked Up at Coney (Metropolitan Magazine, Feb/Mar 1923)
The Aforementioned Infant (Munsey's, Mar 1923)
It Seemed Reasonable (Munsey's, Apr 1923)
Old Dog Tray (Munsey's, May 1923)
The Matador (Munsey's, June 1923)
A Hesitating Cinderella (Munsey's, July 1923)
The Postponed Wedding (Munsey's, Aug 1923)
With Unbowed Head (The Century Magazine, Aug 1923)
This is Life (The Nation, Aug 15 1923)
The Marquis of Carabas (Munsey's, Sept 1923)
Out of the Woods (Munsey's, Oct 1923)
Benedicta (Munsey's, Dec 1923)
Nickie and Pem (Munsey's, Feb 1924)
His Remarkable Future (Munsey's, Apr 1924)
His Own People (Munsey's, July 1924)
Who Is This Impossible Person? (Munsey's, Aug 1924)
Ye Gods and Little Fishes (The American Magazine, Aug 1924)
Mr. Martin Swallows the Anchor (Munsey's, Sept 1924)
Too French (Munsey's, Jan 1925)
The Good Little Pal (Munsey's, Apr 1925)

Flowers for Miss Riordan (*Munsey's*, May 1925)

Sometimes Things Do Happen (*Munsey's*, June 1925)

Miss What's-Her-Name (*Munsey's*, July 1925)

The Long Night (*Ladies Home Journal*, Sept 1925)

The Wonderful Little Woman (*Munsey's*, Sept 1925)

As Patrick Henry Said (*Munsey's*, Oct 1925)

The Worst Joke in the World (*Munsey's*, Nov 1925)

As Is (*Munsey's*, Dec 1925)

That's Not Love (*Munsey's*, Jan 1926)

Rosalie Gets Out of the Cage (*The American Magazine*, Feb 1926)

The Thing Beyond Reason (*Munsey's*, Feb 1926)

Dogs Always Know (*Munsey's*, Mar 1926)

Highfalutin' (*Munsey's*, Apr 1926)

Bonnie Wee Thing (*Munsey's*, May 1926)

Vanity (*Munsey's*, Jun 1926)

The Compromising Letter (*Munsey's*, July 1926)

Miss Cigale (*Munsey's*, Aug 1926)

Blotted Out (*Munsey's*, Sept 1926)

Human Nature Unmasked (*Munsey's*, Oct 1926)

Home Fires (*Munsey's*, Dec 1926)

The Grateful Lunella (*The American Magazine*, May 1927)

The Old Ways (*Munsey's*, July 1927)

By the Light of Day (*Munsey's*, Aug 1927)

For Granted (*Munsey's*, Nov 1927)

Incompatibility (*Munsey's*, Dec 1927)

One Misty Night, (*The American Magazine*, Feb 1928)

Derelict (*Munsey's*, Mar 1928)

Half an Hour Late (*Woman's Home Companion*, Mar 1928)

This Road Is Closed (*The American Magazine*, Apr 1928)

Inches and Ells (*Munsey's*, June 1928)

It Is a Two-Edged Sword (*McCall's*, June 1928)

Too Late (*Liberty*, July 21 1928)

Outside the Door (*The Elks Magazine*, Oct 1928)

Hard as Nails (*Liberty*, Oct 20 1928)

Important Things (*Liberty*, Nov 17 1928)

A Dinner Date (*The American Magazine*, Jan 1929)

Vera's Superior Smile (*Pictorial Review*, Jan 1929)

Saving Up (*Liberty*, Jan 5 1929)

Flow and Ebb (*Liberty*, Jan 26 1929)

Without Benefit of Police (*Complete Stories*, Feb 1929)

The Sin of Angels (*The American Magazine*, Apr 1929)

Dare-Devil (*The American Magazine*, June 1929)

Little Deeds of Kindness (*Liberty*, July 6 1929)

Broken Faith (*The American Magazine*, Oct 1929; *Cassell's Magazine of Fiction*, July 1930)

Carline (*Liberty*, Oct 12, 1929)

Rose-Leaves (*Liberty*, Jan 18 1930)

The Chain of Death (*Liberty*, May 24, May 31, Jun 7, Jun 14, Jun 21 1930)

The Girl in Armor (*Street & Smith's Detective Story Magazine*, Aug 8 1931)

It's All Right for Men (*Liberty*, Oct 10 1931)

Brides of Crime (*Street & Smith's Detective Story Magazine*, Nov 7, 1931)

The Preposterous Mrs. Manders (*Woman's Home Companion*, Mar 1932)

Hound's Bay (*Street & Smith's Detective Story Magazine*, Mar 26 1932)

If It Hadn't Been for Laurel (*Liberty*, Jan 28 1933)

A Man Can Take It (*Collier's Weekly*, May 12 1934)

The Green Bathtub (*Collier's Weekly*, June 16 1934)

The Last Night (*The Passing Show*, July 14 1934)

All She Could Get (*Collier's Weekly*, Sept 15 1934)

"I Could Brighten Your Life!" (*The American Magazine*, Jan 1935)

The Bride Comes Home (*Cosmopolitan*, Feb 1935)

The Root of Evil (*Collier's Weekly*, Apr 27 1935)

Nobody Would Listen (*Mystery*, Aug 1935)

Somebody's Cynthia (*Collier's Weekly*, Aug 3 1935; *The Passing Show*, Nov 2 1935)

You Never Can Tell (*Collier's Weekly*, Dec 14 1935; *Grit*, June 1936)

Unscathed (*Ladies Home Journal*, Jan 1936)

Lost (*Redbook*, Feb 1936)

Cross Purposes (*Collier's Weekly*, May 30, 1936)

Can Do! (*Pictorial Review*, July 1936)

Scandal (*Woman's Home Companion*, July 1936)

Night Life (*Redbook*, Sept 1936)

Third Act (*Pictorial Review*, Apr 1937)

Drifting (*McCall's*, May 1937)

Wedding Day (*Cosmopolitan*, Sept 1937)

The Nicest Little Lunch (*Cosmopolitan*, Nov 1937)

Echo of a Careless Voice (*McCall's*, Jan 1938)

Illusion (*Good Housekeeping*, Aug 1938)

They Take It So Lightly! (*Cosmopolitan*, Oct 1938)

Two Passes for the Show (*Liberty*, Nov 5 1938)

So Sort of Proud (*Good Housekeeping*, Mar 1939)

Money Can't Buy It (*Liberty*, Aug 5 1939)

Open That Door (*Liberty*, Aug 26 1939)

Blonde on a Boat (*The American Magazine*, Dec 1939)

Late Date (*Cosmopolitan*, May 1940)

Proposal (*McCall's*, May 1940)

On Yonder Lea (*Good Housekeeping*, Aug 1940)

Tropical Secretary (*The American Magazine*, Feb 1941)

Tomorrow's Not Soon Enough (*McCall's*, Mar 1941)

What It Takes (*Grit*, Mar 9 1941)

Loved I Not Honor More (*Liberty*, Apr 12 1941)

The Fearful Night (*The American Magazine*, June 1941; expanded to *The Obstinate Murderer*)

Another Baby (*Woman's Home Companion*, Nov 1941)

Not Goodbye But Au Revoir (*McCall's*, Oct 1942)

The Kiskadee Bird (*Cosmopolitan*, 1944)

The Old Battle-Ax (1943; abridged, *Liberty*, Mar 18 1944)

Bait for a Killer (*Collier's Weekly*, Sep 30 1944, as "The Blue Envelope"; *The Saint Mystery Magazine*, Mar 1959; *The Saint Detective Magazine* [Australia], Nov 1959; *The Saint Mystery Magazine* [UK], Oct 1960)

The Unbelievable Baroness (*The American Magazine*, 1945)

The Net of Cobwebs (*Collier's Weekly*, Jan 6, 13 & 20, 1945)

Funny Kind of Love (as by Elizabeth Saxanay Holding, *Boston Sunday Globe Magazine*, Nov 11 1945)

"Be Careful, Mrs. Williams" (*Cosmopolitan*, July 1947)

People Do Fall Downstairs (*Ellery Queen's Mystery Magazine*, Aug 1947; *Ellery Queen's Mystery Magazine* [Australia], Aug 1949)

Friday, the Nineteenth (*The Magazine of Fantasy and Science Fiction*, Summer 1950)

Farewell, Big Sister (*Ellery Queen's Mystery Magazine*, July 1952; hardboiled satire)
The Death Wish (*Cosmopolitan*, Feb 1953)
Shadow of Wings (*The Magazine of Fantasy and Science Fiction*, July 1954)
Glitter of Diamonds (*Ellery Queen's Mystery Magazine*, Mar 1955; *Ellery Queen's Mystery Magazine* [Australia], May 1955)

The Strange Children (*The Magazine of Fantasy and Science Fiction*, Aug 1955)
Very, Very Dark Mink (*The Saint Detective Magazine*, Dec 1956; *The Saint Detective Magazine* [UK], Oct 1957)
The Darling Doctor (*Alfred Hitchcock's Mystery Magazine*, Mar 1957)

Other Stark House books you may enjoy...

Clifton Adams Death's Sweet Song /
Whom Gods Destroy $19.95
Benjamin Appel Brain Guy / Plunder $19.95
Benjamin Appel Sweet Money Girl /
Life and Death of a Tough Guy $21.95
Malcolm Braly Shake Him Till He Rattles /
It's Cold Out There $19.95
Gil Brewer Wild to Possess / A Taste for Sin $19.95
Gil Brewer A Devil for O'Shaugnessy /
The Three-Way Split $14.95
Gil Brewer Nude on Thin Ice /
Memory of Passion $19.95
W. R. Burnett It's Always Four O'Clock /
Iron Man $19.95
W. R. Burnett Little Men, Big World /
Vanity Row $19.95
Catherine Butzen Thief of Midnight $15.95
James Hadley Chase Come Easy–Go Easy /
In a Vain Shadow $19.95
Andrew Coburn Spouses & Other Crimes $15.95
Jada M. Davis One for Hell $19.95
Jada M. Davis Midnight Road $19.95
Bruce Elliott One is a Lonely Number /
Elliott Chaze Black Wings Has My Angel $19.95
Don Elliott/Robert Silverberg
Gang Girl / Sex Bum $19.95
Don Elliott/Robert Silverberg
Lust Queen / Lust Victim $19.95
Feldman & Gartenberg (ed)
The Beat Generation & the Angry Young Men $19.95
A. S. Fleischman Look Behind You Lady /
The Venetian Blonde $19.95
A. S. Fleischman Danger in Paradise /
Malay Woman $19.95
A. S. Fleischman The Sun Worshippers /
Yellowleg $19.95
Arnold Hano So I'm a Heel / Flint /
The Big Out $23.95
Orrie Hitt The Cheaters / Dial "M" for Man $19.95
Elisabeth Sanxay Holding Lady Killer /
Miasma $19.95
Elisabeth Sanxay Holding The Death Wish /
Net of Cobwebs $19.95
Elisabeth Sanxay Holding Strange Crime in Bermuda /
Too Many Bottles $19.95
Elisabeth Sanxay Holding The Old Battle-Ax /
Dark Power $19.95
Elisabeth Sanxay Holding The Unfinished Crime /
The Girl Who Had to Die $19.95
Russell James Underground / Collected Stories $14.95
Day Keene Framed in Guilt / My Flesh is Sweet $19.95
Day Keene Dead Men Don't Talk / Hunt the Killer /
Too Hot to Hold $23.95

Mercedes Lambert Dogtown / Soultown $14.95
Dan J. Marlowe/Fletcher Flora/Charles Runyon
Trio of Gold Medals $15.95
Dan J. Marlowe The Name of the Game is Death /
One Endless Hour $19.95
Stephen Marlowe Violence is My Business /
Turn Left for Murder $19.95
Wade Miller The Killer / Devil on Two Sticks $19.95
Wade Miller Kitten With a Whip /
Kiss Her Goodbye $19.95
Rick Ollerman Turnabout / Shallow Secrets $19.95
Vin Packer Something in the Shadows /
Intimate Victims $19.95
Vin Packer The Damnation of Adam Blessing /
Alone at Night $19.95
Vin Packer Whisper His Sin /
The Evil Friendship $19.95
Richard Powell A Shot in the Dark /
Shell Game $14.95
Bill Pronzini Snowbound / Games $14.95
Peter Rabe The Box / Journey Into Terror $19.95
Peter Rabe Murder Me for Nickels /
Benny Muscles In $19.95
Peter Rabe Blood on the Desert /
A House in Naples $19.95
Peter Rabe My Lovely Executioner /
Agreement to Kill $19.95
Peter Rabe Anatomy of a Killer /
A Shroud for Jesso $14.95
Peter Rabe The Silent Wall /
The Return of Marvin Palaver $19.95
Peter Rabe Kill the Boss Good-By /
Mission for Vengeance $19.95
Peter Rabe Dig My Grave Deep / The Out is Death /
It's My Funeral $21.95
Brian Ritt Paperback Confidential:
Crime Writers $19.95
Sax Rohmer Bat Wing / Fire-Tongue $19.95
Douglas Sanderson Pure Sweet Hell /
Catch a Fallen Starlet $19.95
Douglas Sanderson The Deadly Dames /
A Dum-Dum for the President $19.95
Charlie Stella Johnny Porno $15.95
Charlie Stella Rough Riders $15.95
John Trinian North Beach Girl /
Scandal on the Sand $19.95
Harry Whittington A Night for Screaming /
Any Woman He Wanted $19.95
Harry Whittington To Find Cora /
Like Mink Like Murder / Body and Passion $23.95
Harry Whittington Rapture Alley / Winter Girl /
Strictly for the Boys $23.95
Charles Williams Nothing in Her Way /
River Girl $19.95

Stark House Press, 1315 H Street, Eureka, CA 95501
707-498-3135   www.StarkHousePress.com
Retail customers: freight-free, payment accepted by check or paypal via website. Wholesale: 40%, freight-free on
10 mixed copies or more, returns accepted. All books available direct from publisher or Baker & Taylor Books.